D1521812

Also Available From Jacy Morris

Fiction:
The Abbey
The Enemies of Our Ancestors
Killing the Cult
The Pied Piper of Hamelin
This Rotten World
This Rotten World: No More Heroes
This Rotten World: We All Fall Down
Unmade: A Neo-Nihilist Vampire Tale (as The Vocabulariast)

Non-Fiction:
Let's Get Drunk and Watch Horror Movies: 50 Horror Movie Reviews and Drinking Games (as The Vocabulariast)

Music:
All Hell Breaks Loose Soundtrack with Jeremy Brown (Available on iTunes)

Movies:
All Hell Breaks Loose (Available from Wild Eye Releasing in 2015)
The Cemetery People (Coming Soon)

The Enemies of Our Ancestors

By
Jacy Morris

Prologue:

The Night Whispers

Kochen walked through the night, his bare feet testing for sharp rocks before he put his full weight on the ground. In this way, he moved through the black-chilled air. Wind blew through his obsidian hair, and his dusky brown skin raised gooseflesh in response. Kochen looked up and saw the outline of the canyon's rim against the night sky, the faint hint of blackness against a dark blue. More stars than he could count looked down at him. It was the time of the Lynx moon, the time of the bobcat. Its full, round face rose into the sky, bringing with it the onset of spring. He could smell the change in the air. Though he was only six-winters-old, in a world where seasons meant everything, he had learned the signs of change at a young age.

He walked through the empty farmland, away from the mud and stone houses that his ancestors had carved and molded into the cliff, his toes sinking into the loose brown soil. Kochen lived on the lowest terrace of the village nestled among the cliffs, so he needed no torch to descend down the variety of stone ladders that led from the highest level to the rough stone ground. He had simply walked out of his family's small room where his mother and father

1

slumbered, inched down a single, thirty-rung ladder, and he was on the ground.

The farm soil had already been broken up for the spring. The soil felt cool and soft against his toes as he plodded through the loose farmland, avoiding the budding shoots of corn. He stopped to relieve himself, pulling his loincloth to the side. His urine steamed in the night as it pattered to the ground, impossibly loud.

Behind him, he heard someone doing the same. He turned to look and saw his father.

"What are you doing out here?"

"No, what are you doing out here?" his father shot back.

Kochen had been told over and over to not wander far from their house to relieve himself in the night. No one had ever explained why; they just said not to.

"I had to go. Besides, it's good for the crops." Kochen finished up his work and let his loincloth fall back into place. His father did the same. Kochen walked in his direction, and his father cuffed him on the back of the head.

"That is for thinking you know it all. Get your skinny rear-end back into the house."

Kochen ran in the night, lest his father's ire turn into more than just a simple cuff. He was usually slow to anger, but tonight he seemed different.

"Next time, you go from the ledge like everyone else."

Kochen heard the words, but dared not give a response on the odd chance that it would be seen as disrespectful. As Kochen put his first, rough hand on the ladder, he heard a noise, a low rumbling. It was not a noise he had ever heard before. It echoed through the canyon and across the farmland. A gust of wind blew the hair on his head backwards as he turned around to see what was making the noise.

In the faint light of the moon, he could see the blue shine of his father's skin running towards him. The tilled farmland was darker in the night than the untilled earth of the canyon floor, and when his father reached the edge of it, the earth opened up. A shape emerged, maggot-white, and twice as tall as his father. At first it seemed like a massive white worm, erupting from the ground, but then he noticed the arms Twisted and corded with segmented veins, the creature's arms were all twisted muscle and bone. In place of hands, the shape had sharp spikes, hooked like the backwards limbs of a praying mantis, and its eyes were black bulbs in a misshapen skull that was covered in skin the color of fresh-washed mushrooms..

Before he could even scream a warning to his father, the creature had shoved a claw through his father's middle, the other claw wrapping around his throat. Kochen's sob caught in his own throat, as his father descended into the ground in the embrace of the creature. The soil parted for him, and it was as if he had sunk into the river instead of the farmland of the village.

Kochen climbed the ladder, and reached the edge of the limestone landing. He sat on the edge, his feet safely on stone, watching and waiting for his father's hand to appear from the ground. It was a good harvest that year.

Chapter 1:

Predictions

As he spoke, Kochen stood in the dirty pit of the pulpit, low in the ground with the eyes of the people on him. He spoke of doom and despair, things that none of them wanted to actually hear about, but which he felt compelled to speak about. He was just about to tell them the prophecy he had dreamed the night before, when Lansa rushed over, shoving him off into an alcove against his protestations, the smoke of the fire still wreathing his head.

"Be quiet," she said. She turned her back on him and walked back to the people, her arms in the air as if to tamp down their fears.

By now they had grown restless. Some of the younger ones were crying into their mothers' skirts. A part of him felt bad for scaring them; another part wanted them to know the truth about the way the days would grow. Lansa wanted none of it. Kochen often wondered how Lansa had become priest if she was not willing to share the words of the spirits with the people. It was whispered among the other priests, Harcha and Birren in particular, that she didn't even believe in the spirits. In Kochen's eyes, this had always made Lansa seem like a fool. Kochen had, after all, seen one of the Great Ones with his own eyes.

"You'll have to forgive Kochen. He hasn't been feeling well lately. Too many bad dreams." After they heard that, the crowd looked at him. They knew. They were reminded. His past would never be left behind. He was like the village itself, a fine place to look at, but with a crushing weight of rock always hanging over it. Kochen's rock hung over his head, preventing him from gliding forward into leadership of the tribe. Their eyes twinkled with sorrow when they beheld the poor crazy boy that they had all known as a youth.

He had failed again in their eyes.

****

Young Kochen sat before the priest, his eyes unfocused. His hands trailed in the dust of the ground, the walls around him seemingly composed of wind. The woman across from him, sat down on her knees, her feet tucked under her. Her shaved head gleamed in the sunlight streaming through the south-facing window, dust motes borne into the air by the heat of the sun's rays.

Her eyes were laced with red veins, and they bugged out of the hollow pits of her face, surrounded by high cheek bones and a nose that looked like the beak of a vulture. Maybe that's what Kochen was, a meal for a vulture, a corpse waiting for the priest to feed on him.

"What happened?" she commanded.

Kochen had no words.

She slapped him across the face. "Do you know who I am?"

Kochen knew her. There were only three-hundred people crammed into the cliff houses, and maybe a hundred more in the surrounding areas. How could he not know Lansa, the high priest?

Kochen looked up at the woman kneeling in the dirt across from him, his eyes glistening with tears that refused to fall. "I know you."

"Where is your father?"

Kochen didn't have the words to describe what he had seen. He simply looked at her, anguish swimming in his eyes. She slapped him across the face again.

"Tell me," she bellowed.

His face stung, but still he could not find the words.

"Did the Stick People take him?"

Kochen shook his head.

"Did he run away?"

Kochen shook his head again.

Lansa grabbed him by the arms. "I know this is painful, but I need to know if the village is in danger. What happened to your father?"

"Bimisi."

The priestess sat back on her heels, her mouth opening and closing like a fish. Then she laughed, her voice echoing throughout the sanctum. Kochen would never forgive her for that laugh.

Lansa stood. She leaned over Kochen, towering over him, her red-veined eyes seeming to bug out until it seemed like they were going to fall out of her face. She placed her hands on his upper arms, squeezing tightly. "Don't joke, child. Speak the truth."

"Bimisi," he said again. He thought she was going to smack him again, but she didn't. She dusted her skirts off and held out her soft, dry hand for him. He grabbed it and together they walked outside.

****

When the crowd parted, and his own thoughts drifted away like the mist of morning breath. Lansa stood in front of him, her shaved head shining in the morning light, bits of stubble appearing here and there. Her eyes did not shine. They were dull, worn by age, and filled with ire that was aimed in his direction.

"What did we talk about?"

6

Kochen clenched his jaw, and looked at Lansa. "You talked. I listened. I never agreed."

Her face softened. "What are you trying to do?"

"I'm trying to save us."

Lansa looked at him. She suddenly seemed more tired than ever. The flesh under her eyes was pouched and baggy, leaving her with the look of a mourning wife. It was merely a look though; priests never married. The sagging flesh couldn't hide the concern that was hidden in her eyes. Lansa looked upon the folk as her children, and she often claimed she simply had too many people to worry about, but she loved every moment of it. Well... almost every moment of it.

She seemed to despise the moments of the day where Kochen was doing anything that was not specifically sanctioned by Lansa. She seemed especially hateful of his visions.

To be fair, none of his visions had ever actually come true, but he was sure they were visions, and that, eventually, they would bear fruit.

Lansa put her hands on the side of his face and kissed him on the cheek. "Kochen. We don't need saving."

Lansa walked from the sanctum and left him standing in the dirt-floored room, watching motes of dust dance in the air... trying to predict where each one would land.

Chapter 2:

The Hunters

Lonpearl lounged in the morning sun. They were late, but it was a good thing. Lonpearl walked up behind his daughter, placed his hands under her arms and lifted her into the air. Her giggle shot through his heart in a way that he could only think of as warm.

Stot appeared with a red clay jug of water in her hands. She smiled at him, the apples of her cheeks bunching, and her teeth shining in the gloom of their house. Earthen walls and a dirt floor, decorated with mats of woven corn silk, but Stot was the greatest decoration.

"Well are you going hunting or not?" Stot asked.

Lonpearl shrugged his shoulders. "I thought we were, but who knows? They take their time."

"If the farmers were as lazy as you hunters, they'd be planting seeds in the snow," she said.

Lonpearl tossed Hubra in the air, her little arms and legs shooting out, trying to find anything solid to hold onto. Lonpearl caught his daughter in his arms, soaking in her laugh. "Is it such a bad thing to have me around for just a little longer?"

Stot smiled, "I can't wait until you're gone."

"Oh, really?" he said as he placed Hubra on the ground.

"Yes," Stot said, glaring at him. Lonpearl set Hubra on the ground, and prodded her through the door and out onto the landing with gentle hands. With Hubra outside, watched by the inevitable elders sitting on the terrace, Lonpearl turned and wrapped his arms around his wife, squeezing her tight to his body, and kissing her. She pounded on his chest with her arms, but it was a show. Soon they were locked together, one creature with two heartbeats.

Farway's voice interrupted their efforts to give Hubra a sibling. "Time to go, Lonpearl," his raspy voice yelled through the mud walls. Lonpearl sighed. As he stood up, his penis jutting into the cool air, Stot grabbed him and gave him one last caress, smiling, mischief in her eyes. Lonpearl groaned out loud, grabbed his spear, and shifted his clothing to try and conceal his bulge before he stepped into the sunshine of the third terrace. "I love you," he said over his shoulder.

"You're just hoping I'll be here when you get back," Stot said.

Lonpearl shook his head and then pushed open the wooden door that led out to the village.

"You have the worst timing," he told Farway as he stepped out into the warming air of the cliffs.

Farway squatted on the ground, his scarred body rippling with muscles, his hair wound with trinkets of successful hunts, feathers, claws, and teeth. He poked Hubra in her tummy, sending waves of laughter through her. Lonpearl snatched her up, kissed her on the cheek and then pushed her back inside the house.

"It's not my fault you guys wait until the last minute to make love."

"No, but it is your fault that we waited around so long," he shot back.

Farway threw a muscle-corded arm over Lonpearl's shoulder, "Maybe you'll hunt better, knowing what's waiting at home for you."

Lonpearl laughed. "Or maybe I'll just stick a spear through you and come back here on my own."

9

Farway put his hands over his heart, feigning injury. "What would you do without me, Lonpearl? What would any of you do without Farway?"

"We probably wouldn't spend three night out of every ten sleeping out of doors away from our wives."

Farway waved his hand in the air. "Bah, wives make men soft."

"I wasn't soft just a minute ago," Lonpearl shot back. Their laughter echoed over the cliffs as they began their descent, grasping onto the rough wooden rungs of the ladders that led from the third terrace to the second. "When are you going to settle down, Farway?"

"The wild is my mistress," he said.

"You should hear yourself sometimes." Lonpearl jumped off the ladder and landed on the ground, using the butt of his spear to break the impact.

Farway did the same. "What would I hear if I should hear myself, Lonpearl?"

He almost said the truth. He almost told Farway that he would hear a fool and a coward. Farway was afraid to live. The village was not the place for him. A wife would only drive him further away. He was only comfortable away from the village. It wasn't so much about the hunt as it was about getting away, escaping, but to what? Farway was a fool for not seeing this much about his own nature. But Lonpearl was not the type to throw these truths in another man's face. Show a fool his reflection in the water and he will dispute it. Let him find out on his own, and he will remember his face forever. "You would hear Farway, the greatest hunter that ever lived, talking about making love to the wild."

"That does sound ridiculous." Farway hopped over to the next ladder and began climbing down it.

"Have you given any thought to settling down?" Lonpearl asked. "There are several ladies here that could do with some company, and you're getting past the age where

10

anyone your age is available. If you wait too much longer, the only single lady around will be Lansa."

"There is plenty of time for that. I'm not ready yet. Besides, I bet Lansa is great in the dirt."

Lonpearl shook his head. Farway seemed to believe that tomorrow would always come, that the sun would always rise, and that Farway himself would always be young. Lonpearl watched as the women going about their chores stopped to look at Farway's bare chest, bronzed, criss-crossed with scars and layered with hard muscle. Some merely glanced out of the corner of their eyes. Farway was a marked man, the most prized catch of the village, but he refused to sit still for the spear.

As they reached the floor of the valley, the others were waiting. There was Ghulish with his severe face and his shaved hair with the little lock of hair hanging off the back. Hinler smiled at him, his two front teeth missing, and his long black hair tied into braids. His face was wide, perhaps the widest in the village. There were many more, but together, these four made up the leadership circle of the hunters.

Everyone took their cues from Farway. His physical superiority could not be matched, and outside of the village, he was their leader. Ghulish came second, his closeness to Farway meaning that he always had his ear, though the dark words he whispered were seldom known by anyone other than Farway, his influence was great. Hinler could sway the opinions of many with his wide smile and his cheerful manner. He was respected and liked by all. Lonpearl came fourth, his sway won by deeds, the ability to track, and the wisdom that he showed. Though Farway was the leader, should Lonpearl set his feet in the ground and reject one of Farway's ideas, most of the men would side with Lonpearl. He seldom used this power, and this gave him even more sway among the hunters. Should he need to make a point, the men would listen.

"Can we go now?" Ghulish spat, his clipped speech and inherent cantankerousness floating through the air on his words.

"Yes, let's move out," Farway said. "before Lonpearl decides to go back and finish what he started with his wife." There was a round of laughter, and then they began marching. It was a loose formation born of freedom, twenty sets of feet flattening the earth beneath them. Though Farway was in charge, they were each their own person, each their own leader. They chose to follow each other for the good of the village, for the good of the hunt, and to put food on the fire. It was an easy company, and they drifted out of earshot of the cliffs, time and stress disappearing with every step.

In the distance, Lonpearl thought he saw someone walking towards the river. "Is that Kochen?" Lonpearl asked.

Hinler put his hand over his eyes to block out the glare of the sun. He squinted and said, "No, that isn't Kochen."

"How do you know?"

"Because that guy is carrying two pitchers. When is the last time you saw a priest carry anything?" Hinler slapped him on the arm and moved away as Lonpearl cast one last look into the distance. He could swear it was Kochen.

Farway turned west, and the rest of them followed, away from the river.

Chapter 3:

The First Vision

Kochen stepped lightly over the scrub brush as he made the hike down to the river, a thick pole made from one of the long-gone pine trees that used to grow on the mesa slung over his back. The river seemed close, but it was just an illusion, like the full moon on a cloudless light seeming to hang just out of arm's reach. With nothing between himself and the river besides bushes and the occasional stunted willow or cottonwood tree, he knew he was in for a hike.

Kochen shifted under the weight of the oak pole, trying to balance two clay jugs hanging off either end of it. The pole was straight now, but when he returned, the branch would bend from the weight of the water and the jugs... as would he. Though he was close to manhood, the musculature of his arms had not fully developed and lines of ribs showed through the brown skin of his chest. He had the soft body of a priest. The other villagers pointed at him and laughed as he set out with the buckets draped over his shoulders, flexing their own muscles and calling him a woman.

He had been spared the life of manual labor. It's the one thing his father's death had bought for him, a lifetime above the rabble, perched atop the canyon, learning the ways of the world from Lansa and the other priests. He didn't mind the farmers and hunters having fun at his expense. He understood it. He had been one of them before his father died, laughing at Doulk, the young priest, now not so young, as he was sent about the village on errands that were more about building character than actually accomplishing tasks. Now it was his turn. The village's farmers pointed at Kochen's soft hands and barely brown skin whenever he clambered down from the high perch of the priests on some errand in the village. When he had passed, the farmers would go back to pulling weeds and dead leaves from among the crops, their hands and knees buried in the rich earth. It was almost as if somewhere, there was an unspoken pact that young priests were to be mocked until they attained adulthood.

The sun beat down on Kochen's hair. He thought the heat from his head was going to bake his brain as he walked. Sweat poured down into his eyes and dripped from the end of his nose. Off to his right, he spotted a brief glimpse of color. He turned around to see how far he had come from the village. In the distance, he could see the limestone and mud houses of the village rising up out of the ground, the four terraces of the village were distinct, ladders leading from one of the village's platforms to the next. The people were tiny spots of brown standing still on the farmland, their movements lost among the wavy haze created by the hot air between them.

Kochen placed his burden on the ground and walked to where he had seen the flash of pink. Behind a gnarled cottonwood, he spied a stand of cactus, their branches looking like green paddles reaching towards the sky. Each branch was composed of a series of paddles, and at the end of each of the last paddles grew fruit, pink ovoids covered in tiny, sharp spines. Kochen pulled the fruits off the branches, careful to avoid pricking himself. He dropped them in the jugs and continued his journey away from the village and towards the river.

When he reached the water, he squatted at the edge of the clear water and rolled the prickly pears in the sand until the spines were all broken off and the skin of the pear was smooth. He rinsed the smooth fruit in the water. A warm flat rock next to the river called to him, so he sat and looked off into the sky, savoring the first bite of the pear. The tiny seeds swam in the juice of the pear as he chewed the soft flesh. The boy looked to the sky and watched thin wisps of white clouds swim through the blue sky overhead.

When he was finished eating, he tossed the remains of the pears in the water and watched them float down the river. Then he stood up and walked to the edge of the river, dunking the first jug under the water. He listened to the gurgling as air and water fought to take each other's place.

****

The people stood on the edge of the bank, watching in quiet, as they tried to drown him. Bubbles of air gurgled up from underneath the water, his skinny arms trying to fight off the hands that were holding him under. When his arms could fight no longer, and his vision began to turn black, he began to wonder what was on the other side. Would his father be there? He began to hear the deep rumble of another presence somewhere underneath the water. The rumble rose, and just as he was about to make sense of the rumblings, Lansa pulled him out of the water.

"You are my son now. You are the son of the people. You will serve. In time you will be the voice of the spirits, but first you must learn to listen to them."

She dragged Kochen to the riverbank and laid him among the hot stones; water bubbled out of his lungs, and he coughed and gagged for an eternity, begging to take sweet gasps of air. He could not, until his lungs had emptied themselves of water.

The village watched in silence as he retched. His first mother stood there, eyes red and raw, not for the loss of him, but for the loss of his father. She did not care about him. His loss was a gift, a promotion of status that freed her from having to raise the child on her own. Now she could marry again and create something more suitable. In time she would, and when Kochen passed her in the dusty paths of the village, she would avoid looking at him, her eyes averted as she pressed her new children on, her hands on their shoulders prodding them along.

Kochen saw this all in his mind's eye as the spots swam before his eyes and he struggled to catch his breath. Comets of flashing black and white swam in front of the world, and then the world changed. The white limestone cliffs began to darken and turn red. Blood fell from the sky, and where it touched the people, their skin split open, peeling away from the flesh underneath. The lucky few threw themselves from the cliff, falling on the ground, breaking bones and spilling their blood into the farm soil.

The unlucky tried to run inside, as their skin was flayed off of them by the bloody rain. Kochen thought, *There's not a cloud in the sky.*

****

It was the first vision of his life. When he had woken on the riverbank, screaming about the end of the world, the villagers had been terrified. Lansa had shaken him into silence and forbid him from talking. The other priests hid their agitation behind still eyes, but that night in the safety of the sanctum, they had grilled him over and over about what he had seen.

He was unpracticed and unable to recall the details that were important to the vision; their questions rained down upon him one after another, and with each passing moment, the vision drained from him like water from a knocked over jug. Some water would remain, but most of it would run into the sand of the ether to disappear forever.

Kochen pulled the jug from the water and placed it on the sand. He groaned at the weight of it. Carrying one jug would be tiresome; carrying two was apt to kill him. And this was the first trip of many. Lansa was not one for idle punishment. She would make sure he remembered this one. Kochen was torn as to whether Lansa's infrequent punishments were a blessing or a curse. On one hand, this prevented her from ever punishing him for inconsequential things, but on the other hand, when she did decide to punish him, he knew he was in for some torturous task that she cheerfully referred to as character-building. Kochen wondered if she truly reveled in punishing him the way he suspected she did. She was probably sitting on the upper terrace, laughing at him in the distance.

He submerged the second jug in the water, and when it was filled, he placed it on the ground about five feet apart from the other one. He grabbed the thick pine pole and put the ends through the loose leather loops that hung from holes drilled in the top of the jugs when they were first fired. He squatted underneath the pole and rose on his skinny haunches. He half expected to not be able to raise the jugs off the ground, but they rose easily enough.

The first steps were the hardest, as he had not yet found the balance of carrying two jugs of sloshing water on a stick. The pole would wobble to and fro, and there was a moment when he thought he was going to tip forward into the rocks of the riverbank after he leaned forward a little too far. He managed to right himself, though the strain of doing so taxed his back and his upper thighs to their limits. He began his journey back to the village, the sun rising high almost directly overhead, beating down on his black hair. Other waterbearers began to appear, children of all ages, jugs in hand or balanced on their heads. He was no more than a quarter of the way back to the village when the first waterbearers he had seen started trotting past him. By the time he was halfway, he saw some of the same faces headed back, their jugs empty and mocking smiles on their faces. Their bodies were thicker than his, their eyes cruel and filled with jealousy. This was something they did every day. This was something he hadn't done since his father died, and they reveled in it. They reveled in seeing a priest brought down to their level in the dirt, the heat, and the sun.

He didn't blame them. One had to earn their place in the village, and all he had done for his entire life was see bad things... in real life and in visions.

Chapter 4:

Do It Right

The village was bustling by the time he reached it. The women were watering the crops, corn, beans, and squash, all layered together the way the ancestors had taught them. A steady stream of children filed from the river back to the farmland where they dumped their loads into a large clay cistern, and the men were nowhere to be seen, except for the old men who sat with their old wives, if they were still alive, on the terraces. They peered down at them, secure in their position. They had put in their time to make it to elder status, bending their backs for years. Many of them had crafted parts of the village, expanding it to make room for growing families years ago, using their hands, hard rocks, and their own sweat to transform a cliff face into a place that could accommodate hundreds of people. They had earned their right to bake in the sun like clay figures, staring down at them from the cliff's roughhewn terraces.

Kochen could feel their eyes as he approached the cistern, jugs dangling low as his back bent forward under their weight. Sweat ran into his eyes, and the sun glared down at him along with the eyes of the elders. He felt as if he were on display for the entire world to see. Even the women in the field were probably eyeing him out of the corner of their eyes as they watered the ground and plucked weeds and dead leaves off the crops.

Careful not to spill the precious water in the pitchers, Kochen squatted to the ground, sliding out from underneath the wooden pole. He rubbed his hand over his neck. He couldn't tell, but he was sure it had left a nice indentation back there. He lifted up one pitcher and tipped it over the edge of the cistern, careful not to spill a drop. Water was sacred. Spilling it was not.

When he finished dumping most of the second pitcher, he held it up to his mouth, letting the cool water wind its way through his mouth and into the cold pit of his stomach. When he had gotten every drop he could, he lowered the pitcher to find Lansa standing in front of him, her stern face judging him silently.

"You must move quicker."

She didn't say anything else. She simply turned on her moccasin-clad heel and left. He could feel the eyes of the elders upon him, weighing and calculating. Without wiping the sweat off of his brow, he bent over, adjusted the pole in the loops of the pitchers and began the long trek back to the river. His muscles ached, and his right shoulder felt as if it were going to fall off at any moment... he bet Lansa would demand that he walk to the river and fetch water even if it did. That's the way she was.

****

Footprints. There were footprints in the sanctum. This was to be expected. That they needed to be wiped away every night was not. When he asked Lansa why, she had muttered something about tradition. Another priest, Harcha, told him the real reason.

"The sanctum is holy," Harcha said. "If you want the spirits to appear, there must be no sign of man, no footprints to say, 'This is the house of the people, not of spirits.' Though the spirits guide us, they cannot abide us. This is why they communicate through visions. While we

20

slumber, we are most susceptible. The nearer they are... the more susceptible. For these reasons, we must take care to abolish all signs of our passing. The sanctum must never be personalized, it must never show even the print of a single toe in the dust."

"Why must we depend on the spirits?" Kochen asked.

Harcha looked at Kochen as if he had sprouted a third eye in his forehead. "The spirits guide us, and keep us safe. Through our growth and prosperity, they grow and prosper as well."

"Does Lansa believe this?" he asked.

Harcha smiled. "One never knows what another believes. We only know what they say they believe."

The answer was unsatisfactory to Kochen. "But if you had to guess."

"Lansa does what she needs to do."

Kochen stopped asking questions. Sometimes getting a straight answer out of Harcha was like trying to suck water out of a stone. Harcha was a believer. He believed in the spirits, worshipped them even. Bimisi was one such spirit. It could not abide the presence of the people. It had punished his father and changed Kochen's life forever. Harcha's description of spirits did not mesh well with Kochen's actual experience with them.

For this reason, when Lansa handed him the cottonwood branch to brush away the footsteps of the people, he only half-heartedly did the job, starting at the far entrance to the sanctum and shuffling backwards. What did he care if the spirits didn't come near? Why would he want the creature that killed his father to visit him at night. He didn't care, but Lansa did. As he flopped down on his fur mat in the sleeping quarters of the sanctum, Lansa rose, and walked to the door to examine the work that he had done. The room was filled with snores, and just as he was about to fall asleep, she grabbed him by the hair and pulled him to his feet.

"Do it right." She shoved him into the sanctum and handed him the branch. Kochen yawned and stared at the entirety of the sanctum. It was a rough square room, large with a low ceiling of rock and a floor made of dirt. Redoing the floor would take forever.

It was late; he wanted to sleep. He went through and did what he thought was a good job, smoothing out anything that looked like it could have been made by a human. When he stood up, his lower back ached from being bent over for so long. As he spun around he came face to face with Lansa. She pointed to a few spots that he had missed. Then she grabbed his arm and pulled him through the sanctum, pointing out a handful of other spots among his freshly swept floor. When she was done, the entire floor of the sanctum was freshly covered in their footprints.

"Do it right," she said. This time, Kochen took his time, his knees in the dirt, he moved backwards, erasing all signs of their passing. When he stood at the exit to the sanctum, he turned around to look at the ground. It was unmarred, as if no one had ever been there before.

Lansa walked up behind him, and put her hand on his shoulder. "Now we will dream," she said into his ear, the snores of the other priests threatening to drown out her whisper.

That night, Kochen dreamed again. A vivid dream, full of terror, and something else... the faint hint of triumph. When he awoke, the dream vanished quickly as if it were a puff of winter breath. His mind was not yet trained.

****

The walk back to the river wasn't that bad. The pole and the pitchers had seemed heavy when he first set out that morning. After having carried the full pitchers back to the village, he had formed a new definition of heavy in his mind. Now they were positively light. He smiled at the children that passed him, clay jugs balanced on their heads. A few even smiled back.

Of course, by his fourth trip back to the river, he was no longer smiling. It took too much energy to smile. Each time he would return to the village, and Lansa would appear, telling him to be faster, be quicker. Each time he headed back he was more exhausted than the next.

He finished dumping the water from his fourth excursion into the cistern. The elders on the terraces had wrapped themselves in blankets, the shade of the canyon descending upon the village itself. The air buzzed with evening insects, freed from the oppressive heat of the day. He could smell the smoke of the fires and see them rising from twenty different spots along the terraces. As he went to place the jugs back where he had gotten them that morning, Lansa appeared again.

"Once more," she said simply before turning away again.

"It will get dark soon," he replied.

"Then you better hurry," she said coldly without even looking at him. She climbed the ladder to the first terrace, and pulled the ladder up behind her. Kochen looked up at her for a second, and then looked at the angle of the sun. What he saw did not please him.

Chapter 5:

The Stick People

Kochen walked briskly, his toes kicking dust, dirt, and rocks as he scrambled towards the river. His breathing came in ragged jags, and the cool air sent a chill across his sweat-soaked body. He paid no attention to the weight of the pole or the jugs. He fell a few times, stubbing his toe on a rock once and hooking his foot underneath an exposed root the second time. Each time, he split a knee until blood ran down both of his shins. Had he paused to look, he would have seen tiny rocks embedded in each of his knees.

His body shook from strain, and as he neared the river, he could see the blue waters darkening, the bottom of the river disappearing in the failing light. He dropped the jugs to the ground harder than he wanted to, hoping in silence that he hadn't cracked them. He grabbed one and thrust it under the water, waiting impatiently for it to stop gurgling.

The air escaped from the jug slowly, and then slower, and then it stopped escaping at all. His heart pounded in his ears like a drumbeat, picking up in intensity. Kochen's eyes rolled back in his head, and he fell to the ground.

****

They passed in the dawn, thin, weary, and covered in paint. The mists of the river cloaked them, and they waded silently through the frigid mountain runoff, not making a sound. When they emerged, they were painted black and white, their sticks held in their hands and murder in their eyes. They came for fighting. They came as the hand of death. At this time of the morning, the villagers would be in the field, the hunters already gone to range up and down the river, scrounging for food and hunting down prey.

The Stick People held their sticks in front of them, deadly spears, bows, and clubs all made to maim. They crept silently through the brush, their black and white war paint blending into the blasted landscape.

****

Kochen sat up, pebbles buried in his face. He brushed them off, and then looked at the last sliver of light as it faded behind the canyon. The sun was gone, the sky glowing orange in farewell. The canyon could be a dangerous place when the darkness came and it would be dark by the time he reached the village. He held his vision in his mind, trying to picture every detail as he had seen it. The vision had been different than the others. He sensed the immediacy of the vision, and he no longer worried about the darkness... he just wanted to get back to the sanctum and tell Lansa... but first he had to get there.

Kochen had no idea how long he had been asleep, but he felt as if it couldn't have been for more than a moment. In the fading twilight, he loaded up the jugs and plunged up and down the low hills of the land, water sloshing back and forth, spilling more than he wanted to, but not quite caring at the same time. He knew full well, there was a chance that Lansa would send him out again to fill the jugs, but he counted on his message being more important.

He skidded to a stop as the village rose above him, fires glowing orange in the night and the smell of grilling fish and smoke spreading over the canyon. The brown earth of the farmland stood between himself and the cistern. Stalks of corn reached for the sky, jutting out of the earth like his hair out of his scalp in the morning.

His moccasins sank in the soft earth, as he moved quickly towards the cistern. On the edges of the cliff faces that hung over him, he could see elders holding torches, encouraging him.

"Hurry, Kochen. Make haste. The night is coming," Dantish yelled from the third terrace, his brown hand waving at him, all tendons and bones.

He dropped his load carefully, standing next to the cistern, just on the edge of the farmland. As the last drop of water tumbled from the pitcher, the last light of the sun disappeared entirely, and the twilight came upon the village, torches glowing on the cliff face. He set the clay jug on the ground, hoping to never see another one in his life.

Like a crooked old man, he sprinted across the farmland, hoping to beat whatever menace lurked under the fertile ground. The elders had stopped calling to him, an awkward and expectant silence overtaking the still evening air as they watched his stooped lope.

His thighs burned with exhaustion as he ran through the field, the dry leaf blades of the corn rows slapping against his face. Kochen was in sight of the ladder when he tripped for the third time that day. He turned back around, expecting to see the white claw of Bimisi reaching for him the way it had reached for his father. Instead, he saw the leaves of a stalk of corn seemingly alive, curling back onto their stalk, as if their sole purpose in life had been to trip him and send him tumbling to the ground. He didn't believe his eyes, but then, belief was a ethereal construction, and by the time the corn stopped moving, he had made up his mind that what he saw was real.

In the distance, he could hear a strange sound, a rustling sort of noise, combined with a rushing sound, as if the river were just a few feet away. The corn began to shake on the farmland, and Kochen rose to his feet, hesitating, even though he knew he shouldn't. He could feel the tremors through the deerskin on his feet. He ran. Despite the days trials, Kochen found energy that he didn't even know he had. When he had gone twenty feet, he looked behind and saw the ground swelling upward as if something hidden was moving under the soil. He did not look for long. He ran forward, leaping into the air, and landing on the ladder. He climbed as fast as he ever had, and then sat on the edge of the cliff face watching the corn sway in the breeze. The sound was gone. The mound of raised earth was nowhere to be seen. There was only the crackling of fires from the village and the sighing of the wind through the canyon.

The elders said nothing. They nodded their heads and walked back towards the cookfires, their ancient skin yearning for the heat of the flame.

When Kochen was sure that nothing was going to climb out of the ground, he pulled up the ladder, and went to find Lansa.

Chapter 6:

Listen. What is that?

He found Lansa next to the fire, staring at the flames as they moved about, spewing smoke into their eyes with every shift in the wind. A thick bobcat fur was draped over her shoulders, its dotted pattern reflecting the light. Her eagle-like nose cast a large shadow on the right side of her face as she turned to look at him.

"You made it." Lansa handed him a clay plate with the still steaming leg meat of a desert rabbit left on it. As tired and hungry as he was, Kochen did not reach for it.

"Eat. There is time enough to talk later. You must rebuild your strength. You have more water to carry tomorrow."

Kochen sat on the ground, his muscles knotting and unknotting in his thighs and his back. The hot meat was welcome, but the water was even more welcome. Every time Kochen would try to talk to Lansa, she would tell him to hush and drink more water.

The fire burned into the night, and eventually the day caught up with Kochen; the flames swam in front of his eyes, and he could see the Stick People dancing in them. The heat from his sunburned skin kept him warm. When he woke in the morning, the fire was merely ashes, and someone had laid a fur over his body.

Smoke still guttered up into the brightening purple sky. Kochen sat up, rubbed his eyes, and went to relieve himself over the edge of the cliff face. Mists covered the canyon floor, and he remembered his vision. *Where is Lansa?*

The village was just coming to life as he sprinted along the paths, waiting at the bottom of each ladder as elders slowly made their way down them to reach the fields. He climbed as fast as he could, hoping to reach the sanctum to discover Lansa and the other priests waking from their sleep.

As he climbed the last ladder, he began to arrange his thoughts. He skidded to a stop in the dust. Lansa and Harcha were talking in low hushed tones, her shaved head almost brushing Harcha's bald, bulbous skull. Kochen had to wait until their conversation was over, as interrupting Lansa would likely set off another round of "character-building." The wait was long, and he had to fight to keep himself from interrupting, but he needed Lansa and Harcha in the best of moods when he told them about his dream. Eventually, Lansa looked over at him, bid the priest she was talking with to wait for a second, and then said to Kochen, "Shouldn't you be walking to the river to fetch some water?"

With that, she began speaking to Harcha again about winter stores and crop yields. When she noticed that Kochen was still standing there, annoyance flashed across her face. "Do you have something to say?"

"Can I speak to you in private?" he asked.

"You know we have no secrets here. Speak."

With that, Kochen spewed everything he had seen. All of his plans of sounding intelligent, calm, and collected fell to the wayside as he tripped over his own tongue to get the entire vision out. When he was finished, Lansa did nothing. He had expected her to go screaming through the village, and call the men and women back to the safety of the village's cliffs. Instead, she placed her soft hand on his shoulder and led him to the back of the sanctum. Harcha looked at him, a sad look in his eye.

29

When they were alone, Lansa looked at him, disappointment in her eyes, and said, "You were heat sick. The heat caused you to see things that weren't there."

"That's not true," he replied, hurt by the implication that what he had seen hadn't been real. "Don't you believe in visions? Don't you believe in the spirits?"

Lansa smiled down at him, the way his father used to smile down at him when he would say something particularly stupid. "Visions and spirits are just stories parents tell their children."

Kochen knew differently.

****

Father sat on the edge of the cliff face, his feet dangling over the side and his rough hands carving chunks of flesh from a squash. It was winter, the nights were cold, and he and Kochen were both wrapped in furs, far away from the cookfires.

"Do you believe in the spirits, Kochen?"

It was a trick question. He knew it was. Father always tricked him. He would ask Kochen questions, always knowing the answers, and then tell him why he was wrong. Kochen had given up trying to figure out what his father wanted to hear. Instead, he chose to tell the truth. His father was going to tell him what he wanted him to learn either way.

"No."

His father looked at him, surprise etched on his face. "How can you not believe in the spirits? Look at all that is around you. The stars overhead, the fields that grow food, the river full of water, it's all here for us. The spirits did this."

"I've never seen one," he replied.

His father nodded his head and smiled. "You are skeptical. That is good. I don't want a gullible son. Gullible children often find themselves in trouble thanks to their friends. I don't have to worry about that with you." His father wrapped an arm around his shoulders. "But I'll let you in on a secret. The spirits are real."

Kochen leaned back and looked at the sky, a shooting star flew across the dark blue night sky, screaming in and out of existence in the blink of an eye. "How do you know?"

"They've talked to me."

Kochen laughed at this. "What did they say?"

"They don't say anything. They speak to you in pictures and feelings."

Kochen giggled some more. He was pretty sure his father was trying to play a trick on him.

"No, it's true. Close your eyes," his father said, his white teeth smiling in the moonlight, as he popped a chunk of squash into his mouth.

Kochen did as he was bid.

"What do you see?"

Kochen closed his eyes, but all he saw was darkness. "I see darkness."

"What do you feel?"

Kochen thought with his eyes closed. "I feel happy, not like laughing happy, but full belly happy."

His father leaned in close and Kochen felt the warmth of his breath on his cheek. "That's a spirit. Jamyong, the night spirit. He flows through you now, blessing your body. He robs your mind of sight, fills your heart with contentment, and then breathes his hot breath into your furs, lulling you to sleep, so you can wake up the next day and do the spirit's bidding."

"What does Jamyong look like?" he asked.

"Ah, you still want to see one, don't you?"

Kochen nodded his head "yes" and opened his eyes. His father leaned back and looked up at the stars, popping

31

another chunk of squash into his mouth. "Aren't you going to tell me?"

His father shook his head.

"Why not?"

His father's face was serious, like the limestone cliffs, without a curve in sight as he spoke, "Spirits are shy. They don't like our eyes. They do things for us, and all we have to offer them is our belief. They feed off it, growing fatter and fatter. When the people stop believing, they show themselves... and you don't want that to happen."

"Why?"

Despite the fact that Kochen was sure his father was most definitely playing a trick on him, he continued to listen. "When a spirit shows itself, a blood price must be paid."

"Why don't the priests speak of this, Father?"

His father waved his hands in dismissal at the rooms at the top of the cliff. "The priests are no closer to the spirits than you or I. They would have you believe in their special powers, but we all have the power, if we are able to stop and listen. They don't tell you because they don't want you to know that you have every right to live as high in the village as you wish."

Kochen thought about this for a minute, then asked, "If we have the ability to live wherever we wish, then why don't we have a room at the top of the village?"

"Because the others are gullible, and the priests have them fooled into believing that they are special. But you want to know something?"

"What?"

"The spirits are coming. The blood price will be paid. It has been too long, and the villagers have been grumbling about the priests, bossing us all around."

"How do you know?"

"The spirits showed me... in a vision."

****

His father's vision had been partially correct. He now rested in the ground, feeding the spirits, the blood price paid in full. Many in the village still doubted the tale that Kochen had told that early spring morning after Bimisi had dragged his father into the ground. Kochen never knew if Lansa was one of them, but that morning he found out. Lansa may believe in the spirits, but she didn't believe in visions. She didn't believe in him.

He made his way to the river in the aching orange of the morning sun, pole slung over his shoulders, pitchers dangling from the ends. His back was pure pain, his neck was raw where the pole rested, and his shoulders felt like they were constantly on the verge of cramping.

It crossed his mind to drop the pitchers and find his own way in the wilderness, just drop it all and survive on his own. But his life had been easy, and the world was harsh. Survival was not something the priests had taught him. Picking fruit and berries would be fine, but hunting was something the priests were forbidden to do. The moment he had been abandoned by his mother and taken in by the priests, he had been forbidden from killing. His visions were real; he knew that, and the world was slowly coming to focus in his budding mind. Killing would not be acceptable for him. He needed the visions. He needed to guide the people. Unfortunately, Lansa stood in his way... and without the cold act of murder to free him from her practicality and disbelief, he was doomed to toil, fetching water, carrying messages, and listening to the visions of those that had no visions at all.

Kochen found it odd that the priests still lived by a code ordained to please creatures that many didn't believe existed. Those who harmed animals muted their abilities to communicate with the spirits, or so the priests said. In the morning, the priests would awaken and share their visions.

33

Most were about things that were solidly predictable. Farway's men would be successful in the hunt, the rains would come, so-and-so's baby would arrive soon. He was surprised that they didn't just wake up and foretell the rising of the sun in the east.

He found himself at the river. As he set the pole on the ground, he plunged the first jug into the water, pretending it was Lansa, the last gasps of her life emerging as bubbles in the river. When he set the jug aside, he felt pangs of guilt. Lansa was Lansa, and that was a good thing to be. She was strong, wise, and kept the village in good health. Her knowledge of herbs and medicine were second to none in the village, and they all profited because of it. Lansa kept nothing for herself. When Farway and the hunters returned from the hunt, it was her right to select the pick of the hunt. She always took a modest portion, not the worst, but not the best either.

As he squatted in the sand of the riverbank, he submerged the second jug. A hundred feet to his right, a naked girl about his age dove into the water, startling him. Kochen stood there, trying to decide if he was going to alert the girl or try to sneak off without her noticing. In the end, he decided to act like a startled deer. Her black hair shone in the morning sun, and she floated on her back, kicking her legs, her breasts cresting out of the water. The jug had stopped bubbling for some time before she noticed him staring at her.

She smiled at him, and as she walked from the water and tossed her dress over her thick-waisted body, he had the impression that she was actually pleased to see him. He smiled back.

Kochen's first sign that something was wrong was the sound of snapping twigs. Simultaneously, Kochen and the girl looked to the east to see painted warriors streaming out of the woods on the opposite side of the river, silent but

34

for the occasional snapping of old tree branches, spears and bows held in their hands.

On the opposite riverbank, he saw a man clad in bearskin leggings hop up on the ancient bole of a long dead tree. He held his bow out on front of him, and as Kochen locked eyes with the man, an arrow hurtled at him. Kochen ducked out of the way, and the bearskin warrior smiled at him, perfect white teeth shining in the sun.

The warriors were a third of the way across the waist-deep water when the girl reached him. Together they ran, he freely, her with her dress up around her thighs, their feet aching against the sharp rocks of the valley.

"Run," he told her. "Run or you'll never run again."

Without stopping, she peeled the dress off in one smooth motion. The girl was far faster than he was. She was bound to reach the village minutes before him. He watched her brown buttocks jiggle in the sun. He kept his eyes locked on them, even as they disappeared into the distance, behind a stand of stunted willow trees. Even then, he saw them in his mind's eye.

He was still thinking about them when he stepped on a jagged jut of volcanic rock that shredded his moccasin and imbedded itself in his foot. Kochen fell to the ground and chanced a look behind him. Through the shimmery hot air, he could see warriors approaching, spears held high. The paint ran from their bodies, but their faces were still white, the color of death... the color of spirits.

Kochen turned his attention back to his foot, and he began to tug on the rock. The pain was awful, and when he touched the rock, agony swept through his body. The thought of a hoard of Stick People bearing down on him took root, and the panic began to rise in the back of his mind. He had to do it. He had to pull it out. With one hand he reached under his foot and grasped the rock. He had time to take one deep breath, and then he yanked on the shiny black obsidian. Blood spattered to the ground, the

35

sound of the drops masked by his howl of pain, and when he next looked up, after the tears had cleared in his eyes, a man with a ghostwhite face stood over him, eagle feathers laced throughout his long black hair. He grinned at Kochen. Kochen smiled back, and then the man raised his arm up, and brought it down, turning Kochen's world into blackness.

****

Loudest Laugh stared down at the boy. *Was he the one? Was he the reason they had come to this spirit forsaken part of the world?* If he was, Loudest Laugh hoped that he hadn't hit him too hard. The club in his hand felt heavy, and he longed to hear the wind rustling the leaves of the trees.

He squatted to the ground and looked at the boy's face. It was soft, unwrinkled. He was certainly no grower of plants. The boys hands were softer than his face. Loudest Laugh placed his fingers to the side of the boy's throat. The pulse was there, strong, pressing against his fingers rhythmically. He would be fine.

Ever Sleep stood next to him looking down at the unconscious boy on the rocks. Blood jetted from the wound in the boy's foot. "Is that him?" Ever Sleep asked.

"I don't know. Bind his foot." Loudest Laugh stood up, and spotted He Who Makes the Drum Beat. "I think I found him."

The leader strolled by him, his face covered in white paint with bands of red swirled around his eyes. His barrel-chested body seemed as if it were hewn from rock. He did not pause as he said, "Think and know are two different things." With that, He Who Makes the Drum Beat and the rest of the warriors continued past him.

Loudest Laugh hissed through his teeth. The slight would not be forgotten. "Help me bind his wound," he said to Ever Sleep.

Ever Sleep laughed, as he jogged away. "I didn't come here to heal wounds. I came here to make them. Have fun babysitting." Ever Sleep turned and ran after the war party, white paint dripping off of his body in the bright sunlight.

Loudest Laugh looked back at the boy on the ground, rage thumping in his chest. He grit his teeth, and fought the urge to smash the boy's face with a rock. He was just a boy, a still living boy. There would be glory today, but it wouldn't be his. Loudest Laugh pulled his waterskin from his belt and cleaned the boy's wound. When it was clean, he bound the wound with strips of leather, squatted down and hoisted the boy over his shoulder, confidant that he had missed all of the fun.

Chapter 7:

Burdens

From her perch on the highest terrace of the cliff, Lansa was the first to see the girl appear from behind the trees. Her brown skin was covered in sweat, and her face was filled with terror. *What had the boy done now?*

Lansa had reached the ladder that led from the top terrace to the third terrace of the village, when she spotted something else in the distance. There, in broad daylight, men moved silently, their white faces barely discernible over the blasted rock and scrub brush that carpeted the valley. Were it not for the fact that the war paint had washed off many of their torsos in the river, she doubt she would have noticed them at all. As it was, it was as if an army of headless people were approaching under the morning sun, their face paint blending into the blasted background.

"Drums!" she yelled waving to catch the attention of Doulk, the youngest priest, who was praying on the cliff-face. He hopped down from his perch and ran to the war drum that rested underneath a stone overhang. Without hesitation, he began beating on the drum. The boom of the drum danced across the valley, and it wasn't long before the people below were flooding back to the cliff face. The drum was a sign, a sign that death was in the valley.

Lansa climbed down to the bottom terrace as fast as she could, not even stopping to spare a look at the approaching army. Now that they had been clearly spotted, they were in full flight, spears and bows held at the ready. When she reached the bottom of the terrace, a group of elders were already there, pulling up children as they climbed the ladders, tears streaming from their faces, fear etched into them the way time etches itself onto the face of the old. Lansa grabbed the last ladder she had climbed down, and placed it over the edge of the bottom terrace, it's rocky flatness suspended some twenty feet above the floor of the valley that the river had carved long ago.

Most of the women and some of the men were up the ladder when the naked girl appeared, lathered and wild-eyed. The men moved aside to let her climb. Lansa was the first to help her off of the ladder, where she collapsed in her arms, slipping to the dirt.

"Where is Kochen?"

The girl looked at her, no more than fifteen, "I don't know." Lansa's heart skipped in her chest. She stood and looked out over the valley floor. The far end of the cornfield was shaking violently as the Stick People made their way through the fields. She tried to see him, but he was not there.

The frontrunners of the army burst from the corn, their spears held at the ready, and fell upon the last handful of men to climb up the ladders. They turned to fight, using what they had, sticks, thick pieces of wood used for digging furrows in the farmland. The clubs were no match for the sharp, fire-hardened spear tips of the Stick People. Blood splattered to the ground as the men screamed in the heat of the day, dust puffing up from the feet of their attackers.

"Pull them up."

The men who had reached the terrace began to pull the ladders up. They placed them on the terrace and then watched as the men down below began to chant, and wave around their weapons in triumph, standing over a handful of dead bodies.

For Lansa, it was all too familiar.

****

Lansa's new dress was still stiff. It would be weeks until the dried deerskin became supple and broken in. She hated it, but she had grown out of her previous dress. She moved through the field of corn, looking for her mother.

She stopped to talk to Gulfik, a kind old man who was missing some teeth, but who had never uttered an unkind word to a child in his entire life. The children of the village had come to love that broken-toothed smile. "Have you seen my mother?"

Gulfik looked down at her, and for one of the few times in his life, he had no smile to give her. "No, dear. She is not here."

Lansa didn't understand. She would have many exchanges like this throughout the day, but it wouldn't be until her father returned from the hunt that she would understand why.

"Where is mother?" she asked.

"She no longer cares to live here," he said simply. He hugged her against his sunbrown chest. Then he looked her in the eyes. "She is gone. Her mind is elsewhere."

"What do you mean?"

"If you want to see her, then climb to the Up Top, where the Corn Men dwell."

Lansa didn't like the look in her father's eyes. He had always been cold, and somewhat pragmatic, which is why the hint of sadness in his eyes looked out of place. The deep frown lines around his mouth were strained, and she could tell that the words he said were hard for him. "Maybe she will care to come back if she sees you. I have already tried."

The next day, as the sun rose over the cliffs, she began her climb. The way was steep, but she had always been a good climber. Any child who grew up in the village

40

became good at it. Sometimes it was the only way to obtain any sense of privacy, of solitude. The village was big, but perhaps not big enough. One was never more than ten feet from another person, or two or three. The steep, rough rocks of the cliff face led to all sorts of nooks and crannies where a society-tired child might find a brief respite from duty and chores.

So she climbed, the orange sun of the morning lighting her way. There were breaks along the way, and as she reached the halfway point, she sat on an outcropping of granite, her legs dangling over the edge. She looked down into the field, and she could see the people, their backs bent, tending to the corn, pulling weeds with their bare hands, ripping sickened nubs off of the cornstalks, and arranging the bean vines to curl around the stalks of corn.

Sweat ran down her face, and her stiff dress was more of a curse than a gift. She contemplated taking it off and climbing to the top without clothes, but she was past the age where that was considered proper. She spit over the side of the granite. Somewhere underneath her was the Sanctum. The angle wasn't right to see down that far, and if she wanted to see it, she would have to turn her body around and hang over the ledge, her head peeking over the side. The thought made her stomach turn inside out, and as she lifted herself up, she noticed that her arms lacked the strength they had in the morning. She knew she could get to the top, but she didn't know if she could get back down in the same day.

She was about to head back down when she saw the villagers running through the fields, her people sprinting towards the cliff face. No, wait... they weren't all her people. Some were different, their faces painted. Everywhere they encountered her people, they would fall, as if they were playing some sort of game, but she knew differently. The people didn't play games once they reached a certain age. Through the howling wind of the cliff, she imagined she heard their screams as tiny blooms of red blossomed among the fallen villagers. Most of them reached the safety of the cliff face, and when the horrible show was over, the attackers stood on the farmland, hooting and hollering up at the people of the cliff.

Lansa decided to climb to the top. She didn't want to know or see what was at the bottom. With her rough farmhands, she grabbed an outcropping of granite and began the second half of her journey, thankful for the focus required to scale the cliff, because it kept her mind off of the slaughter below.

Near the top, her legs began to tremble as if with a mind of their own. There were no ledges to rest on, and her body was strained as far it would go. All she could do was press on, and hope that her legs would hold out until she reached the top.

The sun was past the high point of the day, and it would be falling soon. She knew she would have to spend the night on the Up Top. She hoped her father wouldn't worry, that he wouldn't think she had been stolen or killed by the attackers below. As she reached for her next handhold, she found a flat precipice covered in rough, dry grass. With one last burst of strength, she was there, hauling her legs over the edge, and rolling over onto her back to look at the sky. Her new dress was covered in grime, but she didn't care. The hot sandy soil was comforting, and she stretched her legs out while watching the clouds pass by in the sky.

She could feel the muscles in the back of her legs trying to cramp, so she sat up and began stretching them out. As she rotated her world upright, she noticed the handful of dirty shacks built on top of the cliff. Old deerskins and woven high-desert grass kept the elements out. Smoke rose from a hole in the middle of the shack, and the smell was odd.

Lansa was curious, but not curious enough to ignore the view of the valley behind her. Standing on the edge of the cliff, she could see the village far below, the farmland sloping into shale and stone, until it met the sandy river bank. On the other side, she could see a mirror image, only the cliffs on the other side of the river were more red than grey and white. She looked south, and saw the shape of the river mirrored on the edge of the cliffs. It continued forever, and she wondered where the river ended.

From inside one of the shacks, she heard coughing, so she turned her back on the view. Behind the shacks, scrubland ran towards the horizon, disappearing in a wavy haze of heat. Other than the occasional tuft of tough grass and a stunted tree here and there, there was nothing to see. She took her first hesitant step towards one of the shacks, regretting her decision to climb to the top of the cliff, but knowing that she was too tired to head back down.

As she reached the entrance, she moved a hanging deer hide to the side to reveal the interior. The shadowy interior was lit by a flickering fire that was more smolder than flame. There, next to the fire, in the arms of a wrinkled old man lay her mother.

The old man looked at her, his face sunken in around his toothless mouth. He was a Corn Man. A magic maker. The pot hanging over the fire was no doubt filled with corn mash, ready to be put into a jar and buried. He raised his head and bid her to sit across the fire from him. She did as she was told. Her mother didn't stir.

"You've come for your mother."

Lansa nodded her head.

"What makes you think she wants to go back down there, where the backs are bent, and the reward is birthing children and preparing meals?"

"She loves me." The Corn Man smiled at this, his ragged pink tongue poking through his withered gums.

"Maybe she does. But what is love?"

43

Lansa had no answer for this.

The Corn Man smiled some more. "Love is responsibility. Love is something that takes, takes, takes, and never gives. Love is a burden. Do you understand?"

Lansa felt guilty. She felt the truth in the Corn Man's words, felt them in her bones, but didn't quite know how to put her feelings into words.

"Up here, on top of the world, we simply are. We do what we want, when we want. There are no rules. The spirits do not even bother us here. There is only corn, only *tilnac,* only dreams and waking dreams. What can you offer your mother?"

Lansa was still thinking about her answer when her mother awoke. Her eyes were dead to her, and for the first time, her mother seemed like a total stranger. She sat up, leaving the old man's embrace, her mother's breasts dangling against the rounded paunch of her stomach. The Corn Man watched her, his eyes knowing, and tilted in an amused fashion. Her mother rose, exposing the old man's wrinkled and gray nakedness. She sat on her haunches, and began to grind some corn on a slab of cold granite that had been worn smooth over time.

"Mother."

Her mother stopped grinding to look at her. Her face was blank. "Your father needs you. You should head back home."

"It is too late."

Her mother went back to grinding corn. When she had ground up a fair amount, she gathered a clay jug and began chewing the cornmeal. She squatted and chewed, staring at Lansa, a hollow gaze, unmarked by emotion. Every once in a while, she would spit chewed corn juice, yellow and milky, into the red clay jar.

The Corn Man watched her mother, oblivious to Lansa's presence. Out of the corner of her eye, Lansa could see him quicken. Lansa froze in place. Her mother looked at her. "Wait outside."

Lansa rose from the ground and went outside. She reached the edge of the cliff, and then crawled to the edge and looked over it. In the world below, fires glowed in the darkness, their smoke rising high, even above the level of her own head. Near the river, more fires burned; the attackers had not gone.

She wondered what they were like, these attackers. Were they people like her? Did their mothers leave them to be the wives of Corn Men, chewing up corn, and spitting the juice into jugs. The villagers told tales of the Stick People, savages intent on nothing but murder and pillaging. Their crops, gained through toil and labor, would be ravaged, and then they would disappear, back to where they came from.

Groans and grunts emanated from the shack behind her. She had heard the noises before, but this time she didn't find them comforting. They made her nauseous, and she tried to will the sun to rise in the east. After a few minutes, the sounds ceased, and her mother came out with a clay cup filled with milky liquid. "Drink this."

Lansa held the cup up to her face. It smelled sweet. She drank a sip of the *tilnac*, it's sweetness soon followed by a sourness and a flush of warmth in her chest. Her mother sat down next to her, still naked and unashamed. She grabbed the clay cup out of Lansa's hand and drank deeply of it.

"They're dying down there," she told her mother.

Her mother looked up at the sky, cradling the cup between her breasts. "What goes on down there is no concern of mine."

"But what about father?"

"I wish him well, but we are finished."

"What about me?"

45

"You deserve better." An old toothless man pulled the deer-hide flap of his shack to the side and looked out at them.

"Come," he demanded. "I have need of you." Her mother rose, and drained the contents of the cup. She patted Lansa's head and walked meekly into the shack. There were more grunts and groans. Lansa fell asleep on the cliff face before the next round stopped.

When she awoke, a jug with a rope attached to it was sitting next to her. She understood what to do. Without saying goodbye, Lansa picked up the jug and stretched her muscles. They were sore, but not so sore that she couldn't climb back down the cliff and into the valley. The way down would be easier, but just as dangerous, and with a jug of *tilnac* slung over her shoulder, it was even more so.

Lansa cried for the first half of the climb, the unending wind of the cliffs drying the tears in her eyes before they could reach her cheeks. Her hands were cut and scraped and her moccasins were shredded. When she reached the halfway point, she stopped and set the jug on the outcropping of granite. She lay on her stomach and inched forward to see the world underneath. It was filled with smoke and fire. She looked above and thought of the Corn Man's words. *Love is a burden.* She felt it now, clinging to her as if she were carrying twenty jugs of *tilnac*. Her love was a burden. Loving her mom, caring for her, wanting her father and her mother to be one again, these things weighed her down, sapped her energy and kept her from feeling right.

Lansa stared down at the village, standing now on the balls of her feet, her toes hanging over the precipice. She could feel her love drawing her outward, into the air. *It would be so easy.*

She backed away and picked up the jug, continuing her descent. Lansa understood the Corn Man's words now. Her mother had been weak, too weak to bear her burden of love. She had retreated to the Up Top where the Corn Men fermented corn and produced *tilnac* for the rituals of the priests, trading the burden of love for a life of chewing, spitting and fucking for the wrinkled rejects who lived on the plains, their teeth long ago rotted away from the chewing of corn kernels.

Lansa's burden was heavy, but her back did not bend under its weight.

When she reached the floor of the topmost terrace, she saw many injured villagers curled up around fires, blood oozing through poultices made of grass and spider webs. Many of them were covered in coarsely stitched wounds, tied shut with the dried and cured intestines of animals. She hiked up to the door of the sanctum, and found a priest there. His name was Fesh, and he seemed older than the mountains to her, his shaved head gleaming in the evening sun, the only part of him that didn't seem wrinkled. She held the jug out to him, and he looked at it, knowing.

"Thank you, Lansa." She turned to walk away, but he put a hand on her shoulder. "Come with me." Lansa followed him as he descended the terrace ladders, his ancient body still limber enough to descend the ladders on his own. On the bottom terrace, they ducked under the edge of the wall, to avoid the arrows of the Stick People below. They could not avoid their mocking calls which were loud and insulting. They reached a hut and crawled inside through the door.

Bodies were arranged on the ground, including that of her father, his brown chest did not rise or fall, and tears fell from her eyes. Fesh placed an arm around her shoulder, and from then on he would guide her to become the leader that she was and to cope with the burden of love through discipline.

****

47

Though her burden was heavy, and her mind throbbed in alarm at the prospect of Kochen's safety, Lansa did what she was supposed to do. She directed the people to the second level of the village. They climbed as fast as they could, and once they reached the top, the wounded and tired villagers collapsed in the dust, sweat covering their bodies.

The men walked to the wall of the terrace, ducking down, lest a stray arrow pierce their bodies. They gathered around clay bowls filled with gray river rocks, washed smooth by the river. The men called them Nom's scales after the river spirit. They loaded them into thin strips of supple leather, and the air whistled as they twirled the leather-cradled rocks above their heads.

The Stick People below began to climb the rock face, and as they reached the first terrace of the village, the men let fly from the terrace above, striking them with the smooth rocks, drawing blood and breaking bones. Some Stick People continued to climb, while others sought to escape Nom's scales which resulted in mass confusion. From above, the villagers rained more stones down upon the men. The volley was greeted by a handful of arrows, but more Stick People had fallen to the ground, some never to move again.

Lansa watched it all from the third terrace, safely out of range of spears and arrows. She yelled her commands down to the men below, the muscles in their shoulders bunching and relaxing with each twirl of their slings. The Stick People were not many, and that night, they were less. As the sun moved overhead, she hoped that they would be able to keep up the pace. She hoped that Kochen was alright. She hoped that her burden would not be lessened by the time the night was through.

Chapter 8:

Bound and Delivered

His ankles felt like fire. His arms felt worse. But his foot hurt the most, the leather bandage cold from his own blood. When he opened his eyes the world spun in front of him, and he noticed corn all around him. Kochen was tied to a stake shoved into the ground, his arms spread wide on a crossbar. The sun was going down, and all around him, he saw cornstalks and Stick People looking up at him, their faces hidden behind paint and their long hair strewn with feathers.

A broadchested man with bands of red swirled around his eyes came up to him, the face paint giving him an angry appearance, though the lines of his face betrayed a calm demeanor.

"You are awake."

Kochen tried to focus on the man, but the best he could do was nod his head and groan as his chin sagged to his chest.

With the smooth end of a gnarled club, the man lifted his head and looked him in his eyes. "Are you the one we're looking for?"

Kochen was confused. "Why would you be looking for me?"

The man's eyes squinted at him, "You are the water hauler, the boy who dreams."

"I am Kochen. I am nobody."

The man laughed at him. "We shall see. When the sun goes down, that is when we will know the truth."

Kochen shook his head. Somewhere in the foggy remnants of his addled mind, he remembered his father. He remembered Bimisi surging up out of the ground and stealing his father into the underworld. "We have to leave here. Bimisi will come after dark."

The man laughed. "Your cliff spirits are nothing. If your spirits were so strong, you wouldn't need to live in a cliff, hiding from real men, real warriors." The man spat upon the ground and walked off. Other Stick People sat around, eating raw corn, and looking up at him, curiosity in their eyes.

The man who had knocked him out, the man with the white face paint laughed at him, his voice ringing through the night.

Bimisi would come... and the Stick People would die, along with Kochen.

****

Lansa and Kochen stood on the uppermost terrace, the morning sun baking down on them. "Where is your father, boy?"

Young Kochen stood there, his toes in the dirt. The words would not come. He had already told her the truth. he didn't know what more she wanted to hear.

"Where is your father?" Lansa commanded, her voice sharp like rocks and as unyielding as the cliff face that stood behind her. She nodded to a wizened old priest who stood to his left. The man bent down and looked him in the eye. Roughly, he grabbed Kochen by the neck and slapped him across the face.

The slap stung, but Kochen had felt worse from his own father. Still the words did not come. There was another slap, followed by another.

"Tell us what happened."

"Bimisi," he said when his face was red and warm and tears flowed from his eyes.

The priest that held him stepped back, doubt on his face. He looked to Lansa for guidance. Under her beak nose, Lansa chewed on her lip. "Where did you hear of Bimisi?"

Kochen could recount countless tales his father had told in their own house around the fire. "My father told me."

Lansa smiled at him. "He always was a storyteller, and now it appears his son is too." Kochen didn't like the way the priestess talked to him, and he didn't like the look in her eye.

"If you won't tell us what happened, then you will bake in the sun until you do. The sun has ways of making men tell the truth, and when your lips are cracked and so dry that not even blood will come out, and your eyes are shrunken in your head, then we will have the truth of you."

She nodded at the priest, and the man shoved Kochen out the door. On the Sanctum terrace there was a rock, smooth and hot. On this rock, Kochen was laid, hands and wrists tied to posts dug into the ground. Next to him, the old priest sat. His name was Vint. He would keep Kochen company through the coming days.

The first day Kochen cooked in the sun underneath a blue sky. His body dripped sweat from everywhere. Even his eyes felt like they were sweating. The whole time, Vint sat next to him asking, "Where is your father?"

His mother came by on that first day. She looked down at him with contempt in her eyes. He could barely make out her face as she leaned over him, covered in shadow, the sun beating into his eyes through the veil of her hair. "Help me, mother," he said.

She spat on him and left. The sun was hot, but not as hot as the wad of spit that dried on his chest. It burned there. Even after the spit had evaporated underneath the searing heat of the sun, Kochen could still feel it burning. Tears sprang to his eyes as he called out for his father.

Vint asked again, "What happened to your father?"

Kochen answered again... "Bimisi."

When night came on the first day, he collapsed into sleep. A fur was thrown over him, as nights on the cliff could be bitter cold, even when the day was hot. Underneath the fur, his sunburned body radiated heat, and if his hands or legs had been unbound, he would have happily kicked the fur to the side. He began to cry. He tried lifting his head to guide the tears to his parched lips, but it was no use. He laid his head back down and drifted off into sleep, comforted by the thought that they had at least thrown a blanket over him.

When he awoke, Vint was there, sitting in the orange morning sun, drinking water from a jug. Kochen was so thirsty that he swore he could actually smell the water.

"I have to make water," he said.

"Vint looked at him, and for a second there was a glint of pity in his eyes, and then he said, "So make it."

He did.

In the afternoon, when the farmers took refuge from the overhead sun, they climbed up and ate their lunch around him, joking about the smell of piss, and by now shit, that hovered over Kochen's sunbaked body.

Their words were cruel. *Look at the father killer. Look at the boy who betrayed his father and speaks of spirits. Kochen is cursed. Even his mother spat upon him.*

That night, Vint left him again. His tongue felt like it was made of compacted sand, and there wasn't an inch of skin that wasn't burnt. Before they threw a fur over him, one of the farmer women walked up to him and rubbed his skin with a salve that smelled like rancid meat. It was in fact the fat from rancid meat, meant to quell the fire that his skin had absorbed from the sun. Kochen's tongue was too dry to make words and thank her. Without a sound, she grabbed her bowl, and descended to the terrace below.

Kochen's night was full of discordant thoughts. Though he begged for Jamyong to appear, he did not. Though his body was exhausted and tired, sleep would not come. The Night Spirit would not come. He felt nauseous, and in the middle of the night, he turned his head and vomited to the side, the vomit sliding into his long black hair.

In the morning, Vint appeared, his eyes dark, circles ringing them, a jug of water in his hands. "What happened to your father?"

By now Kochen was delirious. His story was garbled, mixed. Later, the priests would say that the sun spirit had inhabited Kochen's body and made him tell the truth. When Kochen finally awoke some days later, washed and covered in the oils of rancid meat, his mind put back together, they told him what he had said. Kochen said his father had run away from the cruel people of the village, to live a life where he could be free. When pressed about Bimisi, he had said there was no Bimisi... he had made it all up because he was ashamed to be left behind.

This is what the village believed. Kochen believed that Caldus, the sun spirit, had entered into his body, and told them the story they wanted to hear, the story that would release Kochen from his bonds. As he hovered on the edge of madness on the morning of the third day of bondage, he had looked east at the orange sun, and he had seen the shape swirl, wings unfolding from the bright ball of orange, fluttering through the purple morning sky, a maw of flame and fire opening and calling his name.

****

Panic was alien to him. Kochen's life had been one of toil and acceptance. Hanging suspended on a cross in a field known to harbor the spirit that had killed his father was actually something of a relief. It would soon be over; when the sun disappeared over the horizon, the Stick People would find out about the Cliff People's spirits. They would find them strong and cruel. They would find no quarter. Kochen knew he was likely to perish with them.

The Stick People watched him, spears in hand, as if waiting for some great show. The sky deepened to a dark purple, and he knew the time was almost near. The throbbing in his head had ceased, and the drums from the cliffs had stopped a little bit ago. Stick People waded through the cornstalks, returning from battle, some sporting bruises and broken bones, but most still fit to fight. A couple carried bodies slung over their shoulders. In the fields, they pulled down stalks of corn and built their fires.

The Stick People made simple meals of dried meat and fish from the river. Dried corn was produced from somewhere. Over the fire, they placed kernels of corn on a clay slab covered in oil. With poles, they moved the granite slab over the fires, heating the kernels until they hissed and finally popped. They whooped and hollered, fighting to be the ones to pick up the kernels of popcorn off of the ground.

Kochen was no more to them than background as they went about their business. No food was offered, nor would he accept any. He hung in the air, his ankles and wrists numb from the experience, a puddle of blood forming on the ground from the wound in his foot. The cool night air washed over his body, his torso uncovered in the night chill. He watched the Stick People. They seemed much like his own people. Broad in face, brown skin, hair black as panther fur. Their bodies were squat and stocky. Put them in the fields, and they wouldn't be discernible if it weren't for the face paint on their bodies.

Kochen saw their leader, the tall muscular man who had spoken to him before. His voice was different, commanding and full of confidence. The words the Stick People spoke sounded just like Kochen's own language, but they were subtly different. The man sat watching him, his red face paint hiding his expression. Kochen stared at him across the fire as the first stars appeared in the sky. It wouldn't be long now.

A low rumble began in the ground, and the sounds of revelry stopped. The Stick People stood in place, trying to figure out where the rumble was coming from. They looked around as the ground began to quake. Kochen was rocked back and forth on his pole. He hoped it would be over soon and that it would be quick.

In the distance there was a scream. Kochen squeezed his eyes shut, not wanting to see Bimisi, the monster that had haunted his dreams for the better part of the last decade. In the end, he couldn't help it. A scream off to his right was so close that it startled him, his eyes snapping open and looking around in the firelight to see the source. He was just in time to see the bottom half of a man topple over, spilling blood into the fertile soil.

To his left, he heard a familiar voice shout, "Cut him down. He comes with us."

Stick People rushed to him, pulling on the cross that they had driven into the ground. His own weight had driven it deeper into the ground, but his weight was no match for four warriors. Hanging with his feet parallel to the ground, the four men ran, carrying him through the fields bound to a cross. Above the corn stalks, Kochen could see Bimisi hunched over, claws at the ready, gliding through the corn, stalking its prey.

The Stick People's leader ran before the warriors carrying him, his broad shoulders combining with the corn around them to block out everything in front of him. They emerged from the corn into scrub brush and broken rocks.

The noise of the farmland seemed to stop on the other side of the farmland. As the men turned around, they could see the white shape of Bimisi hunched over, claws splitting men in half, but there was no sound.

To the left and right, Stick People stumbled from the corn, some with their faces covered in blood, others fine but clearly frightened. Most were simply confused. The leader strode over to Kochen and looked him in the eyes. "You think your spirits are strong?" The leader laughed. "Then come, you must see ours."

The leader turned his back on Kochen, and addressed his people. "We have what we came for. The spirits will be pleased. We head for home."

"But what about the bodies?" the white-faced warrior with the booming laugh asked.

"If you want to go in there and get them, you may do so."

The warrior did not want to go get the bodies.

Chapter 9:

A Realization

The day's battle had been long and hard. The men of the village slumped on the second terrace from the bottom, their shoulders sore from a long day of slinging stones and pushing Stick People from the cliff's walls, where they tried to climb to the next terrace. Women and elders ran back and forth, bringing the men food and water. Children gathered rocks and placed them in the clay bowls around the men. Nom's scales had vanished halfway through the day. When this battle was over, she would have the children collect more, as the more jagged rocks from the cliff had a tendency to not fly as true as the smooth rock from the river.

Lansa was cleaning an arrow wound in a man's shoulder when the noises began, a deep rumble followed by the screams of many. The village rushed to the terrace edges and peered down into the valley, but all they could make out was the smoke and flame of the Stick People's campfires amid the corn. By now, the Stick People had probably destroyed one-third of their crops. It was going to be a lean winter, but that was in the back of her mind. In the forefront, Lansa was trying to understand what was happening. *Why were the Stick People screaming?*

Perhaps Farway's men had returned from where they were hiding and snuck up on the rear of the camp. If so, they were doomed. The sheer numbers of the Stick People were far more than Farway's twenty warriors could possibly defeat. They could set the cornfields on fire, but it would be better to let the Stick People climb the ladders and murder them one by one. Were the crops completely lost, the village was in for a long hard winter. They had seen them before, but without the corn, their village would wither and die until the next spring... if any of them were left. Hunger did strange things to a village.

A villager pointed at a monstrous shape that appeared near the edge of one of the campfires. It was there for just a second, white skin towering over the cornstalks. *Bimisi.* The word spread among the villagers, whispered in hushed tones. Some elders turned their back on the scene, not wanting to see the shape lest Bimisi come for them, but the screams continued in the night. Lansa could not believe her eyes. The shape, Bimisi, spirit of the harvest. It was impossible. It couldn't be.

Lansa sank to the ground, her mind a jumble. The spirits. Could she have been wrong all this time?

****

Her father's body had been torn to pieces when the Stick People had reached the first terrace where the bodies were being stored until they could be placed in the ground. Several other bodies had experienced the same fate. When the Stick People retreated after being repelled on the second terrace, the elders had moved among the lowest terrace and gathered the pieces, putting them with the bodies that they thought they belonged to.

After they had all been arranged, the children were finally allowed to leave the sanctum and see their fallen loved ones. The remains had been sewn into a deerskin casing that covered her father from head to toe so that only his face was visible. To her, it looked like the cocoon of a caterpillar. At any moment she expected her father to rise from the ground, sprout wings, and fly off into the sky.

This did not come to pass, and Fesh implored her to pray to the spirits to guide him to the next world. The next world... what use was the next world to her? She was trapped here with a father wandering a new world and a mother abandoning the one that Lansa still lived in. Who cared about other worlds? Still, Fesh was a priest. He knew the spirits.

She prayed on her knees, beseeching the spirits to bring her father back, anointing each prayer with tears and sobs so that they might fly into the heavens to be heard.

Rocks and pebbles dug into her knees, even through the tough leather of her dress. The sun beat down on them, just as merciless as it always was. Those around her joined in adding their voices and their wails to the skies, but there were no signs, not even a cloud for an elder to point out as a signal from the spirits. It was still and hot.

When Fesh attempted to comfort her by laying his hand on her shoulder, she looked at him with hate in her eyes.

"Why do you glare at me?" he asked.

"The spirits do not listen. The spirits are not real."

Fesh sucked in his breath taken aback by her words. "The spirits listen. The spirits are helping you as we speak."

"What do you mean?"

"You will come with me. The doubt in your heart is a sign of a lost soul. I will not allow it. Your father was a good man; his blood will not perish. You will carry on the line."

"Why should I go with you?"

"You can decide yes. You can decide no. But the spirits have told me what way you will choose. When you are ready, climb the ladders." With that, Fesh turned and walked away.

When he had gone, Lansa sat there, watching her father's bloated face. She saw it for what it was, a rotting piece of flesh, the spark of life gone from it forever.

Whether the spark that made that flesh her father was walking in a new world somewhere mattered not to her. Later that day, as they lowered her father into the ground, she vowed to turn her back on the spirits forever. What good were they if they couldn't keep her and her family safe?

For the next few months, Lansa lived in the cold, empty house that her father had inhabited. The elders spent their time trying to talk her into becoming the wife of some of the young men of the village. She had no desire to serve them. They had all become Corn Men, toothless lusters who wanted nothing other than what was between her legs.

If she was going to go that route, she would climb the cliff and live in the Up Top with her mother. But she didn't want that route; instead, she had toiled season after season in the fields, grinding corn, carrying water, picking weeds. She did the work of a woman, earning her share and keeping her fire warm in her lonely house. She grew. She flowered. She remained apart.

Fesh continued to visit her, his ancient age never slowing him down. His visits were welcome. In him, there was no ulterior motive, just honest friendship and the dauntless surety that one day, she would join him in the sanctum.

"They want you to marry."

Lansa laughed. "There is no one in this village worth marrying."

"Do you want to find another village?" Fesh asked.

"They are all the same."

"Perhaps the spirits here do not agree with you."

Lansa's mind had been made up about the spirits long ago. "The spirits have nothing to do with this."

"Then why do you resist? It's as if you are drowning in a river with no way to swim, but you slap away every hand that reaches to pull you out. Do you wish to be unhappy?"

Lansa thought about Fesh's question. Her toil. Her denial of company. It was all designed to keep her from ever experiencing the joy of happiness. What had it gained her? Nothing. She was too prideful to admit the truth. "That's foolish. Why would I want to be unhappy?"

Fesh smiled, a twinkle of knowing in his eye, "I don't know. I was hoping you would tell me. Maybe an evil spirit snuck into your ear in the night."

Lansa looked at Fesh, biting her tongue about spirits. When Fesh left, making his long climb up to the top terrace, Lansa laid down in her furs and stared up at the clay roof of her dwelling, her mind swirling with thoughts. As warmth filled her furs, and contentment took over her body, she thought to herself, "If there are no spirits, then there is no afterworld. Better to make the most of the world that I have now than to waste the one life I have." Then her mind was robbed of sight.

****

When the morning arrived, fires still smoldered in the makeshift clearings the Stick People had made in the corn. The men of the village walked quietly, listening for any signs of life, their breathing heavy, their nerves raw. Lansa walked with them. Where they found Stick People, they frequently did not find all of them. Arms were missing, legs were missing. None lived.

The men, seeing an opportunity, strung the remains up on crosses and planted the crosses in the ground to keep the vultures away from the corn. They would feast on the readily available meat on the crosses.

No one said the word Bimisi, but looking at the ragged wounds of one of the Stick People, they could not help but think it. Here a man of twenty winters rested, the other half of his body ten feet away. The skin where his legs should be was ragged, his intestines pooled on the earth.

If the teachings of Fesh were true, their harvest would be amazing this year... and it only cost them a handful of lives. But, that remained to be seen. *I would rather have our people back,* Lansa thought. The thought was selfish. A bad harvest would see the village lose more people than what they had lost in the murderous attack of the Stick People.

Cheers went up among the people as the corn parted to reveal Farway and his hunters, their faces grim, their eyes like coal. She knew without talking to him that Farway craved revenge. The only real question was would she let them have it?

The Stick People were thorns in their sides, but they were like the seasons, here one day, gone the next. They were like the wolves who only prayed on the sick or weak, allowing the herd to grow and replenish itself. Were the village under constant siege by them, they would have perished long ago. The Stick People struck, took what they wanted, and then moved on. She understood this, and had even made her peace with it, but Farway wasn't likely to be so easily placated. His will was like the sun, ever-present and unchanging. It would take some tact to bring him around to her thinking, whatever way that might be. As Farway approached, she sought to stall for time.

"We want justice." Farway stalked through the rows, a spear in his hand. His hair fell about his shoulders, and his body was criss-crossed with scars. He was at one time considered attractive, the pride of the village, until the hunt got in him. Now he cared nothing for the gentle ways of civilization. Farway and his men spent weeks out in the wild, trapping, hunting, and killing whatever they could find. They always came back, but there were many in the village who wished they would just stay gone.

"You shall have your justice in time," Lansa said.

Farway planted his spear in the ground. "Justice is fleeting. We want it now."

Lansa eyed Farway, an eyebrow cocked. "Fools rush into the river. Wise men check the speed of the current. Which one are you, Farway?"

"I am a warrior."

Lansa smiled. His simplicity would be admirable were he a farmer. As one of the most dangerous men of the village, it seemed he was always on the edge of an atrocity. "Then you are not a complete man. In order to help this village, you must be more than a warrior. You must be equal parts wise, brave, and foolish. Right now, you say you are a warrior. What good is a warrior? Anyone can pick up a pointy stick and wave it around. How will you help this village?"

"I will give to them what they gave to us. Death."

Lansa smirked at Farway's ridiculous boast. "In doing so, you would bring the Stick People down upon us. Though you say you are a warrior, you are untested. Taking down a bobcat is much easier than taking down a man. You are outnumbered, your handful of men are dwarfed by the numbers and savagery of the Stick People. If you want to run off to your death, then please, feel free, but don't take your men with you."

Doubt had crept into the eyes of Farway's men. Andras, the four-fingered, nodded his head at her words. In him, she had an ally. Andras wasn't much though. Where was Lonpearl? He was a natural leader. If she could sway his opinion, she could sway Farway. She scanned the hunters for Lonpearl, but did not see him anywhere.

Farway could sense that Lansa was stalling, and he eyed Lansa with suspicion, sensing some sort of trickery. "What would you have us do?"

"I would have you do something that will be very painful for you, something which goes against your very nature."

63

"And that is?"
"I would have you wait."

Chapter 10:

Homecoming

Lonpearl and the others had waited, out of sight of the warriors. Their numbers had not been great, but the Stick People had outnumbered their little band of warriors 3 to 1. Lonpearl had to fight hard to keep Farway from plunging into the cornfield and throwing all of their lives away. They could have done some damage, but the odds that any of them would have survived would have been minimal.

Ghulish's harsh face matched his words, as he steadily whispered in Lonpearl's ear. "You coward. Your wife and child are up there now. Who knows if they are alive? And you want to sit here and wait it out. You make me sick, coward. You're no better than a coyote, fleeing from its hard-won meal at the first sight of man."

They huddled behind a ridge of rock, their faces peering over the edge, unable to do anything but watch. Ghulish's words did not fall on deaf ears, and Lonpearl knew that he could be throwing away the lives of his family. His mother, old and forgetful, his daughter too young to understand, and his wife, beautiful and understanding, were nestled among the cliffs, spear-tipped death waiting in the cornfield. No, Ghulish's words were not unheard.

The tide of the hunters was turning against him, and Lonpearl thought he could hear Farway grinding his teeth to nubs, his jaw clenched like the biceps of men locked in an arm wrestling match. If Farway gave the word, they would storm in there, their spears ready, and plunge them into the hearts of the Stick People huddled around their fires. They could take them by surprise, but in the end, every one of them would wind up as food for the fields.

"Let's go..." Farway began, but then his words caught in his throat. In the firelight of the Stick People's campfires, they saw the great white shape among the cornstalks, the rest of the hunters knew that Lonpearl's wisdom had won the day, with the exception of Ghulish, who always saw Lonpearl's patience as a sign of cowardice.

The shape moved among the cornstalks, coiling and springing like a worm fresh from the dirt. The torso of one of the Stick People flew into the air, arcing in the blue-night sky to become a shadow blotting out a tiny section of stars. It landed on the ground, lost among cornstalks that came alive with shadows surging through the corn.

"Bimisi," Lonpearl said, the word falling out of his mouth without him being conscious of uttering it.

"Bimisi," Ghulish said, mocking Lonpearl, his voice tipped with anger.

"Are you blind, Ghulish?" Farway hissed. "It's right there."

Ghulish had no retort; he simply stared at the scene, his spear gripped in his hand. A group of Stick People burst forth from the corn, their voices erupting in mid-scream. The screams carried across the night air to their ears, and every time another warrior stumbled from the corn another screaming voice would be added to the chorus. The night was filled with shrieks, their intensity fading as the Stick People disappeared into the darkness.

When they had gone, Ghulish said, "Let's go and see."

Lonpearl fought the urge to argue against Ghulish, but he didn't have to struggle for long as Andras spoke first, pointing his four-fingered hand at Ghulish for emphasis. "If you want to go down there, go ahead. That was Bimisi. I'm waiting right here until the sun comes up."

"You're all cowards," Ghulish said as he flipped over onto his back and stared up at the night sky.

"Let's get some rest," Farway said. "Tomorrow, the hunt begins."

****

When they awoke, they had stumbled upon the carnage of the cornfield. Limbs and bodies were strewn everywhere, and there didn't seem to be a spot of earth that wasn't stained with blood. Lonpearl steeled himself for what he might find in the village. While Farway and the others pushed through the cornstalks, Lonpearl sprinted to the first ladder, climbing it as fast as he could, aching to see his wife and child. If anything had happened to them, Lonpearl would make sure that the hunt began in earnest.

Climbing the ladders that led to the upper terraces had never seemed so slow. Were Stot and Hubra lying in pieces down below? Were they even now lying on their deathbed? Lonpearl had no wish to find out from someone else, so when he landed on the third terrace, he ran past the elders on the terrace to the door of his dwelling and threw it open.

In the darkness of the dwelling he heard shifting, and then she was there, her face buried in his chest. Hot breath and tears rolled down his brown skin, and his heart, which had somehow clawed its way to the back of his throat, dropped into the pit of his stomach. Lonpearl wanted to say something, anything, but there was nothing to say. He didn't have the words to tell Stot what he was feeling.

"Daddy?" a small voice said from the corner of the room. Lonpearl wiped the tears from his eyes, and squatted down on his knees. His daughter, with near-black eyes, tottered out of the shadows and walked into his outspread arms. "Why is everyone sad?"

Lonpearl laughed, tears running down his cheeks. His wife looked at him, and warmth spread through his body. He felt guilty to know that his wife and daughter were alright, while others in the village were mourning. He felt guilty knowing that some people had lost family members, and then he remembered his mother. "My mother?" he asked Stot.

She smiled and nodded, "We're all fine."

In the darkness of his dwelling, Lonpearl breathed his first free breath since they had first spotted the fires in the cornfields the afternoon before. From a distant part of the village, Lonpearl heard wailing, the wrecked voice of a man whose life had been ripped apart. He hugged his daughter even closer.

****

It was afternoon when Farway showed up at his door, a scowl on his face, his spear jammed in the dirt at his feet. "Lansa means to make us wait," Farway said.

"And you want to go after the Stick People? Maybe patience is the right way."

Farway shook his head, his long hair shimmering in the daylight of the terrace. "Our people are dead. Ghulish and Markon have both lost their fathers. They want revenge. Would you deny them that?"

"If it means no one else dies, then yes."

Farway looked at Lonpearl, disbelief in his eyes. "Would you say the same if it were your wife and your daughter?"

Lonpearl had no answer for Farway. The thought was too uncomfortable to even think about. He was saved from having to make the decision by the approach of Ghulish. His normally harsh face was made even worse by the red-veined eyes of sorrow that bulged in his face. He had the air of one who was about to snap.

"There you are!" he yelled at Farway. "Why are we still here? We should be gone from this place."

Lonpearl said nothing. He knew grief when he saw it. Farway turned and put an arm around Ghulish's shoulder. "We will avenge your father, and all of the others that we lost yesterday. Isn't that right, Lonpearl?"

Farway looked at Lonpearl with a twinkle in his eye. It was a dangerous twinkle, the glimmer of chaos deep in his pupil, daring him to tell Ghulish that there would be no revenge. It was not a dare that Lonpearl was up for.

"If Lansa and the priests say that revenge is the path we must take, then I will walk that path with you. If she says otherwise, then I will wish you luck." Ghulish stared at him, the word "coward" scrawled across his face. Farway smiled at Lonpearl, who turned his back and went inside, closing the door behind him.

Chapter 11:

The Blind Seer

The Stick People trudged throughout the day, poking Kochen in the back with their spears whenever they felt he wasn't walking fast enough. His hands bound in rope, Kochen plotted his escape, though it was more to pass the time than out of any real hope of evading his captors. They had bound his foot, but the pain was still intense. He tried to stay brave, masking his limp so as to deprive them of the satisfaction of seeing him in pain The muscles in his neck hurt from gritting his teeth before every step, but so far, he had not cried out once. It was a little victory, but it kept him going.

They were many, and they fanned out, picking up fruit and slaying animals as they went, hanging the carcasses on their belts to be cleaned later when they made camp. The sun beat down upon their brown bodies and black hair as they followed the river north. The terrain was much the same as at home, but every twist of the river brought a new sight to his eyes. He had never been this far from the village before. Few people besides Farway's men ever went further than the river bank to the east.

Kochen grunted as he was poked in the back by a sinewy man with a crooked nose. Kochen imagined whirling to grab the spear from the man, swinging it around and cracking him across the crooked nose. Then he would run and jump into the river... though he was not an excellent swimmer, he figured he could ride the current back to the village. With his hands bound, this was out of the question. Perhaps tonight he would find a sharp rock and begin trying to get his hands free.

The Stick People were fit, fitter than many of the people in his village. They had walked all day and didn't even seem tired. Meanwhile, Kochen's hair was plastered to his head with sweat, and he routinely stumbled over rocks that seemed to pop up just in front of his feet whenever he would take his eyes off the ground to study the sights around him. This would inevitably draw another rough prod from the crooked-nosed man behind him.

Time continued like this for most of the day until the sun reached its zenith. They sheltered under an overhanging rock, while the heat of the midday sun beat upon the shelf, trying to get at them. Kochen sprawled in the dust, too tired to find a suitable rock to help him begin his daring escape. He rested his head on a large stone, letting his sweat run cold in the shade and cool his body. His eyelids hung heavy over his eyes until he could keep them open no longer.

****

His dreams were dark, exhaustion opening the way to a deep place that was unfamiliar to him. Tentacles reached to him in the darkness, lacy tendrils of shadow probing the darkness to find him. Were these visions? Or were these just the dreams of a tired boy forced to march for miles? Blood splattered upon the ground, and when he lifted his eyes up to see the source, droplets covered his face. They were still warm.

Kochen woke up screaming, a man in bearskins stood over him, a now empty waterskin dripping its last drops of water onto the dusty ground. He laughed, a loud booming laugh that echoed off the rocks, "You looked thirsty." How the man kept from cooking alive in those bearskins was a mystery to Kochen.

Kochen's face and hair were dripping wet, and his heart felt like it was going to beat its way right out of his chest.

"Loudest Laugh, go play your jokes on someone else," the leader of the Stick People said as he handed Kochen a full waterskin and sat down next to him.

"He looked hot," Loudest Laugh said defensively, but he walked off into the day, laughing with a gray-haired man and a spindly fellow who looked like he was made of sticks and skin.

"Tell me about your village." The warrior never looked at him; he always looked off into the distance, as if always waiting for some sort of attack. Even when they were walking, he had that far off stare. Kochen would bet he had the stare even when he was sleeping.

Kochen drank greedily from the skin, the water hitting the pit of his empty stomach and cooling his core. He ran his tongue over his cracked and dry lips, getting them wet, and then spit some water on the ground. "Why do you want to know?"

"I ask so that I don't have to take. You know things. Tell me these things. Life will be easy. If you don't tell me the things I want to know, then life will be hard."

"There isn't much to tell."

"Do they know about you?"

Kochen laughed. "They know that my mind isn't right. It's different, and around me hangs a cloud of death."

"Do they know of your visions?"

He did not want to tell him the answer. The villagers knew he thought he had visions, but no one actually believed the things the visions foretold. He wasn't a seer; he was a dreamer in their eyes, nothing but a child with a big imagination that tended towards a dark bent. "Visions are not real."

The chief rocked back and spat on the ground. "What good is a seer who won't open his eyes?" He handed him a handful of dried meat and then walked away. "Eat."

The dried meat wasn't bad; he had no idea what it was, but it tasted pretty good, and when it was time to walk, he was ready. He was blistered, tired, and still in need of a sharp rock, but he was ready all the same.

Chapter 12:

Around the Fire

Lansa kicked off her moccasins and sat in the dust of the sanctum. The fire filled the room with smoke, and the other priests sat around her in a circle, their eyes leaking tears. To the side, Farway and his men sat awaiting the decision of the priests.

"Farway wants to go after the Stick People," she announced. She produced a jug of *tilnac,* put it to her lips, and took a long drink of the milky fluid. She passed the jug to her left to Harcha, who took a drink and passed it around some more. Thus it went until it had come back around to Lansa.

There was silence among the priests. As smoke billowed around their heads, Lansa looked at Harcha first. The eldest of the priests, he was also the most even-tempered and logical. Harcha ran his hand over his bald head. He cleared his throat, tears running down his face from the smoke. "Revenge leads to revenge leads to revenge. What have we to gain but pride from this action?"

Birren spoke next, her stout body curled over to try and catch her breath, sweat gleaming on her shaved head. "Pride is the downfall of humanity. To chase pride is to chase the wind. To feed pride is to waste food. I say, 'No.'"

The next to speak was Doulk, the youngest priest among them. His temper was present, and the other priests listened only half-heartedly to his words. He was still learning. The only reason Lansa let him speak was to expose him to the wisdom of the other priests. Doulk said, "The spirits demand retribution. Our blood has been spilled. It must be repaid in kind."

None of the priests rebutted him, letting his unwise wisdom hang in the air with the smoke. The smoke would purify their thoughts, drown the bad advice, and leave only the good. It was either that or they would all pass out, and Farway would have to put out the flames, douse their heads with water, and let them try again on the next evening.

The last of the priests, Caubrey, spoke. He was half-mad, touched by the spirits, and frequently incapable of formulating anything but the most rudimentary of plans. Occasionally, something mind-blowing would fall out of his mouth, which is why he had been foisted upon the priests. When he was a child, he had run through the village proclaiming that the sun was burning out that evening. No one had paid him any attention. Even at that young age, the people could see that he was different. So when the eclipse happened that evening, he was proclaimed a prophet and his family happily insisted that Caubrey be taken under the auspices of the priests. Useless in the fields, incapable of hunting, but still functional enough to live, the priests had taken him in, more out of pity than anything else. But his mind was magic, and if the spirits were real, it was clear that his half-empty brain was a conduit for them on that night.

"Revenge is not at stake. The future of our tribe walks on two legs with the Stick People. The spirits howl at his loss. It is as if our two peoples are at war, our spirits balanced evenly on a plane with their spirits. The plane teeters on the curve of the world. The seer is the key. The balance will shift to one or the other." Doulk coughed heartily and then pitched forward into the dirt. The others looked at him, black spots dancing before their eyes.

Birren spoke first, "Kochen is just one person. How can we be sure that he is even still alive? They could have cooked and eaten him for all that we know."

Harcha said, "The risk is too great. Should Farway's men fall, we will collapse like a man without a spine. Kochen is one. We are many."

Doulk took the chance to seize on Caubrey's prophetic words. "If the spirits speak through Caubrey, then we must send Farway after them. We must have retribution. If what he says is true, then the entire future of the village depends on it." Doulk's body was racked with coughing and he too fell over.

Lansa watched them all. She picked up the jug of *tilnac,* took a drink and spat the mouthful into the fire. It glowed red, and Lansa opened her eyes as wide as possible, trying to see the future in the brief red flare of the fire, though she knew she would see nothing. The flames danced in front of her, warmth flowing through her body, but there was nothing in the flames except glowing coals and smoke. She rose from her sitting position and walked over to Farway, looking at his scarred face. It was red around the cheeks, and veins popped out of his temples. It was if he were a pot, barely containing the frothing edge of boiling water.

"You will go to the Stick People. You will take back what is ours. If you can do so without bloodshed, then so much the better. If you must wet your spears, then that is what you will do."

The smile that Farway gave her was frightening. She knew that the spears would be wetted. In that smile, there was no other intention but slaughter and murder. Farway was the best at what he was; the council had spoken and Kochen would be coming home. Yet, she couldn't help feel like something was wrong here. She watched as Farway and her men hooted, their eyes round with future-seeing. Their faces racked in grim smiles, while their arms pumped in the air. They cheered for it. They cheered for death. When the skin melted from their faces, Lansa stood still, wondering if the smoke had gotten to her more than she thought. Then Farway turned to her. His face was not a skull, but a mask of dripping red, his eyes turned black, and the slashes on his body numbered in the hundreds. Maggots dripped from his wounds. She didn't know what it all meant, but this was the way with visions. Lansa collapsed to the ground.

****

Farway helped Harcha carry Lansa to the back room of the sanctum. They bundled her up in furs, while Birren attempted to wake Doulk and Caubrey from their smoke-induced slumber. The overcome priests awoke, coughing and gagging. With Birren supporting them, they stumbled to the back of the sanctum, where they too curled up in their furs. Birren began to sweep away the signs of their presence, grunting and groaning at the effort.

As Farway and his men prepared to leave, Harcha called him to the side.

"Kill only if you need to," Harcha said, commanding him as if he were there to take orders from priests.

"I need to," Farway said.

"Kochen is the key. He is special."

"Do you believe that mud-brained priest? Truly?"

"Caubrey knows things. Kochen knows more. He foresaw the attack on the village. Had we listened, no one would have died."

Farway didn't quite believe Harcha, but then why else would they allow him to head out on his own to exact vengeance on the Stick People? "I will bring Kochen back... if he is still alive. I cannot promise that no one will die."

Farway made to leave, but Harcha grabbed his arm, holding him in place. "Promise me."

Farway looked at the silver-haired priest, resisting the urge to punch him in the face. "I do not make promises I do not intend to keep."

With that, Farway and his men were gone, their torches disappearing into the scrub brush. Harcha watched them as long as he could. They drifted North, the wind of change following in their wake.

****

Farway and his men did not go far that first night. He simply wanted to be away from the village when Lansa awoke. She had the ability and tendency to change her mind. That the priests even gave their blessing at all came as something of a surprise to Farway. He had been sure that they would deny the request, at which point, he had fully intended to head off anyway. It was better this way, but he wasn't going to give Lansa time to think it over.

Farway's men made camp underneath a rock overhang that was out of sight of the village, though not terribly far away. Lonpearl built up a fire, and then searched the rocks with a torch to make sure that no snakes were present. His face was shadowed with worry, and in his mind, images of his wife and daughter flashed. When Lonpearl was satisfied, the men lay under the stars, far away from meddling priests, mundane villagers and the like.

Farway looked up into the sky tracing the shape of the Panther in the night sky. Darbery they called it, the fierce spirit of the hunt. Darbery had no time for sneaky ways. Trickery was the realm of the coyote, not the Panther. They would pounce upon the Stick People, take what was theirs, and leave enough scars to keep them from ever coming back to the cliffs.

In his dreams, he waded among the dead, every thrust of his spear impaling another foe. The blood washed around his feet, and fires burned throughout a foreign village. When he awoke, he was sure it was a vision.

With the dream of a dream dancing in his men's heads, they set out to search for signs of the Stick People's passing. It wasn't hard. They did not appear to be concerned about being followed. This was their fatal mistake; Farway would make sure of it.

They continued up the river, heading north. Farway nibbled on dried snake, as Markon yammered on in his ear.

"Did you see me in your vision?"

Farway smiled at him, and filled in the appropriate details, "Yes. You were there. Their women clung to your legs as you stabbed down their men."

"My wife isn't going to like that," Markon laughed. "Was I injured?"

"Nothing major. Just a few slashes here and there to make you look more manly... like me."

Markon laughed. "I hope I have a vision tonight."

Farway looked off into the distance. "You just might. The spirits are with us. They follow in our footsteps, guiding our every move."

At that moment, there was a scream. Farway and Lonpearl moved to the sound. Remlithica, the son of Farway's older brother sat on the hot rock of the river bank, holding his ankle. Two holes dripped tiny amounts of blood on the skin just above his ankle bone.

"It was the rattlesnake," Remlithica panted.

A rattlesnake jittered at the end of a spear; it's tip through the snake's head. With his stone knife, Farway knelt on the ground and cut a line between the two holes on Remlithica's ankle. Remlithica screamed and groaned, when Farway placed his mouth over the wound, sucking and spitting out the bitter poison, but the swelling continued.

"You have to head back," Farway told him.

"Nonsense, I will be fine."

"Look, it swells even now. If you don't get help from the priests soon, they'll have to cut off the foot. If you go now, you'll make it. They can help you. If you go with us, you will surely die."

Remlithica was disappointed when Farway and his band melted into the distance. They never looked back, nineteen warriors, heading off into a sea of the unknown. Remlithica hobbled back to the village, his ankle on fire. Despite Farway's proclamation of the spirits' blessing, Lonpearl couldn't help but feel that it was an inauspicious beginning to their journey.

Chapter 13:

The Price of Clarity

Lansa's lungs burned when she awoke. Each breath brought a cough, and chunks of phlegm danced around in her mouth. Harcha brought her a pitcher of water, and she washed them down. Her sleep had been fitful, and as it faded from her mind, she tried to etch the details in her memory, but it was like grasping water in a fist. All she remembered was the wetness, and the dream disappeared into the morning light.

"I had a vision last night," she told Harcha.

Harcha looked at her, his old face equal parts surprised and disbelieving. "What of?"

"I can't remember," she said, pressing the palms of her hands against her eyes. "But it was terrifying."

"You've never had a vision before."

Lansa took a sip of cool water. "I'm telling you I had one last night?"

Lansa sat up, and began to rise as Harcha told her the bad news. "Farway left last night."

She fell back to the ground. "Then it is too late."

"I told him not to kill any of them unless he needed to."

For a brief second, Lansa felt a glimmer of hope. "What did he say?"

Harcha swallowed and said, "He said he needed to."

The priests sat in silence; the sounds of the villagers waking and beginning their day drifted up from the terraces

81

below. Birren's snoring filled the back room of the sanctum.

"Falling stars! Falling stars!" Caubrey sat up, his face in his hands, sobbing.

Harcha and Lansa shared a look. It was true.

"What does it mean?" Harcha asked.

"I have to see the Corn Men."

****

Lansa's climb to the top of the cliff was long and arduous. Her arms felt like dead grass when she reached the top. She reclined in the sandy soil on her back, staring up at the blue sky, the sun high above her, radiating heat onto her brown skin. The smell of the Up Top was the same, smoke and sourness, as if the land itself were sick.

No one came out to greet her. The Corn Men were notoriously anti-social, which is why they chose to live in a place that was so inaccessible. Except for the occasional corn delivery by the most gifted climber of the village's children, they had little to no contact, except when someone decided they no longer wanted to be a part of the village, as Lansa's mother had decided when she was a child.

She didn't want to be here, didn't want to know what had happened to her mother. She had never asked the climbers about her, and she had never made another attempt to climb to the Up Top on her own since the day her father died. For all she knew, her mother was long dead, buried in the loose sand on top of the cliff.

There were five huts on top of the cliff, dilapidated old structures made of ancient white wood with animal skins draped over the framework to keep out the roaring wind of the Up Top. Smoke came from three of them, and she slowly approached the first, the one she had seen her mother lying in, a dreamy look on her face. The Corn Men made *tilnac,* a sour and sweet liquid that allowed the priests to have more clarity in their visions. She knew that they drank more than they produced, but it didn't matter. They were out of sight and out of mind. Harcha had once suggested that they cut off all contact with the group in that logical way of his. She would have none of it. Whether the Corn Men wanted to be a part of their society or not didn't really matter to her; they would always be a part of the village, even if they themselves failed to acknowledge it. She knew that her mother's presence on the Up Top had much to do with the way she felt.

Lansa hesitated at the door of the hut, her hand trembling on the deer-hide flap that kept the world outside. *What if she was in there?* She threw the flap aside and entered. Instead of the old wrinkled man that had used to live there, there was a younger man. She knew his name from the past, when he had been a young man toiling in the fields below.

They had called him Jib. He was as lazy as he was cantankerous, even as a youth. The days he had gone without food because he had not done any work were more than could be counted. Only when he had been on the edge of starvation, his ribs sticking out of his skin, and his kilt sagging off of his emaciated hips would he head out to the farmland and begin toiling. It was no surprise to anyone when they saw him climbing the cliff one day.

No one called him Jib anymore. Corn Men didn't have names. They left everything behind when they decided to climb over the cliff, names, property, clothes. The man that had once been Jib looked at her. What remained of his teeth were brown from chewing corn all day, and his skin hung in loose flaps of pale brown, sweat beaded on his brow.

"Lansa. I am surprised to see you here. It has been a long time."

"Hello, Corn Man."

83

The Corn Man spit into a bucket, corn activated with saliva, the kiss of the spirits, turning the juice into something more, something magical.

"Why are you here? Why does a priest climb so high? Have you gone through the last batch of *tilnac* already or have you come to join us?"

"I come for guidance." The Corn Man stared at her in silence, a brief look of disappointment flitted across his face and then it was gone. He waited for further explanation. "Last night I had a vision, only I can't remember it."

"Visions. Dreams. You are sitting in the shack of dreams."

Lansa didn't know what the Corn Man was talking about. "Can you help me recover my vision?"

The Corn Man spit another wad of spit into a jug. "Help is good, but I care nothing of your ways down below. Your vision has naught to do with me. What price are you willing to pay?"

Lansa knew this was coming. The Corn Men did not just reject society, they rejected it and demanded payment for any infringement on their freedom. Only the most backwards people ever seemed to climb the cliff. Common interaction with them seemed to bring out the worst in The Corn Men. "What do you want?"

"When I first came here, there was a lady among us. She was not the most beautiful lady, but she was a lady all the same. She made the time here... more bearable. When she died, so too did a part of us. Now we are sad. We stare at the cliff, and imagine flying... to a different place, one that is more agreeable."

"Say what you mean to say."

"We want a woman."

Lansa shuddered at the thought of sending any of the female villagers Up Top. "The Up Top is for those that don't want to belong; it always has been. The Up Top is a choice. I cannot just send someone up here and condemn them to live among you to satisfy your urges."

"Then we are done. Recover the vision on your own."

For a second, Lansa wanted to smash the jug across the Corn Man's face. He truly cared nothing for the village. The Corn Men protected the secrets of the *tilnac*, along with other secrets that Lansa could only guess at. She didn't know what bargain had been struck, how the Corn Men had come to be, or what role they served in this world, but Fesh had always told her they were important. If it hadn't been for Fesh's words still rattling around in her skull, she would have had this spot wiped out of existence years ago when she had come into power. There was no getting around it. The Corn Men and the priests had grudgingly existed side by side since a time past remembrance. They knew things that the priests did not. They were from an old time, their history passed down mouth to mouth. If she wanted to know the vision, she would have to acquiesce. But when Farway came back, she would make sure that the priests and the village would never have to bow down to the Corn Men again. She would take from them their secrets, and send their huts tumbling into the canyon, along with every brown-toothed degenerate that stood in her way.

"Name your price."

****

One girl... that was the price. A girl to satisfy their urges. She told them she would ask for volunteers, but first she must secure her vision, fix it in her head the way a footprint is saved in the mud. She had no intention of following through on their payment.

The man that once was Jib was joined now by two other Corn Men, old and toothless, their eyes red from consuming *tilnac*. Lansa did not know their names. Their hands ran across her body, covering it in a strange blue mud. It was cold at first, but then it began to dry, shrinking at the same time, so it felt as if her entire body were being hugged tight all over. It was comforting, and were she not repulsed by the stench of the creatures around her, she would have closed her eyes and fallen asleep.

When her body was covered, they squatted around her head and began chanting. Their song became a dull buzz, and then it was over. She saw the Corn Men were chewing something in their mouths, large bubbles forming on their lips, gray, hazy bubbles that appeared to be filled with liquid that swirled like smoke. Their faces disappeared, replaced by the hazy gray bubbles. At any moment, she thought they would burst, but they continued to grow, the haze inside swirling faster and faster. When the first of the bubbles pressed against the skin of her cheek, it burst, as did the others. Rancid liquid splashed across her face. Instinctually, she screamed, and the liquid crawled inside her mouth as if it were a living thing. Her vision turned milky gray, and she could feel the liquid rushing through her body.

The faces of the Corn Men were gone, and it was as if she were inside of a cloud. The light pulsed and flickered, and she felt the rush of the wind as she was borne through the sky. She was falling, the air moist and clinging to her arms. The gray parted, and she saw below her the village, or what she imagined the birds above the village saw. Below her were the squat huts of the Corn Men, from this height, built perilously close to the edge of the cliff. To the East and South, the river cut like a snake through the canyon. Below her the villagers crawled like ants in the daylight.

The ground was rushing up at her, and she began to scream and flail her arms to right herself. It did no good. The canyon walls flew by as a blur, and then she thumped into the rich farmland, but there was no pain. Lansa pushed herself off of the tilled brown turf, and looked around her. The sky darkened and clouds parted. The stars pulsed with light, brightening, and brightening, until she thought they were going to burn her alive, and then they began to darken. They turned a sickly pink color, like that of blood floating in a pool of water. Then the pink darkened to red, and blood fell from the stars. One by one the stars darkened until they fell from the sky. They landed among the villagers spinning, shooting out darkness that ripped the skin from them. They ran screaming around the village, raw masses of muscle and flesh covered in red as the stars spun on the ground.

The ground beneath her bulged, and she lost her balance. It rose in a mound shape, and then the great white worm, Bimisi, erupted from the ground, dank earth cascading down his white sides.

It hovered in front of her face, its misshapen head and beady black eyes hovering inches from her. Then her head felt like it was going to split open, as a voice began to speak in her head. The voice did not speak in words, but emotions that threatened to split her mind open. It was a message that could not be conveyed using only words... it's meaning bound to the dreamplane. Her eyes dripped blood as she stared at the empty eyes of Bimisi, and then she awoke.

The first thing she noticed was the pain. The second thing she noticed was that her vision was fading from her mind, the way the image of the sun eventually disappears after you look at it. The images were already gone by the time she noticed the Corn Men were each chewing one of her fingers with their brown, broken teeth. Three fingers... the price for a vision whose message couldn't even be conveyed by human thoughts.

It was silent in the hut except for the crackling of the fire, and the whistling of the wind on the Up Top. She watched the Corn Men as they ate her fingers in silence.

She held her right hand up to her face. At least they had left index finger and her thumb. It was an expensive price, but one she had felt she had to pay. Though she wouldn't be able to explain the sense of urgency to the rest of the priests, she now had a course of action, and the rest of the priests would follow or die.

But first thing is first, she thought, *the Corn Men have to go.*

Chapter 14:

The Circle of Life

After three days of marching, the landscape had changed. The blasted rocks of the mountains had become thick forests, the canopy of the trees rising up into the sky and blocking out the sun, except where a few rays managed to fight their way through the branches and the needles. The Stick People walked slowly, placing their feet softly in the blanket of pine needles that covered the floor. They were careful to avoid stepping on dry branches.

Kochen was covered in a layer of sweat. The humidity in the forest was oppressive, and though it felt cool, the air seemed to cling to him. It was as if the trees were breathing and he was walking through their moist breath.

After an hour of walking in the forest, Kochen had lost all sense of direction, and all thoughts of flight fled from his mind. He no longer looked for sharp rocks. His captors no longer tormented him, confident in the fact that he would never find his way out of the forest.

The man who walked beside him had said as much when Kochen had asked him about the size of the forest. He had replied, "The forest is not so big, but it's magic is. A man could walk across it in a day, if they were smart and knew how to navigate the trees. For one such as you, it is endless. You could walk all day and wind up where you started."

They had not talked after that. The men had begun to coalesce and take on distinct personalities. In addition, they had begun treating him better. Food was more plentiful, and he now had his own waterskin, which they had filled at a cool brook that slowly wound its way through the trees. He had splashed water on his face, staring at his reflection in the water. He wondered if Nom lurked in the depths of the brook as it did back home. Was it watching him? Did he protect the Stick People as well as his own?

Through listening to the Stick People's conversations, he had learned the name of the leader. He Who Makes the Drum Beat... that's what they called him. It was a strange name to Kochen's ears. The people in the village had all been given names that sounded nice, simple, but the names of the Stick People were complicated.

On the fourth day of marching, when Kochen had asked his captor about it, he had shrugged, and said, "Names are given at birth, but true names are earned after manhood. He Who Makes the Drum Beat has always been special. When he speaks, we listen. When he commands, we follow. When it is time to make war, he will always come out on top. He is the drum, and we are the dancers."

"What is your name?" Kochen asked.

"I am called Coyote Tongue."

"Why do they call you that?"

"Because my tongue is always wagging. I've said too much already."

It was the most conversation he had heard for days. Actually, it might have been the most conversation he had heard since his father had died. Lansa and the other priests weren't the most talkative bunch. As he was pondering this fact, the forest opened up, and the trees parted way into a massive clearing of hard-packed earth dotted with wooden huts that were built into the ground. The village was large, and smoke from the campfires hung in the air, captured by the trees surrounding them.

Women, children, and elders erupted from the huts, running to their loved ones and embracing. They were human after all, his captors. They did not appear to be the monsters they had when his father would tell him stories about the Stick People. Kochen watched as He Who Makes the Drum Beat spoke to expectant wives and mothers, grief flooding their faces at the news of their loved ones' deaths. He Who Makes the Drum Beat was brief with each of them. Women and family members flocked around the grieved ones. The homecoming was a bittersweet occasion.

Kochen was ushered through the village, the children eyeing him with curiosity and awe, their brown eyes big and round. The women kept their distance as their captor led him to the heart of the village, some of them giving him dirty looks, as if he were the one that killed their men.

The largest hut was in the center of the village, and sitting at the entrance of the hut was a wrinkled old man, his face covered in white paint, the hollows around his eyes painted black. He looked like a skeleton, waiting to sink into the earth. A necklace of large, sharp teeth hung around his neck, and in his lap he cradled a stick that was possibly the most elaborate piece of carving that Kochen had ever seen. The man's face was blank, his expression further clouded by the face paint. He Who Makes the Drum Beat grabbed Kochen by the arm and ushered him into the elderly man's presence.

His eyes were closed, so that the black paint made it seem as if he had no eyes at all, just two gaping black hollows. Silver hair hung splayed across his shoulders. Around the hut, there was complete silence, and even the smell of fire didn't seem to approach the area. They stood in silence. *This is it. This is when I die.* Kochen didn't know why he felt that way, he just did. Various scenarios flitted through his head, awful images that gained in horror with each new iteration. By the time the old man's eyes snapped open, he was sure he was having a vision of his own death where he was standing on a pile of burning sticks, tied to a pole, with burning flames crawling up his body while women and children flung rocks at him with hate in their eyes and curses on their lips.

"Welcome, seer."

It was not what Kochen had expected.

****

Outside of the village, Farway watched as Lonpearl climbed a tree, moving like a squirrel from branch to branch. Lonpearl had always been the best climber of the bunch. He had spent the majority of his youth climbing to the top of the cliff, delivering sacks of corn, food, and firewood to the Corn Men. One day, when Farway was too young to hunt, he had skipped his farm work and watched Lonpearl scale the cliff, leaping from one jut of rock to the next, a satchel full of corn slung over one shoulder. He moved without fear, and Farway admired him for that. Farway had always felt most comfortable with his feet on the ground.

Now Lonpearl was hidden in the tree watching the village from his lofty perch. Farway's men sat around the base of the tree, eating dried meat and berries that they had scavenged while moving through the forest. A campfire was out of the question, and they had already detailed their plan. Unless Kochen appeared to be in danger, they would wait until the Stick People had settled in and put their spears and bows away; then they would sneak in at night, killing anyone who happened to get in their way.

"What about women and children?" Ghulish had asked.

"We do not kill women and children... but if they get in the way, and it comes down to us fighting a whole village or us killing a woman or child, then that is your decision. The consequences are yours to deal with," Farway replied.

The sun went down quickly in the forest, hidden behind the treetops. Darkness filled the night, and the sounds of drums began to reverberate through the forest. Farway and his men sat in darkness, waiting for their time. Lonpearl appeared at his side. He wasn't sure if he had dozed off or if Lonpearl had just been so quiet that he hadn't even noticed him.

"What's going on in there?" he asked him.

"They are having a feast," Lonpearl replied.

The thought sickened Farway. "They're having a feast. They're celebrating killing our people. Let them have their celebration. Tonight, they pay for it all."

Lonpearl seemed shocked. "I thought we were just going to grab Kochen and get away."

Farway thought about it. "No, they're going to die."

****

Kochen sat across from the old man. He had been silent all night, so Kochen had remained the same. Instead, Kochen watched as men began piling up wood taller than a man. So much wood. How would life be different for the people of his village if they had this much wood around?

They piled it up as if it were nothing. The light began to fail, and then one of the men dumped an armful of dried pine needles into the middle of the standing logs. He placed a torch to the pine needles and they flared up, sending a cloud of smoke rushing through the air. The wood caught quickly, and the fire burned so bright it was all he could see, making it so that even though there was daylight, it seemed as if night had already come.

Elderly men produced drums and began pounding out a rhythm. The entire village gathered around the fire, sitting in the dirt or on logs. Children appeared with their mothers, and Kochen and the old man watched without saying a word, close to the circle but apart, so that they seemed invisible. He felt as the spirits must when they spied on the world of man.

The dancing began. The men went first, twirling about the fire to the beat of the drums, their feet alternating between kicking up puffs of dirt and pounding the ground flat. They sang as they danced, the words unrecognizable, almost as if they came from the past. Emotion, drums, fire, Kochen became lost in the fire.

His eyes locked onto the flames as the men whirled about. The drumbeat seemed to disappear, but he still felt it pulsing in his chest. The singing lost all pretense of meaningfulness and became a stream of consciousness in the back of his mind. His mind wandered, dancing with the flames the way the men around the fire danced to the beat of the drums.

Their bodies melted away, and a gout of flame shot into the sky where it formed a flaming circle. At the top of the circle, a giant eagle eye floated in the night, glowing purple from within. On the left side of the circle, at a right angle to the eye, a single ear of corn sprouted out of the flame. On the right side, the flames formed a constant parade of shapes, some recognizable and some not. First, he thought he saw Bimisi. Then he thought he saw Caldus. There were a hundred shapes, but he only recognized those two.

At the bottom of the circle, the flames took the form of his own face, and then more faces appeared alongside it. Kochen didn't attempt to make sense of the fire or the images they made. He soaked it in, the flames burning in his eyes, pulsing to the beat of the drum. Everything was harmonious and as it should be.

Then the corn shriveled and died. The circle of flame was broken and the weight of Kochen's face pulled the circle into a straight line, so that the ever-changing spirits hovered directly above the human faces. The eagle eye blinked once, and then it was gone, the purple light extinguished. The morphing shapes converged upon the faces, until they had consumed each other. In the night, all that was left was a tiny spark. Then, it too was snuffed out.

****

The Eye That Shields watched the young man slip free of his mind. Though his eyes were there, they were not there as well. This had always been the way. The secret to waking vision rested in the heat of the flames, in the shifting light of coals, and the beat of humankind. The Eye That Shields had slipped away like this weeks ago, gone in his own mind, only to see the face of the boy sitting across from him.

He was a slight boy, almost effeminate in his skinniness. His hands were soft, and his face had the look of confusion and frustration about it. He was youth incarnate, and The Eye That Shields had begun to question his vision.

He Who Makes the Drum Beat padded over to him, his footsteps indiscernible above the din of the drums and the singing. He sat down next to The Eye That Shields, and they sat and watched as the boy locked in on the fire.

"Is he the one?" He Who Makes the Drum Beat whispered.

"I had my doubts at first, but he is gone now, talking to the spirits."

"What does he see?"

"You see what I see... in this case at least."

He Who Makes the Drum Beat walked away, while The Eye That Shields pulled a pouch of tobacco from his

95

waist. He pulled his stick from his lap, a hollow stick carved with all of his accomplishments, marking time and progress and his inevitable march to the afterlife. He filled the end of the stick with tobacco and placed it in the fire briefly to light the dried, shredded leaf. He inhaled deeply, waiting to find out what the spirits had told the young man.

How would this man save his people, as the Spirits had told him that he would? How would this boy do anything?

****

Though the vision had come on steadily, it's ending was abrupt, and he questioned whether he had truly seen anything. Around the fire, the women were dancing while the men sat and ate pieces of meat from some sort of charred beast that seemed alien to Kochen. Their women moved among the firelight, their breasts glowing orange in the glare. Their arms were adorned in copper bangles that clinked along with their movements, shining in the light.

His mind wandered, pondering the meaning of the vision. Meanwhile, his body wandered as well, seemingly stuck in the circle of women, their eyes locking into his so that he couldn't tear his eyes away. He felt... moved.

"What did you see?"

Kochen jumped. It was the voice of the old man, gravelly and worn with age. Kochen didn't respond, not out of spite, but because he had no way of putting the vision into words.

The old man handed Kochen a stick and he pointed to the dirt, "Draw."

So Kochen did. Though the flickering flames made it hard to see in the night and the shadow of the heavy-breasted women threatened to break his concentration, he drew the circle with the stick. The vision seemed to coalesce in his mind as he drew. When he finished, he stood above two drawings, and he had no inkling of how to explain them.

For the first time that night, the old man rose from his seat. The drums stopped, and the dancing stopped as well. The women parted away from the fire so that the light could fall over the drawings Kochen had etched in the dirt.

"Do you know what this is?" the old man asked.

Kochen shook his head.

"This is the circle, the circle of life." The old man pointed at the second drawing, "But this... this is what happens when the circle is broken. The circle becomes a chain of death, the world becomes unbalanced, and we will all find ourselves consumed. The Creator will close his eye to us, and we will all be lost."

"What does it mean?"

The old man sighed heavily. "It could mean much. Now is not the time to discuss such matters. Sleep, and in the morning, we shall talk more and puzzle it out together."

Kochen wanted to talk to The Eye That Shields for longer, but he was exhausted from days of marching. Coyote Tongue led him to a hut. It was small and held the dank odor of disuse, but Kochen was glad to fall on the straw mat covered in furs. He didn't even have time to pull the furs over top of himself before he had drifted off to sleep. He didn't hear the sound of a wooden bar being slid into place. All he heard were the echoes of drumbeats as he drifted off. Somewhere in the village, a woman was wailing, mourning for someone that must have been important to her.

****

Lonpearl stood in the branches of the tree. He had taken a nap earlier in the evening. The other men were sleeping now, resting for what was to come that night.

He peered into the village, preventing his eyes from focusing on the flames, lest he lose his ability to see the dark shapes moving in the night. Their village seemed very much like their own in the cliffs. The people smiled and laughed. Their drums were strong, and thankfully, he had not seen them put Kochen on the fire.

He wondered about them, and how they lived in this forest, but most of all, he wondered what the night would have in store for them. Would they have to wet their spears tonight? Lonpearl didn't want to, but they all listened to Farway. Farway was the best hunter the village had ever known. He was fearless, and most of the men looked up to him. Lonpearl admired certain aspects of Farway, but he recognized his lack of wisdom.

He had already heard hushed protests from a few of the other hunters. Killing women and children would anger the spirits. They would be cursed. They might never make it out of the forest alive. Lonpearl was of much the same opinion, but no one said anything to Farway. It would be no use, his jaw was clenched. The best they could manage was tacit disapproval.

Still, the men were angry about the attack on their village, and there was no doubt that some of the Stick People would die tonight. Some of the hunters had lost family members, cousins, brothers, uncles. In Ghulish's case, he had lost his father, a proud man of elder status who refused to quit working the fields. The other farmers had told of how Ghulish's father had let the younger men go before him, volunteering to be the last man up the ladder. Ghulish would take some lives tonight, of that Lonpearl was sure. Even if Ghulish hadn't lost his father, he would have still found some reason to kill.

Lonpearl didn't know if he had it in him. He had watched them take Kochen to the far side of the village from his vantage point, but he didn't see where they had put him. His best hope was to sprint through the village as fast as he could, locate Kochen and pull him out of the village while sounding the retreat. In this way, he hoped to limit the amount of blood that would splash upon the soil.

The noise of the village began to settle. The drums were put away, and first the women and children disappeared. The men sat around the fire telling stories, no doubt of their bravery in battle. Soon they too began to drift off one by one, followed by the sounds of lovemaking. More Stick People would be made tonight to replace the ones they sent to the afterlife. Would they grow up hating Lonpearl's village and the people in it? Would this be the start of a never-ending war? Or would it be the opening assault in a war that would consume one or the other? His thoughts were dark, and Lonpearl didn't like where they were headed.

He thought of home, of his humble quarters on the third terrace, where Stot and Hubra were waiting for him. His wife's smile and the milky breath of his daughter were comforting thoughts. As the sky lightened, and they could see the smoke hovering in the sky, he knew it was time. When they returned, he would become a farmer so that he could stay at home and grow old watching his daughter learn the world.

Chapter 15:

Infiltration

The night was dark. The only light visible came from the moonbeams that filtered through the treetops and the coals of the fires, burning hot but low in the central firepit of the village. Lonpearl inched through the village on his toes, listening to the snores of villagers. A small wind found its way into the village, and on its breeze he caught a whiff of burned meat.

The others moved around him, silent, toes first, taught as a bowstring drawn back, ready to release at a moment's notice. Lonpearl approached the first hut just as the sky began to lighten and fade into a dark blue. He moved silently past the hut, waiting with anticipation for any sort of sound, any sort of alarm.

He wasn't sure where they had stored Kochen, but he knew it wasn't on this side of the village. From his vantage point in the ancient pine tree, he had counted close to sixty huts in the village with three to four occupants per hut, sometimes more. That put the village at close to three hundred people against their nineteen. Of course, maybe only a fifth of those people were warriors like themselves, but still... that put them at a three to one disadvantage with a group who didn't seem to lack experience in the art of war. Their own experience was limited to slaying bobcats and stray deer. Humans were a different type of hunt.

All they had going for them was surprise, and that would only last so long before they were overwhelmed. At the worst, that would mean almost total destruction for them and some pretty significant losses for the Stick People. He could feel the pressure mounting with each hut that he passed. In his mind, he prayed to Darbery, the spirit of the hunt. *Make my footsteps silent. Keep my prey unaware. Allow me to sneak into the herd, and pull my prize without being seen or heard.* He repeated the words over and over, watching every step along the way.

When he had reached the other side of the village, he began to examine the huts. Farway stood to his right, waiting with impatience for Lonpearl to make the call. Lonpearl shrugged his soldiers. The look on Farway's scarred face was one of frustration. Lonpearl knew he had to do something before Farway did, so he pointed out a random hut in the general area where he had seen them take Kochen from his vantage point in the ancient pine tree.

Ghulish and Markon, the youngest hunter, stood on either side of the hut's wooden door. It was held shut with a simple latch. Lonpearl, Farway and the rest of the hunters, stood ready should anything go awry. Ghulish reached out, his hand trembling, and placed his palm on the latch. Markon nodded his head, and Ghulish pressed the latch down and pulled the door open. The inside of the hut was dark except for the glowing of coals, smoke escaping through a hole cut in the ceiling. Lonpearl waited for a scream from inside the hut, but there was nothing.

Time seemed to stretch, and Lonpearl thought his eardrums were going to burst from the sound of his own heartbeat thumping in his ears. Then they appeared, their spears dripping blood. Lonpearl wanted to know what had happened, but none of them dared talk, lest they bring the entire village down on their head.

With a glance, Farway inquired about Kochen. Ghulish and Markon shook their heads. Farway glared at Lonpearl in response, as if to say, "Their deaths are on your hands." They moved down the rows, the pressure mounting on Lonpearl. In his mind, he imagined himself sleeping with his wife and daughter, strangers with spears hovering over him in his sleep. It was horrifying. He hoped the next hut he pointed out would be the correct one.

He pointed to another hut, virtually identical to the last hut. By now the sky had become even lighter, and it wouldn't be long before the sun was up, with the villagers to follow soon after. They rushed to the next hut in the gray morning light. Two different men lined up next to the hut's door. Hinler and Ondus stood next to the door. Ondus counted to three with his fingers, grabbed the latch and together they stormed inside. They heard the sound of a scuffle, and a brief gurgling, but then there was nothing. When they emerged, they shook their heads, their spear tips dripping blood into the dust.

In the brightening morning, Lonpearl spied another hut, the doors now becoming visible in the light. He rushed over to it, cursing himself for not having seen the hut before. As he was lifting the bar off of the door, he heard a cough somewhere in the village. Time was falling through their fingers. He set the wooden bar on the ground and lifted the latch.

It was dark inside, as there was no fire built in the hut. Lonpearl inched into the hut, his spear at the ready. He looked down at his feet, waiting for his eyes to adjust to the darkness, hoping against hope that the shape at his feet was the form of Kochen, and not someone else. The shape shifted and sat up, a beam of light illuminating the face of Kochen.

"Lonpearl? I dreamed of you," Kochen said sleepily.

"We came to get you out of here. Get to your feet, and move quietly, we need to leave before the village awakens." Lonpearl turned to leave. He was at the door before he noticed that Kochen was not behind him. He still sat on the ground, staring at Lonpearl, his legs tucked underneath his furs.

"Come on. We don't have much time."

"I'm not going with you."

Farway bullied his way past Lonpearl. "I'll die before I leave you here."

Farway gripped the boy by his arm and pulled him to his feet, clamping a hand over the child's face, "Move your feet. We're not going to die because you want to betray the village."

Kochen struggled against Farway's grip. Without even thinking, Farway spun Kochen around and delivered a solid fist to the back of his skull. As Kochen began to crumble to the ground, one arm stiff and hanging in the air, Lonpearl caught his toppling form and slung him over a shoulder. Swiftly, they made their exit through the village.

As Lonpearl neared the far end of the village, he looked over his shoulder to see Ghulish and Ondus pulling lit torches out of the coals of the village fire. He watched as they tossed the torches in the air. They flew through the sky in an arc, landing on the roof of two huts. They caught fire in seconds, the dry, wooden dwelling being no more than kindling to the fire spirit.

With Kochen slung over his shoulders, Lonpearl turned and headed into the forest, the morning brightening their way. He ran as fast as he could, which wasn't very fast at all. Kochen felt a lot heavier than he looked. In the distance, he saw the first carving they had made in the trees, pointing him in the direction that he was to go. With any luck, the fires would burn, and the Stick People that lived in them would escape unscathed.

They had made it out. They had actually escaped without waking the entire village. Farway ran next to him, his deep breathing sounding ominous. An aura of disappointment hung around him, as if he had secretly been wishing for someone to rise and sound the alarm. They ran on, following the fresh markings they had made in the bark of the trees. They would run home. They would run all day and walk at night. It was what they did. Even taking turns carrying Kochen, they should easily outpace the Stick People.

Chapter 16:

A Course of Action

He Who Makes the Drum Beat awoke with a start. He heard screaming and wailing. At first, he thought it was just the echoes of his dreams, and then he realized it was real. Startling his wife and children, he burst from his hut, naked and with a spear in his hand. He saw one of his warriors sitting in the dust, his arm burnt up to the shoulder. In his arms, he held the scorched corpse of a child, his hut smoldering behind him.

Bits of charred skin curled on the flesh of the man's arms, and he grimaced in pain, sobbing. His wife stood behind him, her shrieks echoing throughout the village, bouncing back off the trees, and sticking in his ears, where they would remain until the end of his days.

To his left, another such scene was playing out. Only, there were no survivors, just burnt masses of flesh that used to be people; smoke still rose off of them where they sat in the ruins of their hut that had burned down around them. Their flesh still sizzled among the coals of the hut. The hut had belonged to a pair of elders. Their passing was not so sad in that respect, but no one should have to burn alive. The thought horrified him. That they were still holding each other in their arms did not make his stomach turn any less. A crowd of people had gathered around, holding each other and wailing.

From the back of the village, he heard another scream, and a woman came running out of a tent, her hands clasped to the sides of her face in shock. He Who Makes the Drum Beat was closest, and he went inside, throwing the door wide. Lying in a pool of blood was Coyote Tongue and his wife. They had been stabbed through the throat. By the size of the wounds, the attackers must have used spears.

His rage boiled, and when he emerged from the hut of Coyote Tongue, he called for the people to search all of the huts. He walked to the hut where the young seer from the cliffs had been stored. The door was open, and when he looked inside, it was empty.

As he walked back to his own hut to put on his clothing, he began to understand what had happened. After throwing a fur over his shoulders, and comforting his wife and children, he walked briskly to the hut of The Eye That Shields, throwing open the door. He sighed a breath of relief when the old man sat up in his furs, his hair sticking out every which way. He had been worried that they had killed the old man as well.

"What is it?"

"You should come outside. Things are bad."

The Eye That Shields rose from the ground, his body nothing more than bones wrapped in skin. He would have to talk to him about taking an apprentice soon. He was too old, and the knowledge contained in his head and soul were too valuable for the village to lose. If the Cliff People had stolen into the wrong tent in the night, then it could all have been gone, millennia of knowledge and wisdom wiped out with one spear thrust. Things were changing. The Cliff People had never retaliated like this before. They would have to adapt. They would have to change as well. The Eye That Shields would need a second eye, but today was not the day that he would push the issue. Today was a day of sadness and mourning.

On the morrow, the time would be more appropriate. It would be a day of rebirth and renewal, and a more timely day to broach the issue.

The Eye That Shields coughed up the evening's smoke, wrapped himself in his furs and stepped out into the morning air, shambling along, the chains of age dragging on the dusty ground of the village.

"Burned people," he said as soon as he had stepped outside, before he had even seen any of the bodies. The Eye was old; he had seen and experienced much before He Who Makes the Drum Beat had even been born. Though no one had burned alive in the village since his birth, The Eye had seen and been a part of much worse.

The Eye's face was filled with sadness as he stumbled through the village. Tears flowed from his eyes when he saw the burned huts. He squatted in the dirt and placed a hand on the burned warrior's shoulder. The warrior looked at The Eye and moaned, "Bring her back. Bring her back."

"She is gone, my friend. She will not come back."

The warrior continued to plead with him as he walked away, repeatedly yelling, "Why didn't you see this?" The Eye That Shields had no answer.

"What should we do?" he asked The Eye.

"Where is the seer?"

"He is gone. His people took him, burned these huts, and made their escape."

The Eye walked back to his hut, and sat in the dirt. He closed his eyes and sat silently. He Who Makes the Drum Beat waited for his words. It could be a long wait. He began to stoke the coals of the fire. Loudest Laugh appeared from the back of the village. His face was grim, as he spoke. "There is another family dead in the back. Sun Racer and his wife and two children, dead in their hut."

He Who Makes the Drum Beat simply nodded. That was not good enough for Loudest Laugh. "What are we going to do about it?"

As he placed more kindling on the coals and blew on them, he waved Loudest Laugh away. At first, the warrior made to leave, but then he spun around, not content with waiting. "We need to go now. These people have murdered our women and children. They snuck into our village, killed our families and then walked away. Why are we waiting?"

He Who Makes the Drum Beat blew on the coals before speaking. "We wait for the word of The Eye That Shields. He will know the way."

"He is an old man. His time is past. Spirits no longer rule here. The spear does."

He Who Makes the Drum Beat blew on the coals. They were red hot, and flames sprouted along the dried twigs that he had formed into a teepee shape. He stood up, his knees cracking at the effort, and grabbed Loudest Laugh by the face. "Hear me, Loudest Laugh, and listen. Keep your tongue in your mouth, and let The Eye do his job. He is the mind, we are the hands and arms. He will tell us the path we must take, and if you don't like it, you can ask the spirits yourself." He Who Makes the Drum Beat pulled a knife from the sheath at his waste and held it up to Loudest Laugh's eye. He pressed the rough obsidian edge against his cheek.

"What do you say? Do you want to ask the spirits?"

"No. I'll wait for The Eye."

"Good." He Who Makes the Drum Beat put his knife in his sheath. "Let me know if you change your mind. We could always use an eye on the other side." He shoved Loudest Laugh away from him, and went back to stoking the fire. He knew the heart of Loudest Laugh, and it was much as his own. Loudest Laugh could afford such an outlook. He had only himself to look after. He Who Makes the Drum Beat had an entire village of people depending on him. Though he knew Loudest Laugh and his close friends would be gone within the hour, he had no choice but to wait for the wisdom of The Eye. Silently, he wished Loudest Laugh and his men luck. He sat on his knees, forced the sobbing of the village out of his mind, and stared into the fire.

****

The fire danced in the evening. He turned the spit, watching as the meat darkened, sizzling and popping over the flames.

"Not so fast, Machia," his father's voice said to him. "Nice and slow, so that it all cooks evenly. Uncooked meat can kill a man as easily as a spear."

His brother laughed at him. With squinty eyes and an unruly laugh, his brother was always looking for ways to bring Machia down. Machia did not care. It was all his brother had. The girls did not like him, and most of the boys did not care for him either. He was all bluster, quick temper, and cruelty. He wasn't sure how he had gotten that way, but he sensed that his own success might be the cause of it.

His father smacked his brother across the back of his head. "Instead of giving your brother a hard time, learn from his mistakes. Appreciate him. Try to do things like him. Even if you are half as good as him, you'll still be better than most." Machia winced on the inside; this was also part of it. Always the favorite, Corbath had always been held to his standard, and failed miserably.

His brother looked at Father with hate in his eyes. "I am not Machia. I am my own person. I do not need to learn anything from him."

Machia shared a look with his father. No matter how many times his brother Corbath had been disciplined, he always came out the same... only slightly more sour. It seemed there was nothing that would satisfy him. He wanted the world, but didn't want to work for it. When Machia tried to explain how he had become the best young hunter in the village, all Corbath did was wave his hand at him in a dismissive matter and say, "I will be better than you, Machia. I don't even have to try."

Machia saw his brother for what he was, a lazy blowhard who would always take the easy road. Still, he was his father's son, and his own brother. So when Corbath would find himself in the middle of a fight, Machia would appear to clean up the mess, peacefully if he could, with his fists if he had to.

When the rabbit was evenly cooked, they divided it up. Machia gave Corbath the best bits as a balm for his ego. No thanks were given. They lay down in the forest, stoking the fire up high, and when their father's breathing became deep, and only the sound of the owls and the coyotes could be heard, Corbath turned to him and said, "I hate you."

Machia closed his eyes and said, "Hate me all you want; I'll always be your brother."

Even after they had grown old and earned their adult names, He Who Makes the Drum Beat would occasionally see Loudest Laugh looking over at him, across the evening fire, his eyes repeating the phrase that he had uttered so long ago. "I hate you."

His brother was on his own path, a path that weaved over a yawning cliff, a path that would pull Loudest Laugh out of his shadow or send him plummeting to his death, taking who knows how many others with him.

****

The voice of the old man broke him out of his contemplation. He Who Makes the Drum Beat shook his head, letting the thoughts of his lost brother fly into the sky with the ashes of the fire. "What did you say?" he asked The Eye That Shields.

The entire village was gathered around. Graves had been dug for the dead, and they had long since been buried underneath the oldest of trees, their bodies living forever in the massive, thick-trunked pines that rose hundreds of feet into the air. They would always watch over them, looking down on the village, and protecting it... although not from the people of the cliffs apparently. Before He Who Makes the Drum Beat could continue further down this line of reasoning, The Eye That Shields spoke again.

"We must go."

The villagers listened in silence, their tears dried with the passing of the sun. "Very well. We will gather our things and head after them."

"You don't understand... *we* must go. You and I, to the cliffs."

He Who Makes the Drum Beat wiped his brow. "The Eye never leaves the village. This is the way it has always been."

"Times are different now. Things are changing. If we wish to preserve our way of life, we must adapt, so that we may preserve it. If I stay here, all is lost. I have seen it."

He didn't doubt The Eye, but it didn't feel right. Nothing had felt right since they had made their way to the cliffs and found the boy they had been looking for, right where The Eye said they would find him. Though he hadn't left the village in decades, he had described to them exactly where and when to be, and it had worked. He had not mentioned anything about a giant beast that lived underground, but visions did as visions must. They were all tainted with the tricks of the coyote.

"But we will never catch them, I mean no offense, if we have to drag you along with us."

"This journey is not about catching them. This journey is about doing as we must. Do I wish we had the powers of our forefathers? The power to turn into an eagle or a wolf? Of course, but those ways are lost now. Now I am only what I am, an old man, trying to save the world. You can do as you wish. This has always been our way, one man choosing his own fate, but I have seen what I have seen, and if you leave me here, the world will die."

He Who Makes the Drum Beat hung his head. Though he relied on The Eye's wisdom, it was seldom what he wanted to hear. "Pack your things. We leave before the light dies. Water Like Breath, Questions the Sun, build a litter for The Eye. When it is ready we go."

The Eye departed, as did the men who would accompany them on their journey. There were many of them, but Loudest Laugh was not there. Several of Loudest Laugh's cronies were conspicuously absent as well. By now they were probably sprinting through the forest, hell-bent on catching up to the Cliff People. It was as it was, and there was nothing he could do about it now.

As He Who Makes the Drum Beat walked back to his hut, his wife and children joined him. He put his arm around Kula, his wife, the warmth from her slender shoulders feeling good beneath his rough hands. He stooped to pick up Inuola, and then plopped him on his shoulders, giving him a bird's eye view of the village. Kula held their infant daughter in her hands. Together, they walked back to their hut.

His preparations would be quick. He had little in the way of possessions. Other than his family and the security of the village, He Who Makes the Drum Beat cared for little else. Within five minutes, he had gathered all of his things. The litter wouldn't be put together for a while, so they ate food, and he told stories of his adventures to the home of the Cliff People.

Inuola laughed at his tales, his eyes growing round at the telling of the great beast that lived under the ground. Kula smiled, and in his heart, he felt the pull that most leaders feel from time to time, the desire to abandon it all and just focus on worrying about his own family. It was a fleeting sensation, but it's why he was a leader. His family was why he cared about the village. They were the reason he had gone to the cliffs in the first place. The spirits had said, "Do this or perish." Looking down at his infant daughter and his growing son, there really was no decision to be made.

The same could be said for today. He could sit here, let the circle of life fall apart, but what happiness he gained now would be gone within a matter of years, maybe even sooner. What sort of life would his children have then. What if he should fall ill or get injured in a battle? What would be their fate? He trusted the spirits, so he put all thoughts of a comfortable life at home out of his head.

When he was done with his story, he passed the infant child to Inuola, and told him to go play. When he had gone and closed the door behind him, he wrapped Kula in his arms and together they whiled away the last few moments before the litter for The Eye That Shields was ready.

****

The Eye That Shields looked over the hut that he was leaving behind. It was the oldest in the village. The layer of char around the roof of the hut was thick and scaled like a great black serpent. The furs and sacred implements were as old as the hut itself, older than even him. But he would miss none of it. It had been years since he had left the village. He had been but a young man before he was elevated to his current role.

Before he had taken on the mantle of spiritual leader for the tribe, he had ranged far and wide with a group of hunters from the village, encountering countless people from the shadows, slipping into their villages, looking around, and then slipping back out again. It had been a thrill, and he fondly regarded those days of high adventure. Perhaps he would have one more. He would not miss his things, but he did hope to see them again.

The old man gathered up his counting stick, his pipe, and a leather bag full of various herbs and remedies, and stepped outside. He watched as men hugged their wives and children, some crying, some hoping to see their loved one return soon, but all somber. There was no such embrace for him. The life of the spiritual leader was a solitary one. His predecessor claimed it was to keep a leader from attempting to sway the direction of the village to benefit his own family. It made sense.

Part of him wondered what it would have been like to have had a family of his own. What would his child have been like? Would it have been wise like himself, brave like He Who Makes the Drum Beat, or hotheaded and abrasive like Loudest Laugh? Loudest Laugh... where was he? He didn't see him among the warriors saying their farewells, nor did he see any of his friends.

The Eye That Shields pulled aside a passing warrior, his spears in his hand, and various gear thrown over his shoulder in a satchel. "Where is Loudest Laugh?"

The man, Footstep in the Dewy Grass, looked as if he wanted to be anywhere but there. He looked around, hoping to be saved by someone else, and then finally he sighed. In a husky voice, he said "Loudest Laugh gives chase. They left this morning."

The Eye That Shields let go of the man's arm, and he gratefully walked away, thankful to be away from The Eye That Shields. *That damn fool, always looking for glory where only sorrow can be had.*

Hobbling, The Eye That Shields made his way to the litter that would bear him away from the village. Part of him was embarrassed to be such a burden, to be carried around like an overgrown baby. The dull ache in his knees made that part shut up quickly. He looked at the litter with doubt. Two young pine branches, stripped bare and lashed together with deer-hide thongs. A fur had been draped between the sticks, holes punched in its edges, and the thongs wound through the holes to secure the hide to the branches. It wasn't pretty, but it should make for a fine litter.

"Would you like to try it out?" Water Like Breath asked.

No, I don't want to try it out. "It would be my honor. Thank you." The Eye That Shields squatted down, his knees screaming in protest, then he rolled himself onto the litter, his possessions clutched in his arms. Water Like Breath and Questions the Sun lifted the head of the litter up off of the ground. They dragged it around the village, testing it out. He laughed along with the villagers who saw him, and then they were off, running through the forest, their goodbyes said and done, the mission before them, and the light growing dim.

His litter bounced and jostled every which way, the warriors running as fast as they could. He looked up to the sky and watched as the treetops passed by. Were it not for the constant bouncing of his lower half, he could have fallen asleep. The pain was great, and his joints did not react kindly to all of the jostling, but he bit his tongue. It was the least he could do for slowing the men down and causing them such hardship.

Chapter 17:

Coming Down

As Lansa lay on the edge of the rock precipice, she knew what she must do. She would not send a woman to the Corn Men. Their time was over. They had broken the pact. The Corn Men were there to serve, and in return, they were delivered firewood, corn, and food. They were not there to make demands. If she were to give a woman to the Corn Men, she was sure the village would be damned by the spirits.

They had to go, but how to do it? The village was a superstitious place. They would take her vision at her word; she was sure of it. But there were those among the village that would not take kindly with the break in tradition. Dantish came to mind. He was old, not the oldest person in the village, but he felt like it. He was intractable, sharp as an obsidian spear, and always filled with questions.

Dantish would be difficult.

Lansa looked over the edge of the granite outcrop, the pain in her hand shattering her train of thought. She looked down at the village, and saw an exact replica of what she had seen in her vision. It was a long way down.

Her missing fingers throbbed, and she had exhausted herself making it to the outcropping. Her body was covered with sweat, and the wounds where her fingers had been burned. The strain of climbing with a two-fingered hand was too much. She would not be able to make it to the floor of the uppermost terrace without aid, of that she was sure. If she were to fall and perish, so would her vision, and then, so would the village.

She squirmed herself around, so that her head was sticking out over the edge of the outcropping, the same one that she had spit off of as a youth. She had come full-circle. Lansa silently cursed her mother. Were it not for her, Jib would have never had any idea of what it was even like to be with a woman. In her own way, her mother was as responsible for their impending doom as anyone.

"Help!" she yelled over the side of the cliff. None of the shapes looked upward, so she yelled some more while thoughts tumbled through her head. The secrets. The powers of vision. These things could not be lost. Though the Corn Men's existence on the Up Top would soon be over, Lansa knew that they were an important part of their world. The *tilnac* was important. They would need the secret of it. She would pry the secret from their lips in whatever manner she could. She would pry all their secrets out of them, even if it meant their death.

"Help!" she screamed again. Below her she saw the jaunty and odd shape of Caubrey stop and look upwards. She waved her good hand at him and yelled some more. Caubrey waved back and smiled at her. He seemed content with just waving at her, until another familiar shape walked over to see what he was looking at.

The squatty bald shape raised a hand to her brow and looked upwards. It was Birren. Finally. Lansa thought she was going to be stuck on the rock all day, waving aimlessly at Caubrey and his cracked brain and toothy grin.

"We'll get help!" Birren yelled, the words barely audible over the gentle breeze. Lansa rolled over on her back, and dreamed of ways to pry information out of the Corn Men, while the sun baked her skin.

****

It was hours before two young men showed up, coils of rope slung over their shoulders and waterskins on their belts. Their hairless bodies shone with sweat, as they bent over, testing rocks to tie their ropes off to. When they had found two spots that were adequate to support her weight, they asked her to stand, and with blinding efficiency, they coiled the ropes around her legs and her waist. She couldn't remember the last time anyone had touched her anywhere, and the sensation made her long for more, it made her wonder what other traditions the priests and the village had been stubbornly holding onto.

They stood back to admire their work, testing the knots on the harness, and then came the hard part. Lansa stood on the edge of the granite outcropping, looking down at the village. By now, the entire village had showed up to watch the proceedings and find out if they were going to have to find a new head priest. She recalled the last time she had stood on the edge of the outcropping, deciding whether or not to kill herself. Had she made the right decision? She didn't know. All she knew was that she was saving her village, saving her people, saving the only family she had after her parents had abandoned her to death and Corn Men.

She squatted down and sat on the edge of the outcropping, her legs dangling into the air, her head swimming as she thought about what would come next. She turned around and looked at the boys behind her. The ropes were laced around their bodies, around their legs, around their waists, and over their arms.

"You hold that rope tight now," she pleaded more than commanded. They nodded and smiled at her, clearly enjoying the prospect of being heroes for the day. With that, she turned and looked out over the river valley. Such a wide world. Why did anyone want to bother them here in this out of the way place. Was Kochen out there? Was he having a vision of this very moment?

Lansa took a deep breath. It was no use wondering. She could sit and wait forever, but she had things to do. She leaned out over the edge, and her stomach flew up into the back of her throat as she left the outcropping and fell into the air. It was a short fall, but it was enough to make her start praying to the spirits before the rope caught, and she found herself dangling in open air, the world spread out around her.

She clung to the rope, as if she could climb up it were she to suddenly start falling. Below her, the villagers looked up at her, their hands over their eyes, to shield the sun, their heads tilted back. Had any head priest ever lived through such embarrassment? The wind roared through her ears, and the ropes dug into her thighs and waist hard, as she gripped the rope with her one good hand. It was pain upon pain, but it wasn't the worst she had ever felt.

****

He had been a handsome man. His skin was more red than brown from the hours he spent in the fields. Though he was fully capable of hunting, he didn't like to be away from the village. He said he enjoyed the smell of the earth, the feel of the sun on the back, but most of all, the sight of her bent over.

He was a dirty man, classless, but somehow beyond class. His honesty was refreshing. She had never known anyone in the village who talked like him. She had watched him in the fields, the round, hard muscles of his chest bunching, as he dug furrows in the spring ground. She felt it when she watched him, she felt the part of herself that she thought had been dead years ago. In addition, she felt something else, a confused feeling warming the flesh between her legs.

At night, she explored the area, imagining him there, his rough hands running all over her body. In the cold, empty home of her parents, she had dreamed of him like she had never dreamed of any man before. They watched each other from the fields, him smiling at her, her imaging what was under his kilt.

Then it had happened. He came to her, in the night, his hardness throbbing in her hand, in her mouth, in her loins. The pain of that first night was bittersweet, the blood frightening. But he came back, and it got better and better.

They made no secret of their relationship. But no one said anything. They just smiled, and turned their eyes the other way when they would exit Lansa's dwelling, sweat plastering their hair to their heads.

He was married already, but she didn't mind. His wife was younger than her, but he complained of her coldness. She was always pushing him to go on the hunt, to get them a bigger portion of the spoils. Lansa had no complaints. She would starve with him if he wanted her to. He was her nourishment; she was his.

When she became pregnant, the visits stopped. As her belly swelled, the smiling stopped. People no longer turned their eyes when she walked by. They stared at her, accusations in their eyes. His wife stared at her, hate burning in those cold brown eyes of hers, but worst of all, he began to ignore her. In the fields, she would smile at him, but his eyes would slide right over her as if she weren't even there.

She had never been more lonely in her life. The movement in her belly, which had been so comforting at first, became a hateful burden to her. Even Fesh, her one friend, stopped coming to see her. What she did was against the spirits he had said. She was breaking the circle between husband and wife. She was an outcast to the spirits.

Lansa knew pain. She knew it tenfold when she finally gave birth. She knew it a hundredfold when she walked to his dwelling and knocked on the door. She knew it a thousandfold when she handed the child to him, and said "His name is Kochen."

****

Priests were not allowed children, and she had been fine with that. When Kochen had been abandoned by his supposed mother, who was not really his mother at all, Lansa's heart had skipped a beat with hope. It was meant to be. The village had kept Kochen's secret for years. The day that Lansa had climbed to the Sanctum and abased herself before Fesh had been all it took. Fesh took care of it. Word was spread, and Kochen's father and the woman who Kochen thought was his mother never spoke of it.

It hurt Lansa to see how Kochen's supposed mother treated him, but it was part of the bargain. Priests weren't supposed to have offspring, but she had vowed to give him up, and Fesh had relented, eschewing tradition to save her life. Though the villagers had turned their backs on her, she had volunteered to protect them, to protect her Kochen, even if it were from a distance and even if he could never know she was his mother. When Kochen's father had died, and Kochen had been given up to the priests, she thought her dreams had come true.

She had been hard on Kochen, harder on him than she had wanted to be. But the village still knew. They still knew he was Lansa's, though no one said anything. She had to show him the hard side of her love, or she would lose face in the eyes of the villagers. If she lost face, she would lose power. If she lost power, someone else would be in charge, and how could she be sure that Kochen would be safe then?

As she descended into the village, she could feel their eyes again. The village was not safe, not with the Corn Men on the Up Top. If Farway and his men were successful, and they brought Kochen home, they would

121

find a village that was much stronger than when they had left it. Kochen's new home would be a place of safety. She would steal the secrets from the Corn Men and use them to protect Kochen. When the time was right, and Kochen was grown into manhood, he would take over leadership of the village, armed with his visions, the spirits, and the secrets of the Corn Men. He would be a god among men. She would make sure it would happen, or she would destroy the entire village trying.

Chapter 18:

Laying Traps

They thundered like wounded elk through the forest, heedless of the sound they made. Branches snapped, pine needles flew, and stray branches were broken off if they were in the way. Normally, they would move silently, like the sun across the sky, but they were already behind.

Loudest Laugh breathed through his nose and out through his mouth as he ran, the way he had been taught as a youth. The men to his left and right were with him, every step of the way.

To his right, Ghost Hair's powerful legs pumped, his spear held at the ready. His gray hair flew backwards, and his wide face was set in a permanent sneer. To his left Sky Toucher loped along, his lanky body moving effortless through the day. To Sky Toucher's left, his brother, Snake Tears jogged along, sweat dripping off of his chin and down his chest. He was the worst jogger of the group, but he would be invaluable should it come to fighting. Two clubs were strapped to his back, evil chunks of ancient wood that were carved with symbols of strength. Loudest Laugh had seen Snake Tears open a man's skull and then take off his jaw with just two swings in the Cliff People's village. It had appeared to be effortless for him. The clubs weren't a traditional weapon, but ever since they had taken them from an unsuspecting village two nights' run from the forest of their homeland, he had taken to them as if he were born to wield them.

They ran with purpose, knowing that glory would be theirs if they were successful. They had tasted glory before, but it was the silent type of glory, the glory of four men sneaking into a village in the middle of the night and spiriting away a woman. It wasn't the type of glory that they crowed about among the villagers, but they felt it just the same; the ties that bound them were strong, and they never gave each other a false face. They called themselves the Last Honest Men, and this was their chance to put their names in the stories. This was their time, and years from now, whoever took The Eye That Shields' place would find him or herself sitting around a fire telling the tale of how Loudest Laugh and The Last Honest Men had tracked down the murderous Cliff People and made them pay for their crimes.

Sky Toucher was the first to see the markings. He knew the forest like the back of his hand. He had never been comfortable among the tribe, though he was bound to it, just as they all were. He had grown up, exploring the woods, living there as much as he could. He spent as much time in the tops of the trees as he did in the village. The villagers sometimes joked that Sky Toucher had a pet name for every tree. If he did, he had never mentioned them, but he could spot any disturbance in his forest. Today, he had spied fresh scars on the bole of a pine tree. The sap shone in the sun.

Sky Toucher walked to a tree, placing a hand on it, and he looked around the forest.

"Do you want some privacy?" Ghost Hair asked.

They laughed, but Sky Toucher ignored them. He looked at the ground and off into the distance. Then he bolted off into the woods. Loudest Laugh took a deep breath and then ran after him, leaping a decaying tree trunk in the process. Snake Tears and Ghost Hair did the same. Men had been known to break their ankles in trying to use the dead trunks as leverage to leap into the air. Place your foot on an old rotten trunk and attempt to leap off of it, and you'd likely find yourself with a broken ankle when your foot sank into the rotten tree corpse. It was one of the first things they were taught as young men on the hunt.

They skidded to a halt to find Sky Toucher with his hand placed on another tree, looking about, reading the world around him.

"Isn't the other tree going to be mad that you're cheating on her?" Snake Tears asked.

"There's plenty of me to go around," Sky Toucher shot back.

Loudest Laugh laughed loudest, his voice echoing back through the trees. In an instant, he was serious again. "What do you see?"

"They are escaping along the same path we used when we came back from the Cliff People's village. They tracked us here and carved these marking to find their way back. They are running."

"As they should," Ghost Hair chimed in.

Sky Toucher squatted down on his knees and looked at the ground. "There are many of them. Many more than us." He pointed off in the distance. "If they continue the route that we took, they will switch back and forth, wasting time, perhaps a whole day."

Loudest Laugh smiled. Stupid Cliff People, they hadn't realized that they had spent half a day moving among the forest, twisting this way and that without ever really going anywhere to confuse the young seer so that he might not escape. If they retraced their route, they would find that they had done little more than spend the entire morning stepping over their own footsteps.

"We can catch them then! At the edge of the forest, we will set our trap, spring upon them, and leave them to feed the trees," Ghost Hair crowed.

"Come on, let's move. I bet an hour with your wife that I get the first kill," Snake Eyes yelled as he took off into the forest. Ghost Hair scoffed at him, and chased after Snake Eyes whooping and hollering.

Loudest Laugh smiled before he trotted after the others. It would all work. They would have their glory. This time they would have glory they could talk about. This time they would make a story that would be told for the ages. They ran.

****

The forest shot by them, until they emerged on the plains. Two days from the village, their bellies full of meat and fish, the stench of the village and its inhabitants far behind them. They ran through the flat land under the full moon, its light showing the way among the scrub grass of the plain. They had come through the forest, over the foothills and appeared on the plains without thinking twice about it, The Last Honest Men, their intentions carried in their hands and slung over their shoulders.

The buffalo were running. The sound of their bleating in the night was great, and the ripe smell of their herd carried over the plains. They stalked forward, spears at the ready. They would only get one chance in the night to take one of them down.

Loudest Laugh still remembered the tales of his father, talking about how to bring down one of the giant beasts. Sitting around the fire, he had told them of a time when the tribe had ranged far and wide, exploring the world around them. They had found little of interest besides other people speaking strange languages, but the buffalo... he remembered the buffalo. He could still see his father staring into the night sky saying, "The meat was like nothing man was ever intended to eat. The fat of the hump tasted better than any bear, deer, or rabbit you or your brother will ever taste."

Though his father was past the age of exploration, he had always yearned to go back, bring down a buffalo and taste it one last time. His father was gone. He Who Makes the Drum Beat had taken his place, and now Loudest Laugh was the laughingstock of the tribe. He had pushed so hard to be the replacement, to take the mantle that his father left under the trees when he had coughed himself to death. The people of the village wouldn't have it. The elders cast aspersions on his character, making him out to be some sort of thoughtless monster. His brother said nothing, but he won the vote of the elders anyway.

Well, tonight he would do something his brother had never done. He would kill a buffalo and taste the meat that his brother never would. In the night, they inched forward, low and slumped over so as not to startle the buffalo. They were grazing lethargically, but the slightest noise would send them careening across the plain, their hooves thundering across the black soil, the waist-high grass hissing against their hairy hides.

Their prize stood on the edge of the herd, a medium-sized buffalo grazing off to the side. They crawled up behind it, their spears at the ready. Loudest Laugh's legs ached from the tension, as he moved closer and closer. He could smell the musky hide. He glided through the grass like a snake, his spear arm cocked and ready. Sky Toucher stood a hundred feet away, an arrow nocked and ready to finish the job. Snake Tears had his clubs slung over his shoulders for once, though he very likely could walk up to the buffalo, crack it over the head, and kill it. He had agreed on a more expedient rout. Ghost Hair stood in the distance, low to the ground, waiting to throw his spear should the animal bolt at their approach.

Loudest Laugh and Snake Tears were within arm's reach when the first spear struck home, just behind the buffalo's neck. It sunk deep into the meat, as did Snake Tears' thrust on the opposite side. The beast was off like an arrow loosed from a bow. Sky Toucher took his shot, the arrow thumping home in its side, and yet still the beast ran onward.

The rest of the herd was agitated by the smell of blood on the prairie, dripping down in nightblack rivulets. The wounded buffalo surged forward, right into the path of Ghost Hair. He rose up out of his crouch and threw another spear into the thick hide of the buffalo. The herd was swarming. The night became an echo of thunderous footfalls and Loudest Laugh had to dodge the charge of a monstrous buffalo. He fell hard on his shoulder, but rolled to his feet. In the moonlight, he could see the silver mop of Ghost Hair running in the night, chasing the buffalo they had wounded.

They followed suit, the cold night air filling their lungs and escaping as steam. By the time they had stopped running, the sound of the herd had lessened, and soon they were alone, on the trail of the lone buffalo. It was a wounded and scared thing. It snuffled heavily at the ground; its footsteps became less sure. It could no longer run.

As Ghost Hair neared the wounded creature, it made once last charge at him. He dodged out of the way easily, and then it toppled over on the ground, breathing heavily. They admired the beast they had taken down. It hadn't been the biggest, but it had certainly given them a good fight. Sky Toucher ended its misery with a well-aimed arrow, and Ghost Hair knelt to the ground to thank the spirits for the gift.

The thundering of the herd was all but gone. The night was still. Loudest Laugh stared around the plain. There was nothing here, just wild grasses for the buffalo to feed on. He looked around the valley, bathed in silver moonlight, watching the grass sway like rippling water under the unceasing wind. In the distance he saw something... it was fire.

Loudest Laugh pointed it out to the others. "Should we see what it is?"

"Why not?" Snake Tears offered.

"We have all this meat," Sky Toucher said.

Ghost Hair grunted, "Go. See. I will stay here and claim the meat."

Loudest Laugh was not surprised by Ghost Hair's lack of curiosity. He had always been the most prudent of the bunch. He was silent and spiritual. He enjoyed the wilds of nature, and had no use for the village itself, but it was not safe in the wild for one man alone, so he had become a part of their band, offering countless tips of survival. For him, having them leave him alone for a few minutes would be a gift.

Loudest Laugh, Snake Tears, and Sky Toucher crept through the sea of grass, keeping their eyes on the fire. It was burning low, and it was mostly coals by the time they reached the clearing. Strange structures were built in a circle around the fire, conical shapes made from deer hide and wooden poles. The hides were decorated in a profusion of colors that had a cheering effect on Loudest Laugh. He didn't know why he liked the shapes, he just did.

Having satisfied their curiosity, they were about to leave when Snake Tears pointed out a structure that was set apart from the others. It was not part of the circle. Through a series of hand signals, they agreed to investigate the lone structure. They stayed low, and they made no noise that wasn't drowned out by the flapping wind.

As they reached the edge of the structure, they flopped down on their bellies and lifted up the edges of the deer hides, hoping to see what was inside. Inside it was dark, and there was little light to see by. A tiny shaft of moonlight shot through the top of the structure where the wooden frame's poles met. Loudest Laugh could see nothing, and then the shape shifted, furs fell to the side, and he glimpsed the erect brown nipple of a breast.

He crawled under the hide of the structure and made his way to the breast as if it were calling him. Snake Tears and Sky Toucher stayed back, looking around the small village for any sign that they were being observed.

When he was within arm's reach of the breast, he sat there, not knowing what to do.

"Are you going to rape me?" a voice asked out of the darkness.

Loudest Laugh jumped, startled by the rough voice in the night. "No, we just wanted to see."

The woman sat up, moving her face into the moonlight. A dark eye glittered in the night, and she said, "You have seen. Now what?"

He giggled for just a second. "Now nothing."

The woman smiled, half a smile, the right side of her face was slack and unmoving. The woman threw back her furs, and revealed her naked body. "You must want something, or else why come so close."

Loudest Laugh had no words for that, and for the length of time it took a medium-sized log to burn, no words were needed. When they were done, he emerged outside adjusting his clothes. The woman emerged with him, and they ran off into the night, The Last Honest Men and The First Honest Woman.

****

Sky Toucher climbed to the top of the tree, his bow slung over his back. The tree was not the tallest, or the widest, but it offered the best vantage point and was situated over a narrow gully that the Cliff People were likely to travel through.

When they were escorting the young seer from the cliffs, they had travelled through here. Ghost Hair backtracked and found that the marking in the bark was the third to last marking. If they were truly making their way out using the markings, they would come right through the gully.

Loudest Laugh sat underneath the branches of a young pine, its needles close to the ground and shadowy. The pine was close enough to the south end of the gully for their plan. He covered himself in loose branches and needles to hide his shape from the Cliff People's eyes. Snake Tears and Ghost Hair did the same on the north end of the gully, while Sky Toucher looked down on them from his perch, his lanky limbs looking like extensions of the dead branches of the tall pine.

He sat and waited, listening for any sign of the Cliff People's approach. He could hear nothing but his own breath. Even the trees were still for once. The birds were quiet, and the insects had stopped.

A hand grabbed his foot, and he kicked at it, flipping over and pulling his spear free to find Niviarsi half-smiling at him.

"You should see your face."

"Bah." Loudest Laugh rolled back over, and remade his bed of needles and sticks. Niviarsi slid into the space next to him, doing the same. He felt her warm skin against his underneath the needles.

She had been with him ever since that night on the plains. She was a proud hunter and a fierce lover. Her face had been frozen years ago when she was but a teenager. Her people told her she was cursed by the spirits, and no man had wanted her among her people. Loudest Laugh was thankful for that.

When he went into the village, which was seldom enough these days, she would wait outside, hunting and living on her own. The people of the village were small-minded. Just as she had been shunned by her own people, the village was not likely to accept her into their midst. Her deformity and the fact that she came from a different people was bad enough, but the fact that she hunted and

131

seemed more manly than many of the men from his own village would not be tolerated. He was amused by the thought of watching the soft women of his village try to put her in their dresses and make her prepare dinner for the men.

Niviarsi was not soft. She was tough, violent, and self-reliant. He loved her for it. The other members of The Last Honest Men admired her for it as well. Loudest Laugh's greatest hope was to win the honor of the day, and invite Niviarsi back to the village with him, where they would have no choice but to accept the lover of such a brave warrior. They would have no choice.

Chapter 19:

In the Woods

Disaster struck soon after they were outside of the village. Dravid broke his ankle. It happened as he went to jump over a fallen tree. He was in full flight, placed his foot on the side of the tree, and attempted to use it to leap into the air; however, his foot sunk into the decayed wood, and he went sprawling forward, his ankle bent at an awkward angle.

They crowded around him, discussing what to do. Lonpearl set Kochen against the fallen tree. Kochen rubbed his head and generally kept quiet. He was not yet himself.

"What do you want us to do, Dravid?" Farway asked.

Dravid groaned in pain, before he spoke. "You want me to tell you to go on without me, like some sort of hero in a story, but I do not wish that. I want to live. I want you to get me out of here. I want to see home."

Farway nodded. It was not the answer he wanted to hear. It was the honest answer, and one worthy of respect. "Lonpearl, what is your counsel?"

Lonpearl thought before he spoke. His wisdom was respected among the men, so his voice would sway the decision, one way or the other. "If we leave him here, we go on, knowing we left Dravid to die. It is something that I cannot bear on my conscience, but we would get Kochen home, and be able to prepare for the Stick People. If we take him with us, there is a chance that we all die."

Ondus, one of the more hotheaded of the warriors, spat back, "We know the options, Lonpearl. What do you think we should do?"

Lonpearl looked down at Dravid, anguish etched on his face. "We take him with us. Carrying two is the same as carrying one. We all take turns, we move always, and maybe we all make it."

"Dravid is much heavier than Kochen," Hinler pointed out.

Lonpearl regarded Hinler coolly. "I didn't say it would be easy."

Farway squatted next to Kochen and looked him in the eye. "Are you in there?"

Kochen shook his head to clear it, which was a mistake as it sent spots spinning in front of his eyes. "I am here."

"Can you walk?"

Kochen didn't have the words to reply, he simply lifted his feet to show the men the wounds that were on them. Blisters the size of a baby's fist covered the balls of his feet. They were open and raw. The bandage over the gash on his foot was soaked with blood. The march to the village had left him damaged and in pain.

"You are soft, Kochen. If you hadn't been playing priest your whole life, we could all run right out of here."

"I am aware of who I am."

"Then you have no reason to be angry with me since I only tell you the truth." Farway spun on his heel, and moved away. "Carry them."

Ondus and Hinler helped Dravid onto the shoulders of Ghulish, and Lonpearl picked Kochen up easily enough, and they set out again, avoiding rotted logs, and skirting around them.

"Don't let Farway bother you," Lonpearl said over his shoulder. "He is a wild animal, always concerned with establishing his place among the other animals. He has no time for civility."

Kochen, hanging over Lonpearl's shoulder, and not completely comfortable with the situation asked, "Why does anyone follow him?"

Lonpearl thought about it for a moment, and replied, "Farway is never going to be your best friend, but he does what needs to be done when it needs to be done. He is reliable, unchecked, wild. These are qualities you need to be successful in the hunt. In the village, these gifts are burdens. The men that follow him know what he is outside the village. The men that don't, well, outside of the cliffs, they would be falling over each other to be led by one such as him."

"Well then get me back to the cliffs, so he can get put back in his rightful place."

Lonpearl laughed. "What do you think we are trying to do?"

They moved through the forest, Ghulish running ahead and spotting the slashes in the tree bark, setting their path. From his vantage point, Kochen had an excellent view of the ground. He admired the forest floor with its pine needle carpet, thick brown earth, and a variety of small plants surviving among the shadows of trees, content with what little light and life the big trees left for them. The sound of birds was pleasant, and unlike the cliffs where every bird there would rather pluck your eyes out as soon as look at you, their calls were not harsh and jarring to the ear. The forest was filled with their twittering, a sweet high-pitched music. If all of his blood wasn't pooled in the front of his brain and his ribs weren't being jarred by every one of Lonpearl's footsteps, he would have been happy to fall asleep.

They had been traveling for an hour when Lonpearl called for a switch. That Lonpearl could carry him for an hour was amazing. Kochen thought back to when he had to carry the water jugs. Maybe if they could find a stick, Lonpearl could balance it over his back with himself and Dravid dangling off of the ends like two jugs of water. Kochen smiled at the thought.

"What are you smiling about?" Ondus said, as he stooped to fling Kochen over his shoulder. Ondus had a strong smell, not unpleasant, but not pleasant either. Kochen was trying to make up his mind about the smell when he spotted something out of the corner of his eye. "Look. Over there."

Ondus looked where Kochen was pointing, and then dropped Kochen on the ground. The forest floor was soft, but not soft enough to keep the fall from hurting. The hunters watched as Ondus walked through a stand of pines to emerge in a small clearing with a downed log. In the middle of the moss-covered, half-rotted log, there was a hole, the type of hole that would be made by someone trying to use the log to launch himself into the air. It was Dravid's log. "I think we are going in circles," Ondus announced to the rest of the group."

Farway muscled his way forward, shoving his way to the front of the group. "What are you rambling about, Ondus?"

"Look," he said, pointing at the log.

Farway's face was one of disbelief. He stalked over to the log, refusing to believe what he thought he saw. "No. This can't be."

Andras, the four-fingered, said what they had all been thinking. "We're going in circles."

"They must have wandered all throughout this forest, trying to lead us off the trail."

"How can this be, Markon?" Farway asked of the hunters' best tracker.

Markon shrugged his shoulders. "It's not like the cliffs here. In the cliffs, you pick a landmark and make your way towards it. Here, the trees all look the same. How am I to tell one from the other?"

Lonpearl was starting to get nervous. If the trail had been circling around for an hour, just how far had they come since they had destroyed the village. Even now, an entire village could be bearing down on them. "We need to move. They could be here any moment."

"Not yet," Farway said. "Lonpearl, up the tree. See what you can see."

Though his back and shoulders ached from carrying Kochen for an hour, Farway's plan made sense. If they could spot a way out of the forest, then they could save themselves some time and maybe put some distance between themselves and the Stick People. Lonpearl examined the trees quickly but carefully. He choose a tree with a trunk that was as big around as ten men holding hands, then he ran and leapt onto the tree, hugging it, and ignoring the scraping of tree bark on his chest. He climbed, using the trees ancient and thick bark to go higher and higher. By the time he was halfway, he could no longer see the hunters below, and his arms were burning. All he wanted to do was rest on one of the branches, but he knew that time was important. Sweat rolled into his eyes, stinging them, but still he pressed on, climbing from one branch to the next. The branches were denser near the top, and he had to figure a way to worm his way through them, but eventually, he reached the wobbly apex of the tree.

He poked his head up, like a prairie dog in the desert, and beheld the vast expanse of the forest. He had chosen his tree wisely. It was one of the tallest in the forest, and it gave him a full view of the entire area. He marveled at the lush green forest as it spread away into the distance looking like nothing more than a carpet made of green clouds. The sun rose high overhead, and he could feel its heat strongly. He gave a quick prayer to Caldus, and then he noticed the vision of home in the distance. Miles away, he saw the edge of the forest disappear, and he saw the rugged terrain of home sloping upward in jagged rocks and hills. The forest ended as if a perfect line had been drawn between their homeland and the land of the Stick People. The sandy soil shone as a yellow-brown smoothness on the juts and spurs of their rocky homeland. From so far away, it seemed like a dream, the haze of the heat appearing as a gray film between home and his eyes. But it was there. He knew the direction, and he simply had to not lose his bearings upon descending the tree. If they could run straight, they could be out of the forest in three or four hours, if he had judged the distance properly.

Lonpearl descended the tree, carefully placing his feet on the branches, straddling them, and then dropping down to the next set. Climbing down a tree was frequently harder than climbing up. Lonpearl equated the process with human nature. Striving for something was physically harder and exacted more of a toll, but the strain was hardly noticeable. Losing your spot at the top was seldom a graceful endeavor; many people tended to plummet all the way to the bottom, never managing to climb back up. Lonpearl had tried to explain this to Farway once when they were just young men going out on their first hunt. The look of confusion on Farway's face had always pained him, and Lonpearl had never quite found someone that he could explain these things to, so he kept the thoughts to himself, and he let the thoughts nourish his soul.

As he reached the bottom of the tree, he dangled off the final thick limb and dropped to the ground, rolling so his knees didn't bear the brunt of the impact. The men looked at him expectantly.

"Home is in that direction." He pointed to the south. "If we run straight for three, maybe four hours depending on terrain, we can be out of the forest by the time night falls, and then we can march in the open air."

They took off running in a line, letting the carriers of Kochen and Dravid set the pace. The forest blurred by for hours. Kochen was lost in his thoughts, dangling upside down, when the men began to hoot and holler. Kochen craned his neck to see what the commotion was all about. Through the trees, he could see sunlight, but not the muted, filtered rays that managed to snake their way through the branches of the tall trees around them. It was the sunlight that he was used to, full, bright coverage that would have them sweating in minutes. Kochen didn't quite know how he felt about the fact. He was happy for the men that he was with, but part of him wished he was back in the Stick People's village, talking with The Eye That Shields, learning their ways, and understanding who he was supposed to be. He didn't want harm to come to any of them, and that was the hardest burden to bear. He knew this was all headed in the wrong direction; you didn't need to be a seer to see that. During the last exchange, when someone new had offered to carry Kochen and Dravid, he had heard one of the men reflecting on how awful he felt killing a woman while she slept.

"I can't get it out of my head," Markon said. "One minute, she was alive, and the next, she was gone... because of me."

Markon's feelings were quickly squelched by Ghulish, "It doesn't matter; she was asleep, she didn't even feel a thing. Stop your whining." Even though Markon stopped talking about it Kochen could still see the hurt in his eye. That type of violence, senseless and unnecessary, never seemed to go unpunished. He had seen men in the village carry grudges for years because of less.

A sharp pain erupted in the back of Kochen's thigh, and the man that was carrying him fell over to the side. When they hit the ground fire shot through Kochen's leg, and he screamed in agony. As he rolled over on his side, he noticed that the end of an arrow was protruding out of the

139

meat of his thigh. When he tried to lift his leg off of Sontang, he found that he couldn't. The arrow had pierced the meat on the back of his thigh and become buried in the throat of Sontang. When Kochen tried to pull his leg free and lift it off the ground, Sontang's head lifted as well. Kochen's leg was pinned to Sontang.

All around him, screams were erupting. He heard the twang of bowstrings, yells of confusion, and the whistling of arrows, but in his position, he could do nothing about it but lie there, his leg pinned to Sontang by an arrow. He decided to lie completely still, in the hopes that another arrow wouldn't find a more vital spot.

****

Sky Toucher saw the men enter the gully. With his lanky thighs wrapped around a branch, his feet crossed underneath, he had a steady position from which to fire his bow. He pulled an arrow from the quiver on his back, nocked the arrow, and waited until every man had entered the gully. When they did, he fired at one of the men at the head of the line, who was carrying another wounded man. His shot was slightly off, but it did its job. The man fell over, his blood flowing into leaves and needles upon the ground. Even better, the wounded man was pinned to the other one with an arrow. Sky Toucher smiled. *Two for one,* he thought.

After Sky Toucher had loosed his first arrow, he saw Niviarsi and Loudest Laugh burst into the south end of the gully, blocking off all escape, their spears held before them. The gully was narrow, so that no more than two people could stand side by side. With their spears, Niviarsi and Loudest Laugh began jabbing at the men at the front of the line. On the north end of the gully, Ghost Hair and Snake Tears did the same. The Cliff People were

140

effectively trapped in the gully, while Sky Toucher peppered their ranks with arrows from overhead.

It was a slaughter.

****

Lonpearl struggled to move to the front of the line and protect Kochen. The hunters could take care of theirselves, but Kochen was defenseless against any sort of attack. He couldn't even manage to walk three days without developing debilitating blisters. As Lonpearl shoved through the men, he heard a an arrow whistle by his head, only to land with a meaty "thunk" in the shoulder of the man in front of him. Lonpearl ducked his head, as if that would do him any good. He turned and risked a look in the direction that the arrow had come from.

There... in the tree. He saw him. A skinny man, a sneer on his face, with his legs wrapped around the limb of a branch to steady himself. When the man took his eyes off of the carnage to nock another arrow, Lonpearl leapt the rock wall on the side of the gully. Without even pausing to look for handholds he clambered up the fifteen-foot gully wall, moving without thinking.

****

Farway shouted for the men to get out of his way. He could see two of the attackers shouting and waving their spears at the end of the gully. When the carnage began, Farway had been near the middle of the pack, so he had to push through the men to even catch a glimpse of who was attacking them. There was a man with gray hair and a rugged face with hollowed out cheeks, waving his spear at his men. The gray-haired man did not push forward and press his advantage.

141

The other attacker stood to his left, two wicked clubs waving in his hands, the air whistling with each swing. One of the hunters rushed the attackers, dodging the gray-haired man's spear and landing a glancing blow on the man with the clubs. It was not enough of a blow to keep the man with the clubs from caving in his attacker's head. Farway grit his teeth as he watched the hunter slump to the ground in a heap, his limbs twisted unnaturally while red slush oozed out of the top of his head.

Farway's vision went red, and he dashed at the attackers, screaming at the top of his lungs. He leapt over the corpse and drove his spear through the throat of the man with the clubs. The man flailed at him from the end of Farway's spear, unable to reach Farway with the wicked chunks of wood. Farway pulled him forward; the jagged stone barbs of the spear's tip stuck in the man's throat, and tugged the club wielder further into the gully. The hunters fell upon the man, stabbing him over and over with their spears. When Farway was satisfied that the light was gone from the man's eyes, he pulled his spear free, taking a large chunk of throat meat with him.

The gray-haired man held his ground, but Farway would make short work of him.

****

Loudest Laugh stood his ground, with Niviarsi to his right. The warriors wanted out desperately, and in their haste, they were bunched up tightly so that they couldn't fight in an efficient manner. Loudest Laugh and Niviarsi jabbed freely at the men who came close.

Every few seconds, one would fall down, an arrow jutting out of their body somewhere. Loudest Laugh looked up briefly to see Sky Toucher drawing back to fire another arrow, but he didn't like what he saw behind him.

142

****

The screams and yells from the gully, covered the noise that he made as he skirted around the base of the tree and approached it from the rear. Lonpearl had climbed up the tree with the ease of one of the bushy-tailed creatures they had seen in the forest. He had avoided touching any of the branches that might alert the bowman to his presence.

He moved quickly and decisively, every second that he hesitated meant the potential for another one of his friends to die. He reached the branch that the bowman was on, and he stepped out on it, immediately alerting the man on the branch to his presence. The bowman spun around at the waist, surprise etched on his face.

Lonpearl pushed him out of the tree. It was a bad fall. With his legs still clinging to the branch, the man had ended up hanging upside down before he dropped. As he plummeted to the ground, he tried to right himself, but the fall was not long enough for him to regain his balance. The man landed face-first on the ground, his back bending the wrong way. He rested there, like the husk of a long dead spider, curled up on himself and unmoving.

****

Niviarsi saw Sky Toucher drop to the ground, and she knew that the fight was over. Without the support from above, they would eventually be overrun. They would be outflanked and taken from behind.

"We have to leave!" she yelled to Loudest Laugh.

He ignored her, continuing to jab into the mass of warriors trying to get at them. He had delivered twenty wounds at least, but none fatal so far. Niviarsi saw the look of grim determination on his face, and she continued to jab right along with him.

"We have to go!" she yelled again, dodging spears flying at her own face.

This time he heard her, but before he could respond, something else happened.

****

Blood oozed from the wound in Kochen's leg. Sitting like a stone, he watched it leak out from the area around the arrow shaft. In lying still, something odd had begun to happen. Time seemed to slow to a crawl, and he watched the red river run down his thigh and drip onto the ground, the drop was suspended in the air and slowly making its way to the ground. In his mind, he heard deep sighing, the breath of one that slept deeply.

He placed his hands on the ground, running his fingers through the dead leaves and dry brown pine needles. The ground underneath his hands was warm, and pulsing. All around he saw men fighting in slow-motion, their movements and words unintelligible. Kochen jammed his fingers into the ground, and in his mind, he saw images flash through his brain.

He touched it... another consciousness in the ground, and for a second, his mind became its mind. After that he could remember nothing.

****

Farway was about to deliver a killing blow when the ground shook underneath his feet. The gray-haired man he was sparring with looked up behind Farway in fright, the fight forgotten. Farway couldn't resist looking behind him to see what had made the blood drain out of his opponent's face, and he almost wished he had simply stabbed the gray-haired man and ran away, never chancing a look at the horror behind him.

At first his eyes couldn't make out what was going on. A pile of mud and rock had seemed to erupt from the ground in the middle of the gully, spewing bodies into the air. It took another glance before Farway realized that the geyser of earth actually seemed to have a mind of its own. It twisted and loomed over Farway and the men at his end of the gully. In its shape, he saw eyes, slit-shaped and glowing green; they looked down at him, and for the first time in his life, he felt insignificant. He was no longer a proud warrior fighting for the future and honor of his village. He had become the prey.

Everybody that could broke and ran. Farway ran the fastest, his legs pumping as quickly as they could. The gray-haired man, Kochen, even his own hunters, people he had been friends with since he was a child, all became afterthoughts. He ran for a long time, his entire body covered in a sheen of sweat.

****

From his vantage point atop the gully, Lonpearl watched as everyone broke and ran. When the ground erupted, Lonpearl fell backwards in shock. He watched as the pile of moving earth picked up Ondus and shoved him inside the mass of stone, earth, and plants. One minute he was there, the next he was part of a living mountain. Everyone scattered, and Lonpearl himself was about to take off into the forest, until he remembered Kochen.

From above, he had spotted him on the ground, motionless, and bleeding. Kochen was the whole reason they had come here. Now people had died. If he left Kochen in harm's way, it would all be for nothing.

Lonpearl slid down the gully wall as slowly as he could. The mountain was drawn to the men that were running, and it moved to the south end of the gully, away from where he last saw Kochen crumpled on the ground.

145

The shifting and sliding of rock upon rock was loud as the mountainous mass moved through the gully. Lonpearl crept quickly and silently, despite the noise. He squatted next to the prone form of Kochen and turned him over to see his eyes rolled back in his head so that only the whites were exposed. Foam dribbled from the corner of his mouth. He attempted to pick him up, but set him down quickly when he noticed his leg was attached to the corpse next to him. Sontang stared up at the forest canopy, his eyes devoid of life. He pulled his knife from its sheath on his belt, and used the rough stone tip to saw through the thin arrow.

When he had finished, he stood up and put Kochen over his shoulder, the nub of an arrow dangling out of his leg. He headed toward the north end of the gully, away from the mountain creature, which was still chasing after those that had long since fled. Without warning, Kochen jerked awake and began screaming. Lonpearl turned around to see the mountainous mass rumbling towards them. Lonpearl took off running towards the bright light in front of him.

The churning of rocks and earth began to get louder and louder as he ran. Kochen's scream rose in intensity as well.

"Run, Lonpearl! Run! It's getting closer!"

Lonpearl imagined the massive hill of earth cresting like the small waves that formed on the river during a storm, and then he imagined the mass toppling over him, burying himself and Kochen in mid-run. He put these thoughts out of his head, and focused on the ground in front of him, soft ground, deceptively treacherous, and easy to trip on.

The rumbling roared and roared. He could feel bits of earth bouncing off of his heels as the mountain closed the distance. Its mass caused the ground to quake and vibrate, and the noise was so loud that Lonpearl could no longer hear Kochen screaming. As he neared the edge of the forest he dove into the sunlight, letting it wash over him. He hit the ground hard, and rolled over on his back, helping Kochen sit up in the process.

In the shadows of the forest the mound stood, looking like nothing more than an out of place hill of mud filled with tree roots, stones, and nothing else. A human hand protruded out of the mound, betraying the true nature of the now still hill. For a brief second, Lonpearl saw a flash of green, as if the mound had eyes, and then the green was gone.

"What the hell is that?"

Kochen stared at it the mound, breathless. "I called it."

Chapter 20:

Aftermath

Loudest Laugh and Niviarsi slithered away from the gully, their eyes wide, and unable to speak. When the earth had bulged out of the ground in the gully, they took the opportunity to slip away. They tiptoed past the twisted wreck of Sky Toucher's corpse and circled around to the opposite end of the gully.

From their lofty perch, they spied the mangled corpse of Snake Tears. They would not cry for him or his brother, Sky Toucher. They were not worth crying for, but they would be missed for their skills and companionship. Still silent, they disappeared into the woods. They walked for an hour before they sat down in the pine needles and leaves to look each other over.

Loudest Laugh had a couple of spear wounds on his wrist and arms, jags of rent flesh that were painful and bloody, but not life-threatening, if they took care of them now. Niviarsi was in much the same condition. One slash had been perilously close to her eye, but other than that, she had never been in mortal danger from the Cliff People.

Niviarsi stood and undid her pants while Loudest Laugh held his arm between her legs. The warm liquid washed over his wounds, clearing out the dust and dirt that had gotten stuck in them. When she was done, he stood and undid his own loincloth, bathing her wound in his urine. They sat in the leaves and were silent, their hands clasped together. They smiled at each other.

"What was that?" Niviarsi asked.

Loudest Laugh looked at her eyes, shining in the forest murk despite the darkness and said, "I don't know. Perhaps it was a spirit. When we attacked the Cliff People, another creature was loosed among us, just as horrifying. It killed many of us."

"Do you think that the seer can call them?"

"If he can, I don't know why he wouldn't have called one to begin with." Their conversation was cut short when they heard some noise in the forest.

They hugged opposite sides of a massive tree trunk and peered around its circular edge to see their people filing by in a slow-moving train, led by He Who Makes the Drum Beat. Loudest Laugh couldn't bear the idea of exposing his failure to his brother. He leaned his head against the tree, waiting for them to pass.

"Hello!" Niviarsi yelled, stepping out from behind the tree.

What was she doing? Having no other choice, Loudest Laugh emerged from behind the tree. His brother smiled at him, until he noticed the wounds that crisscrossed his arms. He Who Makes the Drum Beat walked over to him and embraced him in a hug. It was a rare moment of affection between the two, and he stepped back and looked him over.

"Are you alright?" he asked.

Loudest Laugh hung his head, "I'm fine."

"We found the Cliff People," Niviarsi announced.

He Who Makes the Drum Beat noticed Niviarsi as if for the first time. The look on his face was not one that Loudest Laugh wanted to see. "Who are you?" he asked, an edge of iron in his voice.

"I am Niviarsi. I am a warrior," she announced.

The people behind He Who Makes the Drum Beat murmured in hushed tones.

"So she has a name. Why have you hidden in the woods all these long months?"

Loudest Laugh spoke up, "You knew?"

He Who Makes the Drum Beat laughed, "Of course I knew. You think I would let my little brother wander around in the woods for weeks on end without having someone follow him around? Where are the rest of your 'Last Honest Men?'" he said, a smile blooming on his face.

"Sky Toucher and Snake Tears are dead. We did not see what happened to Ghost Hair."

The smile fell from He Who Makes the Drum Beat's face. "Do you see what your actions have wrought, little brother?" Loudest Laugh did not reply. "You have gotten your friends killed with your rash ways."

"We almost had them," Loudest Laugh shot back.

"But you do not have them. And now two of your friends, two lives, are lost."

"It was the seer. He called forth a creature of horror that killed many."

The Eye That Shields hobbled his way to He Who Makes the Drum Beat's shoulder. "A creature you say? Tell me more of this."

Loudest Laugh was silent as Niviarsi described the creature and detailed their shame. When she was done, the entire camp looked at her and Loudest Laugh, disgust on their face.

The Eye That Shields spoke first, "This creature you speak of is an ancient spirit, one that has long since been forgotten. My predecessor is the only one that ever spoke of such a thing, and even then, I took it more for myth than fact. The creature is known as Vannix, the Spirit of the forest. He is the reason we do not cut down trees... he has not been seen since before my time and before the time of my grandfather. If Kochen has the ability to summon these spirits from their slumber, then it is even more important that we find him, before he unleashes something that will not go back to sleep."

"What do you mean?" He Who Makes the Drum Beat asked.

The Eye That Shields was deadly serious. "I mean that the creature you described is one of the lesser spirits. We have no hope of defeating such a creature... and it is one of the weakest. Should Kochen awaken one of the greater spirits, then our world would be turned upside down."

"What should we do with these two?" He Who Makes the Drum Beat asked.

"Bring them with us. Their hearts are large, but their wisdom is little. They could use some guidance. On their own, they will get themselves killed."

Loudest Laugh let out a sigh of relief, and Niviarsi visibly relaxed, her grip on her spear loosening. As they fell into the back of the line, Loudest Laugh caught He Who Makes the Drum Beat staring at Niviarsi.

"Not her too," he whispered under his breath.

Chapter 21:

Rebirth

Ghost Hair chased after the man. The man ran wildly, stumbling and falling over branches. His arms and chest were covered in a sheen of sweat, and gone was the wild-eyed look that he had seen before the man had buried his spear in the throat of Snake Tears. Now there was only fear. For killing Snake Tears, he would make the man pay.

Ghost Hair had first joined The Last Honest Men at the behest of He Who Makes the Drum Beat. In the beginning, it had just been another task from a man whom he had admired, but as they adventured through the forest and its abutting territories, he had grown rather fond of all the people in the group. They were like children, his children. They might have been headstrong and antisocial, but they were still his children... each one of them worth ten Cliff People in his eyes.

So he followed the man, watched him slogging through the forest, fear still etched on his face as if the creature were still behind him. His weapons were gone, dropped in his haste to escape. His men were gone, scattered to the wind or rotting in the gully. It was only a matter of time before his body exhausted itself and he collapsed. When that happened Ghost Hair would be there, his stone knife in his hand.

****

Farway's mind was not all there. He was only rudimentarily aware of where he was going or where he was. Most of his mind was preoccupied with replaying the events of the gully. He saw his men cut down. He saw the man that he had killed. He saw the giant monster emerge from the ground, picking up Ondus, and shoving him inside the mountain of mud, grass and stone.

He had seen Ondus' face before it had disappeared. His eyes had been huge, and his screaming had been high-pitched and terrified. It was not the type of scream that one could imitate. It was the type of scream that only one who knew they were going to die could issue. Then he had been gone, suffocating inside a giant mound of dirt and rock that could not be hurt.

His mind was fractured, shattered into pieces to protect him from the weight of his own shame. He ran from the truth, never intending to stop. It was behind him... his shame, walking with purposeful steps, always hanging back, waiting for him to stop so it could catch up to him and destroy him completely.

Farway would run. He would run until he could run no more, but he wouldn't stop to face the shame of having abandoned his men, the men that looked up to him, the men that depended on him to keep them safe and lead them to victory. He was a failure.

The sun began to drop behind the trees when he stumbled onto the grassy banks of a river cutting through the forest. It was a shallow thing, calm tranquil, and black. Mosquitoes swarmed around the water, their combined buzzing seeming to whisper to him, and he dropped to his knees in the cool grass of the riverbank, staring at his face in the water. Angular, sweat-soaked, covered in blood... underneath there was the shadow of who he had used to be, a man of weight and purpose, a leader. Now all that was left was a tired man, his honor gone, his face hidden behind his mistakes, blood, and scars.

He was about to dump himself into the water and end it all when a man appeared behind him, his face reflected in the water. He had a knife raised in the air, and as he brought it down, Farway rolled to his left and stuck his leg out, sending the gray-haired man tumbling into the black water.

Farway dove in after him, struggling to pull the knife from the man's hand. He was strong, though he must have had twenty winters on him. Underneath the water, the man kicked him as hard as he could, in his shins, in his balls, in his thighs. As they struggled, Farway wondered why he continued to fight. He had been about to dunk himself in the river and breathe his way to the next world, but that had been on his terms. It had to be his decision. It had to be his choice. So he fought, returning the kicks, his biceps straining as he tried to break the gray-haired man's grip on the knife. In the water, the buzzing of the mosquitoes seemed amplified, their whispers verging on the formation of meaning.

Farway dove under the water, dragging the man down with him. They kicked and thrashed, but Farway continued to make his body like a stone, sinking down, his breath held. The buzzing continued, filling his ears, driving him onward and into the depths. *Kill him.*

His feet touched the muddy bottom of the river, and he had to resist the urge to kick upwards, to struggle for the river's surface and the air on the other side. The gray-haired man had no such inclination and he tried to push upwards, planting both of his feet in the mud and surging toward the surface. Farway held his ground, squatting and yanking at the man, refusing to let him reach the top. The gray-haired man finally let go of the knife; Farway caught it in his hand and watched the man kick his legs up to the surface. *Now. Now is the time. Make him breathe the water.*

Farway shot upwards, propelling himself towards the man, the rough leather-bound handle of the stone knife clenched tightly in his palm. He grabbed the man by the leg; it was a corded leathery thing, and he drove his knife into it. Blood erupted in the water, and Farway kicked upward, breaking the surface and inhaling as much sweet air as he could get into his lungs. As he thrashed about wildly, the gray-haired man managed to punch Farway in the nose. His eyes teared up, and Farway snagged the man by his gray ponytail before he went back under, pulling the man to the bottom with him. He jabbed him in the abdomen over and over with the knife as they sank. His struggles began to weaken, and then they stopped being struggles altogether. Before Farway kicked back up to the surface he locked eyes with the man... two men at the bottom of the river, and though his lungs burned with fire, he watched the light fade from the man's eyes. Funny, a few minutes ago, Farway had planned on it being him. He kicked his way to the top and dragged himself up onto the riverbank.

The buzzing continued, forming words, compelling commands that seemed to make sense.

He sat on the bank, alternating between coughing up water and taking in massive gulps of air. When his vision no longer swam in front of his eyes, he rolled over and looked at the river. There was no sign of their struggle. Even the blood had been washed away. The river rolled on and on, not giving a damn about the two men who had fought for life in its depths. Farway leaned over the riverbank and he saw his face as if for the first time. High cheekbones, beady eyes, and a nose that was askew.

He had been reborn in the depths. Farway had gone in, and a new being had appeared. He was death now. When he felt like he could walk again, Farway rose to his feet and wandered down the riverbank until he found the corpse of the gray-haired man washed up in an alcove in the river, his face planted in mud, blood still leaking out of his body. Fish scattered from the meal that they were making out of the man's legs when he pulled the corpse from the river and the buzzing became stronger, filling his mind until he could not tell which thoughts were his and which were theirs.

With no flint in his possession, he grabbed two sticks and began the laborious process of making a fire. It was nighttime before he managed the first spark. He blew on the spark until it caught some dry moss on fire. He piled on some twigs, and fanned the fire into life. By the time he put the first chunk of meat on the flame, his stomach was rumbling and his body was filled with a sick heat. He stoked the fire until there were gouts of flame that were taller than Farway.

Chapter 22:

Sparks in the Night

Lonpearl and Kochen dusted themselves off, and began the long trek home. With Kochen's arm thrown over Lonpearl's shoulder, they hobbled through the scrub brush that led to the mountains which would lead them to the river and eventually back to the cliffs that they called home.

"It would be best if you didn't mention the whole creature summoning thing if we should stumble across any of the others," Lonpearl said, sweat dripping from his brow underneath the baking sun.

"Why?" Kochen asked.

Lonpearl didn't quite know how to put the idea into words, but he tried anyway. "The spirit saved us, but it also killed some of us as well. Though more of us would have died, some people might not see it that way."

Kochen stood up straight on both feet and took his arm off of Lonpearl's shoulder. "I'm sick of hiding. I'm sick of pretending to be something that I am not. Lansa tells me to keep my visions to myself. No one listens to me, though I warn them of what is about to happen. Now, you want me to act as if I didn't just call a spirit out of the ground."

Lonpearl put his hand up, trying to calm down Kochen, but he slapped it away. "Calm down, Kochen. I'm just..."

"You're just what? Trying to protect me from what other people think? What about what I think? What about what I want?"

Lonpearl had had enough. "We came for you. Who do you think sent us after you? Lansa. Why do you think we came?"

Kochen had no answer.

"Because you're one of us. I'm not saying hide this power forever, I'm simply asking you to not speak of it until we are back among our people. Let the priests figure out what to do about it."

"What to do about it? I'll tell you what to do about it. Leave me alone." Kochen started walking off into the distance, limping on his blistered and wounded feet. Lonpearl hurried to catch up to him, and Kochen shoved him away, tears in his eyes. "Get off of me!"

Lonpearl stood back, not sure what to do.

Kochen wiped his eyes with his arm. "You don't think I know what people think about me? You don't think I know that you think I'm a monster? I know it. I've known it since the day Bimisi killed my father!"

Lonpearl laughed. "I don't think you're a monster, Kochen. I think you are a gift."

Kochen listened, tears still welling up in his eyes.

"I think you're just a kid who has had an awful life, but you're a kid with some special gifts. You can communicate with the spirits. You can protect our people. If you need a friend, I'm it. But if you turn me away, who else is there? Who else do you have, Kochen?"

Kochen looked him in the eye, "No one."

"Then do me a favor and listen to me. If we meet any of our people, don't talk about the spirit. Can you do that for me?"

Kochen nodded.

"Now will you let me help you? We've still got a village of pissed off people coming to find us, and we need to move."

Kochen limped over to Lonpearl, and threw his arm over his shoulder. "Thank you."

They hobbled off into the day, covered dripping sweat in the heat. They made poor time, and it wasn't long until they crossed paths with a few familiar faces. Ghulish and Hinler were the first to find them.

Lonpearl and Hinler embraced, while Ghulish, ever the stodgy one, stood off to the side, eyeing Kochen up and down.

"You made it!" Lonpearl said, genuinely glad to see Hinler. Hinler's wide face beamed back at him. His two front teeth were missing, the result of a childhood accident when he was younger. They had been throwing rocks at the river when one had accidentally hit him in the mouth. Hinler had never told on him, and their friendship had been sealed from there. "I didn't know if I would ever see that toothless grin again."

"It's going to take a lot more than a pile of mud to kill me," he said, still beaming his smile. It faded, and he asked, "Did you see what happened to Ondus?"

Lonpearl nodded his head, "I saw it. It was terrible."

"Where's Farway?" Ghulish asked, tired of the cheerful greeting.

Lonpearl looked over at Ghulish, who happened to be one of his least favorite people. He would have traded any of the men that died in the gully for Ghulish. The sides of his head were shaved, except for a long tail of hair at the back of his neck. He had burned a star into the side of his face when he was a youth. The brand had been done poorly, and it was only faintly recognizable as a star as the two points at the bottom had bled together. When he had returned home, they could hear his wailing reverberate off of the cliff walls as his father attempted to beat some sense

159

into him. They had all laughed at his punishment, and then later at the brand. Gradually the ribbing turned him sour, and he began to fight anyone who said anything about it. He was a bitter person who only ever seemed to get along with Farway. Farway was the only one that cared for him, but since Farway was the leader, he always seemed to be a part of the hunting party.

"We haven't seen him," Kochen said.

Ghulish turned his head to Kochen and spat in his direction. "I wasn't talking to you, you little shit."

Kochen didn't say anything further, but that wasn't enough for Ghulish. He charged Kochen and tackled him to the ground, straddling his chest. "You're not worth one of the men we lost back there, so I don't want to hear another word from you for the rest of your miserable life. If I do," Ghulish pulled a knife from his belt and said, "I'm going to cut your stupid tongue out."

Lonpearl kicked Ghulish off of Kochen. There was a brief struggle, but Hinler helped separate the two men.

"Have you gone crazy? We don't have time for this?" Lonpearl yelled at Ghulish.

"Relax, Ghulish," Hinler added, "we have days to go before we can afford to start fighting each other."

Ghulish spat on the ground and began to walk off in the direction of home. Lonpearl stooped to help Kochen up. "Don't worry about him. He's always an asshole." They set off in the daylight, trying to put as much distance between themselves and their likely pursuers. Ghulish never said a word; he stayed ahead of them, just out of sight. Lonpearl was glad to see that he didn't just leave them in the dust and head off for home on his own.

****

That night they made camp in a cave that they had all been to before. It used to be occupied by a group of wild

160

coyotes before Farway and his men had disposed of them. Ghulish searched the ground for snakes while Lonpearl and Hinler scrounged some old dead branches for a fire. Food was scarce, but Kochen managed to find a stand of prickly pears before the sun went down. It wasn't much of a meal, but anything was better than nothing.

The group was too tired to walk on, though they knew it could mean putting miles between themselves and the Stick People. They sat around the fire, seldom speaking. Their words had dried up in the warm mountain environment, the heat sucking the will out of them. As the night closed in, the air cooled quickly, and it wasn't long before they were huddled around their pitiful fire.

Kochen didn't want to look into the flames, but he couldn't resist. The fire moved hypnotically, and soon the aches and pains of his body were gone, and he was no longer in himself. He could still see Hinler, Ghulish, and Lonpearl, but he was not in the same place.

Deep in the rocks, he heard a thrumming, a beat. He resisted the urge to approach it, not wanting to risk a repeat of this afternoon's carnage. Instead he used his mind to trace the path from whence they had come. With his eyes open but unseeing in the real world, he thought about the path they had travelled, and then without even trying, the world began to blur, flying by as if he were a bird soaring through the air.

The part of his brain that was still back in the cave, staring at the fire, was only a bit of his consciousness. The majority of Kochen's mind flew through the night, over rocks and scrub until it came to the edge of the forest. Without thinking, he flew into the black night, hovering over the trees and scanning left and right. There at the edge of the forest was the orange glow of a large campfire. Kochen willed his mind's eye to hover over it, and it skipped, jumping into place.

Below, among the trees, the Stick People milled around, engaged in various camp tasks. Some boiled water for drinking. Others prepared meals. Around the campfire, The Eye That Shields sat, his face dancing with shadows from the fire, his eyes open but unseeing. Was he searching for Kochen right now, his mind wandering in the sky, scanning for a campfire? Kochen wondered what it would look like if he could see it.

He descended through the trees, cautious, just in case anyone could actually see him in this condition. No one paid him any attention. Kochen commenced the count. In the end, he counted fifty-eight warriors, not including one woman with a nasty cut under her eye and The Eye That Shields. Without knowing the extent of the power of The Eye That Shields, he was little more than an old man to Kochen.

By his estimation, they were little more than four hours behind them. They hadn't gained nearly as much time on the villagers as he would have liked, but with The Eye That Shields along, they had their own burden to bear.

Unconsciously, Kochen turned his eye southward, back the way he had come. He zoomed across the plain, away from the forest. He stopped in the cave, just to check on his own body. It was still there, just as he had left it, but there was something else as well... a glowing light, no more than the flicker of a spark. In his ears, even though he had no ears at the moment, he thought he heard the faint sound of an old raspy voice. The words were indistinguishable, but they seemed as if they were coming from the spark. He moved closer, and the words became louder.

"Stay back!" the spark yelled.

Kochen hesitated and stood his ground, his consciousness floating a few feet from the spark.

"Keep your distance, or it could mean the end for both of us."

Kochen knew for certain that this was The Eye That Shields. "Is this how you found me in my village?"

"A vision showed me where you would be. This is how I confirmed my vision."

"Your men tried to kill me today."

The spark flickered in and out, and Kochen looked at Ghulish, Lonpearl, and Hinler to see if they noticed anything out of the ordinary, but they did and said nothing. They merely sat around staring into the fire, Lonpearl and Hinler talking while Ghulish sharpened his stone knife on a rock.

"Not all who are of my people are of my command. Such are the ones that you encountered today. They wanted nothing more than revenge."

"And what do you want?" Kochen asked.

"I want to help you," The Eye replied.

"Why?"

"I believe you are the key to our salvation and continued survival. I wish to help you, for the good of your people and mine." Kochen didn't know what to make of the old man, but his words had the ring of truth to them.

"Then turn your people around and come to my village... alone."

"I can't do that. My people think we march to war, without them, I would never reach you. I'm not as spry as I used to be."

Kochen thought about it for a moment and then asked, "Can't you just teach me? Through this place?"

"The dreamscape is not the place for such activities. There are things that I cannot teach you in the dream."

"Then we have nothing further to say." Kochen flew his spark to his body and then sat there, unable to figure out how to move his consciousness back into his skull. He travelled through his skull, but when he came out on the other side, his body and mind were still separate.

The Eye That Shields laughed. "You are young. You are untrained and unguided. Without me, you could fade from existence right now. Your consciousness weakens as your body and mind are separate. In time, your spark would fade, and when that happened, your body would shut down. Look at me, even now my spark is dimming."

Kochen looked at the spark that represented The Eye That Shields. It was true, his light was far dimmer now, and he could see it fading even as he watched. A sensation of panic came across Kochen. "How do I get back into my body?" Kochen was desperate now, he had noticed the fading of The Eye That Shields but had thought nothing of it.

"I have to go, but before I do, I will tell you how to get back into your body."

"What is the price of this information?"

"I ask no price. Just trust me."

Kochen's thoughts were becoming, for the lack of a better word, runny. They began to flit around, and he could feel the part of him that was him slipping away. "I will trust you."

The Eye That Shields laughed again. "Good. Now, here is the trick. In order to extinguish the light, you must become the light. It is a painful process, but if you do it correctly, you will find yourself back in your body. Fly into the fire, let the flames wash over you, and your body and mind will become one again. I must go before I lose my own body."

Kochen did not like the thought of going into the fire, but before he could protest The Eye That Shields was gone into the sky like a firefly in the night, his spark dimming and disappearing, lost among the twinkling stars of the firmament. Kochen's thoughts were drifting even faster now, the memory of what he had just been thinking, slipping away from his mind quicker than new thoughts could form. He held onto one thought tightly, and he moved his consciousness into the fire. He felt his mind peel away, shriveling like the outer layer of bark on a pine log.

His thoughts glowed, and with every second, the pain built and built until he felt as if he were going to explode. In the dreamscape, he screamed... and then he was back, sitting in front of the fire. He blinked his eyes, and moved his arms and legs around, just as he heard the hiss of water meeting coals. Just like that, Lonpearl had extinguished the fire. He didn't want to think of what would have happened if he had still been in the dreamscape flitting around the world. Without a flame, he wouldn't be able to get back into his body; he would dim out and fade away like a memory. He would remember that fact.

In the morning, he would ask that Lonpearl and the others not extinguish the fire until they had asked him first. But first he needed sleep. His body was as tired as it had ever been. On his feet, thick dry skin had developed, and underneath raw pink skin was working its way to the surface. Still, his exhaustion didn't come from the marching. He had an inkling his foray to the dreamscape had more to do with it. He closed his eyes, and tried to avoid focusing on the deep thrum of consciousness that reverberated in the rocks.

Chapter 23:

The Hunt

The night was young when Farway had finished his meal. Rather than putting out his fire, he let it burn, the smell of sizzling flesh still filtering through the trees. *Let the forest burn. It is not my home.* He looked down at the chunk of leg meat that was cooking in the fire, his belly was distended, yet he still wanted more of the meat. There was only one thing to do, and that was to run in the night.

His eyes itched, and he rubbed them, discovering that he could see even under the treetops. The world had taken on a yellowish hue. Even the trees were outlined in it, in their deepest darkest shadows. Farway laughed, and then sped through the forest, dodging branches, jumping over fallen logs, and leaping over gullies that suddenly opened up in the ground. It was a new world for him, but the hunger was still there. He felt the meat sloshing around in his stomach. It pained him, but still he wanted more. He knew where to find more. He knew right where to find all the meat that he wanted.

He could hear the whispers of the trees around him. *Punish them; make them pay.* The voices droned on in his ears forming a steady stream of advice, each piece more cruel and twisted than the next. He could feel the trees as if they were alive, their energy pulsing yellowish in the night. As he ran he noticed that he was not tired. By now his muscles should have been fatigued, but there was nothing, just the rhythmic extension and contraction of his legs as he moved through the forest. Sweat covered his body, but he didn't feel tired. When he reached the outskirts of their camp, the meat was no longer weighing him down.

The light from their campfire hurt his eyes, and he could sense them all around, their hearts beating in the night, their flesh soaking in their own juices, waiting to be released and seared on the flames. Farway crouched down among the trees, listening to the voices.

Feed. Bleed them. Turn their flesh black.

****

Niviarsi sat on the outskirts of the encampment, not being welcome in the middle. He Who Makes the Drum Beat had welcomed her, but the stares from the other men in the party were not composed of the same stuff. Some seemed to be curious about her, some clearly had lust in their eyes, and others looked at her with a hatred that smoldered. She did not understand it.

She lay under her furs with Loudest Laugh, to her right caressing the soft flesh of his thigh with her hand. He was fading into sleep when she said, "Am I safe here?"

Loudest Laugh didn't hesitate as he spoke with his dream-thickened voice, "You're always safe with me."

Niviarsi squeezed his muscular thigh for no other reason than she could. Loudest Laugh began to breathe deeply, and Niviarsi propped herself on her elbow, not quite tired yet. She looked around the camp to see bundles of furs lying scattered amongst a dozen or so carefully banked fires. No one was awake, except for one man; he was sitting bolt upright and locked eyes with her. His tongue flicked out of his mouth in a lewd gesture.

Niviarsi reclined, annoyed by the gesture more than anything else. She was used to such rude depredations. In the village she had grown up in, she had been the victim of far worse. Once her husband had died, and she had been

167

stricken with her illness, she had become subhuman to her people. They would never have kicked her out of the village, but not kicking her out and treating her as one of them were two totally different things. At night, the men would come. The same men who during the day wanted nothing to do with her. They would sneak into her teepee and says things like *You are so beautiful; let me make you mine. "* When they were done, they would go, and she would be alone. The next day, it would be as if nothing had happened.

When Loudest Laugh had showed up that night, she thought he was just another of her people, come to profess their love for what was between her legs. He professed his love, and over time, to her surprise, it had become true.

She was still hurt by the fact that Loudest Laugh had never bothered to even try to introduce her to the tribe. He claimed he wanted to protect her from the torment and ridicule of the closed-minded villagers, but she didn't care as long as she was with him. She had experienced worse at the hands of her own people. All she wanted was to be a part of his life, to be there every moment.

Like a wisp of warm breath in the cold morning air, she knew how quickly love could disappear. Thoughts of her long dead husband filled her head. Charming and easygoing, he had been trampled to death underneath a herd of buffalo when the wind had shifted just right. Her grief had been great. He had been the love of her life. She never got over grieving. Her health deteriorated, until one day, she suffered from the crippling illness. Her entire right side went numb, her face drooped, and there was nothing that could be done about it.

She didn't mind the sickness. In her mind, the illness was a visual representation of what had happened to her when her husband had died; she had lost half of herself.

Over the years, she had gradually begun to regain the use of her limbs. While running with Loudest Laugh and The Last Honest Men, the functionality of her body had returned. Loudest Laugh was the cause. He brought back the dead half of her, made it feel alive again, gave her body purpose and warmth. Still, her face never quite fixed itself. She supposed there would always be a dead part of her, buried in the ground with her first husband.

Niviarsi rose from her furs and walked to a dark spot in the woods, she squatted in the woods, listening to the night. She looked back into the camp. Everything was normal. When she was finished, she walked back to the camp, careful so as not to make too much noise. She stopped mid-step as she saw what looked like a pair of feet disappear into the woods. The man that had been looking at her was gone.

She looked around, trying to spy where the man had went, but he was nowhere to be seen, so she curled up underneath the furs with Loudest Laugh. In her dreams, she smiled, and both sides of her mouth worked.

****

They awoke in the morning, as soon as it was light enough to see. The days had been becoming longer, the temperatures rising. Today, the sky started out a brilliant orange as the sun bounced off of the clouds over the horizon. He Who Makes the Drum Beat was eating some dried fish when one of his warriors came up to him. Hardest Yawn told him that in the night, two people had gone missing.

"What do you mean missing?"

"They are not here anymore," Hardest Yawn had said. He Who Makes the Drum Beat followed Hardest Yawn to the spot where two men had obviously bedded down earlier in the night. Their blankets were still there, as were their weapons.

"Who were they?"

Hardest Yawn pointed at another man sitting next to the fire. "Ever Sleep says that last night Fish That Kicks and Under the Mud made their beds next to him."

"Did you see them leave?" He Who Makes the Drum Beat asked.

Ever Sleep, an older warrior with strands of gray in his hair shook his head, "When I woke up they were gone. I figured they went to the bathroom, but they haven't been back and it's time to go."

He Who Makes the Drum Beat squatted down among the furs. He saw nothing among the brown matted fur. He used his hand to push himself into a standing position, and as he did, he felt a strange sensation on his hands. When he looked, there was blood on his hand. As he began looking around the spot, he notice more spots of blood, simple drips, but easily overlooked in the morning light. Near the edge of the clearing, two furrows of earth led into the forest. To the right of those, there was another set, as if two men had been dragged backwards into the forest.

"We do not have time for this. Form a search party."

****

When the search party had been announced, Niviarsi gladly volunteered Loudest Laugh and herself. Loudest Laugh was not happy about it. He had seen the activity as a well-needed chance to rest up, but Niviarsi insisted that doing this would help her endear herself to the men around them.

She had told him about the men around her and the types of stares she was receiving. At first, he had wanted to go out and fight everyone who had looked at her askance, but she had talked him out of it, which was no easy task once Loudest Laugh became upset.

"They will see me as a contributor, as more than just genitalia with a spear if we do this."

"I think you're giving them too much credit," Loudest Laugh said.

"Even if we change the minds of only two people, that's two more people than we have on our side now."

Loudest Laugh had seen the wisdom in her thoughts. Being not popular was one thing; being not popular with no one watching your back was something else entirely. So they had volunteered. The Eye That Shields declared that finding Kochen was the most important task, so the rest of the camp bundled up their belongings and headed out of the forest and onto the great sandy scrub country that led down to the mountains and the river canyon beyond.

The search party included five people: Niviarsi, Loudest Laugh, Hardest Yawn, Ever Sleep, and a young warrior looking for adventure named Hands Full of Ashes. They started with the left set of furrows and traced them through the forest. It wasn't long until they found Under the Mud. It would be long until they forgot what they had found.

Lying on the ground, Under the Mud was obviously dead. His fingers were formed into a stiff claw, and his head was lying far from his body, hidden among a stand of ferns. Blood pooled on the forest floor, white maggots swishing their tails back and forth in the red mess. Hands Full of Ashes threw up into the ferns that made up the underbrush of the forest. Loudest Laugh squatted down and looked at the mess.

"What could have done this?" Hardest Yawn asked.

Loudest Laugh looked at the ragged cut across Under the Mud's neck. It was not smooth, nor did he see any teeth marks. "It had to have been a person."

"What makes you think so?" Ever Sleep asked.

Loudest Laugh did not reply, instead, he stood up. Niviarsi pointed at something and said, "Look at that."

Loudest Laugh looked at what she was pointing at. On the inside of Under the Mud's left forearm, a chunk of flesh was missing. The wound was ragged around the edges, the skin stretched, bruised and maimed around it.

"It looks like something bit him," Niviarsi said.

Hands Full of Ashes wiped his mouth with the back of his arm. "What animal would bite a chunk out of his arm and then cut off his head?"

"Not an animal," Loudest Laugh said, "but a man."

Hands Full of Ashes threw up again.

Loudest Laugh laughed. "They ought to call you Hands Full of Vomit." The others laughed heartily at the joke. "Don't step on those maggots when you leave." Farway turned and smiled as he heard more retching behind him.

****

The next body was much further away. They had to walk for a good chunk of the morning, moving back and forth to find the right tracks. The furrows had stopped some fifteen feet in the forest, where they had found a large puddle of blood, curiously enough, filled with more maggots. From there, they followed a set of footprints that had sunk heavily into the forest floor, as if the person were carrying something... that something probably being the dead or unconscious body of Fish That Kicks. Judging by the blood, Loudest Laugh would wager on the latter.

They would have found the body sooner, but they had lost the trail in a stream, almost as if the person they were looking for knew they were going to come after him. It wasn't the person's tracks that led them to the body... it was the smell.

Niviarsi smelled it first, a crisp, charcoal smelling odor that permeated the air in the forest. The smell seemed to linger in her nose. From there, through the trees, she spotted a thin plume of smoke, black and smudgy in the sky. She tapped Loudest Laugh on the shoulder and pointed the smoke out. The search party fanned out and moved silently, avoiding dry branches and dead leaves. They spread out into a circle with the plume of smoke situated in the middle, and then they tightened the circle, moving closer in an agonizingly slow manner.

Hands Full of Ashes was the first to behold the scene. Loudest Laugh knew this because he heard him vomiting a few seconds later. With their cover blown by Hands Full of Ashes' sensitive stomach, he let loose a cry of rage and burst into the clearing, his club in hand, to find nothing. Some sort of beast roasted over the fire, the meat charred black on the bottom but still red and juicy on the top. It would appear the spit had not been turned in a few minutes.

"He's here," Loudest Laugh declared. They looked around, trying to find any sign of footprints, any sign of the murderer's whereabouts.

Hands Full of Ashes was about to walk into the woods when Niviarsi spoke. "We have found them. They are dead. This is all we need to do."

Loudest Laugh looked at her. He agreed with her words, but he couldn't tolerate another failure. "We will find him, and we will kill him, or we will die ourselves."

"We should just go back," Hardest Yawn said, Ever Sleep nodding his agreement, while the green shade of Hands Full of Ashes' face let Loudest Laugh now how he felt about their endeavor.

"He killed them. He killed them and ate them. We can't just let that go. What if this man makes his way to the village? Hardest Yawn, would you like to return home to find your children in the belly of some madman? What about you Ever Sleep? Do you want your mother being a meal?"

They were scared, but now they were ashamed. Loudest Laugh could see that. He had turned their hearts against their brains, and when he looked at Niviarsi, she nodded in understanding. She knew of his jealousy, his need to succeed and become something more than what he was. It was nothing she had ever said; it was simply understood.

"Fan out."

****

He reclined in the tree, his belly swollen and full of meat. He looked down at his stomach where the skin had stretched. Where once his stomach had been a mass of knotted brown muscle, it was now a round mound of skin stretched tighter than the hide on a drum, seemingly ready to burst without warning.

Yet the hunger was still there, clawing at his insides, trying to get out.

From above he listened to them talk about him. They were coming after him. He couldn't wait to taste them, especially the woman. Her flesh was as tight and muscular as the others, but the breasts... the breasts would be a special treat. He would save her for last.

The sun sapped his energy, and he fell into a deep sleep. Below him, they searched, pushing aside the brush and the leaves for any sign of his passing.

When the sun went down, they would be his. Soon.

****

Niviarsi was becoming concerned. The sun was going down, and they had not found a sign of the killer. They had searched the entire clearing without finding so much as a single sign of the killer's presence. In widening circles, they scoured the surrounding forest, only to find more of the same.

"Maybe it was a spirit," Hands Full of Ashes said.

No one said anything in response. What was there to say? Before the other day in the gully, Hands Full of Ashes would have been laughed out of the forest, but after that day, who was to say what was and wasn't happening? All Niviarsi knew was that she didn't want to find whatever had killed those two men. Whether it meant the loss of face or not, she would have to talk Loudest Laugh into abandoning his quest, which was not going to be a simple task.

"We should go," Niviarsi said. "It will be getting dark soon."

Ten feet away, pushing aside ferns to see the soft forest ground, Loudest Laugh ignored her.

"Did you hear me?"

There was still no response.

Ever Sleep overheard and said, "I agree with Niviarsi. We should head back to our people and tell them what we have found. Who knows, this killer could be circling back for more as we speak."

Loudest Laugh looked around the forest, his eyes far off and his brain working. His trademark smile was absent, and Niviarsi knew it would be hopeless.

"You can head back if you like, but whoever did this is out here, and I'm going to find him. Even if I have to sit in the dark and wait, I'm going to find him."

Hardest Yawn appeared out of the brush and said, "Then you will die."

Loudest Laugh looked at Hardest Yawn. He was a respected member of the tribe, older than most, but still barrel-chested and powerful. He was not someone that you tangled with, and when he spoke, most were smart enough to listen.

"We can't just let this person go free," Loudest Laugh said.

"Would you look at yourself? What are you doing this for? You cared nothing about Fish That Kicks or Under the Mud. What are you hoping to get out of this? Glory? A chance to finally make yourself seem as important as your brother?"

Loudest Laugh said nothing, but Hardest Yawn had his attention. "What good is glory when you're dead?"

"What good is death without glory?"

Hardest Yawn shook his head at this, the orange light of the setting sun filtering down onto his head and making his face hard to see. "You have life. You have a woman who cares about you. These things should be enough. It's time to go home."

Niviarsi moved to Loudest Laugh and put her hand on his arm. "Let's go."

Loudest Laugh looked at her and the men around him. *Cowards.* But if they wanted to go, he would not be able to stop them, and he was outnumbered. The forest was not a place to fight a battle alone, especially not at night. They would go.

"Very well. We will return to our people, but we move out now. Whoever did this snuck into our camp and stole two warriors without anyone hearing a sound. We shall run until the light fades, and then we will move in the dark, until we find our people."

Niviarsi slipped an arm around his waist and leaned up to him, kissing him on the cheek. "You're making the right choice."

Loudest Laugh looked at her and said, "Then why does it not feel like it?"

They lit torches from the smoldering ruins of the grotesque campfire, and then they were off in the night. They had run for half-an-hour when the sun finally disappeared, and the forest darkened, sprouting shadows everywhere.

When their torches burned low, they grabbed more branches off of the ground, and lit them as they went. The night wore on, and they became tired, the cold of the forest leeching into their bodies and slowing their pace.

When it began to rain, they knew that the world was working against them.

****

As the sun began to disappear, the shadows enveloped him, his belly was no longer round, the skin now loosely hanging off of his abdomen, laced with stretch marks. He sat up in his tree, listening, there was nothing but the buzzing of flies and the buzzing in his head.

He dropped out of the tree, falling through the air to land on the ground. The hunger was there, gnawing at his insides. Thoughts of breasts filled his head, and he set out running as the light of the trees filled his vision, their yellow luminescence lighting up the night. On the ground, he could see signs of their passing, disturbed leaves, clods of exposed new earth, and broken branches. They would be easy to find.

The shriveled, loose skin of his stomach flopped back and forth as he sprinted over the ground.

****

Had the rain been a normal rain, the trees would have protected their torches. But it was a downpour like no one had seen in years. Fat drops of rain found their way through the branches, landing and hissing on their torches. They were slowed to a crawl as they sought out fresh dry branches to light, only to find that they were extinguished within minutes by the drops of water that would collect on the underside of the branches, and then plummet to the ground when they became too heavy to cling to the leaves and branches.

Hands Full of Ashes was the first to die. One second he was there, and the next he wasn't. He had been off to Loudest Laugh's right, scrounging for more wood to light as a torch, and when Loudest Laugh turned to see what was taking so long, he was gone. There was no scream, no sign of struggle, he just wasn't there anymore. All that was left was a torching, hissing on the ground as it cast its last light.

They stuck closer after that, keeping up a dialogue so that they always knew where each person was . The movement was slower, and Loudest Laugh could feel the fear rising up in his chest. He didn't want to be here anymore. He didn't want the glory. What he wanted was to get out of the forest as soon as possible, but he knew they were still a couple hours from the edge. It would be a long walk.

They were soaked and cold when they heard the first sign of their pursuer. To their right, branches cracked, and out of the darkness an object flew at them, slapped off of Ever Sleep's wet chest, and fell to the ground. Loudest Laugh held his torch over the object to find a hand. Most of the flesh was stripped from it except for tendons and the flesh around the knuckles. Did the hand belong to Hands Full of Ashes? None of them could tell.

They continued to move, Ever Sleep gibbering uncontrollably, his mind awash in fear. "We're never going to make it. We're going to die here. We're going to be eaten." His voice was frantic, and Loudest Laugh could feel him building to a breaking point. He kept Niviarsi close to his left, her breathing was calm and she did not seem affected by the happenings.

She moved in silence, her feet gliding along the ground, and her eyes peering about the forest in an effort to pierce the shadows of the trees.

"I don't want to be eaten!" Ever Sleep shouted. He threw his torch on the ground and dashed off into woods. The fear had been too much for him. Loudest Laugh fought his own fear, which was mounting at an alarming rate.

"Stay here!" Hardest Yawn yelled after him, but if Ever Sleep heard, he did not respond. In seconds he was gone, lost to them among the driving rain and clinging darkness. To their right, they heard a rushing sound, and Loudest Laugh could have sworn that underneath the commotion he heard giggling. His skin crawled. *What manner of beast is this?*

After that, they moved through the forest in a back to back formation, their weapons at the ready. Loudest Laugh gripped the smooth wooden shaft of his spear, his torch held high to fling the light further. They could see no more than ten feet beyond their own circle at any given time. The rain pelted down upon them, as the wind rushed through the trees.

Loudest Laugh heard it before he saw it. The whoosh of air, the thud, and then the gurgle of someone drowning on their own blood. He spun quickly and grabbed Niviarsi, but she wasn't the one that was gurgling. She looked at him, her eyes wide, but free from fear. Behind them, Hardest Yawn fell to his knees, clutching at the spear that was sticking out of his throat.

From out of the darkness, a creature burst, covered in blood and naked, his face scrunched up and chewing on human flesh. He tackled Niviarsi to the ground, gnashing his teeth at her. Loudest Laugh kicked at the man, but his strength was too great. Niviarsi locked her arm at the elbow, pushing the creature back. His breath smelled of rot, and she could feel the jiggling heat of his belly, as if his abdomen were on fire.

179

Loudest Laugh jammed his spear through the man's shoulder. The man yowled, the rain washing the blood from his body and onto Niviarsi who gasped and sputtered underneath the weight of the man. Using the spear to gain leverage, he pulled the man off of her. He grabbed at the spear trying to pull it free, but to no avail.

Niviarsi rose, spitting the creature's blood onto the ground. She grabbed her own spear off of the ground and drove it through the face of the man. When she let go of the shaft, he hung there, his arms jittering and his legs quivering on the ground. His swollen belly burst and maggots spewed out onto the ground, digging their way into the wet earth in the light of their one fading torch.

As Loudest Laugh pulled his spear free, Niviarsi raised her face to the sky, filling her mouth with water and spitting it out onto the ground. *Funny,* she thought, *the raindrops almost sounded like buzzing.*

Chapter 24:

At the River

They awoke before the sun had risen. The scrape of feet on the rough rocks whispered in the night, startling them awake amongst the low-burning coals of the night's previous fire. Silently they shifted around, taking up defensive positions among the rocks and lying flat in the shadows.

Lonpearl gripped his spear tightly, waiting to see the source of the sound. When Markon and Andras appeared, their backs outlined against the purpling sky, Lonpearl relaxed his grip and smiled.

"Over here," he called. They skittered into the clearing, their breathing ragged and exhaustion etched on their face. Markon, a pale-skinned man with a soft, round face told the tale of their flight from the gully. They had become lost in the forest, and spent the majority of their first night trying to find a way out. When they thought that all hope was lost, they had spotted a fire in the distance and made their way to it. It had turned out to be the camp of the Stick People. They had camped on the border of the forest, and then had run throughout the morning, only stopping briefly to nap in the cave that Lonpearl and the others had used the night before.

When they had awaken, the Stick People had already moved past them, and they had to go around through the hills, lest they be seen by the Stick People. They had yet to sleep, but they knew they were within one day's march of the cliffs that they called home, so they had decided to move forward, checking their traditional camping spots for signs of other survivors. Lonpearl and his group were the only people they had seen. Of the nineteen hunters that had gone into the forest, they were the only ones who had returned, five hunters and a seer.

They broke camp and marched in the light of dawn, Lonpearl taking the lead. Kochen stumbled along between them, limping. His eyes had dark circles underneath them, and he was clearly on the verge of breaking down physically. Though they had stopped somewhat early to give him a full night of sleep, against Ghulish's wishes, Kochen continued to travel afar by the light of the fire. Lonpearl could see the toll that these journeys took, and he still didn't entirely believe that what Kochen had told him was possible.

What was possible was that Kochen was on the verge of falling apart. As they walked across the blasted landscape, Kochen began to stumble, occasionally tumbling to the ground, only to drag himself up. The wound on his leg appeared to be healing fine, they had sewn it together the first night, and the flesh showed no sign of infection, but his feet were another issue. They were raw, covered in blisters, and looked as bad as any case of blisters that Lonpearl had ever seen. On top of that, Kochen appeared to be wasting away. His ribs could be seen through his skin, and even his spine had taken on an odd bony shape. It was no matter. They were only one day away from the village, and as they walked, he could hear the rushing of the river in the distance. Traveling would be easier once they reached it. They could float down the river if they wanted to, but travelling on foot would actually be quicker thanks to the wide, pebble-filled banks of the river. Should the worst happen, they would put Kochen in the water and float down the river, but Lonpearl didn't think he was that far gone.

As they approached the river, the men ran towards it, whooping and hollering before they dove in. The cool water felt refreshing after a day-and-a-half of walking in the blinding sun, their skin baking in the day. They were all suffering from dehydration and exposure, so they rested on the banks of the river, drinking their fill of water and filling their waterskins.

Kochen collapsed at the edge, burying his face in the water and slurping at it greedily.

Lonpearl stripped his clothes off and dove into the water, dunking his head underneath the surface. He screamed in shock as he rose up out of the water. It was freezing, but he loved every second of it. Andras, Markon, and Hinler did the same. He only wished the rest of the hunters could be have been there for the moment. Lonpearl had been holding onto the hope that more of the hunters would make their way home, but he knew that it wasn't very likely. The world was a large place, and it was full of dangers.

Lonpearl wiped the water out of his eyes just in time to see Ghulish standing over Kochen's prone body, his spear drawn back for a killing blow.

"No!" he yelled.

Kochen flipped over on his back and the world froze. The water stopped rushing, and Lonpearl was frozen in his spot. The water had become like rock, and he was stuck in it. From underneath the water, shadows emerged, thick shadows stretching out in tendrils from the now solid water. Ghulish watched them as they advanced, floating in the air and making their way towards him. He stood entranced, his attack on Kochen forgotten. The tendrils danced around him, and then, as if they realized what they wanted, a tendril reared back and snaked at Ghulish, striking his chest. The skin split, and the sound of searing flesh could be heard. Ghulish reared back in pain, his spear dropping from his hand, and he ran off into the sunshine.

The tendrils followed him curling and pulsing, ignoring the fact that the sun should have burned them away.

Kochen was splayed on the ground, unseeing, as the tendrils rode over his body ignoring him and probing into the desert. Lonpearl looked around to see the others in the same situation as him, buried up to their waist in water that did not move.

"Kochen! He's gone! Wake up, Kochen!"

****

It had been pure instinct. When Kochen heard Lonpearl yell he had rolled over on his back and seen the hateful face of Ghulish standing over him, the tip of his spear looking sharp and deadly. His mind melted, pooling in his brain pan, replaced by pure instinct. He reached out with his liquid mind, reached into the depths of the river, and he found what he was looking for.

His consciousness was greeted as if with a mental handshake, and then he and it joined to become one consciousness. His eyes bugged out of his head, and all he wanted was for Ghulish to go away. He reached out to the hunter, and his hands followed... all one hundred of them formed of shadows, water, and mud.

Ghulish ran, and Kochen's clumsy attempt at capturing him using arms that were not his own left him shocked and confused. The consciousness he had linked to probed into his mind and he into its. Scenes flashed before his eyes, nonsensical glimpses of the world that came before. He saw the river, moving through the countryside, dumping itself into a larger body of water, one that he couldn't see the end of, and then he was underneath the water, in a place where the light never went, his breath pressed out of his chest, and the cold threatening to freeze him. It was an empty place, but not empty at the same time. It was home.

Time did not exist here, and the blackness was welcoming. Great shapes swirled in the darkness, formless, innumerable, and uncaring. The blackness enveloped him, heating up and pulsing with dark life that would scream at the sight of light. He opened his mouth and the blackness rushed in.

****

When the river roared once more, Lonpearl and the others were almost washed away with it. One minute it was stone, and the next it was a wall of water, washing him down the river and away from Kochen. He went under for just a second, and when he surfaced, the tendrils were gone, as was Ghulish, fled into the canyon. Kochen did not move, and Lonpearl splashed his way to the riverbank.

The youth was on his back, his mouth open, his eyes rolled back in his head to reveal only the whites. Andras was the first to reach him. He knelt down on his knees and slapped him with his four-fingered hand.

"Wake up, Kochen. Wake up. Are you in there?"

"What's wrong with him?" Hinler asked.

Lonpearl squatted down next to him. "He's somewhere else, I think. We need to get him to Lansa and fast. Help me."

They carried Kochen's body to the river and Lonpearl climbed in one arm tucked underneath Kochen's chin. They began the long float back to the village with Lonpearl holding Kochen's head above water while the others kicked and swam, catching the current where they could.

"Did you see that thing?" Hinler asked.

"I saw it," Lonpearl said, his breathing somewhat labored from the exertion.

Hinler was quiet for a moment before speaking again. "Maybe Ghulish had the right idea."

185

Lonpearl said nothing.

Chapter 25:

A Tale Not Finished

He Who Makes the Drum Beat slogged through the rocky terrain, sweat pouring off of his body. How anyone could live in this environment was beyond him. It was hot, uncomfortable, and the sun seemed to be warmer than it ever was back home. Their war party moved at a solid pace, the men taking turns carrying The Eye That Shields across the rugged terrain, his litter bouncing back and forth over rocks and small shrubs.

The group had been somber ever since the disappearance of Under the Mud and Kicks Like Fish at the edge of the forest. There were whispers in the camp at night that the entire endeavor was cursed, that their mission was not seen favorably by the spirits. No one said as much to him, but as a leader, it was his job to gauge the mood of the camp. Something positive would have to happen soon, or they would be doomed by morale before they even set sight on the village in the cliffs.

They had no hope of catching Kochen and the people who had stolen him away. The day before, a group had stumbled across their campsite from the previous evening. The trackers told them that they were hours behind, and with The Eye That Shields holding them back, they were not likely to capture them. Some of the men had asked permission to set out on their own to intercept the band, but The Eye That Shields had denied them. He had said, "Everything is turning out as it must. Though we may

187

not like the results, it is the way it has to be." He Who Makes the Drum Beat didn't like it any more than his men, but he was just a warrior. The Eye was more than him, though physically he could end the old man whenever he chose, he contained within him the wisdom of the entire tribe. That was something that one did not ignore.

The evening before, prior to The Eye beginning his mediation, He Who Makes the Drum Beat had broached the topic of taking an apprentice. His suggestion had been met with laughter. There was no malice in it, but The Eye simply said, "What do you think we are doing? The boy from the cliffs will be my apprentice."

When He Who Makes the Drum Beat had suggested someone from their own village, The Eye simply smiled and said, "We are all one village, no matter how far apart we may live or how different we may seem." At this point, he had left the old man to his own devices, stoking the fire for him with aged bits of wood from a forest that had long since disappeared. He believed he would see a tree walk before he would ever see The Eye talked into something that was not his own decision in the first place. He Who Makes the Drum Beat hoped that The Eye was right. He hoped that his visions were leading them down the right path, but in his heart he had doubts. The warrior in him wanted to send out the fastest runners and have them capture Kochen before he ever reached his home. The trackers thought there were maybe four or five people with him at most, which was few enough for his trained warriors to defeat.

He Who Makes the Drum Beat was lost in his thoughts when a commotion arose in the back of the procession. He halted in his tracks and turned around to hear cheering as two figures emerged, trotting quickly towards them. He smiled as he recognized his brother and his woman. He looked for the others that had left with them, but they were nowhere to be seen. It was as it had been since the day they had left to search for the prophet, one part good and two parts bad. He would be glad when the child was in their possession and they could return to the forest to hunt and grow fat on their kills. He Who Makes the Drum Beat was beginning to grow weary of the responsibility that hung around his neck.

He moved to intercept the pair, embracing Loudest Laugh and Niviarsi. "It is good to see you. What news do you have? Did you find them?"

Loudest Laugh looked at him, the twinkle gone from his eyes. "We found them."

He Who Makes the Drum Beat was thrown off by his brother's subdued response. The rest of the warriors waited patiently to hear tell of Loudest Laugh's story. "Well?"

Loudest Laugh looked his brother in the eye and said, "They're all dead." A murmur shot through the warriors.

At first the news didn't register for him, and then he thought he must have misheard Loudest Laugh. "What do you mean?"

Loudest Laugh shoved past him and Niviarsi followed, her face wan and tired looking. They marched past the rest of the warriors and continued walking in the direction that the Cliff People had gone. This was not the good news that he had been hoping for; this only made matters worse.

He Who Makes the Drum Beat looked around him, as if looking for anyone who could give him an explanation of what had just happened. The Eye That Shields shrugged his shoulders when he made eye contact with him. Wordlessly, they continued their march, a pall hanging over the group. Conversation was at a minimum and when they came to the cool clean waters of the river that would lead them to the Cliff People's village, they made camp. Not even the sight of the rushing water was enough to liberate the camp from the oppression that hung over it.

He Who Makes the Drum Beat sat down. He would let his brother come and find him when he was ready. Loudest Laugh never came when he was called, only when he was ignored.

****

The night closed in on them quickly. The stars were obstructed by great gray clouds, and even the light of the moon couldn't penetrate them. Loudest Laugh sat huddled next to a fire twenty spans away from the rest of the camp. Niviarsi sat to his left, her clothes tossed shamelessly on the ground. Sweat covered her body, and Loudest Laugh was beginning to become worried about her. It was not a warm night, and there was no reason that she should be sweating.

On top of that, she had grown sullen and quiet during their journey. They never spoke about what happened in the forest, but it didn't seem to bother Niviarsi one bit. The one time he had tried to bring it up she had laughed and told him to stop living in the past. He watched as she ran her hands along her body, smiling at him, beads of sweat standing out on her upper lip, firelight reflecting off of her wet breasts.

"I want you," she moaned.

Normally, this would have been all Loudest Laugh needed, but there was something not quite right with her. Her smile was alien to him, almost a snarl, and the way the fire danced off of her eyes made it seem as if there were another being behind them. "I don't think we should. I think you might be sick. Maybe you caught water-lung in the forest."

"I'm fine," she purred, exposing the parts of herself that would usually drive him wild. They did not do so tonight.

He tossed her clothes at her and said, "I'll be back."

Maybe The Eye That Shields would know what to do. He walked away, ignoring her protests, the language coming out of her mouth would have been a turn-on under normal circumstances, but now they just gave him the chills.

He walked through the camp, avoiding the eyes of the other warriors. He could feel their need to know clawing at him. Some of their stares were accusatory while others simply seemed curious. The smell of roasting meat hit his nose, but he had no appetite. Truth be told, even the thought of meat sent shivers up his spine. The events of the forest were caught in his mind, replaying over and over. It all seemed so wrong, like a fever-dream. He wasn't even sure it had really happened. The only thing he was sure of was that there was something wrong with Niviarsi.

He found The Eye That Shields meditating near a campfire. His brother, He Who Makes the Drum Beat sat to his left, gnawing on the leg of some unfortunate hare that they had found in the canyon. He shuddered at hearing the greasy, slopping sounds of his brother's lips as he chewed the meat.

Loudest Laugh sat down in the dirt. "I need to speak to you," he said to The Eye.

He Who Makes the Drum Beat threw the bones of his meal into the fire where the little bit of fat that was left crackled and hissed. "Leave him be. He's communing with the Spirits."

"I have need of his advice."

"Then you can wait."

"Listen, this is serious."

191

"A lot of things are serious. What The Eye does is always serious, as it pertains to all of us here, not just you and your woman."

"She has a name."

"It could be a while," He Who Makes the Drum Beat replied, ignoring Loudest Laugh's request. Loudest Laugh spat into the fire, and then rose to his feet. "Stay. Tell me about it."

Loudest Laugh froze halfway to his feet. "About what?"

"About where you've been for the last few days. What else?"

Loudest Laugh sat back down. It was not a story that he wanted to tell, but he felt that the story was one that he had to tell.

He started by telling him of how they tracked down the first body, detailing the grotesque state they had found it in.

"Maggots?" his brother asked. "How can that be? Surely he was not dead long enough for maggots to appear."

Loudest Laugh shrugged his shoulders. "I do not know why he was that way, but that is the way that he was. But that wasn't even the worst part. The worst part was the mark on his arm, as if someone had taken a bite out of him."

"Was it an animal?"

"I'm still not sure." Loudest Laugh continued his tale, detailing their journey through the forest and the state of Fish That Kick's body. Then he detailed their harrowing escape from the forest, as they were hunted down one by one by a ravenous creature who seemed to want nothing more than to kill them.

"When he died, his belly split open, and maggots poured out onto the ground. They burrowed their way into the ground. Then we ran without stopping, until we found you."

When he had finished his tale, the fire had begun to gutter out. He Who Makes the Drum Beat rose from his feet, and found a couple more dry branches to put on top of it.

"I know what you speak of," The Eye muttered, his voice weary and weak. "The creature you speak of is a thing not unknown to this tribe, albeit not for a long time, since before the day I was born and since before the day my grandfather was born... perhaps longer."

"Bah. It sounds like the fevered dream of scared fools in the night," He Who Makes the Drum Beat said as he placed more branches on the fire and returned to his seat.

"It sounds like it, but it is not."

"What was it?" Loudest Laugh asked.

"It was a spirit, a spirit best forgotten. It is the spirit of rot, always hungry, always looking to consume and reduce the world to a sea of maggots and death. It uses men to accomplish its goals; it turns them into beasts. Their hunger is insatiable. The meat they eat rots in their stomach because they are no longer alive."

Loudest Laugh was lost in thought.

The Eye That Shields reassured Loudest Laugh, "You did a fine job. The world is a better place without this spirit on the loose."

"But why would it come back now, after all of these years?" Loudest Laugh asked.

"The circle is disintegrating, coming apart. It is becoming unbalanced, and the spirits are looking to take their place, once and for all. I suspect the awakening of the young seer is part of it. Kochen's powers have sent ripples through the natural order of the world. If he is left unguided, there will be more of these spirits... and it will take more than a spear to fight back."

193

The Eye That Shields lay down on his side, and pulled his furs up around his chin.

"There is one more thing," Loudest Laugh said.

"Leave him alone. Can't you see he is tired," his brother chided him.

"I don't think this can wait. Niviarsi is sick."

The Eye That Shields opened his eyes, concern coalescing in the wrinkles around them. "How?"

"She has a fever... and she's... different." Loudest Laugh struggled to find the words, but speaking had never been his strong suit. "She is not the woman I know. Ever since we killed that man, she has been quieter, more subdued, but strange as well."

The Eye leaned towards him, "This is important? Has she eaten yet?"

Loudest Laugh thought about it. "No, I don't think she has. We were busy running, but... I don't know."

The Eye That Shields popped up out of his furs, standing on wobbly hips. "We must see her now. Go, find her."

Loudest Laugh was confused and hesitant. He Who Makes the Drum Beat rose from his feet instantly. Loudest Laugh held his hand out to his brother halting him. "Wait. What is it? What is wrong?"

"Go!" The Eye yelled, his voice hoarse and scratchy. Loudest Laugh jumped when he heard the fear in the old man's voice. He could count on one hand the amount of times he had ever heard The Eye raise his voice at anyone. He moved instantly, walking briskly with his brother at his side. "Bring her to me," The Eye yelled, "before it is too late!"

As they moved through the darkness, He Who Makes the Drum Beat called more warriors to his side. As they approached the fire, Loudest Laugh's heart beat wildly in his chest. When they reached the fire, Niviarsi was gone.

He Who Makes the Drum Beat squatted down next to the fire, and flipped something over with his spear.

"What is it?" Loudest Laugh asked.

"You do not want to see," his brother said.

"What is it? he repeated. His brother stepped aside. On the ground, barely visible in the firelight were two lumps of flesh. One had clearly been gnawed on recently, blood still oozed from the mouth-shaped wounds. On the other lump, he could clearly see a nipple, one that he had kissed a thousand times in the night.

He yelled her name into the night, tears streaming from his eyes. His brother kept him from charging into the darkness to find her, his strong arms wrapped around him, iron and unmoving. It was their first embrace in years.

Chapter 26:

Homecoming

Lonpearl and Andras carried Kochen the last distance to the village. They set him down on the edge of the farmland. This what not the homecoming that they had been expecting. The ladders had been pulled and the cornfield was dotted with crosses, people tied to them, in various states of decomposition. Some of the bodies were bloated, swelling in their own gasses. They recognized some of the faces. Oily, black smoke rose from the top terrace of the village, and the hunters looked at each other, questions on their lips.

As far as they could tell, they had not been seen, so they ducked behind the last rise before the farmland. Lonpearl arranged Kochen's body as comfortably as he could, and they discussed the situation in whispered tones.

"What the hell is happening in there?" Hinler asked with his lispy voice.

"I don't know. Maybe they were attacked while we were gone. That's the only way to explain why all of the ladders are pulled," Andras replied.

"I don't like this," Markon said.

"I don't like this either, but we have to get into that village. There's a war party bearing down on us as we speak. We either sit out here and die, or we go into that village," Lonpearl replied.

Markon looked at Lonpearl and said, "I'm not going in there until I know what we're walking into."

They argued back and forth about what to do until, Andras shushed them. "Do you hear that?"

From the farmland they heard a plaintive wail, weak and barely audible over the wind that rushed through the canyon. Lonpearl swallowed deeply before saying, "One of them is still alive."

They crawled forward on their stomachs, and peered up over the rise, trying to figure out where the noise was coming form. They waited, the only sound in their ears was the cool wind of the canyon. Then they heard it again. Markon pointed in a direction. Lonpearl crept forward on his stomach, crawling through the fertile ground, heading in the direction that Markon had pointed.

The others hung back. "Be quick," Hinler implored.

Lonpearl crawled as quickly as he could, and then he waited to hear the sound again. It did not come for a long time, and when it did, it came as moaning, no words. He crouched and walked among the tall corn until he came upon the bound body of an elder tied to a cross. He knew the man. Dantish, a frail gentleman who had always been looked upon in a positive light in the village. Lonpearl pulled his stone knife from his waist and began sawing at the rough leather thongs that bound Dantish to the cross.

"Help me," he moaned.

Lonpearl said, "Be quiet. I'm cutting you down." The man continued his wailing. He was in obvious pain, and blood ran down his arms where the leather straps had dug into his wrists. When Lonpearl sliced through the last strap, the man collapsed to the ground in a pile of bones and groans. He threw the man over his shoulder and ran back to the edge of the field as low and as quick as he could, just in case any eyes on the terraces were keeping watch over the fields.

Lonpearl set the man down as gently as he could. His eyes were unfocusing, and his lips were dry and cracked. Hinler handed Lonpearl a waterskin and they

197

poured it down his mouth. He drank greedily, and then looked at them. He held Lonpearl's arm and cried, sobbing quietly on the rocky ground.

Lonpearl let him finish, which took some time, and then he asked, "What is happening in the village? Why were you tied to the cross?"

Dantish looked at him, his eyes going wide, and said, "They've all gone mad."

****

The morning the Corn Men were pulled off of their cliff perch was a sad morning indeed. Dantish watched from the terrace where he dwelled as young men, too young to hunt, were sent up the cliffside. The ascent took the better part of the day, and once, when they had neared the top, Dantish became dizzy just watching them, suspended on the side of an unforgiving cliff face. One misstep would be all it took for one of them to come tumbling to the ground. It had happened before, not in a long time, but it had happened.

Dantish had never been volunteered for cliff duty when he was a youth, but even if he had, he would have turned it down. The terraces were bad enough. One would think that after a lifetime of climbing up and down ladders, one would get used to the heights, but he never had. He had seen men and women slip and die falling off of those damn ladders. Once, he had proposed to Fesh, the previous head priest, that they carve steps into the side of the terrace, but Fesh had pointed out that the ladders were their greatest defense against their enemies. So the occasional death happened. It was always a sad affair, and the priests always used the event to further their own agendas, but Dantish saw right through their little games.

Lansa was the latest priest to begin playing games with the village. The day before, she had come down the side of the cliff, halting about halfway down, as she could go no further without the fingers on her right hand. Some climbers had been sent with ropes to lower her to the ground. When her feet were firmly planted on the terrace floor, he recognized the madness in her eyes. Lansa, who had never claimed to commune with the spirits from what the other priests had said, came down the cliff raving and mad about visions and the village's downfall.

Lansa disappeared inside the sanctum and took a few hours to compose herself. When she emerged, she began banging on the war drum. The farmers flooded out of the fields, expecting another attack from the Stick People, but it had been something different... an attack from within. Dantish saw that now.

At first, he thought that nothing would come of Lansa's antics. When she demanded volunteers to bring the Corn Men down the cliff, he had scoffed at her and walked away. Dantish was sure that the other priests would talk some sense into her, and let her see the error of her ways. He should have said something.

Now he sat watching as the children climbed the cliff. It took them a few hours before they crested the lip of the cliff, but they soon emerged. A boy only thirteen summers old tumbled down the edge of the cliff, an old bald man clutched in his arms. Dantish didn't see where he crashed into the ground, but the screams of people from the terrace above let him know all that he needed to know.

He called to some of the elders that he knew. He had had enough. They climbed the ladders to the top terrace, and confronted Lansa.

"Are you mad, Lansa? Why are you doing this. Leave those men alone," he had said.

Lansa's response was to look down her nose at him, and say, "If it is not done. We will all die. The spirits have shown me."

"Since when have you ever been able to talk to the spirits?" The men and women behind him murmured concurring words.

Lansa walked up to him, her eyes bulging, and vein-filled. "The spirits speak when they will it. And they have shown me the destruction of this village. And they have shown me how to stop it. The Corn Men are a blight upon our village. They would have me deliver them a woman for pleasure. Do you want your granddaughter to spend her life getting pawed at by dirty old men, Dantish?" She pointed at another member of the group, "Or you? Does anyone here want to give their daughter to the depraved parasites that camp on top of the cliff?" There was silence. "If you do? Speak now? If you don't, then stay out of the way."

It was a well-played stroke, and Dantish actually kind of admired it, but there's always something to admire about the mad.

The other Corn Men, seeing the fate of the one that struggled were more compliant. Though they spit and cursed all the way down, the boys on top of the cliff managed to successfully lower the two remaining Corn Men to the ground by rope without incident.

Lansa had them tied up and ushered into the sanctum. Dantish and some of the other elders huddled on their terrace, talking about the day's developments. They thought that the worst was over. When the screams began, they knew it was not.

The screams continued through the night, screams that made his skin crawl. In the morning, Harcha and Doulk appeared, dragging the corpse of a second Corn Man between them. They tossed his body off of the top terrace, climbed down the ladder to the next terrace and tossed the body off of that one as well. They did this all the way down to the canyon floor. Then they tied the man's broken and shattered body to a cross and hung him up in the field.

The screams continued throughout the day, and the village found itself divided. When Dantish joined a group of people ready to put a stop to the madness, mostly made up of elders and women, another group appeared in front of the sanctum to stop them. Lansa appeared at the doorway of the sanctum, her clothing covered in blood and displeasure written on her face.

"What is going on here?" she snapped.

One of the elders stepped up and said, "What you are doing is wrong. You must stop."

Lansa looked at her, disgust in her eyes. "We don't have time for this. Put her in the field. If anyone objects, put them in the field as well."

Dantish didn't want to believe that they would do it. He didn't want to believe that his own village could be torn in half within the span of two days, but he looked at the faces of the people standing between their group and the sanctum, and he saw fear in their eyes, blind fear, the type of fear that will allow people to do anything.

When the group surged forward and put their hands on the woman, he couldn't believe it. He stepped forward and put his hands out to stop them, but they were farmhands, their muscles and virility untouched by age. Their group didn't have a chance. They punched him in the mouth, and teeth fell to the ground. The rest was a blur of screaming as they were shoved over the edges of the terrace. He lost consciousness on the first fall.

When he awoke, he was tied in the field, an offering to the spirits, forgotten and surely lost. In the night, he could hear Bimisi moving underneath the soft ground. The pain in his body, the broken bones, they kept him awake, begging the spirits for death.

****

"After that, I do not know what happened," Dantish shook his head as he spoke. "I'm not even sure how long I sat on that cross. All I know is that when I first woke up there were others screaming for help. One by one their voices faded, and then they stopped altogether, until I could only hear my own voice."

They sat on their heels, waiting to see if Dantish had anything else to say out of respect. He was silent. He closed his eyes and rested on the ground, his body a mass of bruises, swollen and cut in a dozen different places. Lonpearl had no idea how the old man had survived a drop from four terraces, but he thanked him for it.

They moved away, so that Dantish could rest. They looked at each other, their faces filled with shock. Hinler ran his hand through his hair, obviously unable to figure out what to do next. Lonpearl knew how he was feeling.

Andras was the first to speak. "We have to send someone in. See what it's like in there."

"Why don't we all just go in?" Markon asked.

"No. That wouldn't work. It sounds as if Lansa has lost her mind. If we go in there, and she sends them against us, we could find ourselves having to cut our way out, or end up like poor Dantish there. Do you want to cut these people down? People you've known for you entire life?"

"I'm not ready to do that," Markon said.

"Me neither," added Hinler.

"Well, then who wants to go in?" Lonpearl asked.

There was no answer... just four people looking in Lonpearl's direction. Being a leader was tough. Lonpearl sighed. It was going to be an interesting day.

****

Lonpearl walked through the cornfield, trying not to look at the faces of the people on the crosses. The crosses were a traditional punishment for the enemies of the village. It was said that their presence would satisfy Bimisi and keep him below ground. At night, Bimisi would appear, and feed on the bodies crosses, thus ensuring a bountiful harvest. Over the last week, the farmland had accumulated more bodies than even Bimisi could feed on.

Lonpearl stopped and shook his head. Just a few weeks ago, if someone had told him that his village was going to be feeding corpses to Bimisi, he would have thought them mad. Things had changed so quickly. He no longer even felt like the same person. He had left the village as a hunter, nothing more. He returned a victim, a man with a world that had been turned upside down, towing the unconscious body of the one person that might be able to right things. The last thing he had expected to return to was a home that had been thrown into chaos, with many of his friends and acquaintances fastened to wooden crosses... to sacrifice them to a spirit.

He almost laughed out loud at the absurdity of his thoughts, and then he looked up to see a familiar face. Lonpearl dropped to his knees. It was his wife. Though the skin of her face was bloated and discolored, he could still tell it was her. He reached out to her, tears dropping from his eyes. He stepped close to her, shaking her foot with his hand, just to see if maybe she were still alive, though based on the smell, he already knew the answer. "Stot?"

There was no answer. His brain pulsed with unfamiliar energies. He had no idea what he was feeling. The sensations surged through him, one after another, all cut with a sadness that hung heavy in his heart. He pushed and pulled at the cross, tears streaming from his eyes. It he moved the cross back and forth, loosening the soil around the base of the cross. Eventually he freed the cross, and he sat over Stot's body.

Her eyes were closed, her limbs broken. Stot pulled his knife from his belt and cut her free of her bonds. Had she been dead when they put her on the cross? Had she suffered in the sun, calling his name? Lonpearl knelt and pulled Stot to his chest, hugging her cold body to his own burning skin.

His mind went to his daughter, Hubra. Was she tied to one of these crosses as well? Surely, Lansa couldn't have gone that mad. Lonpearl let go of Stot, and stood, wiping tears from his face. The village loomed above him, smoke rising from the fires of the village. He gripped his spear and ran through the field, the sun beginning its downward arc. As he ran, he looked at the faces, trying to see if any children were there. Seeing none, he ran faster, his breathing ragged and adrenaline pumping through his body. There were more bodies than he expected. He knew them all.

He skidded to a stop at the bottom of the village, his face looking up. "Lower the ladder!"

There was no response from the village. "Lower the ladder!" he yelled, his throat aching when he was done.

On the top terrace of the village, two faces appeared, poking their heads over the edge. A ladder was lowered, and the people began to climb down it. To Lonpearl, it felt as if he were watching sap drip down a branch. He waited impatiently, visions of his dead wife floating in his head. Guilt ran through his body. Guilt at having left. Guilt at having allowed this to happen. Farway had been a fool. Lonpearl had been a fool for following him. He hoped that wherever he was Farway was as miserable as he was. He hoped he was worse in fact.

His rescuers finally reached the bottom, and peered over the side. Two farmers, men of a significant age, who ought to know better. They were as responsible as Lansa. Did they toss his wife from a terrace, breaking her body, twisting it in ways that it shouldn't twist? They would pay. They would all pay.

Chapter 27:

The New Order

Jib, for he was no longer a Corn Man, moaned on the ground. He had spilled many secrets throughout the course of the last few days, but Lansa knew there was more within him. She had pried from Jib the secret of *tilnac*, the secret of their survival, and secrets about how the world worked. With this knowledge at her hands, she could lead the tribe into a new future, a powerful future. No one would challenge them, not the spirits, not the Stick People, not her own tribe. The enemies of their ancestors would no longer be a problem.

But she wanted more. Jib had been stubborn in imparting his information. Only after she had taken from him his fingers and his toes had the secrets started coming. But he was being stubborn again. Perhaps it was time to give him a break.

"Feed him," she told Harcha. He nodded his acquiescence. Lansa was not fooled. Harcha still didn't believe what she was doing was right, but he was like all of the others, bound by tradition, bound by the laws that their forefathers had set forth. What good were these laws? They prevented their advancement. They kept them in the role of the victim. Well, it was their day now. It was their time be the victimizer.

She drank water from a pitcher as Harcha shoved another one of Jib's own fingers into his mouth. It was brutal move, but the time for games was over. "Chew it, Jib."

Jib looked at her, hate burning in his eyes. Lansa did not care. It was his fault that this happened. The Corn Men had grown greedy and complacent, living off of their village, but never contributing to it.

Lansa longed for another vision, but none had been forthcoming. She had some of the villagers currently making their own batches of *tilnac* to see if the recipe that she had been given would work. It was the only reason that Jib was still alive. Sure, there were secrets that he possessed still, but he was intent on holding out as long as he could. She didn't know what he expected to happen, but as soon as they had confirmed the first potency of the first batch of *tilnac*, they would put him out of his misery.

She wanted the secret of the ceremony that the Corn Men had performed on the Up Top, but this appeared to be one of those secrets that Jib was holding onto to keep himself alive. It would only work for so long.

The sounds of a commotion drifted into the limestone walls of the sanctum. Villagers were shouting. Lansa put the pitcher of water down and walked outside, Birren and Doulk at her side. Birren had taken to the new order of things well, as had Doulk. Harcha was a different story. He would soon be expendable.

When she emerged from the sanctum, she had to shade her eyes from the sun to see the scene that was shaping up before her. It took her a while to recognize the man that was surrounded by a group of her loyal villagers. It was Lonpearl, emaciated, ribs sticking out, and covered in dirt. He waved his spear at the men, demanding to see Lansa.

She was surprised. As soon as the men had left, Lansa had realized how fruitless their expedition would be. What hope had a group of hunters against an entire village of seasoned warriors? That she only saw Lonpearl was to

206

be expected. Lansa was disappointed to not see Kochen, there, but in another way it was a relief. She would be the voice of the people. She would be the bridge between the village and the spirit world. Having Kochen here would have just complicate the situation even further. With the secrets of the Corn Men in her possession, she no longer needed Kochen, but still, she felt a pang of sadness in her breast. Everyone she had ever loved was now gone. Fesh, her mother, her father, Kochen's father, and now even Kochen. All that was left was the village. No one would take that away from her.

"Lonpearl. It is good to see you."

The crowd surrounding Lonpearl parted at Lansa's words, ready to step between Lonpearl and Lansa should he try to attack her.

From Lonpearl's expression, Lansa knew that he was not happy to see her. It would be a shame to have to kill off the last of the hunters. "Where is the rest of your group?"

"Dead," he replied.

"And Kochen?"

"Dead as well. Just like my wife."

Lansa understood. The village's shift had been hard. Change often came with a price, and that price was usually paid in blood. "I'm sorry about your wife. She didn't understand what we are doing here. We have kept your daughter safe. Hubra has been staying with us. Would you like to see her?"

Lonpearl's eyes welled up with unspilled tears. "She's alive?"

Lansa was shocked. "Of course she's alive. Who in their right mind would kill a child? Birren, bring Hubra to her father." Birren waddled away into the sanctum to fetch Hubra.

"You must be exhausted. We'll get some food in you, and you can tell us all about your journey, if you're ready. I know this whole situation must be difficult, but we're glad to have you back. Aren't we?" The villagers murmured their assent.

Lonpearl just stood there, clutching his spear. Lansa sensed that something was wrong for the first time. This was not a warrior returned home, ready to settle in for a night of feasting and storytelling. This was an angry husband, bristling with rage. She could see it in his eyes, behind the blank face, his eyes smoldered, his stare aimed firmly in her direction.

Hubra appeared, holding the plump hand of Birren. She had been in shock for the last few days, her mind not understanding that her mother was gone or why. For most of the first day, she had cried, wailing for her mother. Lansa had comforted as best as she could. Hopefully, Lonpearl could see that his daughter needed him more than he needed his revenge. Even if that were the case, she would probably have to deal with him sooner than later. Hubra would make a great priest. She could be Lansa's successor. It would show the village that there were no hard feelings between herself and those who went against the new order of things.

Hubra ran to her father, and the village looked on smiling, happy to see a positive event for the first time in days. It was good for Lansa to see. Maybe now the village could return to normalcy and settle down for a bit before she consolidated her power. Some of the elders who were still left had tears in their eyes as Lonpearl and Lansa hugged.

Lansa felt moved as Lonpearl ran his hand through his daughter's dark brown hair, tangled and unkempt from lying on the earthen floor of the sanctum and crying. He kissed her on the forehead, his parched lips pursing. Lonpearl held his daughter at arm's length, and then picked her up in one arm. The daughter said nothing.

"We are leaving this village."

Lansa had not expected this. "You cannot leave. You just got here." The village murmured similar sentiments, shocked that Lonpearl would want to leave.

"There is nothing for us here now. We will leave. Perhaps one day we will return."

Lansa wanted to let Lonpearl go, but he was a question. What was really going on in that mind of his? Was this some attempt to double-cross her and the village? "Lonpearl, we need you here. You are a valuable member of the community. Please, stay."

"You have no right to ask anything of me. You should all be ashamed of yourself."

Lansa shrugged. It was as she had expected. "We can't allow you to go. It's dangerous out there."

"You have no choice," he shot back.

"There is always a choice. Stop him." The villagers looked back and forth between Lansa and Lonpearl. She noted the hesitance, and she didn't like it one bit. "I said stop him!" she snapped.

Lonpearl set Hubra on the ground and said, "Climb to the bottom. Run through the fields. Friends will be waiting." He pushed her gently in the back and she moved towards the terrace ladder. One of the villagers moved to intercept the girl and Lonpearl stepped between them, his spear coming up to the man's chin. "Let her go."

The villagers converged on Lonpearl as Hubra's tiny head disappeared over the ledge and down the ladder. A rock appeared, striking Lonpearl on the temple. He was dazed for a second and the villagers made their move. Lonpearl lashed out about him with the spear, stabbing the nearest man in the soft part of his throat. More blood was spilled. To their credit, the crowd did not back away, but they came on even stronger, angry that Lonpearl did not want to be a part of their village.

Lonpearl fought valiantly, swinging back and forth with the spear, using the shaft to stun people and the tip to maim them. The press of the village was too much, and the women at the back let fly with rocks, the most abundant defense of the cliff village. Their aim was awful. Few of the rocks hit him, but the rocks that did began to take their toll. Lonpearl bled from several places, and a particularly well-aimed rock managed to cut open the skin over his left eye. Blood poured into his eye, so that he could only see out of his right eye, but still he fought on. The fight went on longer than Lansa had expected.

Lansa calmly walked down to the edge of the upper terrace and looked over the side. Lonpearl had fought long enough to allow his daughter to get to the lowest terrace of the village. Even now she climbed the last ladder before the canyon floor. *There must be someone out there,* she thought.

A rock caught Lonpearl in the mouth and he went to the ground, spitting chunks of teeth out, while villagers pummeled him with their fists and feet. It would be the last time he ever stood on his two feet again.

"Burn him!" Lansa yelled.

The villagers dragged Lonpearl to the middle of the terrace, his arms and legs kicking and lashing out to be free. But the strength was gone from his limbs. "I curse you, Lansa. I curse you and this entire village! The spirits will come for you!" His words turned to screams as the villagers shoved him into the coals of the terrace's communal fire. He didn't scream for long. His hair caught on fire, snatching the breath from his lungs. The villagers held him in the flames with spears as his flesh-sizzled. Within seconds, his face was no longer recognizable, and his feet and arms stopped thrashing.

"Do you want us to go after the girl?" Birren asked.

"No. I have a feeling that some of Lonpearl's friends are waiting down there." She looked off into the distance, watching as Hubra ran across the field. *Are you down there, Kochen?*

210

Chapter 28:

The Broken Circle

Kochen floated in the cool black void. Unaware of anything around him. The past was here, floating in the depths with him. Was this the spirit world or was this something else entirely? He didn't know. He only knew this was where he wanted to be the rest of his life. Here were the answers to everything he wanted to know... and yet, he found he didn't want to know all that much. The simple fact that he could know if he desired was more than enough to satisfy his curiosity. He was content with floating, existing.

He sensed rather than saw the other beings of the depths. Great beasts with memories longer than his own surged through the deep, buffeting him and sending him spinning through the cool waters. Their thoughts were transparent. To them he was nothing more than flotsam floating through the water.

The waters... the waters... the waters. He remembered against his will. That first vision on the banks of the river, Lansa's hands shoving him under the water, drowning him. He had reached out and been rejected.

"No," the voice had said. "It is not time." Then the vision had hit him. The people ran red through the night, their skin hanging in sheets as the sky fell to the ground. In the depths, he could almost see the blood floating in the water before him.

A shockwave went through the dark, spinning his consciousness out of control. A light bloomed before him, and the face of a man appeared in the flames. "Save her. Save them all," it said. No, not "it." The voice belonged to Lonpearl.

Lonpearl... Lonpearl... Lonpearl... where was he? How did he get here? Kochen's consciousness bloomed, the water unable to suppress his humanity. The shapes in the water became agitated by his thoughts, his patterns, his being. Kochen looked for the way home, but could find nothing.

****

The girl crested the rise, bouncing around as young children do when they run. Her knees were covered in mud, and blood ran down her shins from the cuts produced as she stumbled through the cool farmland. Hinler caught the girl as she tumbled over the edge. Her breathing was heavy, and Hinler cradled her in his arms as she sobbed.

"That's Lonpearl's girl. Where is your father, child?" he asked.

The girl was too hysterical to answer. "The sun is going down. Whatever we do, we do it now," Andras warned.

"Dantish is dead," Markon said from his side.

Hinler looked at the four of them. What hope did they have? What hope of coming out of this alive? They could assault the village, a village that had never once fallen to the hand of man. Or they could sit on the edge of the village, waiting for the Stick People to show up and take their retribution. Neither choice was satisfactory.

"We guard Kochen. Keep him alive." Hinler looked up at the inky, black smoke pouring off the top terrace. "He may be the only chance we have."

They sat on the edge of the farmland as the sun went down. Four hunters, the corpse of an old man, a little girl, and an unseeing seer. Hinler squatted next to Kochen. "Wake up, Kochen. Wake up."

****

The Eye That Shields was anxious. He Who Makes the Drum Beat had wanted to stop, but The Eye had been unable to reach Kochen in his travels last night, so he demanded that they push forward in the night. Their pace had been steady but slow by torchlight. The riverbanks were easier traveling than the rocky wasteland they had come through.

Time crawled by for The Eye, and he must have dozed off, lulled to sleep by the rushing of the river. He had dreams of his youth, dreams of running through the forest with his friends, most of them dead a long time. He dreamed of the river that ran through the forest, and the girl that he lost his virginity to, next to those cool waters with no one around. He remembered how the sun played on her hair through the branches, the feel of entering her. His dreams were short-lived however, and he awoke with a wistful feeling. Questions the Sun was squatting next to him, gently shaking his shoulder and calling his name.

"Wake up. It is time for The Eye to open," he said. The Eye That Shields smiled at the man. He probably thought he was pretty clever. "We are here," Questions the Sun said.

"Where is here?"

"We are within sight of the Cliff People's village. He Who Makes the Drum Beat wishes to confer with you and make plans."

The Eye shivered. It was cold tonight, not a cloud in the sky. All of the day's heat had vanished when the sun went behind the mountains. It was not like the forest at all. It was hot during the day, freezing at night, what would possess people to live here?

213

The Eye That Shields rolled out of his litter, pulling his furs tight against the chill of the night. The air had some bite to it. He could sense the tension in the camp. The last time the warriors had come here, a beast had emerged from the ground and killed several of them. The wound was still raw, and he saw many of the warriors looking jumpy and tense. The daylight would do much to calm them. Dawn couldn't get here soon enough.

He found He Who Makes the Drum Beat sitting around a fire. Loudest Laugh sat to his left, emptiness clouding his face. The Eye felt his pain, saw the worry and the hurt in his heart, and he knew that Loudest Laugh would come through this pain stronger than he had ever been. He was glad that he had learned to love, though he wished he hadn't had to learn about loss in such an acute manner.

That they had been able to keep Loudest Laugh from running off into the night to look for Niviarsi was something of a wonder. That he stayed through the next day was even more wondrous. Perhaps the young man had turned a corner. The tale of his exploits in the forest and his loss had done much to change the tribe's opinion of him, but Loudest Laugh was in no state to reap the benefits of his newfound glory.

The Eye lowered himself to the ground. It was a tough process, as his body had stiffened over the course of the night. Sitting in a litter for an entire day was not an invigorating ordeal. No one spoke; they stared into the fire without saying a word. The Eye had to resist drifting off into the fire. It had been coming to him easier and easier over the last few days. He was not sure why, but it always seemed as if his mind was ready to slip from his body and travel through the world on its own.

"What is the plan?" He Who Makes the Drum Beat said. He was always deliberate and to the point. It was one of the many qualities that made him a great warrior.

"I must find Kochen. I was not able to contact him last night, and since we haven't passed him, I assume he is in the village. I will look, we will find him, and then we will take him, peacefully if we can."

"I am tired of killing," Loudest Laugh said.

"As are we all. This entire endeavor has cost our tribe dearly. I only hope that it is worth it," He Who Makes the Drum Beat said.

The Eye rubbed his hands through his gray hair and said, "If we cannot find Kochen, then we will all die. Any sacrifice that we may make is worth it. Loudest Laugh, will you stoke the fire for me?"

Loudest Laugh moved sullenly, putting dry wood into the fire, where it flared up immediately. The Eye focused on the flames, watching them dance, the coals at the bottom of the fire glowing with heat and flame. The heat bathed his face. He felt himself pull away and then he was off, his mind floating through the night, seeing without eyes.

He moved slowly over the farmland and then drifted up the stone terraces of the cliff village. He moved his mind through the walls of the dwellings. Many of them were empty. People slept in the ones that weren't, children, fathers, mothers, grandfathers, and grandmothers all slumbered. He moved methodically through the terraces, checking each dwelling with nary a sign of Kochen in sight. *Where was he?*

He floated to the uppermost terrace, where he had first seen Kochen slumbering in the night, his spark entering and leaving his body without his own knowledge. That was how The Eye had confirmed his gift. Had he known there would be this much blood, he might have ignored it. Who was to say what would have happened had he ignored his vision from the start? Perhaps Kochen would still be slumbering here, and many of his own people might still be alive. Or perhaps, the circle would have been

215

broken anyway, and Kochen would be dead by now, any hope of righting the balance of the world gone with him.

He moved through the sanctum. It looked different this time. Where last time, the sanctum had been an immaculate shrine to the natural order of things, now the dirt floor was covered in blood, pieces of flesh strewn about like rocks. The head priest sat with his back to her, staring into the fire, her bald head bathed in the orange light. The Eye watched her. He could sense her frustration as she failed to capture the vision that she so desperately sought.

Above her head, he could see her spark, half in and half out of her hair, struggling to pull free of her corporeal form. She had no gift. She would not see anything in the flames but that which she wished to see. Her spark would never be free.

There was movement in the sanctum. What The Eye had initially taken as a bundle of soiled blankets in the corner shifted, sitting up. It was a pitiable man, older than many, but still young enough to not be considered an elder. His body was in a miserable state. The fingers on his rope-bound hands were gone, and his face was criss-crossed with cuts layered over the top of bruises. He moaned pitiably. His lips moved silently, hateful words spewing out of his mouth.

The Eye moved into the sleeping quarters of the sanctum. Three priests were sleeping in the back, huddled under their blankets, caught in the midst of nightmares judging by the twitching and the grunts. One more priest sat in the corner, rocking back and forth, his head buried in his knees which were pulled up to his chest. There was no spark here, just three normal people and a broken-brained man with occasional sight. There was no Kochen either. *Where was he?*

He drifted back through the sanctum, and then he stopped.

216

"I see you," a voice hissed.

The Eye turned to the miserable bundle of flesh in the corner. How was this possible? How could this man see him? He sensed no spark from this one either. The Eye moved on.

"Don't you float away from me. I have something to tell you," the man whispered, anger dripping from his tongue. "Come closer."

The Eye looked at Lansa. She had heard nothing. The Eye had never encountered anyone other than Kochen that could see him in his mind's form. He was curious, so he drifted closer, using caution. He formed the words in his mind, "What is it you would have of me?"

"I am the last of my kind. When I am gone, the circle is broken, and it will never be set right again. I am the last of the Corn Men, the last link between the creator and man."

"What is a Corn Man?" The Eye asked, intrigued.

"We are men but not men. We balance the spirits. Should I die without passing my knowledge on, the balance will shift, and man will be no more."

"Then give your secrets to me."

The Corn Man shook his head. "It is not that simple. The things I know took decades to learn. I cannot give them to you in this time."

"What would you have me do?"

The Corn Man closed his eyes and leaned back in his corner. "I sense you. I see your thread. When I follow it, I see more men. Send them here. Liberate me that I might restore the balance."

"And if I do not?"

The Corn Man's eyes opened, purple clouds dancing around them, glowing in the gloom of the sanctum. "Then you can enjoy the rest of eternity in the pit of the stomach of whatever spirit decides to eat you and your men. Go!"

The Eye shuddered in his mind, the word was said with unseen power behind it. It pained him, shocked him, and when he awoke, he was back in his body, staring at the fire, blood dripping from his eyes and ears. He was out of breath, and on the verge of losing consciousness, but he resisted the urge.

Gasping, he said, "We go tonight. Tonight we battle for our future. We must go now."

He Who Makes the Drum Beat looked at The Eye, not believing his ears. Loudest Laugh looked similarly confused, the depressed look on his face displaced for the moment. They didn't have time for this.

"You heard me! Go! Get the men! Tonight, we either succeed, or we fail. There is no in-between." The Eye rose from his feet, and shouted into the night. "We fight! We fight!"

His voice carried across the camp, sleeping men rose next to their fires and looked at The Eye. They gripped their spears and murmured among themselves.

He Who Makes the Drum Beat stood next to The Eye. "Paint your faces," he yelled. "We take the village tonight."

****

He Who Makes the Drum Beat looked at the painted face of Loudest Laugh. Blacks and whites. He looked like a skeleton. Might he turn into one tonight? He hoped not. His brother was important to him; he didn't want him to disappear.

He Who Makes the Drum Beat dipped his hand into the red bowl of paint. He smeared it on his hand and then rubbed the paint onto the left side of his face, covering it as best as he could, which was a difficult task without water to see his reflection. On the other side, he covered his face in yellow. It was not meant for camouflage, it was meant to make him stand out in the night. One of the scouts said that there were fires on every level, so they wouldn't be working in total darkness. It was late, but the sun would not be up for a while. His men would need to know his orders when he shouted them.

He hefted his spear in his hand and checked the heavy wooden club on his belt. There would be blood tonight. The Eye said there must be. They were looking for a man that they would find at the very top of the village, in the sanctum. They would know him when they saw him. He would be maimed, grievously.

He knelt down on the ground and found a nice-sized rock, about the same size as his fist. He tied a rope around it and then looped the rope into a coil and threw it over his shoulder. The key here was silence and quickness. They did not know they were coming; their own fires had been set out of sight, low and unobtrusive, but the village didn't appear to be all that concerned about invaders to begin with. Speed, silence... these were the tools of the hunt. He was ready.

He Who Makes the Drum Beat walked over to Loudest Laugh, gripped his shoulders with his arm, and looked him in the eye. "If tonight is the last night I have, I am glad to have known you and called you brother."

Loudest Laugh looked at him, smiling. "I wish I could say the same." Loudest Laugh laughed. It echoed through the night, reaching the ears of all those in the camp. He Who Makes the Drum Beat was glad. There he was; there was the brother that he had known before tragedy befell him. He could go into battle now, relieved to know that whatever happened, his brother would still be his brother, whether he survived or not.

They crouched low, placing their feet firmly on the ground, avoiding sounds whenever they could. They moved through the night like deer, skirting around the farmland that contained the beast that had taken so many of his men the last time he was here.

****

Loudest Laugh moved as silently as he could, though he felt anything but silent. His mind was loud enough to wake the dead. *Was she one of them, a flesh-crazed creature like the one that they had killed? Was she out here now? Watching them?* He was distracted. This was not the way to enter battle. The warrior's mind must be free of thought. This was a lesson that his father had taught him. This was what made He Who Makes the Drum Beat such a good warrior, the lack of hesitation, the surety of knowing that whatever you choose to do can be naught but the right decision. He had never possessed that particular talent.

He was lost in these thoughts when he was tackled to the ground, a rough hand placed over his mouth. He did not recognize the face of his captor, and then he saw that there were several of them. A little girl hid behind the back of one of the men, his four-fingered hand resting on her head as she clung wide-eyed to his leg.

"Do not speak," his captor said, placing a knife on his throat. The pressure made it hard to swallow. "If you yell for help, this goes all the way in." They dragged him behind a stand of stunted trees. Loudest Laugh did not know the name of the trees, but they looked as twisted and sick as everything else in this forsaken part of the world.

A half-moon hung overhead, wisps of clouds sailed before it, the wind blowing the clouds to the east. It was dark, but, up close, there was enough moon for him to see by.

"Why are you here?" the man asked him. His face was wide, and he was missing his two front teeth.

"We are here for the seer."

"What do you want with him?" the man asked him, jabbing him in the throat with his dull stone knife.

"He is to save the world." The men around him looked at each other in the night, their faces unreadable in the shadows. The man with the knife to his throat pulled him off of the ground and stood him up. He dragged Loudest Laugh into the proximity of another man who was lying on the ground.

"Does he look like he can save the world?"

Loudest Laugh looked at the face of the man on the ground. It meant nothing to him. Was this the boy that he had captured? Was this the boy that he had seen in the forest, slung over the shoulder of another man? It was hard to say in the dark. "What happened to him?"

"He is gone. As you and your people should be."

"What do you mean he is gone?"

The four-fingered man cleared his throat before speaking. "He called a spirit, and he never came back."

Loudest Laugh looked at the men, trying to figure out if he had heard correctly. *Called a spirit?* Was that even possible? Did that explain the creature they had encountered in the woods?

Against his better judgment, he said, "I know someone who can help."

****

The Eye sat next to the fire, looking into the flames. It was easy to concentrate. The camp was quiet now. There was no one to disrupt him. He had to find Kochen. He stared into the flames. *Where are you?*

The flames danced in front of him, moving back and forth, rising falling, flaring brightly and fading briefly. The wind whipped the flames about, the tips breaking off and existing on their own for the length of a blinking eye. *Where are you, Kochen?*

221

A pair of hands wrapped around his throat. Strong hands, squeezing at his windpipe shut. His arms wheeled about, trying to beat his attacker, but his arms were old, frail, the skin thin as a blade of grass and draped over his bones. They had no effect on his attacker.

The Eye concentrated on the flames. He focused on their movement, he set his mind to the rhythm of the coals. It was his only chance.

****

They pressed up against the rock. Cold and jagged, the stone pressed into his flesh. They did not hear the beating of drums. The village was not watching. They were undiscovered. He Who Makes the Drum Beat pulled the coiled rope off of his chest and played it out so it wouldn't bunch up when he threw the rock. He saw the other warriors doing the same.

He looked above him, trying to find a crevice in the rocks. He spotted a likely one, and began twirling the rock at the end of the rope. He used its motion to send the rock arcing up over the wall of the terrace. It landed with a heavy thunk, and he pulled it towards him, hoping he had hit the crevice just right. He pulled and pulled, feeling the resistance in the rope. When it went slack, he stepped out of the way of the falling rock. It landed in a puff of dust on the canyon floor. To his right and his left, he saw men clambering up the side of the cliff face. He coiled his rope and slid it over his chest, the rock dangling at his hip. He moved to the rope of someone that had been more successful with their own toss, and he began to climb, cringing at every scrape of leather on rock and every pebble that tumbled to the ground, loosened by his ascent.

Hands helped him as he reached the top. They pulled him over the ledge, and he landed gently on the dusty ground of the terrace. Some men were already busy twirling rocks, and trying for the next terrace. He moved quietly, jogging lightly, his men following behind him. Everything was going perfectly.

He Who Makes the Drum Beat paused and looked for his brother. He was nowhere to be seen. Where was he? His worry only lasted for a second however, as one of the warriors fell from the terrace. His rock had not been secured. Footstep in the Dewy Grass would have been fine, just a little bruised, if he had not screamed out in the night as he fell. His voice was sharp, and the night carried it through the village. He had put them all in jeopardy.

From one of the houses, a man appeared, his eyes going wide at the sight of strange men in the village. He Who Makes the Drum Beat threw his spear at the man, striking him in the shoulder, not the throat as he had been aiming for. The man fell backwards into his house, screaming. Even if the rest of the village had not heard Footstep in the Dewy Grass' scream, there was no chance that they wouldn't hear the wounded man's scream. This wasn't going to be as easy as he thought.

****

They moved into the clearing, Loudest Laugh at knifepoint. He only saw her for an instant, but that instant told him everything that he needed to know. Before she dashed off into the shadows, he had seen Niviarsi's face, covered in blood... and chewing. She glanced over her shoulder briefly, smiling at him, her belly distended by the human flesh she now carried in her stomach. Raw, red wounds dripped blood and maggots where her breasts had been, and then she was gone. He knew now that she would always be gone, whether she was alive in the wild or not. The woman that he had known as Niviarsi was dead. She had died in the forest days ago.

"What was that?" said the man holding the knife to his neck, his voice tinged with shock and fear.

"That was a monster. It will not be back tonight, I think." The coldness in his voice was alien to him.

The group moved over to The Eye. Kochen was flung over the four-fingered man's shoulder, while the little girl clung to his leg. Loudest Laugh looked down at the corpse of The Eye. He felt sorrow well up in him.

"Is this the man you spoke of?" the man asked.

"Yes." One of the warrior's hissed through his teeth. Their last hope was lying on the ground, his face gnawed off, purplish marks around his throat.

Loudest Laugh didn't know what to say.

"You are no help to us," one of his captors said. "But we will not let you hurt us." The man holding the knife pressed it deeper into Loudest Laugh's throat.

****

They streamed out of their houses as if they all thought as one. They threw rocks from the terraces above. Men burst from the doors of the dwellings, spears in their hands and wild eyes in their heads.

He Who Makes the Drum Beat pulled his war club from his belt and twirled it in the air. The first swing dropped a man, his jaw askew. Rather than lie on the ground, the man rose again with fevered eyes. He brought the club down on top of the man's head. There was a crack, blood poured out, and the man's feet jittered in the dust of the terrace.

"Get to the next terrace," he bellowed. "Use those bows." Standing on the terrace, shoulder to shoulder with Water Like Breath and Questions the Sun, they formed a wall of death, protecting the men who were firing arrows at the terrace above. The Cliff People came at them, driven by something that He Who Makes the Drum Beat did not quite comprehend, undeterred at the sight of their neighbors and relatives lying in pools of blood on the ground..

Above them, the war drum sounded. There would be no sneaking to the top of the terraces. The entire village was at war, and as he popped the skull of another of the Cliff People, he wondered if any of them would be left at the end of all this.

****

The Eye awoke in darkness, a gray world devoid of life. It was the same, but different. Below him he saw the pallid form of Kochen, his body shrunken in upon itself, lying still on the ground as men surrounded Loudest Laugh, their movements made it look as if they were underwater. Kochen's spark was not there. He looked at his own body, ruined and useless, he would not be going back. His mind was filled with a calm that he had never known. It was only a matter of time before his spark faded. He had to find Kochen before that happened.

He focused all of his energy on the form of Kochen, not his body, but the form of his mind. The Eye built an image of Kochen's spark in his mind, bit by bit, trying to imagine the pattern of pulsing that he had observed a few nights ago for the briefest of moments. Orange light, expanding, contracting, branches shooting out every now and then only to shrink in upon themselves in orange loops of shadow.

Every human had a unique spark. Kochen's was no different. After he had constructed the image, he focused his mind upon it, allowing the rest of the world to melt away. The entire world became a dark void, an emptiness filled with only the constructed image of Kochen's mind. The Eye moved closer to the image, letting nothing exist but it, he called to it with his own mind. "Where are you? Call out to me."

225

There was no response. Wherever Kochen was, he could not hear. "Speak to me!" he commanded with all the focus of his mind forming his words into a sharp, powerful command. The void trembled, and there was a shadow of a response. It was not thought that he heard, but more of an emotion, a feeling of revilement and rejection.

"Speak to me!" he commanded, buoyed by the previous response. The void spasmed, it's blackness lightening, for the briefest instance, and then he was hit with a wave of images, primordial, violent. Their message was clear. Stay away. He had no intention of doing so.

"Speak to me!" he commanded one more time. The void burst, and The Eye was in a different place. It was still a black, lightless place, but he could sense other forms surging around him. It was underwater, his mind floated on the current, and he cast about for Kochen's spark. He was close; he was here, and he was in trouble.

The Eye moved through the water, trying to contain the terror that he felt when he felt the dark beings cruise by him in the darkness. The water swelled, and the beasts' movements created their own currents, tossing his consciousness around in their wake. But how could that be? The creatures must exist in both the spiritual and physical world at the same. As he pondered the implications of such a state of existence, he continued his journey through the waters.

In his mind, he sensed a point of heat in the cool blackness of the void. He focused on this point, drawing closer and closer to it, avoiding the looming shapes in the blackness. "Speak to me!" he commanded.

The voice of his mind shot through the water, sending a shockwave through its inky depths. The beasts around him squealed in rage, thunderous bellows, that would have shattered his ear drums were he in his human form. A wave of blue light shot through the water, and The Eye saw before him the largest creature he'd ever seen. It was a dark blob floating in the water, tendrils as thick as the trunk of any tree in the forest snaked off of its globular mass, thousands of them, snaking off into the distance for as far as the dim light would allow him to see. The shapes he had been passing in the dark were not multiple creatures. They were one creature, the largest creature the world had ever seen, slumbering in the depths of the water, unseen by man.

In the midst of the blob's jellied mass, he saw it, a faint glimmer of orange light floating in the darkness, Kochen, enveloped by the creature. The Eye moved in closer, keeping his mind focused on the orange spark, its light dimmed by the jellied mass around it, looking like nothing more than an extension of the creature's vast and alien body. But it was Kochen. He was stuck. He was fused into the body of a spirit.

The Eye went as far as he could without touching the spirit. He hovered a hair's width from the jellied mass. "Kochen. Can you hear me?"

Very faintly, there was a response, "I can't see. Where are you?"

"You are trapped in the body of a spirit. You have become one with this creature."

"How do I get out?" the voice responded, panic welling up in his words.

The Eye had no answer. He was playing on a field that man had never even glimpsed before, and his own spark was fading. There was only one thing he could think of, and it would mean his own doom... of that he was sure.

****

The sounds of battle neared the sanctum. Lansa stared into the fire, hoping for a vision. None was forthcoming. Through the flames, she saw the Corn Man sitting watching her. He was the reason. He was barring her from communicating with the spirits. He was the reason she was helpless in her greatest time of need.

Lansa rose from her seat, her bare feet trailing through the footstep-marred floor of the sanctum. She squatted down in front of the man. Despite losing all of his fingers, and a hundred other wounds, he smiled up at her, his mouth toothless and stained with his own blood.

"You're doing it aren't you?" The Corn Man did not speak. He simply continued to smile. Lansa grabbed his ear, and twisted it, wiping the smile off of the Corn Man's face. "You're blocking the spirits, aren't you?" she screamed.

The other priests appeared, worry on their faces. She hated the weakness in their eyes. "Block the door. Make sure that no one comes in here." They looked at her, hesitant, doubtful. The look on their faces infuriated her even more. "What are you waiting for?"

The priests looked at her the same way they had for the last couple of days. Lansa could tell that they doubted her, questioning her in their own minds. But they were all spineless and weak, unwilling to do what was right for the village and the people. They wanted to sit in the sanctum and maintain the status quo, tell people lies that everything was going to be alright. But they could be so much more; armed with the secrets of the Corn Men, they would never have to fear anyone again.

Lansa grabbed the Corn Man and dragged him across the dirt floor. He resisted, pounding on her with his stump hands, but Lansa was too strong for him, driven by her own mad fervor. She reached the edge of the pit where the fire burned, and she pushed the Corn Man in. He screamed in pain and then rolled out of the fire.

Lansa put her hands on her hips and sighed. *Was nothing ever as easy as it was supposed to be?* She dragged the Corn Man into the fire once more. The other priests tossed horrified looks over their shoulders, but they stood guarding the door, listening to the screams of the Corn Man as Lansa fought to burn the Corn Man alive.

****

He Who Makes the Drum Beat climbed up the last rope and landed with a thump on the top terrace. He was covered in blood, and bodies already crowded the ledge of the terrace when he first trod upon it. The top terrace was filled with women and children. They pelted his men with rocks. The warrior in him wanted to give the order to kill them, but he was human, so he let the women and children toss rocks at them. His only concern was the sanctum.

He stood outside of it, looking at its jagged rock walls. The door to the sanctum was thick wood, and when he tested the doorway, it would not budge. It was as he expected.

"Water Like Breath, put the women and children in one of those dwellings, and seal it up before they hurt someone with those rocks." Water Like Breath grabbed a few other warriors, and they herded the women and children into a home, along with some elder men and women. As for most of the village's men, they were dead now, lying in puddles of blood, maimed, stabbed. It was a shocking loss of life, and He Who Makes the Drum Beat did not feel particularly elated at the victory. They had never given up. Even when it was clear that they couldn't win, they had come at them, fighting to the death. He shook his head at the loss.

"Let's take down this door," he said to his men. They began pounding on the door with rocks and clubs. This was going to take some time, time that they didn't have. From the other side of the door, they could hear screaming. "Harder, faster," he implored his men, knowing that the balance of their world was at stake.

There was no going back. The Eye pushed his consciousness into the flesh of the creature, pressing through its jellied mass. He could feel the will of the creature push back, but The Eye would not be denied, so he pressed forward into its flesh. It howled, assaulting his mind with images of horror and destruction that The Eye could barely comprehend, but he pressed on, focusing his concentration on the orange spark. He pushed and pushed, and then he broke through into a hollow cavity within the beast.

Kochen's spark hung suspended in the air, the creature's flesh glistening with the light of Kochen's spark. Before Kochen could protest, The Eye surged forward, pressing his own consciousness into Kochen's. The world exploded. The Eye That Shields was no more.

****

Lansa could hear the banging on the door. Time was growing short. Perhaps there was already not enough time. The Corn Man's body was burnt all over, yet he still breathed. He even managed to look up at her and smile, his lips blackened by the fire. She grabbed his head, and shoved his face into the flames, holding it there though her own flesh burned, the pain sending shudders through her entire body. She screamed, and still the Corn Man fought.

When he stopped resisting her, she pulled her hand from the fire. It was not a hand anymore. The flesh was there, but she could feel nothing but pain. The hand did not work, and her mind was in much the same state. She turned to look at the other priests. They stood there, holding their weapons, looking at her to see what she was going to do next, fear in their eyes. The pounding at the door continued, and Lansa waited for the spirits to speak to her.

230

She didn't have to wait long.

****

He Who Makes the Drum Beat looked up to the sky when he heard the roar. It was not a roar that he had ever heard before. He wasn't even sure if it was actually a roar. The earth trembled beneath his feet, and the stars turned pink in the sky.

"We are too late."

Down below, a form had emerged from the ground. He had seen it before. Its white shape had murdered some of his warriors, killing them and dragging them down into the ground. He watched as the form approached the bottom of the cliff, and began clawing its way off the canyon floor. It's tail appeared, coming to a point, pairs of spindly claws and legs scrabbling at the dirt.

The circle was broken. There was no balance. A new enemy had emerged.

In the sky, there was another roar, and a shadow as big as a mountain appeared, winged and terrifying. The stars were not falling; bright pink drops dripped from its head, falling to the ground. One landed a short distance from where he was standing; the dirt melted away. He Who Makes the Drum Beat walked over to the hole and looked down. A pink light burned in the depths, receding further and further away as he watched.

"Don't let the drops hit you!" he yelled to his men, as the shadow circled above. The white creature had reached the bottom terrace. He gripped his spear. "I'll see you on the other side," he said to Questions the Sun. He said nothing back, just nodded and gripped his own spear tighter. "Unblock that door!" he yelled to Water Like Breath. He did as he was told, and the villagers huddled in the dwelling, their arms wrapped around each other, waiting for something bad to happen.

Then the creature above them roared again, pink bile erupting from its mouth in a shower of drops. They fell to the ground slowly, like fireflies hovering to the ground. The drops wouldn't have been hard to dodge, if it weren't for the sheer number of them. It was like trying to dodge individual drops of rain at the beginning of a storm. He watched as a drop struck a young warrior in the shoulder. It bored a hole through him in a matter of seconds, and he lay on the ground writhing in pain, until more drops bored even more holes.

How can we fight something that flies? "Run!" he screamed. The warriors broke, clambering down ropes to reach the terraces below, some dropping straight down, risking broken bones or worse. They would take their chances with the white creature. Perhaps some of them would make it past it. The villagers ran after them. The shadow circled overhead, dripping its rain down upon them.

****

The pounding on the door stopped. Lansa and the other priests waited. Doulk quivered at the entrance, his mind racing. "What was that sound?" he asked, quaking.

"It's a sign," Lansa said.

"A sign of what?" Birren asked.

"The spirits are here to help us." As she said this, pink drops began to appear in the sanctum. They appeared on the ceiling, boring holes through the stone above their heads. They clung to the ceiling and then fell. Birren held out her portly hand to catch one as it dropped to the ground. The drop of gleaming pink went straight through her hand and fell on the ground, where it continued its slow bore into the earthen floor and the stone beneath. She held her hand up to see it better in the light. She could see the fire burning in the pit through her hand. It was then that she started screaming. More drops appeared on the ceiling, and Lansa and the other priests threw the bar on the door, ready to escape the sanctum and take their chances with the Stick People on the other side.

"Don't open it," Caubrey yelled from the back room, fear in his voice, but it was too late.

The exit was completely black, as if the entire world had been extinguished. Harcha reached out towards the blackness, and as his hand touched the darkness, it shifted, and they saw that the light had not been extinguished. The form of a giant creature was blocking the door. It moved around now, turning, and before them the maw of a giant beast reared its head. Lansa only had a second to see the creature's monstrous face, filled with ridges of bone-like shadows and purple eyes that dripped black haze. Then its toothless mouth opened, and a glowing pink tongue emerged from the blackness of its throat. A cloud of pink mist erupted from its mouth, covering the priests in cold warmth that ripped through their bodies, liquefying them.

They didn't even have time to scream.

The shape lingered at the door, and then shot into the air. The sanctum crumbled in upon itself, the stone weakened by the pink rain and toppled over by shockwave of the creature's wings as it took flight. A single black feather drifted to the ground and then dissolved as if it were never there in the first place.

****

On the canyon floor, the white creature cut through the warriors and villagers alike. Whether they set foot on the farmland or not, the creature did not care. The circle was broken. The rules were gone. Death was everywhere, and He Who Makes the Drum Beat, the proudest and bravest warrior of his tribe, found himself screaming at the top of his lungs like the smallest babe of the Cliff People. It was not a war cry. It was a cry of fear, a cry that said, "I am not ready to die."

His legs pumped hard, the muscles fueled by fear and the thought of his family at home. Would there be spirits there, tearing through their village the same way they were here? Where could they run that the creatures could not get them? How do you hide from a creature that can fly and drip poison rain? How do you hide from a creature that can swim through the earth as if it were made from nothing more than water? The sky was not safe. The ground was not safe. Where could they run?

There was no choice. Rather than sit huddled and patient as some were doing, he surged across the farmland, his warriors and villagers running behind him. His breath surged out of him, as he felt the ground tremble beneath him. To his right, the creature leapt out of the ground, snapping up Water Like Breath as if her were an insect unwittingly sitting on the surface of a stream only to have a fish spring forth from the water. The creature landed with a splash, sending clods of earth and stone showering about He Who Makes the Drum Beat's body. Would any of them make it? Would any of them live to tell the horror of this day?

****

Kochen sat up. His body was foreign to him, and a part of him missed the deep blackness. His head pounded when he opened his eyes. He didn't understand what was happening. The sound was deafening, an unidentified roaring, the trembling of the earth, stones plummeting off the cliffs in the distance, and underneath it all, shrieking and screams of horror.

Perhaps he was still dreaming. Kochen rubbed at his eyes and looked around him. In the distance, he saw men running away with familiar strides and shapes. In the dark,

234

he could not tell who they were. At his feet, there was an unconscious man and the body of The Eye. Kochen squatted next to The Eye and shook him. It was no use. His body was cold. His life was over, maggots crawled on his mauled face.

The roar was closer now, and Kochen looked to the sky to see a form circling in the air, pink liquid dripping from its mouth. He watched as it swooped down upon the village, spraying its rain everywhere. Then he saw Bimisi erupt from the ground, chasing the villagers and Stick People running across the farmland.

He understood. This was his vision. The circle had been broken. There was nothing he could do. He couldn't save them.

The villagers hopped over the final ridge at the edge of the farmland, not even slowing down to acknowledge his presence. Kochen didn't know what to do, so he just stood there, peering up over the rise at the oncoming flood of people. He stared at their pumping legs, the dirt and dust flying up at their heels. Pink rain fell from the sky, and screams cut through the night.

Then he was there. Bimisi, his misshapen head bursting free from the earth in front of him. It hovered in front of him, pausing as if it recognized him.

"What are you waiting for?" he asked it.

Bimisi reared back on his thick tail, and plunged forward, his claws reaching for Kochen. Kochen locked eyes with Bimisi, his cold black eyes coming closer and closer. Just before it seemed that Bimisi's claw was going to stab right through Kochen, the beast stopped, and Kochen sensed its thoughts. Snatches of violence and hate came through like a tidal wave in his mind.

Kochen fought back, delivering his own images. Images of sunlight. Images of laughter. Images of caring. Bimisi writhed in the dirt, his tail thicker than five men standing side by side lashing the earth in fury. He sent more

235

images. An image of a woman standing in the river, the sun sparkling off of her hair, the river swirling around her ankles. Bimisi's thoughts were weaker now, softer, less violent.

The creatures thoughts flooded his mind softly. Kochen saw the cliff before there was a village, just a group of families living in a cave, a small patch of brown farmland on the valley floor. There was an image of the families grouped around a hole in the ground. A wriggling baby, an abomination with white skin and a dented head was placed in the hole... and they raked the dirt into the hole, drowning out the baby's cries with earth.

Kochen knew. He knew the truth. Bimisi stopped writhing, and it regarded him with those beady black eyes. He understood. Kochen walked up to Bimisi, his massive head hanging above his own, and he placed his hands on the side of Bimisi's tortured face.

****

Loudest Laugh sat up in the clearing, his head filled with fog and pain. He screamed in fright as he turned around to regard the scene unfolding behind him. The seer was there, the boy visionary, standing on his tiptoes, caressing the face of the murderous creature that had killed so many of their warriors. In the sky, a shadow flew, dripping glowing pink poison from the sky. It looked as if the sky was falling.

"What are you doing?" he yelled to the seer.

He did not reply, but as he watched, the seer's hands began to glow, a bright yellow light erupting from his fingertips and tracing its way through the creatures body. The light was too bright for Loudest Laugh. He raised his arm to shield his eyes against the brightness, catching only a glimpse of the seer's shadow.

236

There was a loud screech, and then the light faded. When he lowered his arm, the creature was lying on the ground, its body still, its swollen black tongue lolling out of its mouth. The white skin erupted in a hundred different places, and then began to shrivel and shrink as he watched. The skin tightening to the bones, as if the moisture were sucked out of the creature, the ribs of its tail jutting up to the sky. The seer walked across the farmland, heading to the village, calling for the creature in the sky to come down.

Loudest Laugh meant to follow him, but a pair of rough hands grabbed him by the arm and pulled him away. It was his brother, He Who Makes the Drum Beat.

"We must go," he said.

"We must see," Loudest Laugh said.

He Who Makes the Drum Beat dragged Loudest Laugh away. Loudest Laugh only gave half-hearted resistance.

They were by the river when the sky lit up, filled with a brilliant white light, a roar shook the world and sent ripples across the river. They ran, wondering what other horrors the night held for them.

Chapter 29:

Rebirth of the Past

Kochen strode across the farmland, the horror of his past gone, decaying upon the ground. For so long Bimisi had been a part of his life, and now it was just a set of thick ribs and desiccated skin lying in the dirt. But with Kochen's victory had come a price, the price of knowledge. The knowledge rattled around in his skull, images of the past, images of the birth of the spirits and their true relationship with humankind.

They were not separate; they were not enemies held in check by the checks and balances of the creator. That was a half-truth, twisted by the blessedly short memories of man. The spirits were man, man at their worst, humans aggrieved by their own kind, twisted and turned into slaves of their own misery, held in check only by the goodness of the bulk of mankind, a reminder from the creator to treat others well.

The priests were not a waste of time at all. They weren't right, but they weren't wrong either. Lansa had been the key, the linchpin to the whole thing, as had the head priests before her who had led the tribe in a moral and just manner. Her crimes, the crimes of their tribe had upset the balance, unshackling the spirits, sending them into a rage.

Above his head, another spirit flew, a newborn spirit, unaware of his own power. Kochen would take care of it, as he had taken care of Bimisi, inhaling his memories, his pain, his past, and leaving nothing but an empty husk.

For the fledgling spirit above, he would offer the same... he would offer release, and in doing so, right the balance of the world once more.

Kochen climbed a rope to the top of the first terrace, walking past the bodies that rotted in the dirt. Twisted bodies, hacked with clubs, axes, knives, and spears, some filled with arrows, some dotted with hundreds of holes. The ground looked porous now, the pink rain continuing to bore its way into the earth.

Kochen climbed to the second terrace, to find more unfamiliar faces. On the third terrace he saw her, his mother lying face up on the ground, an arrow through her chest. Kochen felt nothing for her, as she felt nothing for him after his father died. He simply moved past her and continued his ascent, noting the faces, the carnage. This would all have to be undone.

On the top terrace, Kochen could not resist the urge to examine the sanctum. He had dreamed once of being the head priest and guiding the people of the village to a better life. Were they worth it? Were they worth guiding? Not according to anything he had seen. His village was a travesty, a mockery built on twisted knowledge that had somehow worked for hundreds of years.

Was Lansa in there? What about Harcha? Doulk and Birren? Did poor Caubrey suffer the same fate as the others? What were their last moments like? What had led her to disrupt the balance of the world? Where was the cool logic that Lansa had used to guide the village so faithfully? A thought came to him... he was the reason. He was what had started this all. It all led back to the night his father had died. It all led back to his visions, his ability to see. He would make it right. He would put the world back the way it had been.

A roar split the night, breaking Kochen free from his thoughts. He looked up into the sky to see him floating up there, his shadow blotting out large chunks of stars in the night. Kochen began the ascent in the dark, not worried about his own life. He felt for each handhold and foothold as he climbed the cliff face, his arms straining under his own insignificant weight. He thought about the day he had been made to carry water. He went into that space that is made in the mind when one experiences draining physical labor, that nowhere space where the mind engages in thought rather than expose itself to the pain of exertion and exhaustion.

His mind wandered over his whole past, all the events that had led to today, and where those events would likely lead him the day after next. The truth was he didn't know. He did know that he would never let himself become a pawn in the games of others again. The consequences were too much for him to bear.

He reached the top of the cliff, covered in sweat with the sky beginning to lighten. The shadow circled over the village. Kochen took a deep breath and steeled himself for what needed to be done. He walked back and forth in the sandy soil of the Up Top. Then he ran as fast as his legs would go and dove into the air, his heart leaping into his chest, screaming to release the fear of dying.

He plummeted through the air, thumping into the back of the spirit below. He grabbed a hold of the creature's shadows, bony, black protuberances that stuck out of his body. The creature thrashed, and Kochen focused on the creature's pain. He could feel it radiating from its body. It roared as if it did not want to give up its secrets, but Kochen concentrated harder, opening his mind to the pain that was sure to come.

The creature flew straight into the sky, its wings buffeting the air and the shadows cracking in resistance. Straight up they flew towards the half moon, and Kochen wondered just how high the world went. Suddenly, the creature dropped, plummeting to the ground. Kochen dug his hands into the shadowy folds of the creature's skin, gripping as tight as he could, his heart thumping in his chest. He focused, melding his mind to that of the creature in his hands.

He saw the pain. He saw the outrage of Jib, the Corn Man. Born out of Lansa's rage and violence, Jib had returned, a spirit with vengeance on its mind, an unfinished task in its heart. Kochen and Jib's mind curled around each other, entwining, two thoughts becoming one. Kochen understood. Jib understood. They plummeted faster, the air rushing through Kochen's hair. There would be no stopping.

They landed in the sandy soil of the Up Top, Kochen smashing into the creature's back as it crashed into the ground. There was a flash of light, and everything went black. When he awoke, he could not move. His body was busted and sore. Bones were broken and out of place. But he still breathed. He felt the body of Jib begin to dissolve beneath him, fading away into the sandy soil underneath.

In his mind, he combed through the knowledge in his head, the secrets that Jib had imparted to him. The Corn Men would continue, but for how long? Kochen would balance the world, alone on the Up Top, hoping that another would come to continue the tradition. It was a temporary solution, but temporary was good.

Kochen crawled across the sandy soil, moving Jib's thick bones out of his way. He made it to the wooden shack that had rested on the roof of the world for the last hundred years, and he began his watch. He was no longer Kochen, merely another in a continuing line of Corn Men. He sang his song, mending the ways of the world, sewing the circle back together with his very being. It was to be a lonely watch.

241

Epilogue

He ran throughout that first night, the horror of the river far behind him when he stopped. He spent the next handful of nights camping underneath the open sky, hunting and gathering during the day. Ghulish sat on the edge of his own campfire in this unfamiliar land. It was dry, rocky, and filled with nothing but small brush, snakes, the occasional rodent, and stands of cacti. Ghulish owned nothing except for the knife in his pocket and a spear he had fashioned from a long dead branch he had found on the ground. He had no idea where the branch had come from, as there wasn't a tree to see for days.

He sat on the edge of the fire, enjoying its heat, and wondering what he should do. He could never go home; of that, he was sure. He had thrown his life away, become an exile, and now there was nothing for him to do. Ghulish didn't know what had possessed him to attack Kochen on the banks of the river. He supposed it was just grief, grief at losing close friends to protect someone who was little more than a boy, incapable of anything greater than an erection upon seeing a naked woman.

Ghulish picked a piece of meat off of a field mouse that he had captured in the heat of the day, a small meal supplemented with a handful of fruit from blooming cacti. He was starving. He wondered how long the dry, rocky terrain stretched. He could head back to the forest, pretend that he was a from a different village. Maybe the Stick People would let him stay there. Maybe he should push on through the rocky wilderness and find out what was on the other side.

He was pondering his future, when he heard a noise. He heard the sound of shuffling footsteps somewhere beyond the ring of light his meager fire cast. He stood up and peered into the darkness, his vision insufficient for the task due to staring at the fire.

From the darkness, he heard giggling.

"Who is it? Who's there?"

There was more giggling, this time behind him, the same voice. How had it moved all the way around him without him hearing? It was a woman's voice he thought. *What would a woman be doing way out here all on her own?*

Ghulish hefted his spear, and put on a show of not being scared. "Whoever it is, come out now, and I won't hurt you."

Laughing... unhinged laughing from the darkness.

"You're making me angry. Show yourself!"

There was no sound. Ghulish looked into the murk surrounding him, trying to identify the source of the voice. He jumped when the voice spoke right behind him. "Here I am," the voice said. Ghulish turned around to see a woman, bundled up in furs. She was beautiful, but something was off about her face. It was slack on one side, as if it were dead. Still, a beautiful woman with half a face was better than no woman at all.

"What are you doing out here?" he asked her.

She only smiled, a queer half-smile, white teeth, and a glimmer in her eyes. "I'm cold."

Ghulish put his spear down, and ushered the woman next to the fire. She sat down gracefully, and Ghulish sat next to her. He held the remains of his cooked mouse out to her, but she shook her head giggling.

"Who are you?" he asked.

There was still no answer. She just rubbed her shoulders underneath her furs.

"Are you still cold?"

She nodded her head. "I'm freezing." She smiled at him again, looking at him from the corner of her eyes.

Ghulish scooted closer to the woman and put his arm around her, in an effort to warm her. "Where are you from? Is there a village around here?"

"I am from far away," she said.

They sat in silence for some time, until Ghulish couldn't stand it anymore. "Are you still cold?"

She looked at him, her eyes glimmering in the night, and she put her hand on his crotch. "Yes," she said.

Ghulish couldn't believe his luck. The woman pushed him down on the ground, her back to the fire so that all he could see was her silhouette in the darkness. She fumbled with his loincloth, until she had freed what she wanted, and then she straddled him, riding him in the dark. She was wet underneath, but definitely cold. He attempted to remove the furs from around her shoulders, but she grabbed his wrists and pushed them into the sandy soil.

It was over quickly. He moaned into the darkness, his breath pluming in the air. She leaned forward, and her furs fell open. Something fell and hit him in the face, then something else did the same. He leaned forward, the woman still sitting on his lap and picked something off of his chest. He held it up to the firelight to see its squirming shape. A maggot. His stomach turned and he shoved the woman off of him, she fell backwards, the furs falling off of her shoulders. Where her breasts were supposed to be, there were only shadows against her pale skin.

Ghulish screamed, but not for long. She was on top of him again, dripping maggots from the wounds on her chest, her hands around his throat, that queer half-smile beaming in the night.

"Go to sleep. Shhh. Go to sleep."

****

When she was done, Niviarsi rose from the ground. She searched her lover's body, finding what she needed. With his knife, she began sawing at his body, cutting it into manageable chunks. She roasted them over the pitiful fire, stoking it with her lover's clothing. He wouldn't need it anymore.

When the outside of the flesh was nice and black, she popped the tasty morsel in her mouth, chewing in the silence, her only company the hiss and pop of more flesh on the crackling fire. Her lover tasted great.

She stood around the fire, naked, and she placed her hands on her belly. It moved... she felt it move. She was going to be a mother. She would need more food for her baby, but first... she would need to feed if her baby was to grow strong.

Niviarsi squatted next to her lover and chopped with the stone knife, grunting. The bones were hard, too hard. Fingers were easy to slice off as were testicles, but a different tool was needed for an entire forearm.

She searched in the darkness for a rock, something jagged and heavy. She found one, hard and gray. She raised it above her head and brought it down on her lover's elbow. The crunch was satisfying, but it was not enough to sever the arm, so she brought it down again. Cold blood splattered her bare chest, and she smiled.

When she had finished, her entire body was covered in blood, but she didn't care. She had the fire to keep her warm... and the flesh.

Holding the cooked arm of her lover to her mouth, she took an impossibly large bite. She chewed thoughtfully, and then looked down at her stomach. "When you are born, I think I shall call you Farway."

She felt movement in her stomach, as if the baby growing inside her approved of the name. She didn't know why, but the name sounded right. She took another bite,

and planned the life of her unborn child, Ghulish's grease
running down her chin and dripping on her bulging belly.

###

Be sure to check out

The Abbey

By
Jacy Morris

Here is a sneak preview:

THE ABBEY

He would make him scream. So far they had all
screamed, their unused voices quaking and cracking with
pain that was made even worse by the fact that they were
breaking their vows to their Lord, their sole reason for
existence. Shattering their vows was their last act on earth,
and then they were gone. Now there was only one left. A
lone monk had taken flight into the abbey's lower regions, a
labyrinthine winding of corridors and catacombs lined with
the boxed up remains of the dead and their trinkets.

Brenley Denman's boots clanked off of the roughhewn, blue stone as he trounced through the abbey's
crypts, following the whiff of smoke from the monk's
torch and the echo of his harried footsteps. His men were
spread out through the underworks, funneling the monk
ahead of them, driving him the way hounds drove a fox.
The monk would lead them to his den, and then the prize
would be theirs. And then the world.

He held his torch up high, watching the flames
glimmer off of golden urns and silver swords, ancient
relics of a nobility that had long since gone extinct, their
glory only known by faded etchings in marble sarcophagi,
the remaining glint of their once-prized possessions, and
the spiders who built their webs in the darkness. Once they
were done with the monk, they would take anything that
glittered, but first they needed the talisman, the fabled
bauble that resided at the bottom of the mountain the
abbey was built on.

Throughout the land, legends of the talisman had
been told for decades around hearthfires and inns
throughout the isles. Then the tellers had begun to vanish,
until the talisman of Inchorgrath and its stories had all but
been forgotten. But Denman knew. He remembered the
stories his father had told him while they sat around the

fire of their stone house, built less than ten yards from the cemetery. His father's knuckles were cracked and dried from hours in the elements digging graves and rifling pockets when no one was looking. He knew secrets when he saw them. His father had first heard the story from the old Celts, the remains of the land's indigenous population, reduced to poverty and begging in the streets. His father said the old Celts' stories were two-thirds bullshit and one-third truth. They told of a relic, a key to the Celts' uprising and reclamation of the land, buried in the deepest part of the tallest mountain on the Isles. Of course, they spoke of regeneration and the return of Gods among men as well, but the relic... that was the important part. That was the part that was worth money. And now, he was here, with his men, ready to make his fortune.

He heard shouts, but it was impossible to tell where they were coming from. Sound echoed and bounced off of the blue, quartzite stone blocks, warping reality. He chose the corridor to his right, quickening his pace, his long legs eating up the distance. His men knew not to start without him, but you never knew when a monk would lash out, going against their discipline and training and earning a sword through the throat for their duplicity. That would be unacceptable to Denman. The monk must scream before he died.

His breathing quickened along with his pace, and he could feel the warmth of anticipation spread through his limbs as his breath puffed into the cold crypt air. Miles... they had come miles through these crypts, twisting and turning, burrowing into the secret heart of the earth, chasing the last monk who skittered through the hallways like a spider. The other monks had all known the secret of the abbey, the power it harbored, the relic it hid in its bowels. To a man, they had sat on their knees, their robes collecting condensation in the green grass of the morning, refusing to divulge the abbey's mysteries.

They had died, twisted, mangled and beaten. But still, all he could pull from them were the screams, musical expulsions of the throat that he ended with a smile as he dragged the razor-fine edge of his knife across their throats. Their blood had bubbled out, vivid against the morning sun, to splash on the grass.

When there was only one left, they had let him go. The youngest monk in the abbey, grown to manhood, but still soft about the face, his intelligent eyes filled with horror, stood and ran, his robe stained with the pooled blood of the monks that had died to his left and right. He was like one of the homing pigeons they used in the lowlands, leading them to home... to the relic. They had chased him, hooting and hollering the whole way, their voices and taunts driving the monk before them like a fox. The chase would end at his burrow; it always did.

Ahead, he heard laughing, and with that Denman knew that the chase was at an end. He rounded one last corner to see the monk being worked over by his men, savage pieces of stupidity who were good for two things, lifting heavy objects and killing people. Denman waved his hand and they let the suffering monk go. The monk sagged to the ground, his head bent over, his eyes leaking tears. He sobbed in silence.

Denman stood in the secret of the crypt, a room at the heart of the mountain, the place where legends hid. How deep had they gone? At first there had been stairs, but then they had reached a deeper part of the crypt where the corridors twisted and turned, the floor pitched ever downward. Time and distance had lost all meaning in the breast of the world. How long had it taken them to carve this place, the monks working in silence to protect their treasure? Hundreds of years? A thousand?

The room was simple and small, as the order's aesthetics demanded, filled by Denman and the nine men that he had brought to take the abbey's secrets. Wait, one was missing. He looked at his men, brutal pieces of humanity, covered in dirt, mud and blood. The boy wasn't there. Denman shrugged. He would find his way down eventually.

The walls of the room were blue-gray, stone blocks stacked one on top of the other without the benefit of mortar, the weight of the mountain providing the only glue that was needed. The only other features of the room were an alcove with two thick, tallow candles in cheap tin holders and an ancient oak table.

The smoke from his men's torches hung in the air, creating a stinging miasma that stung his eyes. Brenley Denman squatted next to the monk and used his weathered hand to raise the monk's head by his chin. He looked into the monk's eyes, and instead of the fear that he expected to see, there was something else.

"What is this? Defiance?" he asked, amused by the monk's bravado. Denman stood and kicked the monk in the mouth with his boot, a shit-covered piece of leather that was harder than his heart; teeth and blood decorated the stones.

"Where is it?" he asked the monk. There was no answer. Denman had expected none. Say what you will about the Lord's terrestrial servants, but they were loyal... which made everything more difficult... more exhilarating. Denman was a man that loved a challenge.

He handed his torch to one of his men, a broken-faced simpleton whose only gifts were strength and the ability to do what he was told. Denman knew that he would need both hands to make the monk sing his secrets.

"Hand me the Tearmaker," he said to another of his men. Radan, built like a rat with stubby arms and powerful legs, reached to his belt and produced a knife, skinny and flexible, designed not so much for murder as it was for removing savory meat from skin and fat. It made excellent work of fish, and it would most likely prove delightfully deft at making a tight-lipped monk break his vows.

As he reached out to take the proffered knife from his man, the monk scrambled to his feet and dove for the alcove. Before they could stop him, the monk grasped both of the candle sticks and yanked on them. The candlesticks rose into the air. Rusted, metal chains were affixed to their bases, and they clanked against the surrounding stone of the alcove as the monk pulled on them.

The distant sound of stones grinding upon stones reverberated throughout the crypt. Somewhere, something was moving. Denman glared at the monk. The robed figure dropped the candlesticks and turned to face them. With his head cast downward, he reached into the folds of his robe and produced a rosary. He folded his hands and began to pray, beads moving through his fingers, his lips moving without making sound.

The crypt shook as an unseen weight clattered through the halls of the crypt. Dust fell from the ceiling, hanging in the air, buoyed upwards by the tumbling smoke of their torches.

"What have you done?" Denman asked.

The monk did not respond. Instead, he reached into the hanging sleeve of one of his robes and produced a small stone thimble, roughly-made and ancient. It was shiny and black, the type of black that seemed to steal the light from the room. The monk put it up to his mouth, hesitated for a second and then swallowed it, grimacing in pain as the object slid down his throat.

In the hallway behind them, the grinding had stopped. The crypt was silent, but for the guttering of the torches and their own breathing. "Go see what happened," he said to the oaf and the rat. The other men followed them, leaving Denman alone with the monk and his unceasing, silent supplications to the Lord above.

Denman forced the monk onto the oak table. He offered little resistance. With Tearmaker in his hand, Denman began to carve the skin lovingly off of the monk's fingers. First, he carved a circle around the man's fingers, then a line. With the edge of his knife, he prodded a corner of the skin up, and then, grasping tightly, he ripped the skin away from the muscle and bone, dropping the wet flesh onto the ground. He did this to each finger, one by one. Sweat stood out on Denman's brow, and the monk had yet to scream. He hadn't so much as gasped or hissed in pain. He was turning out to be more work than he was worth. Except for the blood pulsing from his skinned fingers, he appeared to be asleep, his eyes softly closed.

"Where is it, you bastard?" There was no response but for the bleeding.

Denman pulled the monk's robe up around his waist. It was a quick jump, but he was eager to be done with the man on the table. Usually, he would take his time with a challenge like the monk, savoring the sensation of skin ripping from muscle and bone, but he could feel the weight of the mountain about him, its walls shrinking with every minute. Sweat covered his body, and the monk's calm demeanor was unnerving.

Radan rounded the corner at a run, his body dripping with sweat and panic on his face. He skidded to a stop, his boots grinding dust into the blue stones. "We're sealed in here," he said.

Denman looked at the monk lying on the table. His hand gripped Tearmaker tight. "What have you done?" The monk lay there, his eyes closed, a look of peace on his face. "What have you done!" he screamed, jabbing the knife into the monk's ribs. Then Denman saw the monk's hands. Where before his index and pointer finger had been reduced to skinless chunks of muscle and bone dripping blood on the table, there was now skin. "Impossible," Denman whispered.

The monk's eyes snapped open, and finally,
Denman got the scream that he had been waiting for.

Be sure to check out

THIS ROTTEN WORLD

By Jacy Morris

Here is a sneak preview:

THIS ROTTEN WORLD

Two Months from Now

The sun beat down upon him. Beads of sweat ran down the sides of his face. One ran down the side of his nose and perched on the edge of his upper lip. He blew the bead of sweat into the air and grunted as he pulled on the coarse rope. His hands, now callused and blistered after days on the roof, lumbered with robotic automaticity.

His mind wandered as his body engaged in actions that had essentially become second nature. He pulled on the rope some more. In the back of his mind, he registered the coarseness of the rope on the exposed parts of his hands. He had wrapped some shreds of an old shirt around his hands a few days ago, when he first began his work.

His shoulders were red from exposure to the sun. In the past, he would have worried about increasing his risk for melanoma, but not anymore. Now it was perfectly fine to smoke, drink, and sit in the sun for hours upon hours. Hand over hand, he hauled on the rope, leaving bits of skin and blood behind on the frayed, hempen strands. Finally, he hauled his prize up onto the roof, a heavy, blue bowling ball with a metallic finish, swirls upon swirls playing on its surface. It looked like a small planet sans continents. The sun lit every metallic piece of glitter embedded in its plastic. The bowling ball rested in a cradle that he had fashioned out of rope. Crimson drops of gore dripped from the bowling ball onto the loose pebbles that covered the roof of the gas station.

He looked off into the distance, wiping the sweat from his brow. His arm dropped to his side, and the sweat that he had wiped off ran down his fingers and dripped onto the roof. He flexed his aching fingers and looked at the yellow and red gas station sign. $4.19 for a gallon of gas. He had a feeling that it was actually worth a little more these days.

The man pulled a cigarette from a bag that sat on the ground next to a shiny, silver air conditioning vent. He lit the cigarette, looking at the naked lady lighter he had pulled from a house two weeks past. He wondered if he would ever see a naked lady again, a living one at least.

He dropped to the ground and leaned his back against the air conditioning vent. The heat of the flimsy metal burned his skin, but he no longer cared. He took a deep drag off of the cigarette, enjoying the burn of the smoke as it curled its way into his lungs. He looked up at the azure sky, wishing for rain. Hell, a cloud would do just fine... anything for a brief respite from the relentless sun. There was only one thin wisp of a cloud floating through the sky, a mocking wisp with a shape like nothing. He took another drag from his cigarette, and closed his eyes.

He awoke to the pain of burning on his fingers. The man tossed the cigarette across the roof and looked at his ruined digits. Red blisters and pain, exactly what he needed... more blisters and pain. He stood up, shaking off the soreness that had seeped in unbidden during his brief respite.

The man picked up the bowling ball by the rope and dangled it out over the side of the gas station roof. He peeked over the edge, already prepared for what he was about to see. Rotten faces peered up at him, scraps of flesh hanging off of their cheeks, their arms raised up to him as if they were at a concert and he was the object of their affection. But that's not how it was... he was just a meal, standing on the roof of a gas station, holding a bowling ball tied up in a rope. He swung the ball in an arc, releasing it at an angle that sent it hurtling straight down.

He watched it fall, tracking its movement. The zombie's head exploded like an egg. Instead of yellow yolk, red chunks of brain erupted from the shattered skull. He almost laughed as the now headless body fell over to the side slowly like R2-D2 after one of those little creatures blasted him with electricity in the beginning of Star Wars. He would have laughed if it weren't for the fact that two more corpses were shambling down the street, ready to take up watch at the bottom of the wall. A hundred more clawed at the rough red brick of the gas station.

Bodies littered the ground all around the squat building. The moans of the dead drifted through the air. He couldn't wait for the sun to kill him. But in the meantime... he pulled on the rope.

The sun beat down upon him. Beads of sweat ran down the sides of his face. One ran down the side of his nose and perched on the edge of his upper lip. He blew the sweat into the air and grunted as he pulled on the coarse rope. His hands, now callused and blistered after days on the roof, lumbered robotic automaticity.

Be sure to check out

Killing
the
Cult

By Jacy Morris

Here is a sneak preview:

KILLING THE CULT

Chapter 1: A Letter in the Mail

It was the letter that started it all. It was the
proverbial snowball that turned into an avalanche. Matt
discovered the letter in his mailbox one sun-drenched
afternoon after finishing his daily three-mile jog. At first,
he had been ecstatic; the letter was from his daughter, Cleo,
whom he hadn't heard from in ten years. He sat on the
couch with a brass letter opener, his hand shaking with
anticipation. The letter opener was his wife's. It was a
gaudy piece, not the type of thing he would have bought
himself. The handle was shaped like an eagle feather with
the blade in the shape of a claw. She hadn't wanted it when
they got the divorce, but not because it was ugly and stupid.
She hadn't wanted anything. She could still hear her saying,
"You can have it all, Matt. I don't want a single item that
will remind me of you. I just want to pretend like we never
even met." He thought it was a stupid sentiment. After all,
she already had one thing that would always remind her of
him... their daughter.

But that's the way things were. That part of his life
had gone dark, the light snuffed out the moment they drove
away with only their clothes and personal items in the car.
So now, here Matt sat, a letter from his daughter in his
hands... the first communication from his daughter in ten
years. He had dreamed of this moment so often over the
years that he couldn't believe it was finally here. He
hesitated, the blade of the letter opener pressed against the
plain white paper of the envelope. *Bad news or good news?*
he wondered. Maybe his wife was dead. Maybe his
daughter wanted him to be a part of her life again. Maybe

he was forgiven for the past. The idea made him shake, and his ears and face flushed with warm blood simply from allowing himself to hope for such a possibility. He knew his fantasies were pathetic. Ten years was a long time, certainly long enough for a wife and a daughter to forget about a man like him. It was probably just a request for money.

He rose from his recliner, leaving the envelope and the letter opener on the coffee table. He didn't want to open the letter, and he couldn't, not yet. Matt walked to the kitchen to grab a beer instead. He tried not to look at the piles of dirty dishes and the empty Chinese takeout boxes on the counter, but the buzz of flies told him these things were there whether he looked at them or not.

He yanked the refrigerator door open and pulled out a bottle of Budweiser. He popped the bottle cap off and threw it into the open garbage can. It bounced off the pile of garbage and clanked onto the floor. Rejected, just as he had been once. Matt just left it there. That's all it really deserved.

Through the back window of his kitchen, he could see the backyard, a wild and unkempt place that had once been a beautiful playground where beautiful memories were created. He looked at the old rusted swing set and remembered when it had been brand new, right after the move. He saw his daughter, tiny, so fragile, flying into the air and then back down again, in a semi-circle of happiness as he put his hand in her back and pushed her forward for another ride to the moon. "To the moon, Daddy! To the moon!" That's what she always squealed whenever he had pushed her on the swing. Maybe that's what the letter was. Maybe Cleo had become an astronaut.

Matt took a sip of his beer, enjoying its bitterness. It paired well with the bitterness of his old memories. He stood in the kitchen, drinking and letting his regrets wash over him. He killed the beer in fifteen minutes and then set the empty bottle down on the counter next to the others. It was only right. Empty bottles belonged together.

He walked back into the living room filled with purpose. Without giving himself time to second guess, he grabbed the letter opener, jammed it under the flap, and ripped open the envelope. He pulled the letter free and unfolded a single yellow page. The handwriting was small, neat, just as her mother's had been.

He read through the letter once, and then he read it again, looking at every word as if some sort of code were hidden among the words. But there was no code. It was what it was. He sat down in his recliner and leaned his head back, a thousand thoughts running through his head. *What the hell had happened? How could this be?*

Matt picked the letter up again, hoping that he had experienced some sort of temporary brain embolism or stroke, and that this time, the words in the letter would make more sense.

Dear Dad,

I know that's it's been a long time since we talked, and I hope that this letter finds you well. I've gone through some hard times recently, stuff that I won't bore you with, but know that some of those hard times were because you weren't around. I used to be angry with you. I used to be angry that you didn't fight harder for me when you and Mom split. But I know now that it took both of you to rip my life apart.

It wasn't easy for me growing up without a father, especially since you were so great when you were there. But I want you to know that I've gotten over it. I've gotten over it all. I'm in a good place now, a happy place.

The reason you're receiving this letter is because my relationship with you, and with Mom, has prevented me from attaining my bliss... and I want that. I want it so bad.

That's why I sent you this letter. I'm not doing it to make you feel bad, and if you do, please don't. Life's too short to feel anger or hurt. I sent you this letter so that I might close the wound of my past, so that I might better be able to enjoy the present.

This may all seem weird to you, but believe me, the weirdest thing out there isn't me... it's the world. I want you to be happy. I believe that a great calamity is coming, a judgment that will change the face of the world as we know it. Only those that have truly enjoyed life will be spared, so please, Dad, if you do one thing for me, live your life to the fullest, and know that I forgive you, and in my heart, I have found the love for you that was hidden for so long.

Yours truly,
Cleo

Matt read the letter again for the fifth time. He set it on the end table and looked at his dingy living room. The parts of the room that he didn't use were covered in a layer of dust. Old newspapers were stacked on the coffee table even though he had cancelled his subscription six months ago when they had streamlined the format. More empty bottles were stashed around the house, and the floor was so dirty that he doubted he could ever get it clean.

It was the living room of an old forgotten man, but he was only 42, still capable of outrunning 90% of the population. He hadn't slowed a bit physically, but in his mind and in his heart, he had been dead ever since the divorce.

The letter... that damned letter. Something was wrong. It sounded nothing like the little girl he knew, and immediately, he blamed Naomi.

His first instinct was to blame his wife, to say, "This is what happens when you raise your child in such a permissive manner." But Naomi had never been the problem. He had always been the problem. His daughter was twenty now, and she was old enough to think for herself. When life had taken off the training wheels, she had careened into something that he didn't particularly care for, and that was his fault, his alone. He knew it. Cleo had said as much in her letter.

Matt picked up the envelope and looked at it. There was no return address, nor did he expect there to be. The postmark read, "Logansport, IN."

He stood up and walked to the bathroom. It was time to shave.

ABOUT THE AUTHOR

Jacy Morris is a Native American author who has been writing and teaching in Portland, Oregon for years. After working on his own website Moviecynics.com for a decade, under the name The Vocabulariast, he decided to move on from critiquing others' works of art and start creating his own. He has written several books over the last few years including *Unmade: A Neo-Nihilist Vampire Tale*, *This Rotten World*, and *The Enemies of Our Ancestors*. In addition to novels, The Vocabulariast is known to write screenplays and make movies. His first movie, All Hell Breaks Loose will be released onto DVD by Wild Eye Releasing, and he is currently at work on his second film The Cemetery People.

<u>Connect with Jacy Morris</u>

Follow me on Twitter at: http://twitter.com/Vocabulariast

Follow me on Facebook:
https://www.facebook.com/thevocab.ulariast

Follow Me on My Blog:
http://thevocabulariast.blogspot.com/

If you don't feel like connecting, at least do me a solid and leave an honest review. It's the best way to support me in the long run. I'd appreciate it.

Made in the USA
Middletown, DE
23 July 2020

Made in the USA
Charleston, SC
16 December 2012

The Five Books of Jesus
by James Goldberg

For Stephanie & Eric,

James Goldberg

31 March 2013

Cover design by Nick Stephens.
Author photo by V. Elisabeth Westwood.

ISBN-13: 978-1479271306
ISBN-10: 1479271306

The Five Books of Jesus

Author's Note

The gospels are boats that sail on the deep sea of the Hebrew Bible. They were crafted to rest on its stories, to carry their messages with the aid of its strength. As I've studied these four short books, I've been amazed at how carefully they are constructed and how much they offer to those "with ears to hear."

But there is plenty the gospels leave out. They describe few of the individual, internal reactions to events that drive today's novels. They disagree on chronology, geography, and even basic character details—from the apostles' names to the identity of the woman who anoints Jesus. And because they are at odds with modern readers' expectations for specificity and consistency, they are often dismissed.

Whenever we gloss over the gospels, though, we miss their full impact. Jesus and his followers, who lived in a time and place where speech could be deadly, knew how to use language to both conceal and reveal their most potent ideas.

In this book, I've tried to honor not only what the gospels say, but also the way they say it. I've tried to weave different layers of time together, borrowing from ancient prophets, Talmudic sages, and Urdu poets who spoke in eras of oppression.

I have left plenty out—working from four originals with different emphases, it's impossible to do otherwise. But I hope my telling will speak both to those who know the gospels well and those reading the story for the first time.

-J.G.

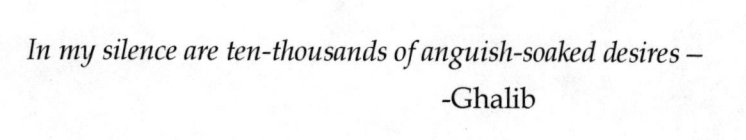

In my silence are ten-thousands of anguish-soaked desires —

-Ghalib

Book One:
Bereshit (In the Beginning)

"For behold, I create new heavens,
and a new earth. . ."

1.

It starts in the desert.

In the beginning of the world, says Genesis, the whole earth was a void and the spirit of God swept over it. This desert out on the banks of the Jordan is no void — even in the night the camels moan and the crickets chirp — but when it does get quiet some say you can still feel the spirit of God sweep by, breathe it deep down into your chest.

A long time ago, the prophet Amos looked out past his orchards and his flocks west of the river to the desert in the east and said *There are days coming* — yes, the vision must have fallen on him the way the sunset can make the desert suddenly cold — *There are days coming says the Lord God when I'll send a famine in the land. Not a hunger for bread or a thirst for water, but for words of the Lord. And the ground itself will grow parched and cracked with your deafness and my absence.*

There are days coming, said the prophet, *when men will wander from sea to sea, from the north to the east: they'll run back and forth, looking for a word from me.*

But they won't find it.

It'll be too dry, he said.

So John doesn't wander from sea to sea. John doesn't run this way or that. He walks straight into the river until it

covers his head then out the other side where the dust gets mixed in his beard. He listens to the camels moan and the crickets chirp, and then to the silence.

The dead prophet Amos smiles. It starts to rain.

*

All through Judea, they hear about it. About the wild man who eats wild honey and speaks wild words that are at once sharp and sweet. All through Judea, after the sun sets but while the last cooking embers still glow, people talk about this lightning in the desert, the way a flash of it can set your life into such stark relief.

The farmers talk about John, wonder about sending their sons to see him—ask themselves if they'd ever come back. The merchants talk about him, wonder what they could buy from some Bedouin to justify making the trip. The contractors and the taxmen talk about him, of this man who earns nothing and builds nothing but knows everything, maybe, that a man truly needs to know. The students and the scholars talk about him, at once drawn to and disturbed by the rumors of a living human being who speaks as if the word of the Lord is a fire shut up in his bones.

Even the soldiers stop telling stories of far-away, half-forgotten homes and of the bloody fields and dead companions who stand between them and those old memories. When the sun sets in the west, even the soldiers look east and talk about whether it's true that there's someone there who can teach you how to start a new and clean life, who can make you feel light again.

But the slum-dwellers of Jerusalem, packed tight into the Temple's shadow, they talk about him most of all because of whispers that make their hairs stand on end, whispers that John says the time they've been waiting for is coming—and if it is, it cannot come too soon. Yes, no time is too soon for the sun to turn dark and the moon into blood and a prince of legends to come and break this world apart.

And through all this talk, the embers cool and dim to ash. Mouths slow and then fall still, eyes wander through the shadows, minds grapple with the pressures of the coming day until, bested, they slink off into sleep.

In the morning, farmers will rise again to their fields, merchants will examine their wares, scholars will take up their scrolls while soldiers take up their weapons and patrol the streets, slum-dwellers will wake to their slums— tomorrow will look so much like today as to make the two, once they are yesterdays, virtually indistinguishable.

Except to those few who wake up with last night's cooking embers still on their minds. Who feel the new day's sun rise in the east and eagerly turn their faces to it, who take the roads up through the hills and who quicken their pace when they see the river moving—as if pulled by the same irresistible force that has drawn them away from their day's labors and toward the desert, toward the wild man whose words divide darkness from light. For those who trace back the route over which evening tales have been told to its source, this day can never be like any other.

*

When John speaks, the words of dead prophets come back to life. This is the first resurrection.

Repent! says John. *For every valley will be made high and every mountain will be made low; the crooked will be made straight and the rough places smooth. And the glory of the Lord will be revealed so that every living thing will see it at once: the mouth of the Lord has spoken it.*

Repent! says John. *Because the day is coming when the proud will be burned down to stubble, when the wheat is gathered out from the chaff.*

Repent! says John. *Because the time has come when the kingdom of God will smash the kingdoms of the earth to pieces.*

Yes: Repent, says John, because your soul has come home to the wilderness, and now it's time to teach your life in the city the things your soul knows.

Then John walks into the river, and you can see the shape he cuts downstream in the current. And that shape is a knife which cuts your heart open, so that by the time you reach the water you're aching to give up all the wrong things you've done. And you tell him: "I can't go on this way," and he says: "you don't have to," so you say: "but how?" and he looks at you hard, so hard you see your life with new eyes, and when he tells you what you have to do, you're ready to make your decision: to walk away now, forever, and staunch the bleeding with an old rag until you can harden your heart, or to step forward, cut your own shape into the current, then lose yourself for a moment beneath the water, immerse yourself in a covenant it is no

small matter to break.

And if you take that path, if you go under and then rise from the water for a new breath of desert air, if you walk up out of the river feeling clean and light, if you sit up on the bank watching the baptisms go by until John steps out of the river again, he'll tell you: "This isn't all. He's coming. And you'll be baptized in fire before the End."

*

Committed to the scriptures as he is, John still makes the scholars nervous. They ask him why he does what he does, and when he answers and the words ring through their bodies, they still ask him to point out where exactly in the text he gets this or that idea, who exactly in the text he thinks he is. They question him as if in search of a scriptural diagnosis: is he the Messiah? "No," he says. Is he Elijah? "No," he says. Is he the prophet Moses mentioned when he recited the law before all Israel the second time? "No," he tells them, "no." Then they throw their hands up and wonder, but don't dare to ask, whether he isn't in fact simply a devil-possessed madman, whether that's why he wears strange clothes and eats strange foods and dwells — of all places! — in this desert.

Maybe it's an inevitable conflict between revelation and education: though each always wants to give the other its due, neither is quite ready to acknowledge the other as a supreme, lest its own integrity be lost in the process.

So the scholars and their students decide it won't be possible to guess whether John was a prophet or a lunatic

until long after he's dead — and that as a matter of principle, it's dangerous to believe in a prophet who is still alive and may therefore easily yet prove to be a false one. It's far better, the scholars tell their students, to wait for death to seal a prophet's message and actions and for generations to pass so that consensus can emerge.

That's when John compares them to desert snakes, who seek out the sun in the heat of the day and bask in it a while, but hide beneath the earth when evening comes and it turns cold.

The scholars explain gently that they are carrying on a grand tradition with an extensive intellectual (not to mention literal) genealogy with which John is no doubt familiar, and that they deserve a certain degree of respect.

John points to the rocks where the snakes love to lie and tells them that if it were necessary, their work could be done by those rocks.

"Why do you talk like that?" say the scholars. "Who gave you the right?"

"Why did you come here?" John says. "Who warned you of the wrath to come?"

*

He arrives as dawn is giving way to morning.

"Why are you here?" says John to Jesus.

"I want you to baptize me," says Jesus to John.

"So soon? I'm not ready," says John.

"But it's time now. I'm sure of it," says Jesus.

John looks at him. The long, deep look John is known

for.

"Are you him? Are you the one?" says John.

"I think so," says Jesus, and they're quiet a while.

"And it's time?" John says.

Jesus nods.

They walk down into the river, which is a bit chilly still so early in the morning, though neither complains. John buries Jesus' face under the dirt-brown of the river water, then brings him back up into the daylight.

And all at once, the sky is bigger and the sun is brighter and there's no room left in this moment for doubt.

A bird swoops down to skim the surface of the water for insects, then rises. Strange that at a time like this anyone should notice that.

Strange that although within a month John is in prison and Jesus is deep in the desert, anyone should remember it.

2.

After John goes to prison, his legend grows even larger. Everyone in Judea talks about him now: the workmen in the quarries who can't help but think about his boldness every time they strike the unforgiving face of the rock, the visiting palace steward and his wife whose hushed tones at night and knowing glancing in daylight say he was right to question their king, the women in the brothels who feel both ashamed and encouraged by a prophet who believes that what has become acceptable for those with power matters less than what is right.

Though John has been shackled, the people hear his voice out of every link in their chains.

To the north, in Galilee, they're also talking about him now. In the same towns where to mention John was a sure sign of religious excess a few months ago, his name leaps from lips to lips over shop counters, across public squares, around dinner tables. By being cast into prison, John has gained the same honor they give the prophet Jeremiah here: only John is alive, potent, and it's impossible to know what God might do with his servant in the next instant. John has captured Galilee's imagination, pulled it taut with long-

suppressed desires for God's hand to be so close again, for everything they've always proclaimed to believe to be true.

When Jesus returns to his home province, people want to see him because he has seen John. People want to touch him to feel some connection to their captive prophet. And when they hear he was baptized by John's own hands, it's hard for them to contain their excitement. Invitations come from this city and that for Jesus to preach in their congregations, and in his voice, it's as if they can hear a little bit of John and it lights something deep inside of them on fire.

But the elders in Nazareth hesitate to invite him back home. Only a few people in town, of course, still remember the rumors about Jesus' mother. Only a few ever whispered about how maybe Joseph had thought twice before marrying her. About how maybe there was some reason why so soon after the wedding he taken her away and not come back until they had a lot of happy kids who looked just like their father. And even the people who remember those old rumors didn't exactly believe them, did they? Always treated Jesus as if there were no doubt whatsoever that he was Joseph's own, never risked evil speaking by repeating unkind speculations.

But evil speaking is counted as a heavy sin for the way it nags and gnaws at the mind. Even after so many years, even without having spread any whispers or fully accepted them in the first place, the elders still feel uncomfortable when they hear or talk about Jesus. So they try not to talk about him, try to avoid the memory of old rumors that this new

saint is Nazareth's bastard son.

And it's not until they've heard and heard from other towns how thrilling it is to hear from this native Nazarene, heard again and again how lucky their town is to count this man-who-John-baptized as one of its own, that the elders are able to push aside their hesitation and invite Mary's son to address the congregation.

And so it is that on a somewhat-belated Sabbath, Jesus returns to Nazareth. He's still thin, the elders notice, from his time in the desert, though they also notice that the new gauntness accentuates the penetrating gaze he's had since he was young. When the time comes he rises to the scriptures and rests his hand on the passage, though he barely seems to look down at it as he calls out the words.

The Spirit of the Lord is on me, because he anointed me: to preach the gospel to the poor, to heal the brokenhearted, to preach deliverance to the captives, to recover the sight of the blind, to free from prison those bound in chains.

To tell you the year of the Lord has come.

Jesus breaks off mid-verse and rolls up the scroll, hands it back to the attendant, and goes to sit down. And even the old farmers who nod off through half the meeting have been elbowed awake now, because this is no ordinary passage, and no one wants to miss what he'll say in commentary about the One who's going to come, and about the days when everything is suddenly and drastically going to be changed.

The elders don't even take their eyes off Jesus long

12

enough to glance at each other. For a moment, the whole assembly seems to hold its breath waiting for words to emerge from that desert-thinned face, to see unveiled what's going on behind those knowing eyes.

"This scripture is fulfilled before you today," Jesus says.

And the words echo through the elders' minds.

*

Here is something true:

The imagination needs to be as strong as the heart, sometimes stronger, because while the heart sustains the body, the imagination sustains the soul. The baker imagines bread so that his hands can be moved to mix and knead dough, the young girl imagines a child and finds reason to prepare for marriage and motherhood, the carpenter imagines the rest his wares will bring before he spends his strength tearing into wood. The farmer imagines a hidden sea above the sky before he entrusts precious seeds to the drought-prone earth; he imagines a hidden sea beneath the soil before he risks his back to dig a well.

The watchman imagines the dawn to keep himself awake through the hour when the very last of his lamp's oil is lapped up by the flame.

The elders of Nazareth are simple men, but they know how to imagine. Sacred words on tiny scrolls stand guard at their doors against the forces of evil. Every seventh day, a queen descends in her glory on their humble homes. Once a year, at least one of them goes up to Jerusalem with his body and down to Egypt with his soul to imagine living in his

ancestors' days, to remember how it feels to be ransomed.

When Jesus reads from the scriptures, the elders imagine John in his cell and their minds stretch back centuries to the days when prophets walked the land. And maybe the taut rope of their minds is enough to draw a portion of the power of those days back again. Maybe their raw belief can be the wick of a lamp that burns from bygone years.

But when Jesus speaks, when he asks them to stretch their minds back to the present and anchor their hopes on him, it's as if they can feel something inside themselves break with a terrible snap.

It is agonizing to believe and believe until it seems your belief has reached the very end of the sky—and then be asked still for more so that your mind is forced all at once to turn back and wonder when it first began to believe too much, to hope too far.

*

The meeting is in an uproar. The elders should be working to keep the peace, but they don't. Some are too outraged to want peace; others too heavy-hearted to stand and call for it.

And so no one restrains the people of Nazareth as they circle Jesus like the animals in the demon-haunted desert used to. "If you're right," the people say, "then let us see some miracles!" But Jesus doesn't answer, just looks half-starved and weak as all the eyes in the room bore into him, looks so much smaller than he did when he read. "If you're a great savior," they say, "why haven't you healed us?"

A man whose son was born blind spits in Jesus' eye.

Another, whose herds have been plagued by a devil for years, reaches for Jesus to bind him with cords.

A few of the elders wonder again if they should step forward to stop the crowd until an old man rises and calls out to Jesus. "Think you're special?" he says, clear and loud, "Then tell us, once and for all"—and though only a few catch the insinuation, an accusation concealed for years carries a special kind of poison—"Aren't you Joseph's son?"

So even the most moderate of the elders decide to leave Jesus to his fate. And it's a woman who's been sinned against and wronged from the time she was a little girl who walks out of the meeting house in search of the first stone.

When she returns, an argument breaks out. Some agree that Jesus the blasphemer should meet his death in a hail of rocks, while others say death should find him as he's thrown headlong down the hill.

*

An important question: does justice live in books or in our hearts?

In either case, of course, it ends up in someone's hands. In this case, in the hands a village congregation whose hearts have just been pushed beyond what they can bear. But because these are thoughtful, God-fearing people, they pause a moment at the hilltop before taking action so that Jesus can speak from the Books in his defense.

"No prophet is accepted in his own country," he tells them first, "and since no miracles happen without shared

faith, I can't help you."

But when a physician fails, the people of Nazareth aren't willing to assume the patient was to blame. They look for a steep spot to throw Jesus down.

"Why do you question God?" he says next. "Weren't there plenty of widows in Israel when He sent Elijah to a foreigner in Zarephath? And what about Elisha: there were plenty of lepers in Israel, but God had him cleanse the Syrian, Naaman!"

But because anger is rarely interested in scriptural precedents, the villagers imagine the way his thin body will bounce off a distant outcropping of rock.

So Jesus stops trying to defend himself and simply walks away, walks away from the angry mob in a moment when, inexplicably, no one is watching him.

Years later someone who was there will remember the moment of confusion when they noticed Jesus was gone, will realize all at once with a sinking feeling that Jesus did work a miracle in Nazareth—that he made himself disappear.

*

After Nazareth, Jesus learns how to keep a secret. When he's invited to read in other cities on the Sabbaths, he takes his passage from Hosea—*I want mercy, not sacrifice*—or from Joel—*Put in your sickle, because the harvest is ripe*—or from the Psalms—*I will open my mouth in a parable, I will utter dark sayings of old*—but avoids blatantly Messianic passages, especially from Isaiah. And when people ask in wonder

what sort of person he is, he just shrugs.

It's the secrets that make him famous in his own right. People can sense when they're not being told something, and so now he's not Jesus-who-was-baptized-by-John, but Jesus, mysterious saint. And it's his name that begins to leap from lips to lips, carrying with it excited speculations, rumors, hushed tones of wonder and awe.

That's when they begin to come to him. The wounded. The haunted. The ones who live off desperate hope alone. They don't know exactly who he is and can't explain to their own minds quite why they believe so fully that he can change them, but they come. Then they'll follow him awhile, because when they see him talking with scholars or students about the scriptures, they don't want to interrupt. And when they see him talking with respectable families, with elders or fathers or brothers or sons, they don't dare approach him, don't dare make their shame known. But sooner or later, the thin man finds a way to slip off for some time to think or pray in a quiet, solitary place That's when they build up their courage and walk up to him, when they open mouths which feel dry all at once to tell him why they have to see him, to tell him things aren't all right, that they're doing the best they can to go on but it's hard, it's very hard, and please. If he wants to, he can help them.

And whenever he looks at them, it's like cool sweet water because the first miracle is that they feel for the first time in so long that they are understood. That he knows the shapes of the scars on their hearts, that they don't have to

17

excuse themselves for having come. Then he reaches out, and touches them: and their demons flee or their limbs gain sudden strength and their desperate hope transforms into wild, euphoric confidence. They want to shout and scream and dance all at once, but he pulls them aside and says: "Shhhh. Your faith has healed you — that's all. There's no need to mention me to anyone."

But when they go back to their neighborhoods and people see the change and crowds gather round — of course they try to keep quiet, but when Jesus' name is among the myriad hypotheses swirling around their ears, how can they help but say, "Yes! Yes! I don't know who he is either, but it was him."

*

Soon fame drives Jesus all the way to Capernaum on the lake's shore, where people walk up to Jesus in the open, bringing their sick relatives or neighbors if they don't need healing themselves. And he touches them and blesses them and talks with everyone as he heals, so that it's not just the old man with fading vision but also the healthy granddaughter he leans on who comes away seeing the world anew. Very quickly, people notice, Jesus grows adept at maneuvering in a tangle of bodies. He avoids stepping on a person who's been lain down behind him while he was attending to someone else; he's expert at keeping his sharp elbows from crashing into bodies that crowd around his sides to watch what he does.

He seems equally adept at dodging questions. The

scholars and students are eager to categorize him: is he simply a charismatic preacher, or a true *tzaddik*, a saint? Is he perhaps, another new prophet? Or an old prophet returned? But he never seems to answer their straight questions in straightforward ways, always seems to steer conversations sideways or upside-down instead, so that the students come out with new questions for their masters instead of answers.

One thing Jesus can't seem to do, though, is find the quiet places in town like he used to. Between the persistence of those seeking relief from their diseases and those seeking relief for their curiosity, no alley is too remote, no roof too out-of-the-way and isolated for the thin man to slip away alone. Capernaum's attention begins to weave itself around him like a basket until maybe the only way he sees to avoid being trapped under it is to get out of town: one evening, Jesus is still out on the streets teaching, healing, dodging, and then in the morning he's gone.

3.

It's quiet on the lake where Simon and his brother Andrew are searching desperately for fish to fill an empty boat and empty stomachs, but the hours have been empty, too, so the only proof they have of their hard day's work is the gleam of the late afternoon sun on the gathered waters. Zebedee's boys pull closer and call out to Simon and Andrew that they're giving up on the lake for now, and that they might as well use the last few hours of daylight to go over every inch of their nets for repairs so that tomorrow, any fish that do swim by won't escape. Andrew laughs, and Simon nods, but they don't follow their friends to the shore. Simon isn't one to give up easily on fish.

Andrew looks out after them absently as he tugs again on the net. The way the light shines off the water hits him all at once with an aching memory of the river Jordan, of the days before his Master there sent him away. He looks across the boat at his brother: the way Simon searches the water reminds him of the night before he left to follow the Jordan downstream in the first place.

They had both longed to see the prophet then, but their faith had to compete with concerns about finances and fish. No matter how quickly they traveled to the south and back,

they knew, their family would struggle in their absence.

"We can wait," said Andrew, "if we're careful, we can save money slowly, and maybe next year —"

"No," said Simon. "For this, you don't wait."

And they sat there in the darkness.

"You go," said Simon. "I can manage. Go now, and see him."

And Andrew looked across at Simon, steady Simon, surprised at his brother's capacity for sacrifice.

"I'll come back as quickly as I can," said Andrew.

"No," said Simon with a force Andrew later found echoed on the east bank of the Jordan. "If he really is a prophet, you stay with him and learn everything."

So Andrew took a length of rope with him as he made his way around the lake and up the river to Bethabara, where he heard John's voice crying out in the wilderness, where he was cleansed beneath moving waters, where a promise made him John's disciple. Every day, he would tie a knot for each new teaching to come from his Master's mouth, and every night he would untie each knot and repeat the saying it had marked so he wouldn't forget, so that when the time came he could bring all his knowledge back to his brother in Capernaum.

Until the day another Galilean came to John, and a bird swooped down across the water. That evening, Andrew asked his Master who the man had been, but John didn't answer. Instead, he looked at the rope in Andrew's hand and said to him: "Go back to Galilee, my son. I thought God

wanted you here, but I was wrong. He wants you to be a fisherman."

Andrew looks down now at his empty net. His brother worked night and day so he could go south. He was a disciple of the famous John; he saw Jesus, the town's new obsession, baptized. And what did he learn, in the end, from all this? That God wants him to be a fisherman.

A fisherman, apparently, who does not catch fish.

He begins to untie and retie loose knots in his net, so that tomorrow, no fish will escape. With each knot, he still remembers something his Master said. Andrew looks across at Simon, who is no longer scanning the waters for signs of moving fish. Simon is looking back instead toward the coast, at a man who seems to be calling them.

They have almost reached the shore before Andrew can recognize the man's face.

"What can we do for you?" asks Andrew.

"I want you to follow me," Jesus says.

"I'm no longer anyone's disciple," says Andrew, and he looks out across the lake, where John says he belongs.

"I'll make you fishers of men," says Jesus.

Andrew and Simon look at each other in disbelief: how does he know? Simon nods to Andrew, says, "Times like this, you don't wait. Go with him."

But Jesus says, "Both of you. Come."

So without pausing to discuss finance or fishes, they go.

*

That night over a campfire on a barren hill, Jesus

prepares a few pieces of flatbread and some fish to share with two sets of brothers: Andrew and Simon, James and young John. After he says the prayer of thanks and finishes his own small portion of the meal, he entertains them with a story: one about a man who discovers that a treasure has been buried under a certain overgrown field. In the story, everyone thinks the man is crazy when he begins to sell everything he owns, and the man doesn't dare tell them otherwise: after all, if he explains what he's raising money for, someone else will buy the field before he can. So the man just smiles and keeps his mouth shut until the money is ready and the land is bought and he can recover the treasure at last.

"What's the treasure?" says James.

"The kingdom of God," Jesus says.

*

Why does he need them? To share his work, helping shoulder the burden of others' suffering whenever he steps into a town?

Or does he ask them to follow him because he knows none of this will mean much in the end if he can't find a few people who can also share his secrets?

*

They've eaten, and they've talked, and they've listened, and the sun has long since set, but Jesus hasn't made any sign of moving off this dry, wasted hill, of spending the night somewhere better than this desert place. When he lies down to sleep, his four new disciples get nervous. Although

they've lived their whole lives in this region, only Andrew has ever spent a night in a desert place, and that was with John and all his disciples down by the Jordan. But tonight there are just the five of them and their Master is asleep, as if there were no reason for concern, even though he must know he is in exactly the kind of place where evil spirits wander when they are looking for a home.

Simon offers to keep the night's first watch and tend the fire. He's had a long, thankless day on the lake, then an unexpected, exhilarating evening on the shore and on this hill, where he's desperately hoping not to lose control of his body and mind during the night.

Simon wakes James before he surrenders to exhaustion, and after listening guardedly to the night winds and the unseen passing of an owl, James wakes Andrew, who doesn't quite make it to the morning without waking John. When Jesus wakes, the first thing he sees is a worried John studying his face.

4.

When everyone is awake, Jesus announces they're going back into Capernaum. Since Zebedee's employees took the boats home, it'll be a long walk, but Jesus says it's better if they go in after dark anyway: it's hard for him to find a moment alone under the sun, but the starlight suits him.

On the road, Jesus asks them questions: what do they think of this scripture or that? How do they imagine the kingdom of God? Why did they follow him in the first place? Simon isn't so sure about his answers: he's no scholar, all he really knows about the kingdom is his own vague sense of longing, and the truth is that he followed Jesus because at the time, it seemed absolutely clear that was the right thing to do.

Maybe Jesus notices Simon's unease, because he switches soon to stories. He tells about a merchant who's bought and sold beauty his whole life, but gives that all up when he finds a perfect pearl, and Simon says, "that's a rare sort of man." Jesus nods, and tells another story: about a magnificent bush, half again taller than a king, where the birds from all around come to nest and to sing: the bush is in a field, which is owned by another beauty-loving man, who

in point of fact did nothing more than plant the smallest of all his seeds in a good spot of ground.

"What's the seed?" asks James.

"A mustard seed," says Jesus, "it was black mustard, I think."

"I mean, what's the seed *really*?" asks James.

But Jesus just smiles.

*

Yes, this is how they walk: Jesus doing most of the talking, Simon and James nodding, asking questions, now and then making a comment while John takes furtive, searching glances at Jesus and Andrew ties knot after knot into the loose threads on his shirt.

They slow down as they get close to town, then have to stop a while and wait until the night has fallen like a cloak over the city. Simon is more than a little embarrassed to be sneaking into his own house with a new master this way, like a thief in the night, and prays quietly as they approach that his mother-in-law won't wake up.

She doesn't, but Simon's wife does. As soon as she hears the first sounds of the five men approaching, she lights an oil lamp she has kept beside her bed the past two nights in case of a moment such as this. She whispers a greeting to the surprised men and ushers them into the house, prepares a sleeping place for them, and offers to leave them her light to augment the moon's if they have more to plan or discuss.

"Just one thing," says Jesus, and he tells her to sit, to stay for it. Then he tells a story about a woman making dough

with just a little leaven, and describes how that little bit of leaven transforms the entire loaf.

After he's finished, Simon's wife takes the lamp back to her room and puts it out. Though it's very late, she lies awake, staring out across the sea of stars, remembering her surprise when Zebedee's servants returned from the lake to tell her they'd brought back the boat her husband and brother-in-law had simply abandoned. Simply abandoned to follow a strange new preacher who speaks with a strange and moving simplicity she loves.

She is dreaming of Simon and Jesus when a rooster's crow startles her awake.

*

Over a breakfast prepared by Simon's wife and her mother and blessed by Andrew, it's Jesus who indirectly raises the issues of finances and fish. "Who starts to build a tower," he asks the four who followed him away from the lake, "if he doesn't have the materials to finish it?" Simon looks a little uncomfortable again, but his wife and her mother speak up: they talked it over yesterday, and they'll be fine. They'll work hard. They're prepared to make sacrifices. Zebedee and Salome have offered to help if necessary. They trust Jesus, they say, and they trust Simon's choice.

Jesus nods his approval, and then begins to speak not of finances or fish but of the flowers that grow wild in a field. A lily, he says, can't afford fine fabric and doesn't know how to sew, but even Solomon's glory couldn't compare to what

God gave the lilies. The lilies, who trust Him for all they need, who are adorned with a beauty spun of pure faith.

*

It's of faith he speaks again before the congregation on the Sabbath, of Abraham who served angels not knowing who they were, of how the angels announced that a long-awaited promise would soon be fulfilled. The things he says drive half the town crazy with curiosity: never mind Abraham's long-ago guests, what's the real identity of this cryptic preacher? Never mind the birth of Isaac and descendants who number as the stars, what long-awaited promise is Jesus really hinting at?

No one brings their sick to him on the Sabbath, of course — only a matter of life and death necessitates healing on the holiest of days — but he ends up being followed back to Simon's house anyway by a crowd of would-be students who hang on his every word. The thing that amazes them is this: most scholars speak as if the scriptures are a mystery and their teachings hold a key, but Jesus speaks as if the scriptures themselves are only the key to a deeper mystery he holds.

*

Within a few days people are coming to Capernaum just to meet Jesus. Many are prospective students, mostly young men whose imaginations have been captured by reports from the cities of a new, imprisoned prophet and reports from the villages of a man who speaks with power and possesses extraordinary understanding. Others come as

patients: they are sick enough to leave home in search of healing, but still strong enough to travel.

Since it's hard to be followed at all times by both a school and a clinic, the two sets of brothers control the crowd: today, James and John are managing the students while Andrew and Simon attempt to organize the sick so they can wait comfortably. They are working their way through the people who have gathered, collecting information—this man has come from Chorazin with an abscessed tooth, that elderly woman has crossed the stream and walked the few miles from Bethsaida because of persistent pains in her leg—when a different sort of patient approaches.

He has come from the desert itself, though years ago he lived in Capernaum. His hair is matted and his eyes are wild and unsettling; there are dirty scars all over his naked body where he has scratched or cut himself as if trying to escape his own skin. And maybe that's exactly what he has been doing, because it's clear to even the travelers from out of town that this man is possessed by an unclean spirit.

*

Imagine spending years in a mind which is no longer entirely your own, which feels unnatural and dull under the force of some unseen occupation. Imagine feeling sometimes angrier than your body can contain and sometimes so empty you don't move for days, but always wrong, so very wrong, and so alone it's as if you are a limb that has been cut from the body of a community which no longer accepts you.

The possessed man screams, and then he weeps as he

approaches Jesus. Simon and Andrew aren't quite sure what to do: they know they're not supposed to touch a man like that now that they're religious disciples, but they also know that if he's wandered into town, something ought to be done. "Leave me alone, you Jesus of Nazareth!" shouts the man, or maybe the unclean spirit who's been part of him so long. "Have you come to destroy me?" he yells, as if Jesus had come to him and not the other way around—then he mutters something unintelligible and blasphemes so loudly the gathered students wince. But Jesus doesn't flinch, he just stares the possessed man down and says in a voice that is quiet but deadly firm, "Be quiet. And leave him alone."

When the possessed man begins to claw at himself, Simon and Andrew forget about ritual purity, diving forward instead to restrain him. He screams again and then all at once he's like dead weight in their arms so that they stagger and nearly drop him, but Simon is quick and keeps the man up until they can find a spot to lay him down. His breathing is heavy at first, but begins to calm once he's flat on his back.

Jesus walks over. The man opens his eyes, which now look remarkably clear. Jesus takes some balm and puts it on the fresh fingernail cuts. The man inhales quickly with the sting, which mostly masks the way some of the students inhale with the shock of seeing the supposed saint touch a polluted body.

"How are you feeling?" says Jesus.

The man swallows and nods. "I could use some clothes,"

he says.

This time nothing masks the sharp intake of breath from across the gathered crowd. Jesus has been teaching them about faith, but when they see that the unclean spirit really obeyed him and left the man, what many of them feel is somewhere between awe and raw fear.

Any man who even the unclean spirits obey is either holy or deadly or both.

Is he a prophet? Is he a saint? Is he a prince of devils? A scourge from God?

If there's more talk about Jesus after this day, there are also more whispers.

*

The whispers gain strength the next week when Simon's mother-in-law collapses on her way back from the well. She tries to stand up and gather the shards of the broken water vessel and go on as if she'd just dropped it through clumsy accident, but she's too weak from the fever she's been hiding and falls down again after slipping on the spill-slicked rock. And though the bystanders are quick to help her up and half-carry her home, they can't help but wonder whether all this is coincidence or a sign, because it seems fairly obvious God is punishing the household that is supporting Jesus.

These whispers rush across the city like a wind, and Simon can hear the chill in the voices that tell him his wife's mother is suddenly sick, can detect the cold tones of unspoken accusation: they touched an unclean man; their Master gives commands to devils; if she dies, the fault is

theirs.

Only the most avid of Jesus' students follow him and the brothers back to Simon's house, enduring the dark looks of the people they pass on the way. Women whose husbands are out in the fields close their doors as Jesus and the brothers walk by their houses. They try to hide their children away from whatever misfortune he may be carrying in his wake.

A neighbor stands in front of Simon's home, steps in front of Simon, who leads the procession's way. "Think twice," the neighbor says, cocking his head toward Jesus, "before letting that one back inside."

"He'll heal her," Simon says, and brushes the man aside.

She's lying on a mat in the courtyard; Simon's wife is kneeling beside her, pressing damp cloths to her head. Simon kneels down beside his wife, takes his mother-in-law's hand. "He's here now," he says. "It's all right."

And then Jesus is kneeling on her other side, taking her other hand — her face softens, and she smiles. He offers her a hand up, as if she's a child who's just tripped, and she looks at him with the same pure gratitude a child might have as she rises. She laughs and puts Simon's hand on her forehead, though he doesn't need to feel the cool of it to know she's been healed. Andrew and James exhale with relief and John sings a little prayer.

"Do you know your son's name?" says Jesus.

"You mean Simon?" says his mother-in-law.

"I'm going to change it to Peter," says Jesus, "because

when the city doubted, your Simon was as steady as a rock."

Simon-Peter's mother-in-law smiles again. "You must be almost ready for dinner," she says, "but it might be late. I'm sorry." And she walks right out the door, past the astonished neighbor, to fetch water she can bring home and boil. Peter's wife politely excuses herself and starts the fire up so it will be ready when her mother gets back.

"With such steadiness around you," says Jesus, "it's no wonder you're so strong."

But as Peter watches the women return so quickly to their labors, as if they are desperate to show they can manage the household alone, he worries that he doesn't deserve his new name, that there are cracks of concern which run straight through the granite faith his Master now expects from him.

5.

Peter dreams that night of fish. In his dream, the lake has risen to his house, so that he doesn't have to choose between following and fishing: he is inviting the sick straight into the courtyard, seating them here and there while they wait for his Master; the lake must follow him because he feels a fish swimming right past his ankle, looks down in time to see the silvery fatness of it. Soon he notices another fish and another, until he is surrounded by fish, swimming as he's never seen them before: not below him, but darting right in front of his face or diving from above his head, or weaving from side to side as they swim in thick clusters around the perimeter of the courtyard. The clusters of fish grow thicker until wherever he walks, Peter can feel their bodies against his chest and brushing the palms of his hands and he knows his family will never go hungry with plenty such as this.

When he wakes, a crowd has already gathered at their door. It's hard to tell in the early morning light just how many are there, or to gauge how many are sick and how many are students. What happened, Peter wonders, to the doubts the town had yesterday when whispers of God's judgment rode a breeze of breath through the houses, shops,

34

and square, up and down the long harbor? Maybe certain desperate kinds of hope are simply ready to flicker at the slightest change from despair to faith, from faith back to suspicion and despair.

James and John are managing the sick today. James sees an old couple in the back and learns that the woman is so weak her frail husband insisted on carrying her most of the way from Chorazin; John leads both of them forward to be the first blessed by Jesus' touch. At the same time, Andrew and Peter turn their attention to the seekers, those who are waiting for the touch of Jesus' words.

Venturing out into the crowd, they can hear at once a shift in the texture of men's speech that can only indicate a large group of Judeans has arrived. Galileans go south when they can for the Passover and a few for other major feast days, but it's rare for so many Judeans to be in Capernaum at once: the very sound of their speech seems to give the place a holiday air, so that within a few hours, Peter predicts, it will be hard to distinguish between people who came to see Jesus and people who came to see the crowd.

"Andrew!" shouts one of the Judeans, and Andrew's face lights up as he recognizes Judas, who also followed John on the Jordan. But before Andrew can introduce his brother and his old friend, James grabs Peter's arm and whispers, "Where *is* he?"

*

Though he dwells now by the lake, Peter begins to realize, Jesus acts more like the western sea: he moves like a

tide, rising into town from time to time then withdrawing again and again to the desert places. James and John work with Peter's wife and her mother to keep the crowd patient and calm while Peter, Andrew, and Judas go out into the countryside searching for Jesus. They hurry out past the fields and the trees to the barren places because, as Andrews explains and Judas seems to intuitively understand, those are the places where Jesus goes to be alone.

Jesus' eyes are closed and his mouth is moving silently when Judas sees him. At once, Judas finds himself frozen in place, moved with the same longing on the verge of tears he felt, inexplicably, when he saw Jesus immersed beneath the waters of the Jordan. Andrew and Peter see Judas standing transfixed and hike up beside him, though by the time they can see Jesus he's finished his prayer and opened his eyes and looks expectantly toward them.

"Everyone is looking for you," Peter says. "A big crowd is gathered outside my house."

Jesus stands up. "Tomorrow we should go to another town," he says.

*

They don't eat the rest of the day. They're far too busy trying to work their way through the sick and making preparations to go and answering questions from people so thirsty for truth they've left their own cities and homes. By dusk, the sick have been blessed and are satisfied—but a thirsty soul doesn't go away as easily as a simple wound, so a part of the crowd follows them when they pick up their

bags and take to the road.

"Is it safe for us to be heading out so close to night?" says a Judean who still has a slight limp from an encounter on the south's robber-riddled roads.

"How much do you pay for two sparrows in Jerusalem?" says Jesus.

"A penny or so, I think," says the man, "though you pay less per sparrow if you buy five or six."

Jesus laughs. "No matter how many are bought at a time, not one of those sparrows can be forgotten by God."

The man has to rush to keep pace with Jesus' long gait. "What's that supposed to mean?" he asks.

"It means don't worry," says Jesus. "You're worth a lot more than those birds."

*

A few of their new followers give up and find an inn at this town or that when they realize that Jesus is going to walk all night. As the first streaks of dawn lend new life to the sky, Jesus stops next to a field to listen to the songs of a dozen birds. He points to a bush.

"Didn't I tell you?" he says to the two sets of brothers, "All it takes to make a home for such music is one tiny seed."

Judas waits until they're walking again to ask Andrew what Jesus was talking about. Andrew smiles, and several of the new followers gather around him as he begins to speak, untying knot after knot after knot.

*

Word of Jesus has spread farther than you can walk in one night, so it's not long before people are bringing their sick to him: children whose eyes are swollen shut from infection, old men with old wounds grown stiff with pus, people with fevers or boils, with aches in their joints or in their bowels. Others come to him without complaints, but with questions. Some hope he can speak to a yearning in their minds; some wonder whether his words are safe enough to welcome. Jesus talks to the curious and touches the sick but seems ready to rest, at last, when the sun sets.

One of the men who walked all day to Capernaum to see Jesus, and then walked all night to stay near him, has a twin sister who married a man from this town. He manages to find her and arrange for the whole party to spend the night in and around their home. In the morning, Jesus leaves a blessing on the house before taking once again to the road.

Outside of town, a leper is waiting for him. The men who follow Jesus take one look at the scaly sores on his face and stop, then step back. They've been willing to risk their health in crowds of the sick, but a leper carries the marks of judgment from God. And who would dare to approach a man who has brought such visible and debilitating punishment on himself?

"I've heard about you," says the leper to Jesus.

Jesus nods, but keeps his distance.

"If you want to," says the leper to Jesus, "I know that you can make me whole."

Jesus starts to walk forward. He stretches out his arm

38

until he's almost touching the leper's ravaged skin and says, "I want to." He touches him. All of the men watch as the leper's skin begins to heal—except for John, who keeps his eyes on Jesus, and who is never quite sure if his eyes were playing tricks on him or whether Jesus, too, was surprised.

The leper reaches up to touch his own face and shouts out for joy, but Jesus hushes him, reminds him what the scriptures say about going to the priest, and tells him and the witnesses not to talk about what happened.

No one quite understands why they should be silent, but you don't question someone who can, apparently, persuade God to rethink His judgments.

*

Respect is, of course, not the same as obedience. Consider the case of a man who asks his two sons to go work in his vineyard. The respectful son says "yes" because he honors the man who gave him life, who nourished him and taught him from his infancy. But it's a beautiful day, and the wealthy father of a beautiful girl invites the young man over for a cup of wine, so decides his own father's vineyard can wait.

No, respect is not the same as obedience. The man's rude son says "no" to his own father's face, putting his own priorities above those of his wiser elders, and he walks away shamelessly with his head held high. Only afterwards, the rude son thinks about his father, thinks about the way the father continues to be patient with him despite their many quarrels over the years, and so it's he who takes his tools to

the vineyard, he who sees how urgent the work there is, while his model brother drinks wine at the neighbor's and would have let the vineyard die.

The leper doesn't question the man who healed him, but this is what he says to anyone who will listen: can you believe that before I made my way to Jesus, my skin was white as snow with leprosy?

*

As Jesus walks from town to town, his reputation becomes a burden. The crowds grow, but the streets and courtyards don't, and soon bodies are always pushing and pressing on each other wherever he goes. One day the thick dust in the air and an elbow to the chest make a sick man cough blood on six people around him. Another day a woman whose cataracts have made her almost blind loses her bearings and gets sick in the churning human mass. Everywhere Jesus goes gets dirty, and ugly, and people grow more rather than less desperate when they see him getting close.

It's not just people in need who contribute to the chaos. Peter, Andrew, James, and John struggle to sort the faith-filled sick and the wisdom-hungry students from those who have come simply to see a famous man. They want to help Jesus heal people, but there are so many now so eager to touch him and to leave with a story worth telling that they will feign disease in the hopes of finding a miraculous and imaginary cure. Soon the brothers are closely questioning newcomers about their supposed symptoms and sometimes

physically restraining over-eager visitors. The more Jesus becomes known for compassion, the more his closest disciples get a reputation for being brusque.

Because Jesus is focused on healing crowds and his closest disciples are focused on handling them, none of them takes much thought for shelter or food. A few of the newer followers notice this and relieve them. Thomas, who arranged for his sister's place after their first all-night walk, makes a point of knowing who has relatives close by, or else of getting into town early to find out whose hospitality can be trusted. Judas, who knows from a childhood of poverty how to find a good price or else drive a hard bargain, always seems to find food and stretch it thin enough to feed the growing group of Jesus' followers—though Jesus himself and the brothers from Capernaum seldom find free moments to eat.

And as hungry hours in packed crowds stretch on and on, the brothers grow less and less patient with people who crowd around Jesus as if he's some strange sight to see, who flock to him like they might flock to a foreign merchant—not to purchase so much as to gawk at his exotic wares.

So Jesus stops going into the towns. Thomas does his best to find shepherds who can direct him to good places to camp. Judas asks them which grasses a man can chew and eat, which wild flowers have nourishing, soup-worthy bulbs.

And though the crowds are far more manageable outside of narrow streets, they keep coming: broken bodies, hungry

minds, and idle onlookers pouring in from north, south, east, and west. People flock together as if they were birds, thinks Judas, and as he surveys the crowds and tries to determine what provisions will be needed, he realizes that even the birds themselves seem to be gathering here, seem to be drawn to this man and his secrets.

6.

An angry shepherd accosts Thomas: one of his sheep has either been stolen or else become confused by the crowds and wandered off. Is this any way to treat someone who freely offered his advice and hospitality?

"Calm down," says Thomas, "it's just one sheep."

"It's my sheep," says the shepherd. "I don't think you understand!"

When Jesus hears the commotion, he asks what the trouble is. The shepherd shouts abuse at him, but Jesus doesn't seem to notice. Instead he asks how long the missing sheep has been gone, asks what it looked like and, if it did just wander off, where it might have headed.

Jesus holds up his hands and announces to the crowd that he won't teach or heal until the sheep is returned.

The students object: they have urgent questions! The sick object: they have pressing complaints! But deep down, they all know Jesus is crazy, so they give up objecting before too long. Many head home in frustration. Others dart this way and that, trying hard to look busy, while still others look for the sheep as if all their own hopes depended on it, as if Jesus will have no choice but to give them what they are looking

for if they can be the first to find what he wants.

As they search, Jesus turns to James, and for the first time since Nazareth, he quotes from the book of Isaiah: *These people run about like hunted gazelles*, he says. *Like sheep without a shepherd.*

*

Andrew, Judas and some students find the sheep, but the presence of so many unfamiliar humans frightens it badly: they have to call over the shepherd, whose voice the sheep knows, to calm it and carry it home. With the shepherd pacified, the sick and the students start to gather again, but Jesus insists on leaving these pastures tonight before more harm is done.

"Where are we headed?" asks Thomas.

"Can you find a place where I won't have to strain my voice so much to talk?" Jesus says.

*

The way the hill curves does the brothers' corralling work for them: everyone who's followed Jesus is gathered by the shape of the land into one place. As soon as Jesus calls for their attention, Thomas knows he's been given good advice: from where Jesus stands, his voice carries over every present body, so that anyone with ears can hear. Only a few of them, though, would need to listen closely to recognize the passage Jesus starts to quote. A few of them, like Jesus, already know it by heart.

The Spirit of the Lord is on me, says Jesus, *because he anointed me: to preach the gospel to the poor —*

A hush falls over the multitude. Jesus stops. Closes his eyes. Starts again.

The Spirit of the Lord is on me, says Jesus, *because he anointed me: to preach the gospel to the poor.*

He looks out at Judas.

"Blessed are the poor," he says, "because the kingdom of heaven belongs to them."

He looks at Andrew.

"Blessed are the meek," he says, "their inheritance is the whole earth."

Then he starts to recite again. *The Spirit of the Lord is on me,* says Jesus, *because he anointed me: to preach the gospel to the poor, to heal the brokenhearted –*

"Blessed are those that mourn," says Jesus, "because they'll be comforted."

"Blessed are those who are starving for righteousness," he says, "because they'll be filled."

He takes a deep breath. *The Spirit of the Lord is on me,* says Jesus, *because he anointed me: to preach the gospel to the poor, to heal the brokenhearted, to preach deliverance to the captives –*

"Blessed are the merciful, because they'll find mercy" he says.

"Blessed are the peacemakers, who remember they are children of God."

The Spirit of the Lord is on me, says Jesus, *because he anointed me: to preach the gospel to the poor, to heal the brokenhearted, to preach deliverance to the captives, to recover the sight of the blind –*

"Blessed are the pure in heart," he says. "They will see God."

The Spirit of the Lord is on me, because he anointed me: to preach the gospel to the poor, to heal the brokenhearted, to preach deliverance to the captives, to recover the sight of the blind, to free from prison those bound in chains.

"Blessed are the persecuted," says Jesus. "Blessed are the mocked, and the whipped, and those cast in chains like the prophets. Blessed are those who men falsely accuse, who people lie and speak evil about."

Jesus falls silent for a moment and surveys the crowd.

"Blessed are you," says Jesus, "blessed are you who follow me in the times which are about to come."

And then his face relaxes and he begins to preach. And he doesn't stop until the sun sets behind him.

*

As they walk away from the hill in the darkness, Andrew is busier than ever untying and retying knots. His thoughts today have been like the thread in his hands: turned upside-down, doubled back on themselves, old lines of thought being crossed and bound together in ways he never expected, and never wants to forget. "Salt of the earth," he whispers, and is reminded of the salty sweat which stains the shirt sleeves whose frayed threads he is tying and untying. "Shining light," he whispers, and is reminded of the way the sun shone over the hill's peak at dusk. Then he turns to the most important knots, the ones he has tied at the four corners of his shirt to remind him of

46

what Jesus said about the law: about murder and anger, peace offerings and making peace, about adultery and lust, about honesty, about justice, and about love.

Thomas is watching Jesus for clues about where they're headed and Judas is watching the crowd and the fields to figure out what they can eat when Jesus calls them to him and tells them not to worry: they're going back to Capernaum.

"Where will we stay?" asks Thomas.

"In two women's faith," says Jesus.

"What will we eat?" asks Judas.

"In the evening, a feast," says Jesus.

Thomas looks skeptical, but Judas smiles wide. It's been a long, long time since he's had a feast.

*

Though Jesus and his followers try to be quiet, Peter's wife hears footsteps, or maybe just breathing, and meets them with the lamp she keeps ready by her bed. She manages to find space in the house and courtyard for everyone, and thanks God that she ground new grain to fill their empty pot of flour the previous morning.

Gossip spreads like a plague, rumor like the wind, but word that Jesus is back in town spreads like a fire: the cooled hopes of those who put off seeing him before his last sudden departure are reignited, and spread quickly to many who hadn't planned on seeing Jesus at all and to others who hadn't imagined how much they would want to see him again.

Jesus hasn't yet left the house when they start arriving—so it fills quickly, until an overflow crowd is packed tightly around the door. The brothers assign some other disciples to keep a space clear around him: if everyone tries to touch him at once, they've learned, dense crowds like this can turn dangerous. Instead, they try to let the sick through one at a time for blessing, taking time for questions and answers whenever Jesus seems to need time to regain his strength. For hours, Jesus teaches and heals and heals and teaches, but the crowd shows little sign of letting up.

In the thick of the crowd, four friends who came early to hear Jesus teach remember another friend who no doubt wished to come. So they give up their places, fight their way out of the house against a current of people trying to fight their way in, and go to the run-down shack where their friend lies on a low woven bed. They try to lift his paralyzed body this way, then that, until they give up and simply grab the corners of his bed to carry him back.

That's when their plan begins to unravel. The crowd is too dense to force a whole bed through. The four are almost ready to take the bed back to the shack and try another day, but the paralyzed man begs them not to give up, not to leave him immobile and alone.

Inside, Jesus is telling stories. A certain man, he says, once received an unexpected but important guest in the middle of the night—the man's heart sang for joy at the chance to extend hospitality to this guest, but it sank when he realized his kitchen was completely bare. What could he

do? Because the man knew how much a guest matters, he snuck out through the back door and rushed to the house of his good friend, knocked as loudly as he could to wake him without waking the whole neighborhood, and called out asking to borrow bread.

"Be quiet!" said the friend, "I'm asleep, my children are asleep, you should be asleep—go back to bed!" But the man kept on knocking, kept on begging, because he knew he couldn't fail that night, knew he would never forgive himself if he couldn't offer this guest, of all guests, something to eat.

"Please," he said, "Please, please, please please please!" and he knocked until the friend let him in and gave him bread just stop the noise.

"Think," says Jesus, "of what Isaiah said: *can a mother forget her nursing child?* I ask you mothers: which of you has ever had a hungry baby who would let you forget?" The women all laugh, and their husbands, too, but Jesus turns serious. "Pray like that," he says. "Pray like the man who wakes his friend at night—pray like a hungry baby who wails until his mother comes."

And a tile from the roof comes off. Two men shout for space and jump down into the courtyard while another two men pass down a bed, jostling the crippled man as they lower him down. They elbow people away, push forward toward Jesus.

The two left up on the roof shout down. "Please!" they say, "Please, please, please please please do something for

49

him."

Jesus looks at the four who have gone to such lengths, and he nods at them. "Your sins are forgiven," he says, and the crowd falls strangely silent.

Some of the men who came from far cities just to hear him, who have willingly followed him on walks that last all through the night, stare at him in undisguised shock and apprehension. To be a keeper of wisdom, a great Master, is one thing—but only God himself can forgive sins. Has he simply misspoken? Does he mean something other than what he appears to have said?

Jesus looks at his followers, and John can't help but notice that he seems suddenly sad.

"What's easier?" says Jesus, "To tell these men their sins are forgiven," and then he turns back to their paralyzed friend, leans down to him and offers a hand, "or to tell this man to get up and carry his own bed from now on?" The man rises and raises his arms up in thanks to God. He picks up the cot—and thick as the crowd is, it parts like the Red Sea to let him out.

And the man whose body has just been healed walks out past followers of Jesus whose confidence in their master has just been broken.

*

Let's give them credit. To forgive sins sounds like a wonderful, generous thing. But how difficult will it be for a man who claims the power to forgive sins to convince his followers to commit some? Don't earthly kings pardon at

their own whims—and aren't earthly kings, as a consequence of this power over justice, almost always corrupt? And how can a man who usurps even the power of divine forgiveness be trusted not to reach for more power still?

Let's give them credit. To believe in someone is terrifying to begin with: only a madman bets both this life and the next on a prophet. And, oh, the ecstasy of that madness! But, oh, how the knife of betrayal stings when it cuts!

They stagger out of the house of intoxicating madness, away from the now-chilling clarity of purpose they've seen in Jesus' eyes. But what is his purpose? Where is he headed? they wonder. What is he really planning? they think. And they cast their minds over everything they've heard him say, weigh it again in the light of his unthinkable presumption.

They shake their heads against a heavy, aching feeling as real as the stupor that follows a night when the wine flows freely until dawn, then ask themselves the most important question of all: how is this man possibly going to be stopped?

*

Word that a group of Jesus' disciples has left him reaches Matthew within the hour through an old woman who has come to pay the latest installment on her overdue taxes. This is the arrangement Matthew the taxman makes in such cases: rather than having debtors beaten or thrown in prison, he allows them to pay gradually—on the condition that with each payment, they bring a fresh piece of news as interest.

One advantage to this arrangement is that anytime something exciting happens, everyone who's behind on payments immediately thinks of Matthew and their taxes: they'll pay what they can at once while they still have something good to share.

The woman relates the incidents of the morning and the apparent crisis to the best of her knowledge, though she's a little uncertain about who was forgiven and why: after all, she was only in the house to see Jesus because she can't hear well. Matthew thanks her anyway and makes a note of her small payment in his records. As he glances over his ledger, Matthew notes with some amusement that Jesus has been good for business: with all the traffic he's brought into town, local people are making more money, and with all his entrances and exits from the city, with all his healings and cryptic teachings, late payers have been unusually quick to run in breathless to Matthew's office with an update and a coin. Thanks to Jesus, Matthew may also be able to buy up the next town's tax collection contract next year.

The thought is bittersweet, because it's his line of work that has kept Matthew from ever seeing Jesus—especially since the Judeans showed up in town. After all, in the south a taxman is considered a collaborator, a traitor to his nation, and people there might shake the dust from their feet as a curse when they walked away from your office. In the north, things aren't so bad: religious families would think twice before marrying their sons to your daughters, but they'll greet you on the street, ask how your uncles are doing, and

if they can, they'll pay on time. Even in the north, though, it's understood: anyone who wants to be holy should steer clear of those who deal too closely with the Romans. So Matthew collects stories about the new local saint, but he doesn't spoil anything by trying to visit him.

Yes, best to let Jesus do his work, thinks Matthew, while Matthew continues to do the work he has chosen for himself: to be a taxman who still quietly studies the sacred books, who bids on government contracts to protect the people from outside brutality and extortion. If the people's hopes come true and the occupiers are overthrown in this generation, Matthew knows he may be murdered in the night. But if the Romans are here to stay—and knowing the methodical persistence of the empire he serves, Matthew will be very surprised if they are not—someone has to be willing to compromise principles of purity and cooperate.

Matthew sighs. He is hardly ever very surprised.

*

That afternoon a crowd approaches the tax office. For a moment, paranoia grips Matthew and he envisions a mob coming to tear his accounting book to pieces along with his skin. But as the crowd draws near, he catches sight of two fishermen he knows and realizes one of the men in the crowd must be Jesus, who they've given up everything to follow.

The crowd seems to slow as it gets closer, as if time itself has been stretched ever so slightly by the force of his curiosity. Will he be able to recognize Jesus? In all the

reports he's heard of Jesus' movements, he never thought to ask what the man's face looked like.

The crowd stops right next to the shade of Matthew's office.

"Are you coming?" a man who must be Jesus says, but Matthew is too confused to answer.

"I want you to follow me," Jesus says, his voice ringing loud and clear. And Matthew is very surprised now to find himself standing up, leaving his ledger unattended, and walking away in the current of an unexpected crowd.

*

Toward the back of the crowd, whispers thick with the accents of the south work their way through the dust-clogged air. "What is going on?" some of the men who have followed Jesus for weeks mutter. He never asked them to follow him, so why did he go out of his way to ask a taxman?

"Maybe the others were right to go," says one disappointed man to his companion.

"Wait," says the companion, a southerner named Simon, "let's not decide that just yet."

*

In the front of the crowd, a minor prophecy is about to be fulfilled.

"What shall we eat tonight?" says Jesus to Judas with a half-smile. But before Judas can answer, Matthew blurts out, "Let me go home and prepare something for you. Teach a few more hours, then come to my house."

"Sometimes, a large number of people follow us," says Judas.

"I like a big dinner," says Matthew. "If you're willing to come yourselves, bring as many guests as you'd like."

Jesus says, "We're willing," and Matthew hurries off to give instructions to his servants.

Judas looks up at Jesus. *And You gave them bread from heaven for their hunger,* he thinks.

*

It's just past dark when a messenger from Matthew's house arrives with word that the food is ready. This is what those who left Jesus that morning see: their erstwhile Master, under cover of night, leads his remaining disciples into a feast in the home of a taxman—essentially a den of thieves. How quickly the descent goes for the corruptible!

"Didn't he teach us that God loves the poor?" they say to each other, "But as soon as we get into town, he cozies up to the rich!"

"Didn't John and his disciples fast on the riverbanks?" they say, "But the man we called Master only yesterday already wants to drink fine wine and stuff his face!"

Let's give those who left some credit: plenty of the men still following Jesus are thinking exactly the same things.

*

The meal Matthew has prepared is superb. He's set out pomegranates, figs, and nuts to start and poured new wine, but even outside the house you can smell the freshly caught fish he's had cooked with olive oil and exotic spices bought

in city markets, plus the festive scents of goat and sheep meat. He's had flat breads and leavened breads prepared, purchased honeys and cheeses and yogurt, kept cucumbers in cool water to bring out at just the right time.

Jesus walks into the house and embraces his host. Servants and neighbors Matthew has employed for the night help seat Jesus' followers: here go the fishermen, here Judas and Thomas, there a few, here a few—but many aren't coming in. Though there's no shortage of room left in the house, they insist on standing outside.

Jesus frowns and apologizes to Matthew for their bad manners. No need to worry, says Matthew. He says he understands. But Jesus says he doesn't understand, and sends Peter, James, and Judas to call in whoever still wants to follow him.

The southern Simon speaks for those who would rather stay outside in the night: "Is this the kingdom he's promised us?" he asks.

But Peter just says, "He wants you to come in."

Simon shakes his head. "I can't," he says. "Where I come from, you don't break bread with anyone who works for the Romans."

"He's one of us now," James says. "You saw our Master call him."

But Simon turns away from James. "I took an oath, Judas," says Simon. "You know that."

"Pray to God to forgive you," says Judas. "Maybe it wasn't the right oath."

"Who is he?" says Simon to Judas. "And who does he think he is?"

"Come and find out," says Judas. "If you want to find out, too," he calls to the men still gathered in darkness, "you'd better come inside."

And Judas walks back into the house, with Peter and James, then Simon and two others following him. The rest stay outside the taxman's house: no feast or teacher can coax them in.

"Don't they know God made us all in his own image?" Jesus says. And he starts to tell a story.

The story is about a king who prepares a great wedding feast for his son and invites all his nobles, but they don't show up. So he sends out his servants to remind them, but they still don't come. The king gets upset. I've killed whole herds for this meat, he says, and pressed a whole vineyard for this wine. If the nobles won't come, send out my servants into every highway, bring as many as you can to this wedding feast! Don't distinguish between the good and the bad, just bring enough guests to fill the house!

They all sit for a moment after the story is done.

"What does it mean?" Matthew asks.

"Do you have any friends?" says Jesus.

Soon Matthew's servants are on the road, calling in every Jew in Capernaum and Bethsaida who ever worked a Roman contract in taxes or construction while some of Jesus' followers take to the streets, calling in to the feast anyone who will listen.

By midnight, the house is packed until every spare surface is taken, every wine-cup full. Jesus' disciples mingle not only with Matthew's colleagues, but also, owing to the late hour when their invitation went out, with every thief, vandal and prostitute in two towns.

*

In the morning, Peter wakes Thomas and Judas and asks how many of Jesus' followers have left him in the past day. Thomas and Judas don't have to make a count. They've already seen who's left. Nearly half, they tell Peter after converting faces into a fraction. Nearly half of those who walked with us through the nights are gone.

*

That afternoon, the city's centurion comes to visit Jesus. Though he's not a Jew, he explains, he's heard about Jesus through Matthew and believes he has real power from his God.

"I have a servant who's in great pain," says the centurion. "Even for me, it's hard to watch."

"Take me to him," says Jesus.

"I've done too many violent things in my life," says the centurion. "I'm not worthy to have you in my home. But you don't need to touch him any more than I need to use my own hands to see an order fulfilled. If you give the word, it's enough."

"He'll be healed, then," says Jesus. Then he adds: "I haven't seen faith like yours in all Israel," and for a few more of his followers, this flattery of a foreigner at their

expense is the thing which is finally too much.

*

There are two parties in Capernaum now, about to become locked in a deadly contest.

Those who have left Jesus take their motto from the Psalms: *My zeal has consumed me, because my enemies have forgotten your words.*

Those who have stayed with Jesus are also thinking of a passage from the Psalms: *I've become like a stranger to my brothers, a foreigner to my mother's children — because the zeal of your house has eaten me up, and the reproaches of those who reproached you have fallen on me.*

All week they argue and seek grounds for conflict with one another, and when the Sabbath comes, they don't rest.

7.

It starts in the assembly.

One of Jesus' former disciples reads from Ezekiel: *And I will judge you, the way women who break wedlock and shed blood are judged; I will give you blood in fury and jealousy.* Then he sits, and speaks about Israel's obligation to keep its covenants, about the dangers of religious laxity in a time of occupation.

Jesus himself reads next, also from Ezekiel: *Will you judge them, son of man, will you judge them? Then tell them the truth about the dark sins of their fathers.* Then he sits, and speaks of the way people persecuted and killed the prophets.

As soon as the meeting ends, the congregation begins to fracture: those without a desire to take sides rush home as quickly as they lawfully can, while others gravitate toward Jesus or his opponents. An old man sits in the center, absolutely still except for lips lost in silent prayer. Then he stands, turns toward Jesus, and extends a withered hand.

Wait until tomorrow, thinks Andrew. He's not dying, he can wait. Don't challenge them by healing him now.

But Jesus looks over at the crowd of those who are against him, calls out, "You're scholars?"

A few of them nod their heads, but most just stare at

Jesus and hope he's about to do something rash. Preferably something that would prove to Capernaum's fickle elders that drastic measures against him need to be taken.

"Here's a question, then," says Jesus, "does the law say to do good on Sabbath days, or evil? Is it better for me to save life, or for you to plan how to destroy one?"

No one answers, but some people who are sure Jesus is dangerous are beginning to worry that he can also read their thoughts.

"Let me see your hand again," says Jesus to the old man, but when the old man brings it up to show Jesus, there's absolutely nothing withered or wrong. The man stares at his own hand in wonder as Jesus says, "It looks healthy. Maybe there's no need to answer my question about the law today after all."

And Jesus leaves the meetinghouse, walking away from one man's faith and others' fury, accompanied by his followers' rising fear.

*

They're all a little relieved when it becomes clear that Jesus is walking out past the edge of town: though there's no conclusive evidence against him, they'd rather get far away from Capernaum now. But they're still more relieved when Jesus stops in a field by the road and sits down: you're not supposed to travel too far on a Sabbath, and it's nice to know he's exercising some caution.

Simon from the south is the first to see three figures approaching in the distance: a few of their old companions

have followed them up the road. He nudges Thomas, who keeps an eye on the men who appear to be doing no more than keeping an eye on Jesus. Jesus is sleeping, though, so the three men who have followed him crouch at a distance and wait.

By the time Jesus wakes, everyone's a little hungry. It's an old custom that you can take grain kernels with your hand as you pass through a field — only if you use tools to cut the stalks is it considered theft. So they pick a few grains each, rub them in their hands to loosen the shells, and then toss them up in the breeze to blow away the chaff from the kernel.

That's when the three men walk up. "You shouldn't be letting them do that," they say.

Jesus glances at them. "Do you think I should tell the wind not to blow chaff from wheat on the Sabbath?"

"They shouldn't be picking and rubbing it in their hands like that," say the three.

"Have you ever read the scriptures?" says Jesus. One of the men tightens his jaw and a second tightens his fist at the insult, but Jesus doesn't balk. "When King David and his men were outcasts and grew hungry, didn't they eat the priests' sacred bread? If such great allowances can be made for my ancestor and his men, can't some small allowances be made for the men who follow me?"

"Is that who you are?" asks the first. "Are you really the One, the Son of David?"

But Jesus just plucks a grain and rubs it in his hands.

"If it's true, we'll come back to you," says the second.

"But we need to know it's true," says the first. "We need a sign that you have the right to do all this."

Jesus tosses the seed in the air, and the breeze blows the loosened chaff from the kernel.

"The only sign given to those who leave the duty God has given them," says Jesus, "is the sign of Jonah, who spent three days in the belly of a shark."

Book Two:
Kibbutz Galuyot
(The Gathering)

"And Jacob called unto his sons, and said,
Gather yourselves together, that I may tell you that
which shall befall you in the last days."

1.

The rumors that get back to Jesus' family in Nazareth are not encouraging. They don't listen too closely to the former disciples who pass through with stories about how his fame has filled him with arrogance. They do their best to ignore the men who come just to look for Mary, to warn her of plots and snares they've heard about from people who want to see her oldest son imprisoned. Yes, they try not to worry about all that: they know about the controversy Jesus can cause, and they've accepted that. No, what worry them are the details they hear from the travelers most hopeful about Jesus.

Mary asks these people a litany of questions about her son: where does he sleep? how many hours is he sleeping? how does he keep warm at night? how does he stay healthy if he's always surrounded by the sick? is he eating enough? Even his most ardent admirers have to throw their hands up against the river of her words and are forced to admit with more than a little shame that they've never paid enough attention to his condition to give her answers.

But Mary is not the kind of woman who gives up. Think carefully, she tells them: what was the last thing they saw

him eat? Nothing? How long were they watching him, how many people would they say were in the crowd? If he never seems to eat while he works, when exactly does he eat? Are his cheeks sinking in? Close your eyes and see him again, she says: was he wearing a robe, too, or just a shirt? Were any patches of hair or skin showing through threadbare spots in his clothes? What about his face, she asks, and grabs one of her other sons to demonstrate: did the skin under his eyes sag here, were there dark spots right through here? — he gets very distinctive marks under his eyes when he isn't sleeping well, she says, they couldn't have missed them.

And the travelers hesitate, insist they don't remember, and then don't want to say — but Mary won't take no for an answer: she asks and she asks until they've dredged up memories they didn't even know they had just to make her stop.

Soon it's Mary who is letting concern for another keep her from eating; soon it's Mary with distinctive dark spots under her eyes, and that's when her sons say "enough" and pack their things to go. James, Judas, and Simon leave their brother Joseph to care for their dead father's business and ask their youngest sister to tend the animals and keep up the house while they take Mary to see her oldest son. If his condition is better than she expects, they reason, she may be content with giving him a mother's short scolding. If things are looking out of control, though, Joseph's sons are stubborn when they need to be and strong as the trees whose wood their father lived by, so they're prepared to

bring their brother home.

*

It's a dusty journey for the family from this village to that, looking for a man who doesn't stay long in one place anymore. Mary hears he's in Nain, but by the time she and her boys get there he's moved on and there are at least four different versions of where he went. In the next village, it's the same and the same in the one after that, so that Galilee begins to feel like a labyrinth of memory mixed with rumor, a maze—or maybe just a mirage?—that has swallowed up her oldest son.

When Jesus was a boy, he wandered off at the end of a family trip to Jerusalem. At first, they assumed he'd just attached himself to Joseph's nephews for the journey home—it wasn't until evening that they searched the camp of relatives and friends and found that he wasn't with anybody at all.

Searching for Jesus now, Mary remembers how she spent the next three days growing more and more desperate, how it hurt more every time they reached a new place where her son could have been but was not. Searching for Jesus now, Mary remembers how the boys cried then at night because they missed their brother, how she told them not to worry, that she knew they'd find him. Yes, she'd comforted them until they fell asleep and she was free to cry herself to sleep in Joseph's arms.

James, Simon, and Judas aren't crying this time, and their determination is a great relief. They quickly decide it's

no use trying to go everywhere people think Jesus must have gone, and decide to pay attention to how much people talk about him rather than what they say. Soon, they're following a trail of talk that grows stronger as they move from where he was toward where he is—until they reach the last village and there's no talk at all.

The strange quiet of this village tells them more about their brother's work than all the rumors and stories they heard on the way. Here, everyone's left their lives: in this garden patch, weeds find unexpected reprieve; by that workbench, wool must wait for the hands of its everyday destiny to spin it into thread. Yes, everyone's gone to the wine house: where the tables have been packed against the walls, where bodies are pressed tighter together than they have been for years by the force of an overwhelming thirst. And though there is no wine being poured today and no space in the house to pour it, eyes drink in the spectacle of miracle, of the impossible rendered ordinary, and are intoxicated; ears savor the strange tastes of this Master's surprising words.

From the outer edge of the crowd, where three dust-covered brothers and their mother stand, it looks like this: all the desperation in this place has risen to the surface like old forgotten wounds which, for no reason, begin again to sting. Decades of remembered pain swirl around their son and brother, who wears a tattered shirt and no robe at all, who is still as thin as if he'd just returned from forty days in the desert, who deposits the darkness he draws out of people's

lives in deep pools beneath his eyes.

Mary cries out a little, then stifles her half-sob and looks away. Simon puts an arm around his mother, while James and Judas put strong arms and sharp elbows to work, inching their way forward in the crowd.

"Who do you think you are?" says a man who tries to elbow himself back in front of them.

"His brothers," says James, pointing toward the distant center of the vortex. "Our mother needs him."

They keep pushing their way through the thick of the crowd, but word travels far more quickly than they can. Soon another James and another Judas, who have been busy making sure no one is trampled today, call out to their Master that his mother and brothers are standing outside, waiting for him. Mary and her son Simon are too far outside to see or hear, but another two Simons near Jesus try to hold the next sick person back and dismiss the crowd—until Jesus shakes his head in an unmistakable no.

"Who are my mother and my brothers?" he says clear and strong enough that even over the noise, James and Judas stop pushing and listen to the voice they've known since they were born.

Jesus looks at all the desperate, thirsty faces in this forsaken, out-of-the-way place. "Can't you see?" he says. "You're my brothers, and my sisters, and my mothers." He finds James's face then, gives him a look like he'd give before telling James to calm down when they were boys. "My family is made up of whoever can accept my Father's

will," he says. And then he moves forward to bless the sick boy two Simons have been holding back.

Outside, so far she can barely see, Mary remembers all at once: after those three days of searching and crying they found him all the way back in the Temple, after three days she shook him and said, "Why did you do that to us? We've been worried sick, looking for you everywhere!" As her ragged-looking son reaches now for the next person to heal, and the next, Mary remembers him looking up at her then and saying, as if it were the most natural thing in the world, "Why were you worried? Didn't you know I'd be doing my Father's business?"

In the wine house, the crowd goes crazy with rejoicing and desire; seeing so many healed so quickly, the villagers start pushing forward again just as James and Judas start pushing their way back out of the crowd and toward the only mother they know.

"It's all right," she tries to tell them, but she can see they're not ready to hear.

"Let's go now," they tell her, their own forgotten pains having risen, as if by contagion, to the surface.

Mary isn't normally one to give up, but she doesn't object. She lets them lead her home: because she can see they're hurt, and she knows there are things she'll need time to explain to them, and because, after all, she worries about more than just one of her sons.

*

That night, Jesus leads his followers out of town, off the

72

road and onto a narrow path worn into the hillside by goats and sheep, until he finally settles on a campsite. He lies down, but John can tell that he isn't sleeping, though he pretends to sleep for more than an hour until even Judas has finished praying and half-closed his eyes. When only Peter is still obviously awake, keeping the first watch, Jesus slips out.

John nudges his brother awake. By the moonlight, they can just see Jesus, just see that Peter has left the campsite and is already following him, and they hurry to catch up. Peter notices them and motions them forward, but Jesus doesn't seem to notice anything, just heads further into the hills, up a slope then over a crest into a still steeper walk up the next incline.

"Where is he going?" James whispers to Peter, but Peter says he doesn't know. They try to keep up, but Jesus seems to move faster and faster as they become more and more exhausted, until he's practically leaping up a mountainside. He moves like a deer, thinks James, a deer that has sensed danger and is retreating to a high place. He looks at peace, thinks John, like a captive who has finally been set free. But Peter only wonders how Jesus can climb so quickly. Peter's legs feel like trees being uprooted with each step, and he wonders how long he can go on.

That's when Jesus turns back for the first time. Peter stops, grateful to finally rest his feet. James and John stop beside him when they see their Master looking back.

"Thank you," says Jesus. "But you don't need to come

any further. There will be times for you to follow me up mountains. For now, just rest."

So they do: they lie down and sleep at the base of the last foothill while Jesus climbs like a deer into the mountain for the night. Back at the camp, Andrew is a little worried when he wakes for his watch to find Peter gone, but when he sees that Jesus, James, and John are gone, too, he assumes they've gone with a purpose.

Early in the morning, Jesus comes down the slope to wake the three who followed him. Then he tells them nine more names, and asks them to come back to the foothill bringing those nine men with them.

*

Twelve men gather around Jesus, who tells them how to heal the faith-filled sick. Twelve men gather around Jesus, who tells them it won't be long before he sends them all through scattered Israel as his messengers. Twelve men gather around Jesus, who blesses them the way a father might bless his sons when he feels he is about to die.

To the Simon he named Peter, who still worries about his wife and her mother, he says, "When you go out, take no money with you: don't even make a fold in your shirt as a pocket for it. Didn't the sea provide fish for you? In the same way, the men you catch like fish will provide you with all you need: with food, with shelter, with a shirt to wear if not always a robe."

Jesus looks at Andrew's shirt and smiles. "You've tied knots into a net fit for your new labor. I charged you nothing

for the secrets of those knots; you charge nothing for sharing them. Then men will see that charity is our Father's currency, and they'll charge nothing when they help you."

Next he turns to James, Zebedee and Salome's older son. "Though God will feed and clothe you as he does the grass, remember that men also walk over the grass and trample it, that they cut it when the first harvest comes. But don't be afraid: whoever finds his life will lose it, and whoever loses his life in this work will find it."

To James's young brother John, he says, "No matter who dies, I'll tell you this: some of you standing here will live to see this world end."

That's when tears start to glisten in the morning light across the face of Andrew's friend Judas, who grew up in a slum hidden under the Temple's shadow. Jesus turns to this Judas: "I've told you privately, but soon you'll proclaim it openly: God's kingdom is here!"

To Philip he says, "Go show them the things Isaiah promised: *the eyes of the blind will be opened, the ears of the deaf unstopped, the lame will leap like deer, and the tongues of the mute will sing: because waters have broken out of the wilderness, streams out of the desert places.*"

And to Nathanael, who cared for his father's crops and orchards, he says, "When you go out, you'll feel like a farmer who plants a seed at night and then wakes in the morning to find it fully grown: when the earth herself does the work, all that's left to you is the harvest!"

"When the time comes for you to go away from me," he

says to the twelve, "find places to stay the way Thomas has done: ask carefully in each town, see who's prepared to receive the blessings of a host." Then he turns to Thomas: "If a house or village accepts you, the peace I send with you will rest on them. But if they refuse you, it will return to you: wrap yourself in that peace and sleep soundly under the protection of the stars."

"But don't think," he tells them, "that I've only come to bring peace to the earth. Because your words will also be like a sword, dividing mothers from daughters, fathers from sons, turning this brother against that one." He turns to the southern Simon: "And when the mouth carries a sword," he says, "what need do the hands have for one?"

And to the other Judas, the one whose big chest holds a bigger heart, he says, "Don't be afraid of what men can do to your body: be afraid of what they will try to do to your soul."

Jesus speaks next to Matthew. "You've kept a ledger with the names of those you bought responsibility for, and you've been ready to forgive their debts when they come to you. But the ledger you'll keep soon for me will be like the Book of Life: won't those who know their debts in that Book want to see you?"

Finally, he turns to the other James he called. "When you look for people who have ears to hear," he says, "remember the story I told in Matthew's house. Son of Alphaeus, I tell you again: the last will be first and the first will be last."

Peter and Andrew, James and John, Judas from

Jerusalem and the southern Simon, Philip and Nathanael the farmer's son, Matthew and Thomas, the broad-chested Judas and Alphaeus's James: these are the twelve Jesus calls to the hill, the twelve he gives his power and makes his messengers, the twelve he will keep as close as if he were a boy again and they were his brothers—until he asks them to leave, and to gather his scattered people once more.

*

Two named James. Two named Judas. Two named Simon. Is it only a coincidence that half of the closest brothers in Jesus' new family share names with his first brothers, brothers who left with their mother only yesterday?

2.

As they approach the camp again, James and John hear their mother. Why she's made the journey out to see them and what has her so animated at the moment they can only guess, but long before they can see her face, there's no doubt it's her. Of all the women in Capernaum, Salome has the most distinctive voice — and the one most likely to be raised when something is wrong. They pick up their pace to reach her.

She embraces her sons, then falls at Jesus' feet. "Come back to Capernaum," she tells him.

This is her news: Jesus' former disciples, having failed to bring him before a religious court, have shifted their attention. They've brought charges against his supporters over every minor infraction of the law. They go from house to house trying to convince people Jesus and his followers are dangerous, tell them not to help Peter's wife and her mother or buy Zebedee's fish. And now, they're urging the ruling elders to expel those who honor Jesus' teachings from the congregation.

"Come back," says Salome. "What are all their words against your might and strength, your dignity and power? If you speak to the ruling elders for us, we'll be given the first

place instead of being cast out."

But Jesus just looks at Alphaeus's James, and doesn't answer.

"Come back," says Salome. "I know you say to love our enemies, but do we have to wait for the Day of Judgment before you're also willing to stop them?"

Jesus looks back at her. "*Those who wait upon the Lord will inherit the earth,*" he says.

"Then we're ready to wait if God's will is that we wait," says Salome. "But come back and confront them if the King of the Universe would have you do so!"

That's when Jesus smiles, then speaks: "Lead the way, you sons of thunder," he says to James and John, "your mother predicts a storm."

*

When angry men first came to the council of five who govern the congregation in Capernaum to suggest charges against Jesus for healing on the Sabbath, two immediately spoke against him and two for him:

"What else can we do?" said one. "We saw it ourselves: he broke tradition knowingly and openly."

"How many years had the man's hand been afflicted?" said another, "After all that time, the treatment couldn't wait a single day?"

That was not the issue, said the first of Jesus' defenders. "If it had been a sheep stuck in the mud, no one would have objected. Isn't a man worth more than a sheep?"

"Besides, there's no proof he did anything," said the

other, who was always a little more careful about his words. "He didn't touch him—and if the man was healed by God alone, who are we supposed to charge?"

But the fifth didn't take sides, preferring a peaceful escape from the controversy. "Why do you come to us?" Jairus said to those who had brought the charges. "This man is not from Capernaum: right or wrong, it's not our place to pursue such a difficult case against a guest."

And, oh, how Jairus wished it had been settled at that! Instead, they'd let that case rest but brought complaint after complaint: about one woman's possible heresy, another man's failure to keep this minor law by that minority interpretation. Before Jesus, Jairus recalled, the council's chief concern had been raising funds to replace the old wooden meetinghouse with a new one made of stone. Before Jesus, no one had argued much about who belonged there.

Still, Jairus is fair-minded enough to admit there are legitimate reasons for concern. Jesus seems like a good man, but if he were to turn his energy toward outright rebellion, he wouldn't be the only one killed. Maybe his former disciples are right to bring case after case against those who follow him. Maybe they're right to want his influence stopped before it brings bitter judgment, divine or otherwise, down on the town.

The proposal Jesus' opponents finally bring to the council is this: why not simply ask people to choose between their loyalty to Jesus and their loyalty to the congregation? If they choose the congregation, all is well. And if they choose

any man over the congregation, isn't that proof enough the man's influence goes too far?

But by that time, Jairus isn't thinking about how to compromise. By that time, Jairus is thinking about his only daughter, a twelve-year-old girl who has grown so pale from sickness that sometimes when she sleeps for a terrible moment it looks as if she's dead. Jairus isn't thinking about compromise because day after day, night after night, sudden bursts of panic for her health hit him like rocks.

Jairus isn't interested in casting judgment right now, because he already feels like he's being stoned.

So he throws both caution and neutrality to the wind, and is the first to come begging when Jesus returns.

*

A girl is dying, but there's a crowd to be reckoned with. Into the streets Jesus' opponents pour to shout abuse, into the streets Jesus' supporters stream to shout encouragement. Young men join the throng hoping things turn ugly, the way Roman soldiers who miss the adrenaline of the Coliseum sometimes bet on fights between stray dogs. Old men pour into the street to ask themselves what happened, how the spell of quiet that once hung over their lakeside town has been broken. Young girls slip out of their homes to see if Jesus can rescue the council chief's daughter; their mothers follow them into the fray, hoping to find them and bring them home again. Thieves join the crowd looking for loose money; drunkards join the crowd in the hopes a celebration erupts; the crowd grows tight around Jesus until his apostles

start to worry about how his ribs will fare in the press.

There's a woman in the crowd who's been bleeding since the dying girl was born. She doesn't want to be here — for twelve years she's been unclean from her constant menstruation and so she's not used to being around people other than doctors at all, let alone a whole town at once. She knows she's polluting everyone she touches, but she can't keep from touching them as she pushes and shoves her way forward. This is not what she imagined. She didn't even want to touch him, didn't need to look at him: if she could just reach the hem of his robe, she'd told herself, it would be enough. Because she believes he can heal her. Though she's believed in doctors before and saints before until it seemed all the wealth, hope, and energy were drained out of her bleeding body forever, the first time she heard a story about him, she knew she had to come. And she knows now that although she's exhausted, she needs to make it just a few more steps, just reach her arm out a few inches farther, and it will all be worthwhile. She'll be healed, and no one will ever have to know what sort of woman they touched. Just a few more steps, just a little longer reach, and twelve years of pain will melt and this pounding in her temples will stop and she can go home and, maybe, finally feel at home in her own skin.

She falls, strangers' knees battering her as she lands on her own, but she can see it right ahead, and just another half inch, so she throws herself forward with everything she has left. Maybe she'll be trampled to death now, in the middle of

a faraway town's road, but she can feel the threads against her fingers and she knows that at least she'll die clean: she can tell at once she isn't bleeding from the inside anymore.

"Stop!" says Jesus, and his voice is so firm that the hecklers stop shouting abuse, the young men stop egging them on. Mothers stop calling out their daughters' names, old men stop shaking their heads, even thieves let the coins they've just lifted fall to the ground in their surprise. The feet around the woman don't come down on her back or shoulders, the shins around her don't slam into her head.

"Who touched me?" Jesus says, as she pulls herself up, as she whispers a prayer thanking God for life and health. His disciples laugh.

"Look around you!" they say. "Who here *hasn't* touched you?"

"No, someone touched me," Jesus says. "I felt some of my virtue go out."

That's when the woman starts to shake. When her relief turns to fear. Has she polluted him after all? Has the long impurity of her body somehow wounded this saint?

"Who touched me?" Jesus says, and she starts to cry.

Now everyone is watching her and so she has to tell the whole story: who she is, why she shouldn't have been here with them, why she wanted so badly to touch him and how she risked their well-being to do it. No one seems to know how to look at her. "But I'm healed now," she says through her tears, "I'm sorry I touched you all, but now I'm clean."

"Don't worry," says Jesus. "Your faith healed you. It's all

right."

But in Jairus's house, it is not all right. In Jairus's house, a girl whose face is pale as death when she sleeps has stopped taking in fresh breath.

*

Into the crowd come servants from the mourning house. "It's too late," they tell Jairus, "she's dead. You can leave him alone." But before Jairus can let out the long wail that is forming inside him, before he can scream the wound in his heart out to fill the open sky, Jesus looks hard at him. "When we go in, don't look at her face: it'll make you afraid," he says. "Just watch me, and have faith."

So Jairus walks in Jesus' shadow like a thief who is sneaking up on fate, or like the prophet Jonah seeking shade from the unforgiving heat of this world. When they get to the house, Jesus asks nine of his apostles to keep the crowd out while Peter, James, and John follow him and the girl's parents inside.

Everyone is crying for her: the cook whose patience she used to test with endless questions, the watchman she'd always ask for a story and a late-night cup of weak wine, the wet-nurse who helped feed her as an infant, and the wet-nurse's son, a childhood playmate she's recently been distanced from.

"Why are you here?" says the watchman. "Didn't they tell you it's too late?"

"She's only sleeping," says Jesus, but the watchman laughs a sour laugh because he saw her chest rise and fall

until it stopped rising at all, then shook her frail body trying to bring back her breath. That's when Jesus makes them go out, so that the house is quiet and he can talk to the parents alone.

"Will you take me to her?" he says, and Jairus doesn't look away, he just nods, and walks to her room, and keeps his eyes on Jesus and off his daughter, just like he's been told. But Peter sees her, and James and John, and they can tell why the watchman laughed — it's a cruel, hard life and it can look so empty at the end.

Jesus leans over and takes her cold hand in his hand. "Wake up, little one," he says, and that's when her father can't help but look at her, at the way her sleepy eyes look up at him. She gets out of bed and walks to her parents, and has just embraced them when John feels Jesus next to him start to collapse.

*

"No more crowds today," says Jesus, as he leans on James and John who hold him on the left and the right. If they carry most of his weight, he seems just able to put one foot in front of the other, just able to keep himself from sinking down to his knees in the dirt.

"Where can we go?" says John, and he envies the birds for their nests and the foxes for their holes. "Where can we take him and be left alone?"

"To your father's boats," says Peter. "Let's see who can follow him to the middle of the lake!"

Peter and Andrew run to bring the boat closer while

eight apostles hold back the crowd so that James and John can help their Master take a short but halting walk to the shore. Twice Jesus nearly falls, and then a third time as they bring him into the water toward the waiting boat—the terrifying lightness of his body on this third almost-fall will linger in John's mind for months. He doesn't even try to lift himself into the boat, but lets them haul him up as though they were lifting a little child, and they lay him down like a child and let him sleep while they sail out toward the middle of the lake, sail out until they can't make out the figures on the land. And Jesus' enemies and friends, the rowdy young men and the wonderstruck girls, the distracted thieves and the disappointed drunks all give up watching from the shore, all return to their homes or the alleys where they sleep and brace themselves against a rising and ominous wind.

"Do you worry about him?" asks John.

"I worry about everything," say both Thomas and Peter at once.

*

The wind pours down thousands of feet from the heights on the northeast to the low-lying surface of the lake, which bursts into violent passion the way a whole block of tenements bursts into flame at the touch of a single lightning bolt. Waves leap up like tongues of fire and lick at the cities on the western shore: Capernaum; Magdala; Herod's new capital, Tiberius.

Off the lake comes hard rain that stings like burning

embers and presses itself through small holes in a roof into the cell where John the prophet is kept. But John sees nothing in the rain. He can hear raised voices in the palace above him, knows that the center of the storm between the king and his wife is his own life or death, but shut away in the city so far from his desert, he can't seem to hear the word of the Lord, can't tell how this tumult will end.

On the lake, Jesus sleeps like the dead; the four fishermen do their best to keep the ship from capsizing while the others bail out the water that fills the boat and threatens to drag them down and drown them.

In the palace, the queen is shouting at her husband. "Don't you care about my shame?" she says. "When I left your brother's bed for yours, I thought you'd protect me. If the king stood with me, who would dare to mock? Who could speak ill of me and escape punishment?"

John the prophet moves his lips in silent prayer as the rain keeps pounding down. *How long, oh Lord?* he says. *How long will you hide your face from me?*

On the lake, Jesus sleeps still. The fishermen shout out their prayers as they work, the others bail as if they were trying to empty the sea.

"Do you want to be killed?" says the king to his wife. "Do you want people to riot in the streets until the earth shakes with them? They count him as a prophet, and the prophets have always meant trouble for Israel."

"You're afraid of him," she says. "I thought you were brave enough to face anyone in the empire, but you're too

scared to face a captive in your own cellar jail!"

The king gets angry then, shouts abuse at his wife and pushes her to the floor. Then he stomps down to the prison, shakes the bars until his arms ache—but John sees nothing in the king's visit, and the king gives up and walks away.

On the lake, Jesus is deep in sleep until Nathanael, who's too honest to be embarrassed at himself, shakes him awake and asks with wide eyes, "Don't you care if we die?"

Jesus gets up without acknowledging Nathanael and speaks straight into the wind, the driving rain, the froth-tipped waves: "Enough for now," he says. "Give us some peace."

And from Capernaum to Tiberius, all at once the storm is gone. Homeless men see the night sky clear again from their alleys and wonder at the brightness of the stars. The twelve look at Jesus in a mixture of awe and fear, wonder for the first time not just who he is, but what kind of being can speak that way to the wind and the sea.

In his cell, John is filled with the depth of this sudden stillness. He wraps his face in a tattered remnant of his robe and rises to speak with his God.

*

What does John say to God, and what does God say back? I don't know.

But after they've talked, maybe, after John is left to study the four walls of his prison until they seem to be falling in on him, doubt sinks in, pools on the floor with the leftover rain.

So when John's disciples come to visit, bringing him

fresh bread dipped in desert honey, John wants to be sure, so he sends them to Jesus to ask.

"Are you the One?" they say to Jesus. "Or will our Master have to wait for someone else?"

"Tell him what the people here have seen," says Jesus. "*The blind see, the lame walk, and the deaf hear. The lepers are cured, the dead raised up, and the poor have the gospel preached to them.*"

John's disciples get excited. They tell him about Herod and his wife, about the rumors coming out of the palace. Is the time soon coming, they ask him, when the words of Isaiah will be fulfilled, when a servant of God will *bring out the captives from their cells, and deliver those who sit in darkness from their prisons?*

But Jesus turns away before he answers.

"No matter how the Jordan twists and turns," he says, "it always ends in the same sea."

And is it only the young John's imagination, or is Jesus' thin face wet with salty tears?

*

That night, Jesus sends the twelve back to the lake without him. The waters are a little rough, but after seeing what their Master can do, they don't question his direction: out they row against short wind-blown waves, straining their arms to make distance. It's slow going, so for a long time they can still see the tiny figure of Jesus, climbing up a mountain to pray for the man who baptized him. Years from now, James will rise from a prison cell, look

into the steel of another Herod's sword, and wonder what Jesus said to his Father this night. "Does he really have to drink this cup?" maybe, or maybe just, "Let his spirit be safe in your hands." Years from now, James will look at steel that shines in his executioner's eyes like this night's moon on the lake and remember the wind, and the sounds of small waves, and the way a boat at night can rock you to sleep.

On the lake tonight, James keeps the first watch, and John the second, and Peter the third. So in the hour just before dawn, it's Andrew who first sees the ghost.

He walks toward them against the breeze, which is strong enough to blow the loose ends of his robe out behind him. He looks as majestic as John did on the Jordan, Andrew thinks, and his heart sinks: is John dead? Where is Judas? thinks Andrew. Judas will recognize their old master.

Andrew tries not to disturb the others as he wakes his friend, but it's hard to keep a secret when twelve men are sleeping on the same boat. Judas wakes quickly and looks out across the water: no, it's not John, he tells Andrew, and Andrew exhales in relief. It looks more like Jesus, he says, and now they're all alert, all staring out over the edge.

As the ghost gets closer, their panic begins to mount. "Who are you?" Nathanael shouts.

"Don't be afraid," Jesus says, "it's me."

"Are you dead?" says Peter.

"No," says Jesus.

"Let me touch you," says Peter, "Ask me to walk out on the water and touch you and I'll know."

"Come then," says Jesus.

And the first step is so easy. It's so easy to climb right over the boat's edge and put your foot down onto the water's shifting surface and yet move forward. Yes, the first step is easy and the second's not too bad, but after that you've got to keep focused on Jesus. You can't let yourself think about the way water pools and swirls and pours, the way it falls down from the heavens on a cool day or disappears in the heat, can't even think too hard about your solid feet, just keep moving them. But then the way the wind blows the edges of his robe. And the sharp white crests of the growing waves. And suddenly your legs feel as unstable as the water beneath them and you know you are going to drown.

There's a hand in your hand and it's not letting go. Jesus pulls you out of the water, because he's alive.

Because he's alive, and because he's the anointed one.

3.

Some say killers and their weapons like to gamble with each other over the next victim's name. And that once the wager has been placed, they grow impatient to see whose blood will be made to redden next as it is brought naked to face the air.

In this empire, the suspense never lasts long. Executioners in palaces keep their weapons unsheathed by their bedsides, because in the passion of night, lives can be spent so casually. And in the morning, the names of the dead are passed between rulers like coins which gradually wear away until no one can remember if they first represented a slaughtered man or city.

In this empire the crucifixions litter the roadsides, advertising the constancy of rulers who bind the world together through daily death and pain.

So why does the king tremble when he gives the order for John's execution? And when his wife, in her unabated anger, lifts the head from a platter to the end of a pike, which she keeps guarded in the square as a warning to those who mock royal blood, why do John's dead eyes give the king such bad dreams?

No one risks his life trying to take the head down, but at night some disciples recover John's body. They wrap it in a camel's skin and they bury him in an unmarked grave in the desert, where they can still feel God speak. Then two of them turn back and find Jesus on a road not far from Tiberius.

*

Though public funerals for the murdered prisoner have been banned by royal decree, in a village not far from Herod's capital, Jesus speaks of the dead.

"What did you go to the desert to see?" he asks, "A man like a reed who would bend back and forth in fear of every storm?

"Let me ask you again," says Jesus. "What did you go out to see? Was it a man who hides from hard truths in soft robes?

"No—you went to the desert, not the palace," he says, and though they're in mourning, the people can't help but laugh. "You've lost faith in the king and were ready for a prophet. And is a prophet what you found on the banks of the Jordan?" Some people shout in agreement, while others start to look nervously around.

"Let me tell you something: you saw more. Isn't it written *I'll send my messenger before your face, and he'll prepare the way?*"

The crowd gets quiet.

"If you're afraid, then pretend you've heard nothing today. But if you have ears to hear, I'll tell you this: God's

kingdom is coming down the path already, and as is written *it will break to pieces all the kingdoms of the earth*. And I'll tell you this: the shameful things this king has done to John won't be done even to the lowest criminal in the kingdom of God."

And the people shake with fear and longing at the things they've heard today.

*

Indecisive as Herod can be, it's hard to imagine that if he finds out, he'll let this speech pass without violence.

"We're ready to die for you," say Salome's sons. "And to kill, if you need us to."

"Is it time to rise up?" says the southern Simon. "I have old friends who will help."

"Is it the time all our ancestors waited for?" asks Judas.

"Let's go back to the boat," says Jesus. "Let's sail out of Herod's kingdom before his men come looking for us."

*

In the boat, the southern Simon frowns. Wherever you flee, he thinks, there's no real escape. He's left the rule of the south's new governor, a man who honors dead and living emperors as his gods, who uses their soldiers as his laws. He's sailing now from the north's so-called king, a Jew who killed a prophet and pitches his tents toward Rome, who never seems embarrassed to rely on the same imperial soldiers as his foreign southern counterpart. On the east side of the lake, they'll reach the ten cities, where Greek settlers outnumber both Syrians and Jews, where Roman soldiers

rule each town without any king or governor at all.

Yes, the real rulers of this world are shields, swords, javelins—and the constant threat of death.

Simon looks across the water toward the shore. A large herd of pigs attests that they're safely in ten cities territory, but a sprawling graveyard below reminds him they're never really safe.

And it's just past the graveyard Jesus tells them he wants the boat to land.

*

As they leave the boat, they hear someone crying. Somewhere in the graveyard there's a living man who's mad with grief, as if he's just buried his wife and his only child. But there are no signs of a funeral party anywhere, nothing other than this one man's cries to tear at the lakeside calm. And as Jesus and his apostles get closer, they can see: there are no fresh graves near where the man lies naked, wailing; his tears fall on hardened earth.

Jesus walks to the edge of the cemetery and calls out to him. The man rises, and John looks away in shame. Though they've come to a land dominated by Greeks and Syrians, the naked man is a Jew.

His hair is long and uncut, as if he'd taken vows like Samson's—vows he can't possibly have kept. The dirt and filth that cover him cast shadows that serve to highlight the strength and size of his body, but his arms and thighs are covered with scars and fresh cuts. In his hand, he still holds a sharp stone.

He shouts out at Jesus like a war-cry, then blasphemes loudly and rushes forward. Jesus starts to command the evil spirits to go out of him, but stops when the man falls to his knees and begs like a frightened child. "Don't hurt me," he says in a voice that sounds strange coming from a man so large. "Please don't hurt me."

"What's your name?" Jesus asks him.

All at once, the child in him is gone. He looks up at Jesus with wild, threatening eyes and spits out the words: "Our name is Legion."

But Jesus sets his jaw, and the man turns childish again. "Don't make us leave," he says, or else the spirits say through him. "It's so hard without a body. Let us go into the pigs, at least. It hurts too much to be alone."

"Go then," says Jesus.

And the man's body falls from kneeling so that he lies completely prostrate at Jesus' feet. He inhales like a drowning man who by some miracle manages to break the surface of the water. "They're gone," he says, "they're finally gone."

And then he weeps again.

"You couldn't have fought them," Jesus says.

"But I should have," says the man.

"There's been fighting enough here," says Jesus.

"But no vengeance and no justice," says the man.

"Have you forgotten so soon?" says Jesus, and he recites: *He who makes peace in the heavens, may He make peace upon us and upon all Israel.*

The man sits up slowly and stares at Jesus. "I was too angry," he says. "I never said the mourners' prayer."

"If a son came to his father's house at midnight," says Jesus, "Would he stand outside in silence—or call out, and be welcomed in?"

"*May His great name be magnified and made sacred,*" whispers the man, "*in the world He created according to his will.*" And as the apostles lean in to listen, he prays for the dead Jews of his city.

"What happened?" Matthew asks after the man finishes praying.

"A Greek child grew sick and died," he tells the twelve. "A rumor spread that our people had been jealous of the family's wealth and that our envy caused their misfortune." The twelve nod. They've heard stories like this one before. "They bribed some soldiers to let them into our quarter one night, but they didn't need a second bribe to get other soldiers to come with them. They robbed and killed and did shameful things to both women and men.

"When I asked for justice, they chained me. When I broke the chains, they chained me again and again. And how could I fight? They were always so many."

In the field above, the pigs are acting strangely. The boys paid to tend them get nervous and back away.

"When they sent me away, I came to the tombs. I swore to avenge the dead: because I couldn't cut the killers, I cut myself."

In the field above, the pigs begin to turn against each

other. Two thousand animal bodies churn as if a storm has swept off the lake onto the land.

"When I slept in the dirt of the tombs, I felt I was where I belonged. A graveyard only makes you unclean if you're still supposed to be alive."

The pigs above begin to run off a cliff. The boys who tend them run back toward the town.

Jesus interrupts the man's story. "Have you said the mourners' prayer for the Greek child?"

*

When prayers have been said for the dead child and for his living parents, they go into the lake to wash the healed man. They bury his scarred and bloody body beneath the surface of the water and bring him up feeling whole again. From the boat, they fetch him the largest of the spare clothes Matthew brought. On the shore, they share some fish and a little bread.

While Jesus and his companions eat, a delegation from the city arrives. The men from the city first survey the pigs' field and see for themselves that it's empty. Then they turn to the group on the shore and see the possessed man calmed, clothed, and healed.

And how should these men weigh signs of terror against signs of hope?

"We respectfully request you to leave our shores," their leader says.

Jesus tells them he and his followers will do so within the hour, and the men go back to their city satisfied.

"Remember this," says Jesus to the twelve, "we are not like the princes of this world: the kingdom of God doesn't come as an occupying force."

*

"Take me with you," the healed man says. "Let me follow you until the day I die."

"No," says Jesus. "Go back to the survivors in your city and tell them what the Lord has done. When the night falls, whisper to those who know how to listen that the kingdom of God is here, and that sooner than they know, it will come to them."

*

The healed man doesn't waste any time or spare any effort. He goes from town to town, from host to host, carrying Jesus' name on his lips. He shows people his scars. Tells them about his demons. Says in what way he was freed and cleansed. If people's eyes grow wide, then mist up, he whispers Jesus' words. Soon whispers start to echo through the Jewish homes scattered across the region east of the lake. What great exorcist, what powerful magician, has come to them?

One day a traveler from the north end of the lake chances to hear their whispers about Jesus. But he, too, has a whisper: Jesus has cast out evil spirits in his town as well, he says, and the spirits obey because Jesus has made a pact with the prince of demons. So the people whisper about this whisper, too: what dark exorcist, what sinister magician, has come?

In Bethsaida, just north of the ten cities and east of Herod's kingdom, Jesus and the twelve are bewildered. They haven't heard this new rumor, so they don't know why it's become so easy for them to sleep in peace, don't know why the people who wait for healing in the day tend to leave so quickly as soon as the night begins to cast its spell over the world. They don't know why even the students hesitate with their questions lately, why no one asks to walk with them until morning anymore. When one young man says he doesn't want to know their secrets, they assume he's talking about the kingdom of God. It's only when scholars traveling from Jerusalem share their accommodations for a night that they learn what people have been talking about.

At first, the scholars simply seem abnormally curt, giving short answers and avoiding the long, lively scriptural discussions and debates that set apart Jews from the rest of the world. As it grows darker, though, the scholars keep their eyes on the door and behave as if Jesus and his disciples all carried long knives beneath their robes.

"What's the matter with you?" asks Nathanael, forthright as always. But the scholars don't speak up for a while, because it takes time for curiosity to bore its way through protective layers of fear. When they look at Jesus, they can see he keeps secrets, and their fear gains strength. Then they look at Nathanael, whose face is not that of a secret-keeper, and they wonder until they can't stop themselves.

"We've heard . . ." they begin, and then struggle for

words. How do you politely ask thirteen men if they're in league with the devil? "What we mean is: everyone talks about your power . . ." and they tell him. They admit they've been afraid to stay here the night, because they're at once frightened of and tempted by what Jesus and his associates might do after dark. They admit that if Jesus has made a pact with Satan, they're impressed by how well it works. Speaking in strictly theoretical terms, say the Jerusalem scholars, does Jesus possess, or have reason to believe one can possess, a special incantation that would use the cryptic names of superior demons to cast out inferior ones? And, again purely theoretically, if one did possess and use such an incantation, what would be the cost?

Jesus laughs — though they can't be sure in the lamplight and the long shadows if the laugh should be frightening, exciting, or relieving. "What sort of prince do you think Satan is?" he says, "What king appoints a son as his heir and then welcomes his rebellion? Don't you remember what happened when the first Herod died? A kingdom divided against itself never lasts long.

"Let me tell you a story," Jesus says, and leans forward. And when Jesus leans forward, everyone leans forward to listen.

"The strongest man in any town does whatever he wants," says Jesus, "because no one can stop him." Then he tells about one city's tyrant, how he makes himself rich off plunder and bribes and sets such a fear in the people's hearts that not even the thieves dare disturb him — they

don't want to be discovered and killed. After some time, though, the strong man has terrorized the city so much that every widow prays for deliverance, and God, hearing their prayers, sends a stronger man to the city to rescue them.

"What do you think the stronger man will do—sit down at a table with the tyrant and strike a bargain? No, he binds the strong man in stiff cords and takes back the people's goods over the strong man's objections!"

It's quiet for a moment as the twelve and the travelers alike puzzle the story out. Are they correct in understanding that Jesus has no secret incantation? the scholars from Jerusalem ask. And his position, even from a theoretical standpoint, is that it wouldn't work to somehow play the evil spirits against each other?

Yes, says Jesus, against evil spirits the only recourse is the Spirit of the Lord.

But they press him further. Isn't there some way around that? they say. If, for instance, the afflicted is too unclean for the Spirit of the Lord to reach, shouldn't there be another way?

Don't go down that road, says Jesus. "Speak ill of me," he says forcefully, "if you still believe that rumor to be true. But if you close your eyes, all that's left is darkness. And if you shut out the Spirit of the Lord and look to demons for deliverance, the unclean can never be restored."

It was just a question, say the scholars. A purely theoretical question.

And since the need for nervous glances toward the door

is gone, they put out the lamp and drift off to sleep.

In the moonlight, Judas waits and hopes and yearns.

"Master of the Universe!" prays Judas, "Has he done it yet, has the strong man been bound?"

And though God doesn't answer, Judas still wonders what it will look like when Jesus utterly spoils the strong man's house.

4.

Jesus gets up early in the morning and leads the twelve to a quiet spot on the stream next to Bethsaida. On the west side of the stream is Galilee proper, ruled by the Herod who killed John, but here on the east side they're safely in his brother Philip's land.

So when Jesus looks west, Andrew has a feeling they're about to head back in the direction of trouble.

"It's time," Jesus says. He takes the twelve and divides them into pairs, as if he had a heavy weight for them to carry and wanted to balance the hands on the right with the hands on the left. "Are you ready?"

"Yes. For what?" says James.

"It's time for you to go on without me," says Jesus. "Then we'll gather again, and you can tell me what you've done."

Now it's not just Andrew who's nervous. Jesus has told them about this before, about how one day he'd send them out to search through Galilee for people who listen, the way children are sent to gather berries as soon as they can distinguish the edible from the poisonous and the ripe from the unripe. But knowing something is going to happen is not

the same as being ready for it, and so the twelve find themselves suddenly full of questions.

"How do we know for certain who we're looking for?" asks Thomas.

"How does a fisherman know which fish to let into his net?" says Jesus, and the brothers from Capernaum laugh: you don't pick what goes into your net, you sort it out afterward. "Just look for the people who are already looking for you," Jesus says. "Remember the lost sheep? It knew the voice of its shepherd."

"What do we say when we preach? What if we open our mouths and nothing comes out?" asks Philip.

"Don't worry about what to keep in your mouth," says Jesus. "Keep a treasure in your heart, and the Spirit of the Lord will bring out jewels when you speak."

"But what if people ask questions we can't answer? We're not scholars—what if people who study the law challenge us and make us look like fools?"

"They'll try to draw you into arguments that last longer than it takes bread to rise—but tell them you don't have time," says Jesus. "Remember the flatbread our ancestors made on their last night in Egypt. Ask the people: when God's Day of Judgment is at hand, where's the need for earthly lawyers?"

"What if soldiers give us trouble?" says the southern Simon.

"The laws of their kingdom say an armed soldier can make an unarmed man carry his pack for a mile," says Jesus,

"But if one does, go two miles to show him that in God's kingdom, it's the strong who will help carry the burdens of the weak.

"The laws of their kingdom say a soldier can slap us with the back of his hand, like he would strike a slave," says Jesus. "But if one does, turn your face so he has to slap you with an open hand, the way he would challenge an equal!"

"How do you know it's time?" asks Judas.

Jesus pauses, takes a close look at him. "When you see a cloud in the west, you know it's going to rain. When you feel a wind from the south, you know it's about to get hot. You know how to read the face of the sky: learn also to see the signs of the times. When you start to see old prophecies write themselves on the pages of life, the Day can't be far."

"So hurry!" Jesus says to them all, "Put your sickle to the grain before the storms come. Cast out the evil spirits, shout hope to the poor. When you find the sick, anoint them with oil like a prophet or a king—because the sick are sacred to God!

"And keep count of who is ready to leave everything to follow us, and where they are," says Jesus, "because one king won't move against another without first counting the strength of his troops."

A thrill passes through the southern Simon's body at this, and he looks around at the others: companions, friends, and fellow-laborers already, he imagines the day when they'll also be military comrades. As he looks, though, he's a little disappointed: no one else seems as stirred by these

words as he feels. Matthew, who's probably terrified at the prospect of fighting, just looks anxious. Philip and Nathanael don't seem to have noticed. Even Peter's looking at Jesus a little self-consciously, and the question that seems to be forming in his mouth doesn't give any evidence of excitement.

"Will you pray for us before we go?" asks Peter.

And Jesus does. He starts the same way as always, the way Peter loves, calling God "my Father" instead of "Master of the Universe" or "Our King." And he speaks like a son who's close to his father, asking humbly that he and his companions will do the Father's will, that when they don't they'll be forgiven and learn to forgive. He begs his Father that their faith won't fail, and when he says "Amen," it's both affirmation and surrender: a witness that he believes the will of his Father will be done, and a promise that he'll accept it.

When he's done praying, Jesus leads the twelve up to the water. And then—believe it or don't believe it, as you will—but I tell you the river parted for him that day the way it parted for his namesake all those years ago.

*

Only two pairs of apostles go straight to new towns: at Thomas's suggestion, the other four pairs start in towns where Jesus has already been. Their plan is this: go find people who embraced Jesus' teachings, ask them if they have relatives in other towns, and preach over kinship lines so they can spend more time teaching and less time looking

107

for people to teach.

But things don't always go according to plan.

Matthew and Thomas make a stop at a roadside village not far from Capernaum where Jesus was received well on his last visit, but find themselves greeted with suspicion. Old friends of Thomas's have been here in the meantime: friends who followed Jesus, then left him. Memory is a strange thing, thinks Thomas: the people in this village have talked with Jesus, but the words they claim to have heard from his mouth sound more like the words his detractors would have left. How could they have forgotten the teachings that so recently moved them? Though their eyes remember, it's as if their ears never really heard Jesus at all.

Judas and Simon travel farther before the rocky hillsides cut at their feet through sandals that have worn thin as they've walked with their Master. Luckily, they too are near a village that had gladly listened to Jesus just a few months ago. They can still remember the dance the villagers held the night before they left, still remember the toasts to new teachings, the promises people made to change.

But no one is celebrating in the village on the day Judas and Simon return. The mood is somber, and the people walk around half-slumped down as they labor in the heat. Judas and Simon try to start conversations, but no one seems interested. Finally a tired-looking woman asks them, "What use are your teachings? John is dead, and your Master has abandoned us." And that's when Judas and Simon begin to understand what happened, begin to see how hopelessness

has hardened into resentment here. They try to plead with people, try to revive their crushed young faith again—but it's hard, thankless work, and they decide before long to move on.

Peter and Andrew come to the village Jesus' brothers tried to take him home from, and everyone's happy to see them again. They're immediately invited back to the wine house, but there's space today to serve real wine and they're offered cup after cup after cup as aging men tell them how their farms are doing, and young men tell them about the thorny paths they're taking in love. Peter and Andrew listen politely, then try to teach—but whenever the brothers stop talking the village men bring up the same things: farms and girls, girls and farms. And it's clear that though they've nodded and made polite sounds, they haven't been listening to the brothers at all. And though it seems each of the men invites Peter and Andrew to stay in his home that night, the brothers announce they have to move on. So late? say the men. "You remember how our Master worked," says Peter. And then they leave and Andrew shudders at the way men can fail to realize what they have forgotten.

Thomas and Matthew, Judas and Simon, Peter and Andrew—each pair will go on to find people who are looking for truth. They'll find places where they can do miracles and have their teachings understood, which is perhaps the greatest miracle of all. But they'll also remember these first villages and know that no progress is immune to time. That if people stop searching for truth, they often lose

even the truth they once had.

*

But Philip and Nathanael will have to learn those lessons from the others, because Thomas's system works better for them than they could have imagined. At the farming village where they stop, even people who missed Jesus when he came can still recite the story of his teachings and give the names of the villagers he healed. The old women who cook for Philip and Nathanael have more questions to ask, and the old men listen with them to the apostles' answers. When the apostles ask who'd be ready to follow Jesus if he needed them, it seems the whole town is prepared to give up crops and take only livestock, pitching tents like the children of Israel as they followed Moses and Joshua. And before Philip and Nathanael can ask about relatives in other towns, the villagers ask them to go and see their family members here and there, say they've sent word in advance that disciples of Jesus will be coming, and offer to send a young kinsman or two with them to witness that what they have to say is true.

How many people will hear about Jesus through each person in this village, Philip wonders. Thirty? Sixty? A hundred?

*

James and John aren't teaching by the hundred: they often go whole days without finding anyone who wants to listen to them at all. But it doesn't matter, because soon someone who's been looking for Jesus finds them.

Her name is Joanna. She's never met Jesus, she says, but

she's been collecting stories about him for some time now. And because she wants those little stories to fit together into a big story, she asks James and John question after question. Some they can answer: where was he born? What's the meaning of his story about the mustard seed? But other questions are more difficult: why are there so many stories about evil spirits recognizing him? Why do they always seem to shout out God's name?

"We don't know everything," say James. "We just know what it feels like to follow him, and that's enough."

"Can I talk to him myself?" asks Joanna.

The brothers hesitate. It's not really safe for Jesus to come to Galilee now, they explain, given what he said about John the prophet just after the execution.

But Joanna smiles. Their Master doesn't have to worry. Her husband, she tells them, is Herod's palace steward. She and her husband know more than anyone would want to about Herod, and they know for a fact that he won't touch Jesus, because he thinks that Jesus *is* John, returned from the dead to punish his killer.

"Is that true?" says James.

"I swear it," says Joanna.

"How can we trust you? How do we know this isn't a trap?" says John.

"Because my husband and I have sworn to serve the king," she says.

"Yes," says James. "That's what we're worried about."

"We work for Herod," says Joanna, "but it's the true

king of Israel we swore to serve."

James and John don't say anything.

"My husband's a very wealthy man," says Joanna. "Tell us what we can do for your Master."

"We'll go ask him," says James, and he promises to meet her again the next week and tell her what Jesus says.

"Meet me in Magdala," she says. "I have a cousin there."

5.

Matthew and Thomas are the last of the twelve to get word that Jesus is now in Magdala and wants to meet them there. In the evening, they say their goodbyes to the people of the town where they've been preaching—as soon as the sun sets, the air cools off, and the villagers go to sleep, Matthew and Thomas plan to go.

Only not everyone does go to sleep. When night falls, a few townspeople linger near the apostles. There's a young man who could barely walk before they blessed him—he's been following them around town for a week and now seems ready to follow them straight out of it. There's an older man whose family died in a plague that left him half-blind: since they blessed him, they haven't been able to get out of his sight, either. There are several students still asking questions. There's a beggar who likes to bask in the generosity that follows Jesus' messengers.

More alarming is the presence of two women. There's the girl who had trouble with an evil spirit and still worries no one will accept her in town. There's the sharp-minded woman who's been widowed twice, both times without children, who always seem to anticipate the next thing

Matthew and Thomas are going to say, who sometimes even finishes their sentences if they take too long searching for words. If the others won't let Matthew and Thomas go alone, if they insist on following them all the way to Jesus in Magdala, it's no problem. But for two unescorted women to travel through the night with them is against both propriety and tradition. So Matthew and Thomas stay, and talk, and wait until almost midnight, and then simply get up to go.

Most of the men follow them. And the women follow them, too. Down the lane, along the main street, and finally out past the village boundary stones. Thomas tries to walk too fast for their female followers to keep pace, but the girl's feet are light and the widow's legs are long. Matthew stops to ask them to turn back, but the widow speaks up first. "I'll take care of the girl. And we don't have any relatives left to be angry with you. No one is worried about our honor."

Matthew turns to Thomas. "Didn't Jesus say we're all brothers and sisters?" he says. "Since we're their nearest relatives, why shouldn't they travel with us?"

And so it is that seven men and two women arrive, just before dawn, at the crowded town on the seaside.

*

"You must be the last two," says a woman Matthew and Thomas don't recognize. She tells them her name is Mary, and that she'll lead the two apostles to Jesus and help the others find a place to stay. Though he won't admit it, Thomas is a little bothered by this: has she taken over his old responsibility? As they make their way across the city,

pausing from time to time for Mary to check on visitors and their local hosts, Thomas realizes she's fulfilling his role quite well: there seem to be hundreds of people here to see Jesus, maybe over a thousand, but there's nothing to suggest they've been sleeping on the streets. She does have the advantage of being local. But still, is it possible she's found a place for everyone?

Mary-from-Magdala brings them at last to one of the town's largest houses, explaining that a well-to-do local woman named Susannah—whose cousin's husband, by the way, is a top official under the king—has opened her home for Jesus' healing and teaching. Though it's clear even from a distance the house's courtyard must be quite large, the street in front is still crowded with people waiting to get in. Many of them seem to recognize Mary, though, and help make way for her to bring in Matthew and Thomas.

Jesus' face lights up when he sees them at the courtyard entrance, but the courtyard is packed with the sick, and Matthew and Thomas aren't eager to push their way through so many fragile people to reach him. So Jesus nods at them and continues healing while they look for the others. They see Judas and Simon, helping keep people from tripping on a paralyzed woman's cot. On the other side of the courtyard, Philip and Nathanael gently guide out a man who's just had his eyesight restored to make more room around Jesus. Closest to Jesus are the big Judas, who keeps people from pushing their way to the healer out of turn, and the little James, who helps them one by one to Jesus when

it's time. But where are Peter and Andrew, James and John?

Matthew and Thomas carefully step over and around waiting people to reach Judas and Simon.

"Where are the fishermen?" asks Matthew.

Judas leans over and tries to answer so quietly that in the noise of the courtyard, no one but Matthew will hear. "They're getting a boat. You're to sleep as well as you can tonight: first thing in the morning, he wants us to go with him to a desert place north of here where we can talk in peace."

It will be almost a full day before Judas feels as if his stomach is sinking down to the bottom of the Sea of Galilee when he realizes he was overheard.

*

This is what Judas sees the next day: in the back of the boat, Jesus is laughing as Andrew finishes a story about how asking locals "who was worthy" in their town to be two preachers' host once got them directions to a brothel. Peter and James are fidgeting with the sail while John leans over the edge of the boat and grabs a fish straight out of the water. Judas stares in unmasked awe at the young man's dexterity, watches the fish try to wrestle its way out of John's hand, splashing droplets of water in every direction. When the fish stops struggling, Judas catches sight of the coast. Something is wrong. He can see the distant, tiny figures of people—a lot of people—making their way like a procession of ants along the beach. His eyes follow the line forward until—right where Jesus had planned to come

116

ashore—he sees them in an absolute swarm.

That's when he remembers. He told Matthew the plan right in the middle of yesterday's crowd. And though no one was there when the apostles set sail before dawn, it seems as though everyone has made it up the shore in the time they've spent out on the lake.

"I'm sorry," says Judas, and he points to the coast.

Eleven men groan and begin to suggest other places to go. But Jesus tells Peter and James to bring them in closer, and Judas watches the people on shore catch sight of the boat, sees the ripple of excitement it sends through the crowd.

"Sheep without a shepherd," says Jesus. "We'll land."

*

Jesus steps out of the boat, picks up some sand and lets it run between his fingers back to the ground. Then he tells a story about two men who built houses: one on sand like this, the other on a rock. Which one, he asks, do you think fared better when they were hit by a great and terrible storm?

And he doesn't stop teaching for the next eight hours, barely even pauses as he tells story after story after story. Every story is like a pearl or a beautiful bead, thinks James: so what is the hidden thread that strings them all into one necklace?

When his listeners seem to be getting tired, Jesus tells funny stories: everybody laughs at the way he staggers around as if he had a giant plank sticking out of his eye while he pretends to try to pluck out a grain of sand that's

gotten in Nathanael's. When the audience seems to be getting too boisterous, Jesus tells unsettling stories: about men who stumble on their way to heaven and then cut off their feet so they can learn to walk.

An hour or so before sunset, Jesus' voice is giving out and he has to take a short rest.

"Should we get back into the boat?" Judas asks. "There's nothing to eat here, and these people need time to get into town before the markets close."

Jesus looks out at the crowd and shakes his head no. "They need to eat together."

Nathanael laughs. "There must be three thousand people here," he says.

"Three thousand strangers now," says Jesus. "But if they break bread together, they can be a family."

"Is this a place where we can do that?" says Philip.

"If we send them out of the desert as strangers," says Jesus, "this whole day will have been wasted. Give them something to eat."

"But where could we buy a year's wages in bread?" says Matthew.

"And what net could we use to bring in a season's worth of fish?" says Andrew.

"Can we at least send some of them home first?" says James. "There's no way we can feed them all."

"How much do you have?" says Jesus.

Judas checks the boat. Five loaves of bread and a fish. Wait—no, it's two fish if he can find the one John

miraculously caught.

"It's enough," says Jesus.

"Then we'll do it," says Peter. "How?"

*

Jesus' first instruction is to organize the people. Get them sitting down in groups of fifty to a hundred. Have a few boys in each group volunteer to help pass the food around.

Jesus' second direction is that each of them should find someone to lend them a basket. It will be easier to feed everyone if they can hold the food in something before they pass it around.

After that, says Jesus, they'll just have to pray. He'll begin with the blessing on the bread, and then they're to keep praying silently as they work until everyone is fed.

After they've divided the crowd, each of the twelve has six groups, meaning there must be four or five thousand people overall. Which makes it easy to find twelve baskets. Jesus says the blessing and gives half a loaf and a quarter of a fish to each of them. They pass the baskets to the young men. And then all twelve apostles silently pray as they watch the young men pass through the crowd.

The twelve keep prayers in the hearts and their eyes on the people getting food from the baskets. The twelve don't look into the baskets to worry about how much is left: they stay focused on making sure no one is passed by and left unfed. And soon they can hear people talking and laughing, can listen to a few singing joyful psalms. If the young men lose track of where they've carried the baskets, the twelve

show them where to go until it becomes more and more difficult to find hungry faces.

"You need to try this," says an old man in the crowd to Andrew, and then puts a piece of the bread straight into the apostle's mouth. It's more moist than a baker's, as rich as the bread at any wedding. As he savors it, Andrew wants to cry.

"It's fit for a king!" shouts the old man, and everyone in the group looks toward Jesus and cheers. Soon the cheer spreads through the whole assembly, and the twelve make their way back out of the crowd and fall down at Jesus' knees—but he tells them to get up at once.

"Go gather the baskets," he says. "No sense wasting what's left."

So they go back, and they wander through their groups, listening to happy people share stories, until they find their baskets. Which are fuller with pieces of bread and fish than when they started.

"You still think we've reached too many people?" says Jesus when they come back. "Still think we need to send some away?"

None of the twelve can find words to answer him, but their awed silence says enough.

"Looks like you each have enough left to feed a whole tribe of Israel," Jesus says, and they smile sheepishly. But Jesus' face seems to turn a little sad when he adds, "You promise me that someday you'll go find enough people to eat the rest?"

6.

Evening winds stir the lake's waters, so it's a rough ride back to Magdala for the apostles who grew up inland. Thomas has the worst time. While the others take turns helping row, he hangs on to the side of the boat against the swaying feeling inside him and breathes through his mouth to keep his stomach from turning at the accumulated smell of old fish.

By the time they reach the city again, well after dark, Thomas wonders if he has enough sense of balance left to walk with Jesus. After stumbling up the streets to Susannah's house, he feels a little more stable, but still drained of strength and will by the trip.

Mary and one of Susannah's servants are rolling out mats for them when they return. "I didn't know if you'd come back tonight," says Mary. "But I'm glad we prepared, because you look exhausted."

"Thank you," says Thomas, though he isn't sure whether he feels blessed or threatened by her competence tonight.

"If you need more time to rest, you can sleep late tomorrow," says Mary. "No one will crowd you here—our city's priests and Levites are leaving in the evening for their

month of service at the Temple, and everyone gathers in the morning to be taught by them first. If you'd like, you can come. But no one will miss a stranger if you stay."

"I'll come," says Jesus, "to honor the Temple and those who serve there. But if any of you need to sleep, rest while you can."

Thomas smiles. Whether he stays or goes, it'll be nice to have a quiet day when the attention is on someone other than his Master. And on a day when the people crowd around the priests, what could go wrong for the twelve?

*

The trouble starts with Judas's nightmare. It's the same nightmare he used to have all the time, though it hasn't come since the day John washed him clean in the Jordan's muddy waters. Until tonight. Maybe it's the guilt he felt yesterday over ruining their quiet meeting place that brings it back. Maybe it's all the talk in the evening about the Temple that stirs up bitter memories of Jerusalem. Or maybe the memories are always somewhere in the back of his mind, and it's because he's at once so tired and so determined to rise early that those dormant memories become nightmares.

In the dream, he's waiting for his sister to get back with water. She's been gone a long time, far longer than fetching a jarful of water should take. Judas can feel his chest tighten with anxiety, can feel it pressing on his bones. This part of the dream is nightmare enough on its own; a sudden panic used to wake Judas some nights before the dream could go on, his body tense and drenched in sweat.

But tonight, the dream doesn't stop. His sister comes in, looking exactly the way she does in his memory. There's a scrape across the left side of her face and a cut on her lip, some tearing at the neck of her tunic. She walks slowly, her shoulders turned in slightly as if she'd like to fold in her arms and draw in her chest, her gait awkward under hidden pain, a kind of pain no one should suffer.

Her eyes are blank; the jar she's carrying is broken.

Judas wants to scream, but the air is trapped in his chest. He shouldn't have sent her out. He should have gone with her. He should have gone with her and taken his knife. He should go out with his knife right now and find the one who did this. Was it a soldier? Some robber? Or else a neighbor — maybe a boy he knows, someone he trusts? Whoever it is, Judas wants to kill him. Judas wants to scream, but the air is trapped in his chest. He's going to drown; he can feel it. He's going to drown in the scream that won't come out.

His sister puts down the broken jar gently by the door. Then she walks to her mat and she lies down and she doesn't say anything. If Judas doesn't drown in his own trapped scream, he'll suffocate in her silence. He walks over toward her, but in the nightmare he already knows. She'll never tell him what happened. Never give him the chance to get the guilt out from under his own skin by plunging his knife under someone else's.

He wakes up shaking. Then he goes to sleep and has the same nightmare again. And again. And a fourth time before morning.

*

By the time Judas drags himself out of bed, the priests and the Levites are already doing the recitation of their genealogies. Judas is tired, and he's starving, but he wants to get out, wants to focus on the day and drive the past from his mind. When Judas gets close to the square and realizes the old priest is reading off the names of each family's ancestors at the time they returned from captivity in Babylon, though, Judas decides he can sprint down to the market and buy some breakfast before joining the crowd.

The run is good. Running forces air in and out of his lungs, proves to him that they're still working. Judas sprints straight back from the market and finds a spot next to Andrew on the side of the road just as the long recitation is ending. When it's finished, the Levites and Magdalenes mill around and talk to give the old priest time to recover before he teaches. Judas offers Andrew half the bread he's bought with money Susannah left for them, and they lean against a wall and start to eat.

"Did you wash your hands first?" says a nearby Levite who's apparently been watching them.

"Sorry," says Judas. "We forgot."

The Levite wrinkles his nose as he hears Judas's accent. "Where are you from?" he asks.

"Jerusalem," says Judas. "City of our kings."

"Is that so?" says the Levite, "I know people up here sometimes forget what's appropriate and what isn't, but I thought men from Jerusalem knew better. Where exactly in

the city is home for you?"

Judas takes a deep breath. He has a feeling it will be better to avoid this question than to have his neighborhood mocked today. "My father's family is originally from Kerioth, just south of Hebron."

"Do they have water there?" asks the Levite, and he laughs loudly. Then he calls several other Levites over: "I just saw these two men eating with unwashed hands." He turns to the nearby onlookers. "If you go down to the Temple, try to remember that you're descendants of Israel, not mannerless foreigners. We see too many of those already—there's no need for our own people to play the part."

Judas tries to slip away quietly, but he doesn't want to leave Andrew alone: Andrew doesn't seem to understand when to slip away quietly and just stands there, as if waiting to be scolded more.

Then a woman says, "Aren't those two close disciples of Jesus? You shouldn't treat them like that."

Judas wonders if it can get any worse. He's brought embarrassment not only on himself now, but also on his Master. He should never have come here. He should never have been born.

"These two are with Jesus?" says the Levite. "Does Jesus know what kind of men are following him?"

"Yes," says Jesus, stepping out of the crowd. He looks at Andrew and Judas. "Yes, and I admire them."

"I admire them, too," says the Levite, "I admire this

one's fishy smell and that one's Jerusalem-slum accent." Scattered laughter passes through the crowd. "But if you've been teaching these men so long, why don't they know yet how to keep themselves clean?"

"Better unclean hands than unclean lips," says Jesus. The crowd gets quiet.

"I'm sorry if you think I'm being rude," says the Levite, "but I'm trying to teach the people here how to honor our God. At the Temple we watch the gates to make sure no one who behaves like your men is allowed in."

Jesus nods. "Then Isaiah told the truth about you."

"You mean the prophet?" says the Levite. "When?"

"These people come close to me with their mouths, and honor me with their lips, but keep their hearts far from me," says Jesus. *"Their worship is not for me, but for the proscriptions of men."*

The Levite takes a step toward Jesus. "Is that supposed to excuse them?" he says. "Or condemn me as a hypocrite for washing my hands before I eat?"

Jesus sighs. "What goes into a man matters less than what comes out of him. Your hands can't pollute you like your thoughts do."

"All I'm asking you to do," says the Levite, "is to teach your men to stop eating like dogs."

But Jesus turns to the crowd. "Whoever has ears to hear, listen to this. He asks you to drink, but only purifies the outside of the cup. He cleans his body, but *sets an ambush in his heart.*"

Everyone waits to see how the Levite will react, but an

126

old priest steps in before he can respond. "Forgive me," the priest says to Jesus. "My nephew shouldn't be treating Magdala's guests this way. But as this is an important day for us, I hope you'll withdraw from our city to prevent any further conflicts." Jesus meets the old priest's steady gaze and nods. He motions to Andrew and Judas to follow him, and they walk back toward Susannah's house without exchanging a word.

For the second day in a row, Judas feels responsible for spoiling good plans.

*

"What happened?" says Mary.

"It's my fault," says Judas. "I forgot to wash my hands."

"That's not why we're leaving," Jesus says.

Mary looks to Andrew. "I'm just trying to understand why the priest was upset."

"We got into an argument with his nephew," says Andrew.

"And everyone was watching," Judas says.

"He just wants his life to go on as usual," says Jesus. "But I always seem to upset people who don't want their lives to change."

Andrew looks down at his shirt and Judas tugs absently at his beard. No one can argue the truth of this, so it's quiet for a moment.

"Why delay?" says Jesus. "Let's leave now."

"Are you sure?" says Andrew.

"I'm going with you," says Mary.

Judas rises. "Where to?" he says.

"Zarephath," says Jesus. "If we've worn out our welcome among our own people, maybe we can find a widow to feed us there."

7.

It's a three days' walk straight from Magdala to Zarephath: two if you're in a hurry. Jesus doesn't go straight or hurry, so it takes him a week and a half.

They spend the first day in Magdala. Jesus has a long talk with Matthew and Thomas, who he's leaving behind to care for his followers here. Mary and Judas pack provisions while the others prepare the boat.

On the second day, they cross the lake and stop in Capernaum because Jesus wants to eat again with Peter's mother-in-law. But a single meal's visit extends to three days when Jesus learns about all the problems for and between his followers in the nearby towns.

In Capernaum, former disciples of Jesus continue to trouble those who still respect him. They bring cases against them to the court and oppose them in commerce. They debate them in the marketplace and harass them on the long walk up the town's harbor. Though Jairus and Zebedee have tried time after time to reach out to them, they refuse to be pacified.

Jesus can't change the opposition in Capernaum, but he visits and comforts those who have suffered because of it,

and he counsels with the most influential of his followers over what can be done to protect the vulnerable.

In Bethsaida, there's not nearly as much trouble with outside critics. But the farmers who listened to Jesus the first time he visited town interpret his story of the unpraised servant one way, while the fisherman, who came to love Jesus on his second visit, interpret it another. They've argued over it since he left, and a few men have nearly come to blows over the difference.

Jesus refuses to say which party in the dispute was right and reminds them instead that *the wisdom of the wise will perish.* Then he tells them another story: about a vineyard where the workers are hired at different times of day but paid the same in the end. Before he leaves, he asks Philip, who's related to half of Bethsaida's fishermen, and Nathanael, whose father is a respected local farmer, to stay for a while as models of harmony and cooperation.

The worst problems are in Chorazin. Two brothers were among Jesus' first followers here, and it was their extraordinary energy that helped change many from simple spectators into true disciples. But the brothers' wealthy father has since died, and there's a bitter dispute between them over the inheritance. For a month, the brothers' boundless energy has been poured into winning the townspeople over to one side or the other of their dispute, and now the city is bathed in the bad blood between them.

The younger brother finds Jesus and explains that he's been wronged. "My brother has a stiff neck and a stubborn

heart," he says. "But you can persuade him to give me my full share of the inheritance."

"Who made me a judge to divide it for you?" says Jesus. "But I'll tell you this: if all of your father's wealth is left to him, and only our Father's wealth is left for you, then you will be the richer of the brothers."

Once he's comforted people in Capernaum, reconciled them in Bethsaida, and instructed them in Chorazin, Jesus and his companions leave the three towns. They almost make it to the border between Galilee and Phoenicia in a single day, and then are delayed another four days in a storm.

*

It's cold and it's wet and the rain is quickly turning the steep hillside roads into rivers of mud when Jesus and his remaining companions find a sparsely-furnished cave that calls itself an inn. The place is already crowded with several merchants from Sidon and Tyre and their servants, but the innkeeper is more than willing to overcrowd his establishment if that means he can profit from the storm.

The only foreigners in Capernaum are the captain and his soldiers, who keep to themselves, so Andrew is both frightened and fascinated seeing so many strange customs at once. He wishes Matthew were here, because Matthew knows how to talk to men from other nations. But even Matthew wouldn't know how to share dishes and sleeping space with them. After all, even in the big cities like Antioch where the taxman has been, the rulers know enough to build

strong walls between the quarters for the Greeks, the Syrians, and the Jews.

And what would happen if they didn't? In the south, Jews have to fight from time to time against Greek settlers who openly desecrate the sacred. And in the ten cities, didn't the Greeks blame all Jews when one child grew sick?

When one of the Phoenician merchants keeps watching Mary, it makes Andrew nervous. He doesn't know what the Phoenician is thinking. Judas must be nervous, too, because he tells the merchant to stop staring at his sister. The merchant stops, and Andrew is relieved—until Judas gets sick that night and Andrew has to wonder whether it's just the food or if the Phoenician is trying to poison him. All through the night, Andrew cares for Judas, who keeps waking up sick from his sleep. And as he tends his friend in the darkness, so close to these strangers, Andrew wishes for a wall.

But in spite of Andrew's misgivings, Jesus and the merchants quickly grow comfortable with each other. And because Jesus is comfortable, Andrew decides to be comfortable, too. Though he never grows accustomed to the way the Phoenicians eat, and he never learns to follow discussions about their trade routes, he begins to enjoy sharing space and swapping stories. He and the others don't mind when the merchants mumble calculations at odd hours, and the merchants aren't bothered by how often these Jewish travelers pray.

One merchant, in particular, grows fascinated with Jesus.

They all know Jesus is a preacher, but only this one wants to understand what exactly Jesus has to preach. And since the rain goes on and on, Jesus has time to explain in great detail, even has time to tell the merchant about old Hebrew prophets he's never heard of.

On their third day in the inn, Jesus tells the merchant a story about a beggar who lies in anguish at a rich man's door. The beggar only wants the crumbs that fall from the rich man's table, but out of spite the rich man throws the crumbs to the wild street dogs, who come and lick the beggar's open sores when they're done. As God is good, the beggar is lifted in the next life from suffering to peace. And as God is just, the rich man is cast down after his death from comfort into torment.

In his anguish, the rich man calls out to Abraham, begging permission to go back to the land of the living to warn his self-satisfied brothers of the sorrow to come. But Abraham says they have the prophets to warn them.

"But my brothers would listen to me," says the rich man.

"No," says the patriarch Abraham. "If they won't listen to the prophets, they won't listen even to a messenger who rises from the dead."

The merchant takes a long look at Jesus when the story is done. "There are beggars all over Tyre," he says. "But no prophets to warn us when we step over them on our way to the docks, or have our servants shove them aside when we unload our cargo." He grows quiet for a moment, then speaks again. "You should come to us," he says. "I think my

people would listen if they heard you teach."

"I can't go where I'm invited," says Jesus. "Only where I'm sent."

But the merchant still offers to send a servant back with them, offers to let them stay in his house. And Jesus still declines the offer, asks what interest an island city of traders who spend half their lives in boats, sailing to the ends of the earth, would have in an Israelite preacher who's never been farther than you could walk in a week. So the merchant lets the matter rest.

That night, Mary wakes with a serious fever. The merchant is lying awake and sees how sick she looks, then sees Jesus cast the illness out. He asks how she recovered so quickly and Jesus speaks of faith. He asks if this has happened before and Peter tells about his mother-in-law. The merchant grows excited. "If you go to my city," he says, "just heal the sick like that and soon everyone will believe."

But Jesus quotes him a proverb from the prophet Amos: *Can an ox plough the sea?* So much separates our people, he says: if I was made for Israel, how can I work anywhere else?

"Then why are you on this road?" says the merchant, but Jesus just smiles and shrugs.

That evening, the merchant starts to fear that the rain will let up and their time together will end too soon, so he asks Jesus questions with an intensity that startles the other merchants. He wants to know what Jesus believes about the future, wants to know whether there's a time when Jesus

will be able to send men to his house. That's when Jesus begins to tell him especially strange old Jewish stories, about walls that collapse without a weapon being lifted, about lambs who lie down beside wolves and a lion who eats straw like an ox while men beat swords into ploughs.

The merchant asks if in those days, the lion will plough the same sea the ox couldn't.

Jesus embraces him. All at once, the rain stops.

*

On the fourth day, everyone sits outside the cave and waits for the sun to dry the mud enough to make travel safe. The merchants repeat invitations to each other's homes, promise to meet again, then wish Jesus and his companions warm goodbyes. They go their separate ways: some back toward their homes on the coast, others farther into Herod's Galilee or northeast toward his brother Philip's capitol.

The curious merchant from Tyre lingers when the others have gone. He thanks Jesus again and again for the time together and the things he's learned. Then he turns to Mary and the eight apostles and gives them careful directions to his home. He's confident, he says, that someday one of them will visit him.

He walks off to the southeast. Jesus watches him go. "That man is not far from the kingdom of God," he says.

*

From the last hills before the coast, the ocean seems to go on forever. From the last hills before the coast, the white tongues of the breaking waves strike Mary as looking

135

thirsty, and she thinks: this is why they say that no matter how many rivers flow into it, the sea is never full.

Maybe, Mary thinks, it's not the wave-tips that are thirsty, but the salty air itself. No one ever told her the world could look or feel so different on the coast of the sea, and Mary sometimes finds herself getting lost in the sensation and falling behind, then having to run a little to keep up.

And while the people here look almost as unfamiliar as the land does, they're neither distant nor unkind. Day laborers are quick to offer travelers a little of their water; passing shepherds are quick to offer advice in their thick, lilting accents on where to stop for a rest to get the best shade.

A few of them have even heard of Jesus through the servants of a merchant who came back this way. But most haven't, and Jesus seems to appreciate the chance to be anonymous. He has time to ask the apostles about their preaching tours, time to ask Mary for details about the kinds of people who gathered around him in her hometown. Who are they reaching, he asks them all, and who else can they reach?

Their conversations slow when the hill path out of Galilee merges into a busy coastal road. Mary is torn between watching the sea and watching the people and animals they pass. At first, it's nice to have so many sights to choose from. When the road turns into narrow steps up a chalky cliff, though, everything begins to seem too close: a passing donkey forces Mary to the edge of the road and she

doesn't like looking down the long, sheer drop to the surface of the sea. She can't seem to help imagining her body falling and floating out, out farther than the eye can see — to Rome, maybe, or to Spain, or else past the pillars they say stand at the end of the world. Yes, Mary imagines her body floating out to a place where there's only endless sea and she shivers as she thinks about how the prospect of violent death can drain all the beauty out of anything.

So although the sight of the ships coming and going from Tyre is still striking, it doesn't fill her with wonder quite the way her first sight of the sea did. And although the sunset over the waters as they approach Zarephath is breathtaking, Mary finds her chest tightening with the fear that they might stumble to their deaths in the dark.

There is very little light left when they reach town, but Mary strains her eyes against the grey to keep a close eye on the path and they all survive. The local people give them directions to a handful of Jewish houses at the edge of town, and there's a family who think they've heard of Jesus and is more than happy to host them for a few nights. Jesus thanks them and asks them not to mention their guests to anybody. He seems to be getting fond of being able to treat his time as his own.

*

That luxury doesn't last long. Jesus and his apostles are sitting outside the house eating breakfast with their hosts when an emaciated Phoenician woman comes up and throws herself on the ground in front of them. "Son of

137

David!" she shouts. "Son of David, remember your father's friendship with our King Hiram!"

"Do you know her?" whispers James to the father of the family they're staying with.

The man shakes his head. "No, but she's dressed the way their custom requires for widows. No doubt she'll tell her sad story—and then she'll ask for money."

Judas cringes. Even the poor have ears to hear: if their host can't be more kind, Judas wishes he'd at least be more quiet.

But the woman doesn't even glance at him: she stays focused on Jesus and presses on. "It's my daughter," she says. "An evil spirit has been troubling her. For almost a year, she doesn't get worse but she never gets better. Almost a year, I've tended to her, done everything I can and she still can't do more than groan. I miss my girl," she says. "I miss her."

Jesus looks at her, but he doesn't say anything.

"I heard you're a healer," she says. "When I saw you, I knew it was true. Lord," she says, and she weeps. "Give me my daughter back."

"I was sent to Israel," Jesus says, and he looks at his hosts. "There are so many of my own people suffering, am I supposed to be responsible for the rest of the world, too?"

But "Please, Lord" is all the woman says. "Please please please please," and she kneels down—as if to pray, or maybe just to beg.

"Your people call mine donkeys," says Jesus. He glances

at Andrew. "And my people call yours dogs." He looks back at the widow kneeling before him. "Tell me: how can we ever help each other when our nations share so little trust?"

The woman looks up at him. "I don't know why men speak badly of donkeys," she says, "when they bear the burdens which are too heavy for us. And not all dogs run wild in the streets: people take some into their homes; they love and take care of them."

"Well spoken," says Jesus, and the hint of a smile passes across his face as quickly as a flying bird's shadow. Then he looks hard at the woman again: "But tell me what you think of this proverb from my country: 'when the children are hungry, you don't give their bread even to the pet dog.'"

"That's a wise saying," she says. "The children should have what they are able to eat. But when the dog comes to lie under the table, doesn't it have a right to the children's crumbs?"

Then Jesus laughs and claps his hands. "This proverb is even better than the first! Take my thanks with you and go home now: your daughter is well."

It's a sign of the woman's faith that her eyes already dance with delight. She doesn't need to see the girl to feel deep relief.

As he watches her go, Jesus turns again to Andrew. "Be sure to tie knots strong enough you don't forget what she said." While Andrew ties the knots, Jesus chants some lines from the Psalms: *How can I leave the way of the judgments you have taught me? How sweet are your words to my taste! Yes,*

sweeter to my mouth than honey.

Jesus finishes his breakfast and rises. He thanks their hosts and tells them he'll be heading back to Galilee now.

"Won't you stay longer?" they say.

"No, thank you," says Jesus. "To tell the truth, we came all this way looking for a meal, and I feel that now we've been well fed."

It doesn't make a lot of sense to travel more than a week for a single breakfast, but what else do you expect from a man like Jesus?

*

When they get back to Philip and Nathanael in Bethsaida, the news is not good. The farmers and the fishermen are fighting again. After a few days of trying to reconcile, the brothers in Chorazin went back to their feud and pulled the people with them, so that no one seems to remember Jesus' promise that the meek will inherit the earth. And in Capernaum, they find the persecution has only gotten worse. Jesus' former disciples have worked hard to trouble all the people their former Master comforted on his last visit.

So Jesus goes out near the lakeside and broods. As he stares out across the water, he seem to fall into a prophetic trance. *Woe to Chorazin, Woe to Bethsaida,* he says. He looks around at the apostles. "If I'd done the same things in Tyre and Sidon I've done here, they'd have repented like Nineveh did at the words of Jonah long ago: the whole city would have fasted, they'd have covered even their animals in

140

sackcloth and ashes. What will those people say to the people here when the Day of Judgment comes?"

No one has an easy answer.

"I wanted to lift Capernaum up to heaven," says Jesus, "but it doesn't want to come. I offered them the kingdom of God, but they'd rather gnash their teeth at us as if they were already in the underworld."

The apostles think of men they used to walk with, men who sat beside them to hear Jesus' words. Men whose hearts seem to have room only for anger now.

"The wind is blowing," says Jesus.

And so they climb into a boat and get it ready to sail, though they feel heavier with disappointment than all the anchors on all the ships in this long harbor.

Of all the nations on earth into which Jesus could have been born, maybe it's true that no other would have given him so much resistance. But if that's the case, it's probably also true that though other peoples would have repented in sackcloth and ashes while he was alive, this is the only nation on earth stubborn enough to remember Jesus after he's dead.

By the time they push off, a little crowd has gathered on the wharf to wish them well. There's practical old Zebedee and his fiery wife Salome; there's Jairus and his healthy-looking daughter, waving goodbye with all the energy of her youth. There's Peter's mother-in-law, folding the same hands that kneaded the dough for their bread in a half-conscious attitude of prayer; beside her is Peter's wife,

whose lantern they know is always full and ready for their next return.

As Judas watches them disappear in the growing distance, he finds himself growing angry. If it weren't for the efforts of a few men who betrayed Jesus, he thinks, Capernaum *would* be close to heaven now. Surely, people like those on the dock could have walked with God like Enoch did. Surely such people could have ridden a flaming chariot straight to heaven like Elijah.

8.

Magdala's fishermen are still out on the lake when Jesus' boat comes in, so it's quiet on the harbor. For a moment, Peter wishes he could push out to fish instead of heading into the city: he knows how to harvest the lake's bounty far better than he knows, even now, how to handle the crowds. But because he made a promise, he doesn't hesitate long. He helps secure the boat and braces himself for the walk to Susannah's house.

The walk isn't far, but it is slow. Women fetching water from the creek leave their work to welcome Jesus back to the city and to tell him about the continuing health of people he healed. While Jesus listens to them, word of his return spreads. Soon a baker comes to Jesus to ask for a blessing and offer him two loaves of bread. Several beggars follow to ask for bread and offer Jesus their blessings.

While the apostles break bread for the beggars, four farmers arrive to thank Jesus, who prayed with them for good late rains on his last visit, for the prosperity of their crops. As they show off a stalk of their barley, a young man limps up, leaning on his brother, and interrupts to show Jesus the puffy redness that's developed around a bite on his

leg.

Peter starts to worry they'll spend the rest of the day on the road.

They move again after Jesus heals the young man, but not far. Two students come with a question about Haman and Queen Esther. An old man has a complaint about a sharp pain in his gut. Several women come up from the creek again, having remembered more news. A father comes running to get advice about his stubborn son.

Peter's ears ache.

The fishing boats start coming in and people from all over the city come down toward the harbor to buy fish. They see Jesus and shout out to friends to come down by the lake to see him. The newly arrived fishermen see Jesus and shout thanks to him for drawing out the whole city to buy.

"It's enough," says Jesus to Peter. "Let's go."

So Peter takes the lead, and they push their way through thick clusters of people up toward Susannah's. When her servant sees them at the gate he lets them in.

Peter is ready for the quiet he expects to find in her courtyard.

But the courtyard isn't quiet. In the courtyard, Matthew and Thomas are meeting with a group of seventy men.

*

When Jesus comes in, Matthew and Thomas stop teaching and start explaining.

"We hope you don't mind," says Thomas, "but there were too many people for us to care for on our own. So we

remembered how you divided the crowd before you fed them, and we called messengers to help us visit and teach the people."

"You've done well," says Jesus. "We can use the help."

"They tell us how your followers are doing in their quarter of the city or their village," says Matthew, "and we send them back with advice and instructions."

"I'd like to hear from them and counsel with them," Jesus says. "But others will be coming here soon, wanting to get in. Where can we go to talk in peace?"

Mary is the first to make a suggestion. "My sister's village is always quiet."

Jesus nods. "Come two by two," he says to the seventy disciples, "without telling others where you're going. Mary will tell us where her sister lives and we'll meet there in two days."

"She'll be happy to host you," says Mary.

*

Mary leaves that night and wakes well before sunrise the next day to help her sister Martha's family sweep the house and borrow neighbors' dishes and gather enough food to offer eighty-five men a simple meal. Though the day's labors exhaust them, and though Jesus and the apostles arrive in the middle of the night, Martha and Mary wake well before dawn the next day to cook.

As they bake bread and boil lentils, their other seventy guests begin to arrive. The first to come sit in the courtyard and the last find space on the roof to listen, but everyone fits

in the house somewhere.

Through the morning, Matthew and Thomas introduce the new messengers to Jesus, and Jesus asks questions about the people they care for and listens carefully to their answers. When he's met and listened to them all, he compliments Matthew and Thomas on their selections and the men on their commitment and strength.

Then he holds up a hand for attention and says something that surprises everybody, Mary and the twelve included: "I need your help, because this is the last time I'm going to tour Galilee."

"What does he mean?" Philip asks Nathanael, but Nathanael doesn't ask Jesus, because Jesus has already started his first story.

The story is about a farmer, who rises to care for his crops on an early spring day just like this. But when he reaches his field, it's even bigger than he remembered and the grain is already white like in summer, suddenly ready for the harvest.

The man runs straight to the center of town, calling out to ask everyone to help him bring in the unexpected bounty. He tells them to bring their sickles and their donkeys and promises he'll send them home with all the grain the animals can carry. The workers come, but every time the man looks out the fields seem still bigger, still whiter. Full bundles of wheat are tied to every donkey on both sides until the animals almost disappear between their loads, but the ripe grain left in the field goes on and on. The man calls

for more help, offering a full day's wage to anyone who will leave what they are doing and help him. But even with a second group of helpers, he can't keep up with the harvest. So the man falls on his knees, prays to the God who has blessed him so richly to send more workers to his field, whether they come from the next village or are strangers from afar.

At the end of the harvest story, Martha starts bringing plates with bread and lentils to the gathered men. She looks to Mary for help, but her sister is too busy listening to Jesus' next story to notice.

This one is about a talented merchant who's already made more money than an ordinary man can earn in five lifetimes. One day, with very little warning, the merchant is called away to a far country and doesn't know when he'll be able to come back. He calls three of his most devoted servants together and entrusts them with most of his wealth: the first servant is given twice his own weight in silver, the second his weight in silver, and the third half his weight in silver. He gives them use of his name and house in his absence, and he tells them to remember him and to prepare for his return.

The first and second servants immediately go to work, investing carefully, trading on their master's behalf. As time passes, they throw themselves into their labors with a growing abandon—after all, each new contract is another chance to hear people speak their absent master's name. Some of their ventures fail, and it devastates them. Most

succeed, and the value and scale of their operations grow.

Though the third servant has been no less devoted to the master, he's more cautious than the other two. He worries that if he invests in a certain kind of good, its price may fall before he can sell it. He worries that if he buys a farm, there won't be enough rain, and that if he buys a fishing boat, it might sink in a storm. He doesn't want to disappoint his master, or for men to speak ill of his master on his account, so he stops speaking of, or acting for, his master at all. Before long, he begins to worry that thieves might come for the money—so one night, when he's sure no one is watching, he buries it deep in the ground.

Having buried the treasure, he returns to his life's routine struggles. He cleans the master's house, though it's used so little these days there's not much to worry about. He cooks meals, though often only for himself since the master, and usually also his fellow-servants, are gone. Still, the rhythms comfort him. Gradually, they surpass his memory of devotion and he stops thinking of his master's eventual return. It proves more enticing just to survive than to wait, and his memory begins to blur until it seems as if at any moment he may forget the man he once waited for.

Trees the first servant planted mature; grapes the second servant trampled develop into old wine. Then one spring, while the breeze pours color into the waiting blossoms, their master returns.

Only the truly faithful, says Jesus, will ever be able to understand how the first two servants felt when they again

saw their master's face. Only the truly faithful will understand how their hearts beat as they ran to greet him, how right the tears of long-delayed reunion felt on their cheeks.

And only the truly faithful will be ready for the question their master asked: what have you done in my name?

The first two show him their ledgers, explain how they've each doubled what they were given, and now it's their master who cries tears of joy. "Well done, my servants!" he says, and then he tells them of his own incredible success, beyond anything they could have imagined. The three of them laugh together, and the master says, "I left you with a few things; I've returned with many things. Then you were my servants; be rulers now in the house of your lord!"

In the next room, the third servant waits. The voice he once knew so well now sounds rough and weathered to him. When the master comes looking for him, his face seems like a stranger's.

What about you? says the master. What have you done in my name?

I knew you were strict, says the third servant. I knew you reap rewards of work that wasn't your own, and I was afraid you'd expect more from me than I can give. So I buried the silver in the ground. I'll go dig it up for you now and return it: to tell the truth, it will be a great relief to have it out of my hands.

"Well said," says the master, "your hands are worthless!

If you felt I was too strict, why did you accept the silver when I left? If you knew I reap the rewards of work that wasn't my own, why didn't you take the money to lenders at a bank for interest?"

The servant doesn't answer. He's forgotten the devotion that once made him afraid to disappoint his master.

And in his silence, the master can tell his servant's devotion is gone. "I don't want to reap the rewards of others' work," says the master, "but I thought you were my own. If you no longer are, leave the silver and take your freedom. You no longer belong to my house."

So the servant leaves a free man, released from the ties that once brought him great joy. That very night, he walks out of the master's house into the darkness, and he never comes back.

*

Martha's children helped when she borrowed nearly every stone cup in the village for her guests. But Martha trusts the children better with empty cups coming from the neighbors' than with full cups in a crowded courtyard, and Mary hasn't noticed her hints to come help, so she's left carrying the cups on her own. Bringing so many cups alone isn't easy: she doesn't want Jesus' men to grow thirsty waiting, so she carries as many at a time as she can, but even she has to walk carefully, watching her step and her balance, to avoid giving anyone a lapful of water or turning a patch of the floor to mud.

As if passing out so many heavy cups weren't trouble

enough, she starts noticing that many of the plates are empty. She doesn't want the men to be hungry, either, so she gathers plates as she hands out cups, trying to remember which groups to bring full plates back to and which men still need to drink. In the kitchen, she tries to guess how many lentils are left so she can tell the children how much more to serve onto each plate. As they fill the plates, she wonders whether she salted the lentils too heavily or cooked them too dry. Her daughter gives her plates to return and more cups to take out and asks her mother whether they'll have to wash all the dishes by themselves. Martha searches for words as she struggles for balance, and finds herself wishing she had four hands to hold all these dishes and three hearts to hold all her thoughts. "If we need to, we will," Martha tells her daughter. And then she goes back out to serve.

As she moves around among the men, one of the plates stacked under her arm starts to slide out. When she shifts to catch it, a cup nearly spills. She notices more empty plates and wonders again if she made enough food. She passes out more cups and wonders whether she borrowed enough. She sees her sister talking with an apostle and again fails to catch her eye, but nearly trips while trying and imagines what a disaster it would be in the crowded, hungry space if she dropped the food and dishes in a heap in the middle of the courtyard. How would she have time to clean up and care for everyone?

And so when Jesus himself stops talking to take a cup from her a moment after her near fall, her whisper to him is

a bit fiercer than she'd intended: "Could you please tell Mary to come and help?"

But Jesus looks at her, not her sister. Looks at her hard, in a way that might be disconcerting if it didn't command her whole attention. "Which Martha should I ask her to help," he says, his own whisper far gentler than hers, "the one who's so careful on the outside, or the one who's so troubled within?"

And the question itself is a strange relief, because it cuts through all the worries she's juggling. By demanding all her attention, Jesus focuses Martha's mind and offers it a calm she very seldom feels.

"There are so many things a person can worry about," he says to her. "But only one thing we all need to. Mary has chosen that, and it won't be taken away from her."

Martha nods, and mumbles an apology: "Of course. I shouldn't have asked."

"No," says Jesus, "to ask was right. Not even an ox is made to work alone: why should a human be? Let me help you."

"You don't need to do that," says Martha, suddenly self-conscious. "No, everyone's come to hear you teach. I don't want to interrupt."

"It's no interruption," says Jesus. "My voice needs a rest: it's better if they watch me teach a while."

And before Martha can object any further, he's taken several cups and half the plates from her. Before she can object, he's following her back to the kitchen and helping the

children spoon out the right amount of lentils and fill the rest of each plate with the right amount of bread before he takes them back to the right people. The seventy look on, bemused, to see their Master waiting on them. Mary suddenly remembers she should be helping her sister, but sits spellbound, trying to figure out what sort of story Jesus is acting out instead.

Not until the last cups have been brought out, until all empty plates have been refilled and returned to the groups who needed more, does Jesus speak to the seventy again.

"When I send you out to do my work, I want you to go two by two. If you yoke yourselves together, even hard work can feel easy. And if you find yourself alone someday, take me with you. You'll know I'm there beside you because the burden will feel too light."

The seventy nod sagely, but it's Martha who will remember this for the rest of her life.

*

Mary joins Martha in the kitchen when the meal is over and they wash the dishes slowly so they can still listen closely through the thin wall as the men ask questions and Jesus answers—or at least responds. It's not always easy to tell how Jesus' responses answer the questions.

One man asks how to handle financial disputes between Jesus' followers, and Jesus responds with a story about a man who's been mismanaging his master's wealth for some time. When the master finds out, this corrupt servant panics. He knows he's about to lose his position, but he's also been

dishonest too long to begin earning an honest living working with his hands, and he's been proud far too long to start begging. So he puts his guile to work one last time, calling in rich debtors and altering their accounts in his master's ledgers. If one owes a hundred measures of oil, he reduces it to fifty. If another owes a thousand bushels of wheat, he marks it down as eight hundred. If he can't keep his job, after all, shouldn't he make a few good friends to fall back on?

"If even corrupt men know the worth of friendship," says Jesus, "why do good men let their disagreements over money rob them of their friends? Tell them to learn wisdom from the children of darkness—maybe then they'll see the light!"

Another one of the seventy points out that significant prejudice against Jesus developed in his village when some of Jesus' followers acted hypocritically. He asks how to identify and remove those whose actions are bringing Jesus' name into disrepute, and Jesus answers with a story about weeds.

In the story, a farmer and his servants spend all day planting wheat seeds in a field. The labor exhausts them, so they sleep soundly and don't hear the footsteps of a jealous rival in the field that night. Even though there are laws against sabotaging another man's wheat by sneaking in ryegrass seeds, the rival fears neither the laws of men nor of God, so he does just that. At first, no one notices, since young wheat and young ryegrass look so much the same.

With time, though, subtle differences begin to appear, and when one of the servants sees them, he bursts into tears. "I thought I checked the seeds carefully," says the servant, "so how did this happen?"

The farmer takes a close look and nods grimly. "It's not your fault," he tells the servant, "I think I know who did this." And he tells the servants about his enemy, who cares for his own profit more than another man's hunger.

The servants have worked hard planting and caring for this field, so it's no surprise they get upset. "We'll work from the first to the last light," they say. "We'll rip out every weed by tomorrow night!"

But the farmer tells them not to, tells them if they rush things now they'll tear half the young wheat plants up with the ryegrass.

"What can we do then?" say the servants.

"Wait," says the farmer. "It will be easy to tell one plant from another when they're full-grown: do your best now to nourish the wheat, and save the final judgments for the time of the harvest."

*

"I have a question," says one of the seventy a little nervously. "What's the truth about the resurrection? The last time I traveled to the Temple, a priest there told me it's just superstition. He says Moses never taught it, and that it's written nowhere in the sacred books."

Jesus laughs. "Did he read about *the God of Abraham, and of Isaac, and of Jacob?* Ours is a God of the living, not of the

155

dead."

"So if eternal life is real," says the man, "how do we get it?"

"You already know," says Jesus. *"Love the Lord your God with all your heart, with all your soul and with all your strength!* and *Don't seek revenge or hold onto a grudge against one of your own people, but love your neighbor as yourself."*

Some of the seventy laugh—even a child should know these two passages. The man who asked, though, presses on. "Who counts in these wicked days as our own people?" he says.

"Yes, tell us!" says another, with a twinkle in his eye. "Is it enough to love our fellow Galileans, or do we have to find room in our hearts for all those people crowded into Judea, too?"

Not all of Judea is crowded, Jesus says. Jerusalem certainly is, but the road from there to Jericho winds down through rock and dust, and sometimes on that road you don't see another living soul for miles.

Jesus looks right at the man who joked about Galilee and Judea. You don't want to take that journey, Jesus says to him, unless you absolutely have to: the men who hide in those hills will do anything to stay alive. Then Jesus tells about a man who's been ambushed on that winding road. The thieves have missed nothing, even ripped the clothes off his back. When he resisted, they beat him and stabbed him and left him face-down in the dust, naked and half-dead.

A chilly wind has picked up by the time a priest from

Jerusalem walks by. The priest is frightened, and he doesn't want to stop for anything, so he tells himself the man is dead, and reminds himself it's his duty to God not to touch a corpse. He steps to the far side of the road and rushes on, hoping the corpse is cold already and the killers far away.

A Levite from the north happens by next. He slows down as he gets closer to the body, notices there's fresh red blood alongside the dried black. He wonders if he should do something, but he knows the thieves in these hills are ruthless, and he wonders if it might be a trick. In his mind's eye, he sees himself walking up to the wounded man: the wounded man turns and grabs him, maybe just to rob him, maybe to slit his throat. The Levite shudders and passes on the far side of the road.

Then comes a Samaritan, a mongrel and a heretic, whose people have sometimes claimed to be heirs of Israel and sometimes persecuted Israel's sons. The Samaritan sees the body on the side of the road and he stops. The light is already going: surely, the Samaritan thinks, this man will freeze to death in the night—if there's any blood left in his body by then. It would be terrible, he thinks, to die alone on a roadside like that: does the man have a wife and children somewhere who will wonder for years if he abandoned them by choice or was kept from home by accident? Who will wonder for years whether or not there's still a chance that he'll come back?

Though the Samaritan knows that thieves may be watching him, he kneels down beside the man to help. He

pours oil and wine on the man's wounds to clean them, bandages them to stop the slow escape of blood. He puts the man across his donkey's back and starts forward again, not letting himself think about danger or knives until he's safely at an inn, until he's looked to the man's wounds again and is confident he'll be all right.

In the morning, the Samaritan has to go, but he leaves two days' wages with the innkeeper. Take care of him, he says, and makes the innkeeper promise he won't hesitate to spend more if necessary. Then he promises the innkeeper he'll come back soon, and that he'll pay whatever else it costs to make sure the man recovers and gets back the strength to return to his children and wife.

Jesus looks again at the man who joked about Galilee and Judea. "Which of the three, do you think, kept the commandment?"

The man takes a moment to search for words. He can't bring himself to praise a Samaritan in front of everyone, but he can't deny the force of this story either. "The one who showed mercy," he says.

"Then forget what Sira's son wrote about who to hate," says Jesus to everyone, "if you want to know who to count as your own people."

And then he turns away and starts to pray for them. "Father," he says, "let your kingdom come. Let your will be done through these men."

And as Jesus prays, they feel God so close it's almost as if they can see Him. And when he finishes praying, they open

their mouths and begin to prophesy without quite knowing what they're doing. They prophesy and start to feel the shape of heaven in their mouths.

In the kitchen, Mary and Martha are also prophesying, and no one is telling them not to.

Mary prophesies about a day when a stone will be rolled aside without the touch of human hands and go on to fill the earth—but Martha prophesies about a cold wind that will sweep across Judea first.

9.

Before Jesus sends out the seventy, he gives them a warning: they'll be like sheep among wolves. They all nod gravely and brace themselves against dangers they vaguely imagine, but almost none of them really understand, because almost none of them have spent enough time alone out in the hills, as Jesus has, to see how wolves hunt.

So they imagine sharp teeth, but don't think about wolves' intelligence and patience. They imagine bristled hair and aggressive growls, but don't realize that wolves hunt mostly by testing their prey for signs of fear and weakness, that wolves are most likely to bite animals only when they panic and run.

The seventy go out to preach. Where they're successful, the twelve follow to heal. Since they're met with few obvious signs of hostility, they forget all about wolves. But their enemies have not forgotten anything. Jesus' critics have simply chosen to save the next confrontation for the right place and time.

*

Jesus and the apostles are exhausted when they arrive in one town late at night, but a crowd still gathers early the

next morning, gaining size as quickly as the light grows with the rising sun. Matthew and Thomas are the first to wake, followed by Judas and Andrew, and the four of them herd the crowd out of the narrow street and into an open space where it's easier to work. In the early morning cool, they bless the fevered. When James and John arrive, they move on to the lame. Next they work to open ears that have become clogged with infection, then, as more and more spectators begin to arrive, they command cataracts to fall away from the eyes of the blind.

Nothing about the morning has seemed unusual in the least by the time they get to the ragged father and his sleepy young son.

"Is one of you Jesus?" the ragged man asks Matthew.

"No," says Matthew, "but he's our Master. What can we do for you?"

"My son needs help," says the man, and then he looks down like he's nervous or embarrassed.

"Don't worry," says Matthew. "We'll take care of him."

So Matthew calls to Thomas and they look over the boy to find out what's wrong. They find old scars, probably from being careless around a cooking fire, as boys often are. They find some dry, irritated patches on his skin, but no infection or fresh wounds. Other than being a bit sleepy, the boy seems alert. His vision and hearing seem fine, and his forehead feels normal.

"What exactly is the problem?" says Thomas. A few people watching seem disappointed and surprised, as if

they'd believed that anyone working with Jesus should know everything without having to be told.

The father looks uncomfortable at the attention he's getting from the crowd. "He's not well," he says curtly, and he looks hard at Matthew. "I thought you said you'd take care."

Thomas is about to say something a little curt back, but Matthew speaks first: "We will. We may not be able to tell what's wrong with him, but God can. And he'll care for those who give him their trust."

The man nods, and Matthew and Thomas move to bless the boy. But for the first time this morning, something feels wrong. When they put oil on his head, he starts to shy away. And when they try to touch him, he pulls away from them and stumbles back to his father.

"What's wrong with him?" calls out someone from the crowd. "Are you healing the boy or hurting him?"

"He looked fine before they touched him," says someone else and the boy claps his hands over his ears.

Matthew reaches toward the boy, but the father stops him. "It's starting again," he says, "it's always like this when it starts."

"What's starting?" says Thomas. "Why won't you tell us what's wrong?"

Someone from the crowd snorts. "Isn't it obvious?" he says, then he turns to the rest of the crowd and speaks as loudly as he can. "These frauds have put an evil spirit into him!"

Something about the speed with which the crowd focuses its attention on this new speaker reminds Matthew of nightmares he used to have, of his old terrifyingly plausible dreams of falling victim to mob violence. "We were only trying to help," he says. "We *are* only trying to help."

"Of course," says the man in the crowd, half to the crowd and only half to Matthew. "I'm sure you've always been a very charitable person. Tell us: before you were with Jesus, what kind of work did you do?"

Matthew's face flushes. He doesn't say anything.

"Funny that you should mention that," says another man, "I heard a rumor he used to be a tax collector." People in the crowd glance at each other: apparently, that particular rumor hadn't reached this town yet. "A generous one, though," the man adds with mock sincerity, "they say all kinds of people were welcome in his house—especially after dark."

Thomas steps forward. "Forget his past," he says. "Let us help the boy."

The first man raises his voice. "A bad tree can't give good fruit," he says to the crowd. "You all rushed here to get something sweet, but did you ask yourself first what sort of tree these men come from? Did you ask who they are or what they teach?"

A hush falls over the crowd. They look at the apostles with new eyes, and then down at themselves with an echo of Adam and Eve's embarrassment.

Something about their sudden shame silences even Thomas, so it's James who speaks up. "You've all seen us heal this morning. By this man's own admission, if the fruit is good, doesn't that mean the same for the tree? "

The second man laughs. "You remind me of Pharaoh's magicians!" he says. "So willing to use false miracles to fight against the authority of Moses and Aaron."

"We honor the law and the priesthood as much as you do," says James.

"Really?" says the first man. "Then perhaps you could explain a few of your Master's teachings."

And now James notices the trap, but it's too late, because the scholars-in-disguise are already trying to tear them apart with a quick series of sharply pointed questions.

*

Matthew is still afraid his past will be an embarrassment and keeps quiet to avoid drawing attention to himself. Thomas still stings at how naive they made him sound and stays quiet. Andrew tries to remember what Jesus has said so he can respond as his Master would, but his tongue feels like it's tied in knots too thick to let him get the answers out in words.

James and John have more of their mother's warm temper than their father's cool wisdom, so they forget that they're fishermen who never quite managed to keep all the different prophets straight and fight for all they're worth. But the two clever scholars draw them quickly into several self-contradictions, a few awkward admissions, and a

misstatement about the law for which they could punished by a religious court.

As the scholars continue to tear apart the brothers' credibility before a still-growing crowd, Judas slips off to wake Jesus and beg him to come help. That's how he misses the talk about the end of the world.

"Do you think we'll live to see a descendant of David back on the throne?" the first scholar says to James.

James wants to shout out that the answer is yes, wants to shake their shoulders as he tells them that this is exactly what they're unwittingly opposing, but he isn't a fool. He knows better than to waste his breath trying to piece together the puzzle of the kingdom of God with men like these anyway, and when there's the possibility that they'll turn him in to the king or the Romans and that his wasted breaths would also be some of his last, a direct answer is out of the question.

"I believe in the coming of the Messiah as much as anyone here," James says.

"Of course you do, but when do you think he'll come?" says the second scholar.

"I'm a fisherman," says James. "If I want to know when it will rain, I don't go around asking. I look at the sky. Is something wrong with your eyes that keeps you from doing your own looking?"

A few people in the crowd laugh at this, and James thinks maybe the tide will turn in his favor after all, but the scholars press on unfazed.

"What do you believe about the Prophet Moses foretold? The one whose words will be binding on the people. Will we live to see that Prophet?"

James sees an opportunity. He can't tell them Jesus is the Messiah without exposing his Master to trouble with the Romans or the king, but he can tell those with ears to hear that the Messiah is close by talking about the Prophet. Since he's not sure how much to say, though, he starts with a simple "yes."

"Do you believe the Prophet has come already?" says the first scholar.

"Was John that Prophet?" says the second.

James hesitates. That makes sense—John must have been the Prophet. But is this another trap? If he says yes, will they report him to Herod?

Andrew speaks up before James can sort out the risks. "No, I was with John on the Jordan. He himself said he wasn't."

Now James is confused. His mother always told him the Prophet will come near the end of this world. And she taught him the Messiah will usher in a new one. So if Jesus is the Messiah, and John wasn't the Prophet—

"Do you know who the Prophet is? Or how we'll recognize him?" says the first scholar.

Now it's John who speaks before James can make sense of what's happening. "He'll speak with authority," he says, "not like you scholars do."

The crowd laughs again, but James is less confident this

time. He feels like he's a little boy again and trying to prove his strength by swimming too far into the lake and nearly failing to make it back.

"That's what drew me to Jesus," says Thomas, as if he's realizing something for the first time. "It was the way he spoke that made me want to follow him all night."

The first scholar raises an eyebrow. "So you think your Master is the Prophet?" he says, "That's strange, because I heard that he himself thinks he's the Messiah."

The whole crowd looks to the apostles and James gets a tight feeling in his chest. They're cornered now, absolutely stuck. They can't back down from what Thomas said. They can't deny the scholar's accusation about their Master's claims, because they've heard how Jesus reads Isaiah and seen how he speaks of David. Saying nothing isn't much of any option at this point because it will make the crowd assume, somewhat accurately, that Jesus' closest followers are spectacularly confused. On the other hand, it's hard to come up with a good answer when you know one wrong word could land you in prison and that another could wake the violence that can so easily erupt out of a crowd this size.

James startles when he hears Jesus' voice behind him. "What is all this questioning about?" Jesus says.

For a moment, both scholars and apostles hesitate, each searching for words that will give their side the advantage. But before anyone comes up with anything, the ragged father speaks.

"I brought my son to you for healing," he says. "But

your men couldn't help. I just want someone to save my boy."

"We were asking when you think the signs of the End will come," says the second scholar. But Jesus just mutters, "how long will I have to live with this shallow and faithless generation?" as he pushes past the scholars toward the boy.

The ragged man's son is picking at his clothes and hardly seems to notice Jesus approaching. Then he looks up at Jesus and moans loudly as he collapses, unconscious, to the ground and begins flailing wildly, spit dribbling out of the corner of his mouth.

Jesus rolls the boy onto his side. "How long has this been happening?" he says to the father.

"Since he was very young," says the man. "Sometimes the spirit tries to throw him in the fire or drown him."

Matthew understands the man's earlier silence now—he was ashamed to admit the nature of his son's affliction.

"Please," the man says to Jesus, "if there's anything you can do, have compassion and help us!"

Jesus looks at him: "I can help if you can believe," he says.

The father looks ashamed again but forces himself not to look away. "Lord," he says, "I believe." He looks down at his convulsing son. "Help my unbelief!"

The boy's limbs are thrashing around and a few people in the crowd, still alarmed by the scholars' suggestion that they've given their trust to a wicked man or a fraud, are about to pull Jesus away from the boy when Jesus

commands the evil spirit to go out.

Peter has just arrived on the edge of the crowd when he hears the spirit's angry cry: "You Son of God!" Some in the crowd wince at hearing the spirit blaspheme; others ask what the spirit just said, though of course no one will take the name of God in vain to repeat it to them.

But the murmured questions stop abruptly and a cold hush falls over the crowd as people catch sight of the boy's still body, robbed even of the motion of breath and his face as pale as death.

*

It's one of the scholars who breaks the silence. "He's dead!" the man shouts, and he glares at Jesus in unmasked accusation.

And if they'd known and loved the boy, if he'd been a prominent villager's heir, Jesus might have been killed then, might have been stoned as a lowly murderer at the hands of the same people who'd come to him that very morning for help. But few are willing to seek sudden and violent justice on behalf of a poor stranger, and so the man's son is left unavenged.

"Do you believe?" says Jesus to the father.

"Anything," says the father back to him.

So Jesus takes the boy by the hand and lifts him up. Color returns to the boy's face and his eyes are clear as he looks at his father and embraces him.

The people in the crowd don't know whether they should be filled with terror or with joy. Their minds are

stuck, unable to reconcile the moment when they thought Jesus had killed a boy with the moment when he seemed to raise him from the dead.

No one says anything. All of them—the sick and the seekers, the scholars and the apostles, the son and the father and Jesus himself—just turn away and walk home.

*

Back in the house, Thomas has a question for Jesus: "Why couldn't we heal him?"

"You can only cast that kind out through prayer," says Jesus.

No one dares to ask the next question: if prayer is required to cast out that kind of spirit, why did Jesus simply act? Why didn't he have to pray?

*

In the unusual quiet of that afternoon, Peter, James, and John sit together behind the house.

"Who do you think he is?" says James.

"I don't know," says Peter. He thinks about what the evil spirit said, what they've been saying every time. He knows it's blasphemous to believe what he is beginning to believe— *for who in heaven can be compared with the Lord, who among the sons of the mighty can be likened to Him?*—but he can't see any other explanation.

"Do you remember the storm on the lake?" says John, and they don't have to tell him they do. Then John sings, "*O Lord God of hosts, who has strength like Yours? You are strong and Your faithfulness surrounds You. You rule over winds and*

170

the rage of the sea: when its waves rise like mountains, You can calm them."

Peter shudders. There's no going back now. There's no going back.

*

That night, seven of the seventy come and tell Jesus about how they've cast out evil spirits in his name. The twelve don't mention how their day has been.

Jesus reminds the seven about how the Lord led their ancestors through a vast and dangerous desert, filled with fiery snakes and scorpions. "Sons of Eve," he says, "I give you power over them. Wherever you walk, nothing will harm you."

That night, Jesus breaks bread with his hosts and his guests while Mary goes out to buy new wine. The seven tell about the villages and towns where they've been. The twelve finally gather the courage to share the story of their failure, and finally tell Jesus about the debate he interrupted. James asks what they should say to people who ask specific questions about the Messiah, the Prophet, and the coming Day of Judgment, but Jesus' only response is that he's grateful to his Father that *the wisdom of the wise has perished, and the understanding of the prudent has been hidden.*

That night, in another house, the scholars also sit down to dinner. Their host is a prominent supporter and advisor of Herod—someone they wouldn't ordinarily count as a friend—but tonight they share his bread and the corners of their mouths become red with his old wine. They drink and

they talk: about conditions in the country these days, about the king's health. They talk and they drink, toasting the king's current trip abroad, circling closer and closer now to the thing that has brought them together, until at last they arrive at the fundamental point.

"We can handle his followers," they say, "but if this movement is going to be brought under control before there's serious trouble, we need your people to stop Jesus."

10.

That night, four of the apostles have nightmares.

In his dream, Matthew is running down an alley toward the setting sun, his heart pounding so hard he can feel it in his temples. He knows he has to get to his office before they come. He needs to protect the names written in his ledger. The slanting light half-blinds him and he trips on one rock, falling hard and cutting himself badly on another, but he gets up and he finds the book and he's relieved to see how many names are still written there.

He can hear shouts in the distance as he uncovers the hiding place he prepared for a time like this. He hears the mob getting closer as he lowers the ledger down and covers it. His pursuers are almost at the tax office when he steps outside and gives himself up: they drag him to the brow of a hill he's never seen before, and he looks down. He's imagining the way his body will break against an outcropping of rock below when he wakes.

Thomas also dreams of danger, but he can't tell what it is he's afraid of in the overwhelming dark — it's a new moon's night and almost nothing is visible, though he can feel someone or something near. Thomas reaches out for the

presence, and it pulls on him, and suddenly they're wrestling. As he shifts his weight and grapples with his opponent, Thomas's fear gives way to a strange familiarity. He used to wrestle like this with his twin sister in the few years when she was bigger than him, spending all his strength just to keep the fight going. Back then, he didn't need to win, only to hold on until her anger broke. Now he's losing his grip and his leg hurts, but Thomas is sure he'll be blessed if he can only keep wrestling through this darkness until the coming of the sunlight.

But when the sun rises in his dream, he still can't see who he's wrestling. And the struggle doesn't stop.

Peter dreams a longing so intense he leaves his boat on the shore and walks up into the hills until they grow into mountains beneath his feet. He walks beside a clear stream: when a voice says "Drink," he cups his hands to lift the cold water to his mouth and laps it up.

That's when he catches sight of the golden calf. Seeing it shining there fills him with a sudden shame. *Hear, O Israel! The Lord our God is one!* he thinks, and turns away. But he knows nothing can still his longing to worship more than is allowed.

Then the snorting and galloping of warhorses fills Peter's ears, and he starts to shake because he knows that soldiers are coming to destroy everything and everyone in their path. It's his fault. He's brought this punishment down on them. He wants to run down the mountain and confess everything to warn the others while there's still time — only the ground

is so covered in snakes and scorpions there's nowhere safe to run. For a moment he freezes, but then he remembers: *I give you power over them. Wherever you walk, nothing will harm you.*

He takes the first step.

Judas can't tell if he's awake or asleep when his sister walks in with a scrape across the left side of her face and a cut on her lip. There's a tear at the neck of her tunic. Judas realizes he can't possibly be awake as she walks slowly across the room, her shoulders turned in slightly as if she'd like to fold in her arms and draw in her chest, her gait awkward under hidden pain. A pain no one should ever have to suffer.

Her eyes are blank; the jar she's carrying is broken.

Judas can't tell if he's asleep or awake when he notices the angel.

"Were you with her?" Judas says. "Why didn't you protect her?"

"I wasn't there," says the angel. "I'm with you. Now. It's too late to change what happened."

"Why weren't you there, then?" says Judas, "Why didn't you protect her?"

"The world is too bad," says the angel. "We can't protect everyone."

"But you could have saved her!" says Judas.

"You think so?" says the angel. "Then whose sister should this have happened to?"

"No one's," says Judas, and his eyes feel so heavy he must be awake, though he's fairly sure he isn't.

"Who should suffer for this world's sins?" says the angel.

"No one," says Judas, more tired than he's ever felt before. "This world needs to end."

"We're waiting," says the angel. "Legions of us: we're just waiting for the sign to come and we'll end it."

Judas's sister puts down the broken jar gently by the door. She goes and she lies down and she doesn't say anything. Judas wants to scream, but the air is trapped in his chest. If Judas doesn't drown in his own trapped scream, he'll suffocate in her silence.

Judas turns to the angel. "How much longer?" he says.

*

Night isn't over when Jesus gently shakes everyone awake and says he's had a dream, and they need to leave now. He tells the seven to go warn the other disciples to be careful for a few weeks, then asks them to care for everyone while he and the apostles leave Galilee. He doesn't say where they're going or why and no one asks as they make their way out of town by lamplight.

When the first streaks of dawn cross the sky like feathers, soldiers come to Jesus' hosts only to find the man they're looking for has taken flight.

*

After they're walked deep into the hills, Jesus finds a place to sit and talk with the twelve and Mary.

He closes his eyes. "The time hasn't come yet, but is close," he says. "Next time, I'll let them arrest me. This time,

we need to escape before they come."

Matthew thinks of his dream. He's been worried about mobs for so long he's forgotten that as one of Jesus' disciples, he might also need to be afraid of prisons and soldiers.

Peter remembers his dream: has Jesus just avoided the same danger Peter sensed?

Neither of them asks a question, though, they just watch their Master and wait. Jesus takes a little dirt—so dry it's practically like sand—between his fingers. He rubs it back and forth so that it falls a few dozen grains at a time, blowing this way and that, spreading in every direction.

"I want to see my mother again before the time comes," Jesus says, and he asks Mary, the little James, the big Judas, and Matthew to go west to Nazareth, traveling quietly and telling no one who they are, to find her and invite her to return with them.

He addresses Thomas, Philip, and Nathanael next. "After I'm gone, an age will come when our people need a refuge," he says. "Best to find a man to care for it now." And he tells them to go east to the ten cities to bring back a certain young merchant from among his followers there.

Then he turns to Judas and Andrew, "Like your old Master, I need you to prepare the way before me." He turns to Simon, "Go with them, and talk about me with your friends in the south." He tells them which route to take to Jerusalem and where to make sure there are people ready to greet him when he comes that way again.

Jesus looks to Peter, James, and John. "I don't want to be alone yet," he says. "Stay with me." He says they'll travel north into Herod's estranged brother's kingdom, that there's something they need to see there.

When he's given each group its assignment, he speaks again to the twelve all at once. "The day will come when you sit on thrones in the kingdom, judging the twelve tribes of Israel. So be faithful, and learn to serve them now.

"Think of me, and I'll be with you," he says. "I'll protect you in the places you go, until your work is done and it's time to meet again in this land."

And—though their bodies are exhausted from the short and unsettling night, though they've been half-asleep for most of the morning's long walk—the twelve are all wide awake now because they can feel God in this ordinary-looking place. Yes, God is unmistakably here, and it surprises them.

But even God's presence doesn't keep them from feeling a little afraid, from having an odd sense of dread at the strange things Jesus told them.

*

On the road north, Peter, James, and John learn this: you can flee from trouble, but not from the things that trouble you.

If anything, their worries grow worse in the isolation of their journey out of Galilee. Though it's harder going, Jesus travels mostly through the open hills instead of the lakeside roads to avoid being recognized. So Peter, James, and John

are each trapped in their own recurring thoughts.

As he struggles up slope after slope, Peter can't help thinking about the golden calf and the shame he felt in his dream. Each time they come within sight of the lake, James wonders how much more he really knows than he did before he left home. And whenever they see a soldier in the distance, John wonders what Jesus meant when he said, "Next time, I'll let them arrest me."

But things get easier on the other side of the river, when they're safely out of Galilee. Jesus no longer avoids the roads, and they teach and heal people in the tiny villages they pass through as they make their way north. Work is a soothing balm for Peter, James, and John: being able to serve drives the doubts from their minds. When they pass through the marsh country, James thinks again of Moses and wonders if Jesus is the prophet he predicted, but there are so many fevers and sick children here, he can't focus on the question for long. When, still further north, they leave the road to avoid Philip's pagan capitol, John wonders what will happen to the people there when the kingdom of God comes, but he doesn't dwell on that question for long, either.

And then they reach the northernmost tip of old Israel, where Peter looks up at the same mountains he saw in his dream, walks beside the same stream he drank from in his sleep. And his questions come back, bringing with them a mixture of shame and awe.

*

Peter, James, and John almost run into Jesus when he

stops walking all at once. He stares up at the mountain in front of them.

Then he turns around to face his three followers. "Who do people say that I am?" he asks.

"At first, most thought you were a great sage or a saint," says James. "After John died, some saw him again in you. Others said you were Elijah returned to fulfill Malachi's words, or some other prophet."

"But who do you think I am?" says Jesus.

"The Messiah," all three say at once. And they wait for his response.

But Jesus doesn't say anything.

"And more," says Peter, his voice trembling a little. He needs to say it out loud. He needs to confess. "You're more than our promised King." He takes a deep breath and closes his eyes: this will be easier if he doesn't have to see Jesus react. Then he gives the full strength of his breath to the thought he's kept hidden in his heart: "You're more than any man—you're the Son of the Living God!"

That's it. That's what he's come to believe. He knows Jesus won't have him stoned, but if he's wrong Jesus will look at him in a way that will make him wish he could pull down the mountains onto himself.

"Blessed are you, son of Jonah," says Jesus softly. Peter falls to his knees. "No one on earth would tell you that: only my Father would have."

James stares and John nods, but Jesus just goes on. "You had ears to hear my Father this time. If you can accept all the

truths he will place in your ears and in your mouth, the forces of darkness will never overcome you. I named you Peter so you'll remember *a stone cut without hands will smash into pieces all the kingdoms of the earth."*

Peter thinks of the horsemen in his dream, the horsemen who ride down from the north.

"When will that happen?" asks Peter, "What's the stone?"

"You'll understand," says Jesus, "three days after my death."

What's harder: for a good Jew to believe that a living man is somehow also a God, or for the man who makes that leap in belief to hear his God is going to die?

*

The next day is the Sabbath, and Jesus is invited to preach in the congregation of a village that stands at the base of the mountain, built on the ruins of what was once an important city. He takes the scroll gently in his hands, opens it slowly, and reads:

I will sing to my Beloved a song of his vineyard. My Love had a vineyard on a fertile hill.
He plowed the land and cleared it, and planted good vines;
he built a tower and a winepress for the harvest that would come.
But when he gathered the grapes, they weren't sweet but sour.
Though he'd tended the vines well, they bore wild fruit.
Judge, men of Israel, between my Love and his vineyard!
What more could the Keeper of the Vineyard have done?

"I knew a man once," says Jesus after he rolls up the scroll and sits down, "who tended a fig tree for his father. For three years, the father waited to taste the tree's fruit, but for three years it produced nothing. 'Why are we still waiting?' said the father of the man I knew, 'The soil is good: if this tree gives us nothing, why don't we cut it down?' But the man asked his father for one more year. 'Let me care for it a little longer,' he said. 'If it bears fruit, we'll rejoice together. If not, we'll cut it down.'"

Jesus stops there and closes his eyes. It's silent in the assembly for a moment.

"What happened to the tree?" says someone from the back.

Jesus opens his eyes. "I don't know," he says. "Before the year was up, some of the father's servants killed his son."

*

The next morning, while James and John are teaching a group of villagers, Peter pulls Jesus aside. He's been looking for a chance to talk to him alone.

"I don't understand you," Peter says.

"But you understand so much," says Jesus. "More than almost anyone else."

"I mean I don't understand why you keep talking about dying," says Peter.

"The wind blows where it wants to. You have to know the wind to know where it's going next," says Jesus.

But Peter is not in the mood for puzzles. "If you have power over life and death, why would you let someone kill

you?"

"Because there are things more important than staying alive," says Jesus, and he starts to walk away.

So Peter reaches out and grabs his arm, pulls him back because he can't let go now, he can't go on without an answer. People in the distance are starting to stare, so Peter leans in close and his whisper comes out harsher than he intends: "Then what's the meaning of this scripture? *I call heaven and earth to testify this day against you, that I have set before you life and death, blessing and cursing: so choose life! that you and your children after you can live.*"

"Don't tempt me," says Jesus. "You're not the first one who's tried to trap me with a question, but it's harder when it comes from you."

"Then stop talking that way," says Peter, and he tightens his grip on Jesus. "If you have the power to choose, choose life! Nothing is simpler than that."

But Jesus tears his arm away. "Get away from me, Satan!" he says. "Whose side are you on?"

Jesus walks over to James and John, who are talking with some of the villagers about faith. "If anyone wants to follow me," says Jesus, "he has to forget his own needs and be prepared to die." Jesus pauses. A villager shifts his weight from one foot to the other and looks at the ground.

"Can't you see?" Jesus says. "If all you think about is how to keep living, you'll find one day that you've lost your whole life. But if you lose your life for me and my teachings, you'll find a life that no one can take from you, not even the

grave.

"Sometimes," says Jesus, "your life is the price of your soul."

Jesus leaves town then and heads toward the mountain. Only James, John, and Peter follow.

11.

Jesus has led them up hills before, but Galilee's hills are nothing like this mountain. At first, they think he's just looking for a solitary place on its steep, forbidding slopes. But after an hour or so of strenuous climbing, they realize he's leading them toward the top of the mountain—though the summit is still far beyond their sight.

When Peter can spare enough breath to think, he wonders if Jesus is still angry. He looks at his Master from time to time, but can never tell if what he's seeing is anger or a raw and majestic determination. In the scriptures it says: *I have set my face like a flint.* Yes, thinks Peter, that's what Jesus has done.

And so he tries to set his own face like a flint. Tries to climb with the same relentless and consuming drive. *The Lord God has helped me, so I won't be disgraced. I have set my face like a flint, and I won't be put to shame.* Up ahead, Jesus keeps climbing. To his right hand and his left, James and John keep pace.

*

They've been climbing for hours and John is hungry. But he refuses to be the first to stop. The first to ask if they can

rest and eat.

*

They've been climbing all day and the wind is stronger and colder the closer they get to the summit. James can feel it slip through his clothing and wonders how long he's made do with the same robe.

*

For the first time in his life, Peter sees snow — not simply as whiteness on a distant hilltop, but as a physical substance lying ahead on the ground. It looks a little like sand. When he reaches it, he takes some in his hand. It feels strange. Cold, yes, but also hot. As if his body doesn't know how it should feel to touch pure color for the first time.

*

They climb over snow-covered rock after snow-covered rock. They fill their lungs with cold instead of air. They can see the whole promised land when they look over their shoulders, but they hardly ever bother to look over their shoulders. They keep moving, keep climbing.

They have almost reached the top.

*

The three apostles' bodies tremble with the cold and their eyes are heavy with longing for sleep when Jesus stops at the top of the mountain. The sun is setting, but his face shines.

His clothes are white, unnaturally white, whiter even than the glistening snow.

*

186

The apostles are struggling to stay awake for even one hour. Their eyes fall closed, and they will them back open. Jesus is talking with Moses and Elijah. They are telling him to take off his white robes and wash them in wine. They are telling him to take off his glistening garments to soak them in the blood of grapes.

*

Peter is struggling to stay awake, so he tries to listen to them talk. Something about Jerusalem. Riding into Jerusalem. And then something about another mountain near Jerusalem.

"Are you ready?" says Moses.

"Yes," says Jesus.

"Can we help you?" says Elijah.

"You're helping me now," Jesus says.

*

James struggles to stay focused. James wants so badly to pay attention. Moses and Elijah are talking to Jesus. Jesus' face shines and his clothes are whiter than snow, his eyes as dark as wine.

*

John doesn't feel cold anymore because there's so much light and warmth coming off Jesus and the two prophets. Elijah burns like his chariot, Moses like his bush. John basks in their presence. John basks in the warmth of Jesus, who is like all the light in the whole world. Jesus is like the sun and the moon and the stars, and the hearth on a rainy night.

*

Jesus wakes Peter, James, and John when Moses and Elijah are about to go.

"It's good that we're here," says Peter through growing shivers. "We should stay here for a while: we'll build a booth for you and one for Moses and for Elijah and it will be just like Sukkot."

But they don't need booths to remind them of the Feast of the Ingathering, because God sends a cloud to shelter them instead.

And in the cloud, they hear the voice of God. Not just feel it, but hear it with their own ears. Unmistakable. Though they've never heard the voice before, they know it at once:

"This is my Son, my Chosen," He says. "Listen."

And they fall on their faces before Jesus in worship and awe and fear.

"Don't be afraid," says Jesus gently. "You can get up."

And they listen, because God himself told them to.

*

The cloud is gone, and they're alone with Jesus now. The sun hasn't set, and the sun doesn't seem to set as they walk down the mountain for hours and hours.

"Don't tell anyone what you saw until everything the prophets said has been done, and I've returned," says Jesus.

None of the three remembers exactly what Jesus talked about with Moses and Elijah, but each of them imagines he'll ask the other two later, and they'll know what has to be done.

All at once, something occurs to James. *I will send you Elijah the prophet before the great and dreadful day of the Lord.*

"What does it mean when Elijah comes?" he says.

"Let me tell you a story," says Jesus. "Elijah came, and they abused him. Herod threw him in a prison and had him killed."

"The John who baptized you is Elijah?" says the young John.

"That's not a story," says James, "that's a fact."

"It's a story for those with ears to hear," Jesus says.

They get down the mountain and into the village just before the sun finally finishes setting.

"Come inside with me," says a familiar-looking man. "I'd be honored if you'd join my family as we welcome in the Sabbath."

Jesus immediately goes with him, but it takes Peter, James, and John a moment to follow. How long have they been on the mountain? Has Time itself abandoned its usual caravan of days and nights?

12.

Apostles return from the north, south, and east to their meeting place in the hills, but Matthew's group is late. As he watches for them, Nathanael grows more and more nervous. Didn't the other nine leave the province for a reason? Aren't they keeping out of sight for a reason now? What might have happened to the one group that stayed in Galilee?

When he catches the first sight of them in the distance, Nathanael forgets caution and stealth and shouts out a greeting at the top of his lungs. He runs out to embrace them, and Andrew and Judas follow. They're already sharing stories and laughing when they get back to Jesus, who interrupts to ask, "Where's my mother?"

"We didn't know if you would all be here yet," says Matthew, "so we left her and Mary to wait at Martha's."

"Good," says Jesus. "Martha's is on our way." And without another word, he heads out. His long, steady stride sets a pace now so familiar to these disciples that walking again beside him feels like coming home.

*

They talk as they walk. Several apostles report briefly on their journeys, but Jesus doesn't say much until Matthew's

turn—and then he's full of questions. Jesus asks all about his brothers and sisters, about how the house he grew up in is looking now, about how his mother did on the journey and what she seems to think of Martha and Mary. He asks whether she's eating well, and whether she seems to be sleeping enough, and Matthew laughs.

"If you cared about your own health as much as you do about hers, I'd have had better answers when she asked those questions!" Matthew says.

After Jesus has been assured that his mother is fine, he asks Andrew, Judas, and Simon about the people they talked to in the south. He nods in approval as they tell him how many of the men they once knew as John's disciples are eager to meet him or see him again. He slows down and asks a few questions as Simon talks about the growing excitement among his old friends.

Thomas and Nathanael share greetings with Jesus from various followers on the far side of the lake, and Philip introduces him to a beardless young trader from Pella, the only merchant who would follow them back. Jesus thanks the three for fulfilling their mission so well, and walks ahead with the lanky young man. Jesus and the trader talk rapidly in low tones, and the apostles walk just out of earshot behind.

Most of them are happy to talk with each other while Jesus walks ahead. Peter tells Andrew about a man on the marsh who had a laugh just like their father did when they were young. Nathanael asks Matthew if he was nervous

spending so long in Galilee after Jesus' dream, but all Matthew seems to want to talk about is the news from the east side of the lake. Philip and James share a salted piece of fish and tell old stories from their villages' harbors.

But John doesn't feel like talking. He keeps thinking about the fire he felt on the mountain and about the truths he has to keep hidden for now, locked deep down in his bones. Until Jesus returns—from what? John tries and he tries, but he can't seem to remember what Elijah and Moses said.

Simon doesn't talk with anyone either. He wants to tell someone how unsettled he feels, but he can't quite explain it to himself. Why should he be bothered by how quick his old friends were to call Jesus *the Star of Jacob*, or by how much they say they're willing to do to help him *bring judgment to the foreign nations*? Is he afraid to have Matthew know his friends are Zealots? Or is he afraid of what his old friends might want his Master to become?

Thomas keeps his eyes on the road in front of him. But he isn't thinking of that road, he's remembering the roads that lead east out past the ten cities. He can't seem to get those roads out of his mind, can't forget how they seemed to call to him to walk out past the borders of the Empire, on past the Tigris and Euphrates and the mountains where king Cyrus was born—but if he doesn't even know where those roads end, how can he explain the depth of his wish to get there?

*

Halfway to Martha's, while Jesus is still talking with the trader from Pella, Philip asks the other apostles a question. "When the kingdom comes, Jesus says we'll sit as judges over the twelve tribes—but how will that work?"

"What do you mean?" says James. "Are you asking which tribe each of us will get?"

Philip shakes his head. "I mean: most of the tribes are gone. How are they coming back?"

"Maybe they're hidden in distant lands. Maybe he'll send some of us out to find them," says Thomas.

"Or we'll fight to free them," says Simon. "Like the judges of old."

"No," says Andrew, "it's written that in the days of the Messiah, foreign nations will bring them back to us: *I will give my signal to the nations and lift up a banner to the peoples, and they will bring your sons back in their arms, and carry back your lost daughters on their shoulders. Kings will be their foster fathers, and queens their nursemaids.*"

"So kings will gather around us?" says Philip. "Who gets to accept children from Caesar?"

"It'll be Matthew," says John. "He has the ledger."

Several of the apostles laugh.

"It wouldn't be me," says Matthew. He knows John doesn't mean any insult by associating him with Caesar, but he suspects others are still troubled by his old life. "It would probably be Peter," he says. "Caesar's the most powerful king, so he would have to report to the most important one of us."

"Is Peter the most important?" says Nathanael.

"I don't know," says Matthew. "He and James and John are the ones Jesus took with him, and they're the first three he called, so it would be one of them. It just seemed to me like it would be Peter."

"Andrew was called before any of them," says Judas quietly.

"Not really before," says Andrew. "At the same time as Peter."

"No," says Judas, "he was calling you because he recognized you from the Jordan. You were the first."

Andrew wants to point out it doesn't really matter, but before he can Thomas says, "Why should the first be most important? Judas is the one who makes sure we eat!"

Andrew laughs, but James doesn't.

"We know the most about the kingdom," says James, "since we've been with him from the beginning."

"If you know more, why haven't you taught us?" says Thomas.

James doesn't answer.

"Do you have secrets? Does Andrew know something about the missing tribes that Simon and I don't?" Thomas says.

"It's my opinion, that's all," says Andrew.

"But James went north with Jesus," says the other James. "Maybe he knows something you don't."

"I don't know how the tribes will return," says James. "Jesus knows, and that's enough. But if we fight, my brother

and I are fighting on his right and left sides. If kings and queens come to return the lost and offer him tribute, we'll be on his right and his left when he receives them."

Simon laughs. "I won't dispute your place in the royal court, but if we're fighting I don't see the wisdom in putting a man who's good with a net on Jesus' right side. I think he'd prefer someone who's faced men before with a sword."

"That's true," says the broad-chested Judas. "Things are different if we fight than if angels fight for us."

"And if the angels fight alongside us," says James, "then faith matters more than experience. Who trusts God enough to be protected from the enemy's arrows? Whose *arms will be made strong by the hands of Jacob's God?*"

"You think your faith will be the same," says Simon, "after you've seen some of your friends kill and watched others die?" He waits a moment, but doesn't get an answer. "Every man has great courage until it's put to the test. We'll see who's brave when the day of trouble comes."

James opens his mouth to respond, but Peter stops him. "I think we've argued enough," he says.

And so they walk on in silence.

*

They're hot and they're tired, but John and Judas still break into a run and race each other to the house when they see Martha's children playing outside. John gets there first and the boys jump on his back. The little girls crowd around Judas instead—they still remember how he shared some dried fruit with them and their brothers the last time he

came.

When Jesus arrives in the courtyard, his mother takes one look at him, turns around and marches off toward the kitchen.

"Don't you want to greet your son?" Martha asks.

"Of course," says Mary, loud enough for everyone to hear, "but look at how thin he is. He needs to eat first so there's something for me to hug."

Jesus laughs. *"Man doesn't live by bread alone,"* he calls after her, *"but by heeding the words of God."*

"By the sweat of your face you should eat your bread," she shouts back. "God says you have to eat."

Jesus laughs again, turns to his disciples, and throws his hands up. "My mother has defeated me!" he says, and he crouches down beside the courtyard wall to wait. Martha's youngest daughter sits on the ground beside him and plays with the fringes on his robe.

Jesus turns to James. "Since we have some time," he says, "maybe you can tell me what all of you were arguing about on the road."

It's not nearly as embarrassing to say something foolish as it is to be asked, after a period of more thoughtful reflection, to repeat it. James doesn't think he can hide anything from Jesus, but he doesn't want to speak up, either.

Jesus looks to the other apostles. "You still want to know who's the most important in the Kingdom of God?" he says.

And though they all shake their heads and mumble apologies, Jesus rises and scoops up Martha's youngest

daughter. She giggles as he puts her up on his shoulder.

"If you can be as small as this child," says Jesus, "then I'll lift you up, too, and you can be the greatest!"

The girl laughs again as Jesus spins her around and the apostles feel shame loosen its grip on their hearts. From the kitchen, the women hear the laughter, and the sisters drag Jesus' mother away from her cooking for a moment to go with them to see what's going on.

They come into the courtyard as Jesus lowers Martha's daughter down off his shoulder and holds her tight for a moment in his arms. "Whoever receives even one child in my name receives the whole kingdom of God," Jesus says.

"Then women are truly blessed," says Jesus' mother, and she laughs. "I've received the whole kingdom straight from heaven now seven times!"

"No wonder they feel so heavy inside," says Martha, and her laugh is as full of joy as the older Mary's.

But Mary from Magdala, who hasn't been able to marry or give birth, just smiles: happy for her sister and all the world's mothers, but also more than a little sad. Then *Rejoice, O barren!* she tells herself, *break forth into singing!* Your day, too, will come, she thinks. The prophets say your day will come.

*

That night, Jesus and the twelve talk about the route they'll take south: between the Jordan and the endless Judean hills. Though they've lived off the generosity of local people alone on past missions, Jesus suggests they take

along some money and a few provisions this time.

Then Jesus lets his twelve tired friends sleep, and sits to talk a little with his mother before he lets himself rest.

"They seem to be good men," she says. "All of them have honest faces. And Martha and Mary are wonderful— they have humble hearts."

"They're all like the salt of the earth," he says. "I'd love them anyway, but I love them for that."

Mary looks at her oldest son. "I wanted your brothers to come with me," she says. "But they didn't want to. I don't know if they're offended or afraid."

"I'll go see them again as soon as I can," says Jesus. "You know I have other things to do now, but I still miss them. I've been wanting to see my James."

Mary smiles. They sit a while quietly, not needing to talk. They've been happy just to sit together since he was very young. She's been happy to sit quietly with him in times of joy or pain or both from the first moment she held him in her arms.

"Do you have to go south now?" Mary asks. "With so many good people around you, couldn't you stay here in Galilee a little longer?"

"Meat can be seasoned with salt alone," says Jesus. He stands up. "But a sacrifice has to be salted with fire."

Then he kisses his mother on the forehead, and he goes to bed.

Book Three:
Vayiqra (And He Called)

"If his offering be a burnt sacrifice of the herd,
let him offer a male without blemish: he shall offer it
of his own voluntary will at the door of the tabernacle
of the congregation before the Lord. . ."

1.

Someday they'll see: the driving wind mingles
the dust of my body with the ashes of the moth
-Sauda

Ages ago, longer ago than anyone can remember, they say the Israelites spent a last night as slaves in Egypt. They packed up their bags, borrowed their neighbors' jewelry, spread lambs' blood on the doorposts, and waited for God's judgment to fall on their oppressors. When it was done — and before any mob came looking from blood-marked door to blood-marked door for revenge — the Israelites got up, and they walked away and away and away for the next forty years.

Every Jew in Galilee knows this story by heart, because each year, just as the cool months give way to spring, thousands and thousands of people pack their bags, borrow a little money from their neighbors with promises to bring back something from the south, and take to the roads toward the Temple in Jerusalem, where the lambs today are slain. And whether they have been on the trip themselves yet or not, every Jewish child in Galilee has heard of the endless crowds there, about how it looks from a distance like all Israel has moved out to tents in the hills and the desert

once again.

In the southern parts of Galilee, children will shirk chores and perch on roofs or in trees to watch the travelers pass by. And is it only pilgrims' clothes they hear rustling below, or also their ancestors'? Does the smell of sweat come from a long day of walking in the heat, or from years spent as slaves in Egypt? When the children sit above the road, they feel time collapsing beneath them.

On the road this year, Salome feels like space is also collapsing: she asks a question to one of Jesus' followers from the marshes upriver and gets an answer from another whose home is near Magdala, west of the lake. She hears about her sons from a woman on her left who comes from the foothills of Mount Hermon and a girl on her right who met James and John near Mount Tabor. On this road, she meets the wives of some of the seventy men Jesus called and blessed and the mothers of other people he healed. On this road, it seems, a sweet sampling of the fruits of her sons' and their Master's ministry has been gathered.

"If only my sons could be here!" she thinks. And she wonders where they are now and how long it might be until she sees them again. She worries about them as she walks, and she worries about them more when she sees the soldiers by the roadside scanning the crowds at the southern edge of Galilee.

Not long after the soldiers are out of sight, a group of men with faces wrapped tight against the dust walk up beside her. Salome quickens her step to move away from

them and keeps her eyes focused ahead, but the men match her pace and stay close. When one of them takes hold of her arm she pulls it away and shouts out a threat—but then he unwraps his face.

"Please don't hurt me," says James. "I forgot how you feel about surprises."

She doesn't know whether to scold him or hug him, so she just laughs. John and Peter and Jesus and the others unwrap their faces and laugh with her.

She shouldn't be surprised that they're here. After all, time and space fall apart so easily on the journey south for Passover.

*

Though Jesus' followers from Galilee are excited to see him, there's no sign anyone else is waiting until the second evening of the journey at a village where the Jabbok flows into the Jordan. Men who were once John's disciples scan the passing travelers, shout greetings to Judas and Andrew, then rush down and hoist Jesus up on their shoulders like a groom, singing and clapping as they carry him off to a feast.

They've prepared for him well: after dinner, the half of the village that isn't busy providing accommodations for travelers gathers to listen to the man who might be heir to John the Prophet's legacy and to savor his strange stories.

He tells them about a woman who loses the precious silver coin that was her whole dowry. Then he asks them: won't she light a lamp after dark so she can sweep every last corner of the house, not sleeping until she finds it? And

when she finds it, won't she celebrate with her friends?

He tells them another story: a man's younger son asks for his portion of the inheritance, sells it for silver, then moves away to a Gentile city and wastes the money breaking every commandment he knows. His sins alone are enough to keep rain from falling over the whole region for a year, and a terrible famine strikes the land.

The young man begs his friends for help and mercy, but their goodwill has gone the way of his wealth. Only one of them offers anything: a position feeding pigs that pays so poorly soon the young man envies his charges their slop.

Hunger and guilt gnaw at him until one day he comes to himself. "In my father's house, even the servants have enough bread," he thinks. "Why should I die here of hunger?" So he leaves the pigs and starts toward his old home.

On the road home, he thinks: my father taught me the right way to go in life, but I left him for the vanity of the world. He thinks: if I were my father's son, I'd have lived the way he taught me—I'm no one's son now, maybe I never was. If I could serve my father for seven lifetimes, he thinks, I'd still be in his debt. But he stays on the road to his father's house, and he practices what he'll say so that his tongue will know how to go on after his heart breaks at the first sight of his father's stricken face. He practices so that he'll be able to plead for work with his father, whose face was a mirror that showed only the truth long before the truth was such a sharp knife.

But all his practice is for nothing. Before he ever gets home his father runs out, holds him tight like a child and kisses his neck. The young man says, "Father, I've sinned against you and heaven!" But the father says, "You're home, now. You're finally home."

The young man says, "I had my chance. I don't deserve another." But the father says, "Bring the ring his mother left him. Bring him shoes and a many-colored robe." The father tells his servants to kill a fatted calf and throw a feast to celebrate. Then he smiles like he hasn't in years and even laughs.

The older son, working in the fields, hears people in the distance start to sing and dance. He comes close to the house and smells the tender meat. "What is this?" he says to a servant, and the servant tells him how his brother has come home, and how his father has welcomed him.

"How is that possible?" says the older son, but the servant can't answer so the brother stays outside until his father comes to see what's wrong. "I've given up everything else I could have followed, everything else I could have had, for you," says the older son. "I've gone wherever you asked me to go and worked long hours every time we've sown seeds and every time we've harvested. And yet we've never eaten even a goat's kid in my honor—why have you given the son who abandoned you a calf?"

"You've had all this time with me," says the father, "and everything I have is yours. So why shouldn't we celebrate with the one who wasted so many years? My son was dead,

and is alive again. He was lost, and now he's found."

*

After he finishes the stories, three scholars approach Jesus.

"You tell very interesting stories," says the first.

"And your reputation as a holy person proceeds you," says the second.

"Although reputations can be hard to live up to," says the third.

"What can I do for you?" asks Jesus.

"Our young patron couldn't be here tonight, but he's expressed an interest in helping support you," says the first. "Financially."

"It's our responsibility to advise him," says the second. "We have no doubt that you're a righteous man and that the honor you're given as a healer is deserved, but we don't know for sure—if you'll forgive me for saying so—whether your wisdom goes deeper than homilies and simple tales."

"What deeper wisdom are you looking for?" asks Jesus.

"We'd like to hear your opinions on some legal issues," says the first. "For instance, there's a woman from near here who recently returned home after spending several years abroad. She claims that her husband died, but can't provide any proof or documentation. She expects his brothers to give her the share of the inheritance allotted to her by the marriage contract, but since there's no proof her husband is dead, should that property be considered hers or held back for now?"

"I don't get involved in property disputes," says Jesus. "But remind them what the scriptures say: *Wait for the Lord, and keep his way, and he'll honor you with an inheritance in the land: when the wicked are cut off, you'll witness it.* If she's broken the commandment and given false witness, she'll find herself without an inheritance on the Day of Judgment. If the brothers break the commandment and covet, they'll find themselves cut off. Tell them, and see if they can resolve the matter on their own."

"What's the use of law," says the second scholar, "if *every man does what is right in his own eyes*? How can you expect them to resolve the issue without a judgment? After all, the property is only one of the concerns. The woman is childless, so if her husband really is dead, she has a right to one of his brothers. The nearest brother says he'd be happy to act as *goel* and marry her, but what if she's lying and her husband—his brother—reappears? A correct ruling could protect the family from serious harm: what do you advise them to do?"

But Jesus just shakes his head. "I advise them to keep the matter away from the courts," he says. "In the courts, a woman isn't accepted as a witness. But when Ruth went to straight to her kinsman Boaz, he believed everything she said."

The third scholar bursts out laughing. "You must be innocent indeed if you believe every woman is as virtuous and trustworthy as a Ruth! If that's what the brother expects, too, you'd better tell me your answer to a different legal

question in advance: how much disappointment does a husband have to endure before he has sufficient grounds for divorce? How many burned meals does he have to eat?"

That's when Jesus grows angry. "Moses gave laws of divorce to a stubborn and idol-loving people, but what was the only teaching on marriage Adam needed?" he says. "In the beginning, God created them male and female and said: *Because of this, each man should leave his father and mother and be joined to his wife, and they should be one flesh.*"

Jesus stares at the scholars a moment, then turns away.

"What God put together, men shouldn't be teaching how to take apart," he says to the villagers before he walks off.

*

In the morning, the scholars return their patron the money he sent with them and tell him about their disappointing encounter with Jesus.

"He's charismatic, but impractical," says the first.

"He's a careless thinker with a short temper," says the second.

"It's a dangerous combination," says the third. "And when it gets him into trouble, you don't want people to come asking you where he got his money from. That's why we brought it back."

But their young patron doesn't let the matter rest at that, so the scholars have to retell the whole exchange, beginning from their first approach and ending with Jesus' abrupt dismissal of the whole field of divorce law.

"I'd like to meet him myself," says the rich young man.

"Do you know where he stayed last night?"

*

Jesus leaves his hosts well before the young man reaches them, but all the pilgrims take the same route from here to Jericho, so the young man hurries to find them.

Since the crowds on the stone road move slowly, he runs through the dirt on the side. Dust covers his cloak, adds color to his thin young beard, sticks to the insides of his mouth and nose, but he keeps running. Pilgrims stop to laugh at the sight: since when does someone so well-dressed and wealthy travel alone with such disregard for dignity? But the young man keeps running: though he's not even sure how he'll recognize him, he knows he needs to talk to Jesus.

The young man moves even further from the road to make his way around a big group of talkative Galileans, then notices there are also a number of Judeans in the mix. He slows down, scans the group, and recognizes a man from his village who was once a disciple of John.

The man next to that man, the one he's listening to so carefully, must be Jesus.

The rich young man presses into the group until he can fall down at Jesus' feet. And when Jesus stops, the whole world seems to stop with him.

"Master," says the young man, "I know you don't give rulings for any earthly court, but I want to know about the court of heaven."

"Then why are you kneeling there?" says Jesus, "Stand

up and walk with me."

The young man does as he's told. "Master," he says again, "how can I inherit eternal life?"

Jesus laughs. "You've sponsored many scholars—I'm sure you know the laws about that inheritance. Have you killed anyone?"

"No," says the young man, a little shocked at Jesus' casual tone.

"Have you committed adultery?" asks Jesus.

"I'm not even married!" says the young man.

"Have you stolen?" asks Jesus.

"Of course not!" the young man says.

"Have you given false witness or cheated anyone in business?" Jesus asks.

"Never," says the young man.

"Have you kept the commandment to honor your father and mother?" asks Jesus.

"As long as they lived, and I treasure their memory," says the young man.

The stones feel strange beneath the rich man's sandals: he's far more used to riding on these country roads.

"If you want eternal life," says Jesus, "you're on the right path."

The young man walks beside Jesus a while. Can it really be as simple as that?

"Is that all you need to do to get into the kingdom of God?" the young man asks.

Jesus glances at him sideways. "You didn't mention the

kingdom of God before," says Jesus. "For that, there's only one thing: give up everything you have and follow me."

The rich young man almost trips on a loose stone. He was his parents' only child. From his mother's side, he has farmland he rents out in four different villages. From his father's side, he has a successful business with agents in ten different towns. "What do you mean, give up everything?" he says.

"Sell it all," says Jesus. "And give the money to the poor. Exchange every treasure on earth for one in heaven, where it can't get lost or keep you up all night with worry. Follow me: sacrifice everything."

Only once before has the rich young man felt this way. When his parents died, grief almost swallowed him, until he saw himself giving to scholars in a dream and woke up with new purpose in life. Why shouldn't he move the rest of his wealth to heaven? When Jesus' road lies before him, what use are the treasures of this world?

But there's another thing the young man has to consider. Though he isn't married now, some day he will be. Though the children he may have are only dreams now, some day they'll be living bodies with physical needs. His mother's fields aren't his own: they belong also to her future grandchildren. His father's business isn't his own: it's also a trust, an inheritance for hoped-for grandsons.

A weight like graves seems to rest on the young man's chest. He knows Jesus is a holy man, and he wants to make the sacrifice Jesus asks for. He imagines himself letting go of

everything but God's favor, imagines himself giving away even the sandals he's wearing so that the rocks cut his soft soles: though his feet bleed, surely something will bloom as he waters the desert with each step.

But he also imagines another life. He imagines a young woman, fair as the moon and clear as the sun, whose face is like the morning when he comes home to her at night. He imagines the pure daughters she'll bear him, and the righteous sons: his parents' grandchildren will grow to watch over their fields, manage their business, and he'll teach them to give generously to both scholars and charities. He imagines himself respected as his hair grays, securing good marriages for his daughters and sons, giving counsel in time to their children. Telling his offspring's offspring the stories of their ancestors.

There are tears on the rich young man's face as he murmurs an apology to Jesus and leaves him. "Thank you for offering me one good life, but I choose the other," he says.

And it will happen almost as he imagined it. He'll find a moon-fair woman and marry her. After some time, she'll bear him two daughters and a son. His fields and businesses will prosper; his children will grow and marry. His life will be sweet, if not always as good as he'd like—until, when his hair begins to gray, the people revolt against Rome but also turn on each other. The rebels will seize his fields and murder his daughters. The Romans will plunder his goods and raze his house and slaughter his wife and grandchildren

and son.

For the rest of his life, he'll stay up half the night, wandering through the darkness looking for them. Trying to find anyone whose death he might only have imagined. Who might have somehow hidden and escaped.

*

The apostles are astonished when the rich young man leaves Jesus. Not because they don't understand why a good person would walk away from their Master, but because as Jesus and the rich young man talked, each of them felt a shadow of what he felt when Jesus first called him. Matthew remembers the way nothing else entered his mind in that moment, the way his body seemed to respond to the words before his thoughts did. Andrew remembers his feeling of discouragement being lifted away, as if by an invisible wind that lifted him from the lakeside to a hilltop. Peter remembers dropping the net, the thick ropes slipping so easily through his calloused hands, never to be taken up again. Even Simon remembers it: when there were so many reasons for him to leave as others did, he remembers thoughts of Jesus pulling him back like the current when you try to walk upstream.

"Why isn't he coming?" asks Andrew, "Didn't he feel that?"

"He must have," says Jesus, "but it's hard for a man with so many riches to join the kingdom of God."

"It's not that hard," says Matthew, who regrets nothing.

Jesus glances at him. "You knew that money didn't

really belong to you, so you didn't belong to it, either. But it's hard for a man who trusts his wealth to come into the kingdom of God, harder than it is for a camel to pass through an opening the size of a needle's eye."

The apostles stare. Thomas looks for a puzzle in Jesus' words, imagines the rich young man spending the rest of his life plucking out a camel's hairs and passing them through a needle one at a time. The futility of the image exhausts him. "Is there any way, then, for a man like him to be saved?" Thomas asks.

Jesus looks around at all the twelve. "How many things have you seen God do that men can't? With God, all things are possible. There will be joy yet in heaven over him."

*

Peter knows he shouldn't be bothered by this, but he is. He thinks of his wife and his mother-in-law, thinks of their faith and sacrifice. Why should a rich man with no family be excused for refusing to do something a poor fisherman has done? Peter knows he shouldn't be bothered, but he can't stop thinking about a story the prophet Nathan once told King David. A story about a rich man who spared sheep that were only things to him and killed a poor man's only lamb instead, a lamb that was all the love and duty in the world to that man.

"We've left everything to follow you—" says Peter, but he stops before he can give voice to his complaint. *A peaceful heart heals the body*, he reminds himself, *but envy rots the bones.*

A breeze comes down off the hills toward the river, giving momentary relief from the lowland heat. Far ahead, Peter can almost see what must be Jericho's city wall.

Jesus turns to Andrew. "How many homes have you stayed in since I called you to follow me?"

Andrew thinks. "A few dozen, at least."

"And how many women cooked for you and cleaned up after you like you were their own sons?" asks Jesus.

Andrew smiles wide.

"How many people have you met who were like brothers and sisters to you?" asks Jesus, "How many houses would you be as glad to see again as your own home? How many fields do you love now as much as if you'd spent your whole life caring for them?"

Peter thinks not just of the villages, but of hills where he's spent the night and risen with the sun in the morning. He thinks of drinking from the dew on the wild grass, of digging up plants with satiating bulbs. All of Galilee is his now. Galilee is his in a way no rich man will ever know.

"Whoever leaves a house or land or loved ones for me and my gospel is given hundreds of homes and lands and loved ones in this life. Your reward is coming in this world already," says Jesus. "So there's no need to be jealous of the lost who are brought back to life in the world to come."

*

They reach Jericho at mid-day. In the winter, the warm, heavy air makes it a favorite retreat for royalty: Alexander the conqueror had an estate built here with plunder from his

siege of Tyre; Mark Antony gave the whole city as a gift to Cleopatra at the height of their romance. After she committed suicide, the city reverted to the first Herod's control. It was a pool in Jericho where that Herod ensured that the last heir of Judah Maccabee would spend the last moments of his life, lost beneath the water in an assassin's arms.

The dates grown outside Jericho are sweet, and the trade in spices from the east is good, but it's still no wonder that many men left those comforts for the desert in the days when John preached there. Jericho is a city stained with too many old sins, too much old blood.

When John was in prison, most of his disciples hoped he would return alive, but from the day of his arrest the disciples in Jericho somehow knew their Master had been taken from them forever. When they finally heard the news of his death, they tore their clothes and fasted like everyone else—but theirs was pure mourning, without any surprise.

But they're no longer mourning. They're eager now to see the man who's said to have a double portion of John's spirit, and they have a feast ready when he comes.

When Jesus approaches the city, John's disciples rush out and bow down before him. They bring him in to the meal, tell him he can eat as slowly as he likes and has no need to be afraid here, because there are already fifty strong men in this city who have committed to do whatever Jesus says.

"Should we send them to Jerusalem with you?" they ask as Jesus finishes his bread and starts tasting dates.

"There's no need for that," says Jesus.

"It's no trouble. They want to help you," they tell him.

"Do they know what I'm doing there?" asks Jesus.

"You don't understand: they'll do whatever you tell them to. If you say 'go up to a mountain,' they'll go up. If you say, 'come back to the valley,' they'll come back without ever having to know why," say John's disciples.

"What about when no one gives them orders?" asks Jesus. "When I've gone, will they look for me three days?"

John's disciples keep pressing him until, washing his hands after the meal, he agrees to let the fifty come, but Jesus' apostles hardly hear the rest of the conversation. Why is their Master talking about being gone?

*

Even the broad streets of Jericho swell almost to breaking with the mass of people who follow Jesus out of the city: his close followers, the extra Galilean pilgrims they've befriended, the fifty strong men from Jericho, and the hopeful disciples of a dead master.

From the city gate, blind old Bartimaeus hears them, unravels the threads of sound in his mind and recognizes the famous name of Jesus. Jesus, the healer. Jesus, the prophet. Jesus, who might be the promised anointed one.

He wishes he could be right in the middle of that cloud of sound, wishes he could make his way safely through the bruising elbows and crushing feet of the crowd to touch the man he's heard so much about. Not that he needs Jesus to heal him as Jesus has healed so many others. No, Bartimaeus

wants to touch Jesus so he will always remember in the most literal sense what it felt like when Jesus was there. He wants to touch Jesus so he can hold on to some connection to goodness on the days when the people are unkind and when the alms are few and when the loneliest place in the world is Jericho's west gate.

But because there's no way for a blind man to safely approach Jesus today, Bartimaeus decides to connect himself with the saint through a song instead. Yes, when the cloud of sound is pressing close, Bartimaeus sings from the bottom of his chest:

David, King of Israel!
David, King of Israel!
David, King of Israel lives forever!

And when the other beggars shout to him to be quiet, to make some room for their cries for charity to be heard, Bartimaeus only sings louder and deeper. Pours every memory from his lost sight into sound to celebrate the hero who, at any moment, may walk past.

Jesus stops. "Bring him to me," Jesus says. "Bring the singer."

So the crowd parts, and Bartimaeus drops his cloak in his eagerness to stumble forward and touch even the hem of Jesus' robe.

"What can I do for you?" says Jesus.

"I just wanted to be near you," says Bartimaeus. "It's already enough."

So Jesus takes the blind man's hand and lifts it to his

own face. Bartimaeus feels the warmth of tears there and begins to shake.

Jesus places Bartimaeus's salty fingers gently on his blind eyes. The water returns at once to those dried-up eyes, and for the first time in years, Bartimaeus can see.

"It's a steep road up to Jerusalem," says Jesus. "I don't want you to trip as you follow me there."

*

On the road from Jericho up to Jerusalem, there's no sign of blood in the Passover season. The robbers' hands are clean, their nails transparent, the sleeves of each assassin spotless. Since the road is too crowded at this time of year for an ambush, they've washed their hands and wiped off their knives, and they've changed into merchants' robes to sell the wares of the last year's victims to the pilgrims who pass by.

In the coming days, wine cups across Jerusalem will serve as monuments for the spilled blood of Pharaoh's Egypt. In the Temple, they'll slaughter a flawless lamb in the name of God, filling hundreds of thousands of worshippers with reverent awe. But in this season of memory, the blood of the road's victims lies forgotten, dried black and mixed with the dust beneath the feet of that man who buys a new coat, that woman whose eyes shine with delight at the bargain she's being offered.

Since Bartimaeus's eyes have been opened, he sees blood everywhere.

He turns to Jesus. "What does it mean?" he asks.

"The time is coming when everything that's been covered will be revealed, and no secret will be hidden," whispers Jesus.

A few steps back, Judas is walking carefully. He can't see the blood like Bartimaeus, but he still knows it's there. The closer he comes to home, the more he's aware of hidden blood, of unspoken secrets.

Judas looks from the carefully washed hands of one robber to the clean fingernails of the next. Though he's sure he's awake, though he'd swear by heaven and by earth that one foot keeps moving in front of the other, Judas starts having his nightmare. His sister is carrying the water. Someone sees her: maybe it's a robber, or a soldier. Maybe it's someone she knows, someone she trusts.

After he's raped her, the man walks away. He must wash his hands before too long.

The world forgets her invisible blood. The world never noticed.

*

They reach a village outside Jerusalem in the evening. It's nice here, nothing like the Jerusalem Judas knows. Pilgrims sit under the shade of trees on the hillside to plan the last part of their journeys while Simon goes out to make arrangements for the next day with some of his friends. Goats bleat contentedly as they graze in the distance, and Jesus gives Andrew and Thomas instructions on where to go in the morning to get him a young donkey that's never been ridden.

Before nightfall, the twelve settle into the house where they'll be staying. Though everyone's excited to be so close to the holy city at last, the long climb has left their legs sore and their lungs exhausted. Soon everyone but Judas is asleep.

Judas is too tired to sleep tonight, too tired to pray. But he's almost drifted off at last when the angel appears beside him again.

"How long?" he says to the angel. "How long until this ends and all the nightmares go away?"

"I don't know," says the angel. "There are legions of us waiting for the sign, but. . ."

"But what?" asks Judas.

"Only God knows when the time is," says the angel. "But many say it's not close like we thought."

"It has to be close," says Judas. "The one we've waited for is here, on earth, already."

The angel shrugs. "Maybe he doesn't have to finish it," he says. "Maybe things don't look ready yet, and he'll leave for now, and let them go on."

"No!" says Judas. "He can't."

"I don't know," says the angel. "All I know is that there are legions of us, just waiting for the signal, but it hasn't come." The angel rises. "And maybe it isn't coming."

When Judas looks over again, the angel is gone. The angel is gone and it's a dark, dark night.

*

In the morning, everything happens for Andrew and

221

Thomas exactly the way Jesus told them it would. They go into the next village and find the place where the road splits — sure enough, the animal is tied by the door there, nibbling on a vine. The next part feels so much like stealing it's hard for them to do, but they follow Jesus' instructions and untie the young donkey. As they start to lead it away, a man rushes out of the house after them yelling, asking what they think they're doing.

"The Master needs your donkey," say Thomas and Andrew, though coming out of their mouths instead of Jesus', it sounds like a poor excuse.

But the man seems to recognize the words somehow. "Of course," he says. "Go ahead."

The donkey is surprisingly cooperative, considering it's a donkey, and it doesn't take them long to get back to Jesus and the growing crowd at the house. The pilgrims are back and the men from Jericho are back, so it's difficult to get the donkey all the way to their Master in the courtyard, but they forget the inconvenience when they reach him.

Jesus' eyes shine today, as if he can see something they can't. As if there's something of untold worth and beauty right ahead, and he's irresistibly drawn to it.

They want to take him there, to help him get wherever he's going.

Without quite realizing what he's doing, Thomas takes the robe off his back and lays it across the donkey as a cushion for Jesus, and most of the twelve quickly do the same.

And after months of watching him walk, the apostles finally see Jesus ride.

Fill yourselves with joy, daughters of Zion! thinks Andrew, *Shout your joy, Jerusalem's daughters! See how your king comes to you: in righteousness, bearing victory. See how he comes: humble, and riding on a donkey's foal.*

But as they start toward Jerusalem, Judas remembers the angel and worries: why is Jesus riding a donkey like a king who comes in peace, instead of a horse like a king who goes to war?

*

When they approach the eastern wall of Jerusalem—God's chosen city—the people who have come with Jesus start to pave the road with their clothes, lining the way for him. And as he draws closer to the city, they start to sing from a psalm:

Blessed is he who comes in the name of the Lord!

We bless you from the House of the Lord!

God is the Lord, let his light shine forth: bind the sacrifice with cords to the altar!

Simon's friends have prepared well. Soon their people join the procession waving palm branches, symbols of the land of Israel. They complement the sounds of the old psalm with their own, adapted overlapping verse:

Blessed is the kingdom of David that comes in the name of the Lord!

Lead us up to the House of the Lord!

Hosanna to God, let his light shine forth: make a sacrifice at

223

the altar!

Some of the men from Jericho and the pilgrims from Galilee take up the new chant. Arriving Judeans and even some Jews from abroad start to gather to see what's inspiring the song. A few join in, though they've never heard of Jesus. They start to throw their coats and sashes down; Simon's friends hand out palm leaves and branches to anyone who will take them.

The cacophony of traffic—camels grunting, donkeys braying, pedestrians colliding, wheels beating on uneven cobblestone—can be overwhelming when the festivals bring half a million people to Jerusalem. But now the force of the song competes even with those sounds:

Blessed is the kingdom of David!

Lead us to the House of the Lord!

Hosanna to God! Hosanna to God! Make a sacrifice at the altar!

Jesus dismounts from his donkey. He has reached the Temple gates.

*

No one watching outside the gate knows what to expect. Will Jesus walk into the heart of the Temple and make a sacrifice at the altar personally, announcing himself as high priest and king? Or will he head straight to the Roman fortress on the Temple's north side and knock it down like Sampson in the temple of the Philistines? Will he call the sick and the lame to the Temple and heal them there? Or will he simply preach to the multitudes of the faithful who have

come to Jerusalem?

No one in the outer court of the Temple has any idea what Jesus will do, either, because no one there even heard the song: the Temple's outer court is the noisiest place in all of Jerusalem this time of year. Cattles' lowing echoes off the high walls, sheep bleat incessantly, coins clank as people exchange profane Roman currency for purer coins. Local guides sing out their slogans in desperate attempts to be heard over hopeful entrepreneurs' loud exclamations of the beauty of their souvenirs. Poor widows lose control of their tempers and voices as they complain about exorbitant prices on sparrows and doves this season, and merchants yell abuse at them as loud as it is vulgar before pushing them away with carefully-washed hands.

Jesus starts to shove.

He goes for the money tables first, flips one over so hard that coins from Rome, Tyre and Tiberias make a cloud in the air like locusts and fall like hail. The local guides and hawkers stop shouting their slogans and dive for the loose coins, but overturned tables crash down in their way as Jesus keeps moving, black hair and beard flaring out like an angry lion's. Using his coat as a whip, Jesus scatters the cattle—the owners shake their fists at him, but chase their heavy goods out onto the porch and then into the lower quarter's tight, hungry streets. Jesus shouts a warning to the dove-sellers and then throws open cage after cage. First dozens, then hundreds, of birds fly out into the sudden freedom and circle above the Temple for the whole city to

see.

God watches one of them as it falls back to the ground.

The high priest's guards rush in, but by the time they arrive herds' worth of livestock are scattered and the floor is littered with coins of gold, silver, and brass. Some of the outer court's best-known merchants are nowhere in sight, others are shouting at Jesus, while still others sit on, fatalistically bemused at the sight of their upended tables and broken plans. Dozens of strong men have poured into the court behind Jesus, armed, as it were, with palm branches.

"Stop!" say the guards. "What are you doing?"

Jesus turns toward them. *"Have you let this house, which is called by the Lord's name, become a den of robbers before your eyes?"*

The merchants look down at their hands indignantly. They don't see a speck of blood.

"What are you talking about?" asks the chief guard.

"I've seen it," says Jesus, and he looks around at scattered wares, straying animals, and angry sellers. "It wasn't supposed to look like this. It was supposed to be a house of prayer for all nations."

There's a big crowd behind Jesus now. Too big and too lively for the guards' comfort. Bigger than the current crowd of Jesus' victims and possibly even more passionate.

Someone is going to have to answer for the chaos of this day, thinks the chief guard, but now is not the time to announce who or how.

"Why don't you come here tomorrow and explain to the high priest and sages what exactly this is all about?" says the chief guard, hoping to avoid a full-scale riot.

"I promise I'll come," says Jesus, and the guards make a graceful but rapid exit from the court, shrugging to disappointed and disgruntled merchants as they go, as the crowd behind Jesus begins to sing:

Blessed is he who comes in the name of the Lord!

We bless you from the House of the Lord!

God is the Lord, let his light shine forth: bind the sacrifice with cords to the altar!

*

But Jesus doesn't enter the inner courts of the Temple today. In the late afternoon, he heads back out of the holy city and up the Mount of Olives. At first the crowd follows him, but he firmly wishes them a good night, and then satisfies them by saying he's looking forward to seeing them in the morning. They wander off in clusters toward their homes or the places they're staying. Even close friends from Galilee let him send them to the villages to get some rest, and at last he's left alone with his apostles.

Jesus sighs and slumps down under a fig tree and looks out at the glare of the sun off the Temple's golden dome. Though it's well before the fig harvest, this tree's leaves are already spread like they do once the fruit starts to come, so Peter looks through the branches to find some fruit for his Master. Then he notices a tear running down his Jesus' face.

"It's no use, Peter," Jesus says.

Peter stops. "What do you mean?"

"Haven't you read the scripture?" says Jesus, "*I will take away the harvest, says the Lord: there will be no grapes on the vine or figs on the fig tree: its leaves will wither, and the good things that I have given them will pass away.*"

"I can get you something else to eat," says Peter. "Should I run up to the market in the village?"

But Jesus doesn't answer.

Andrew sits down next to Jesus and looks out at the Temple and the holy city beyond. "It's beautiful, isn't it?" he says. "The way the gold looks like fire, the marble pillars white like a cloud. Like God's still right in front of us, day and night, still leading us out of the land of bondage. Things will be all right."

Jesus looks at Andrew. "A day of desolation is coming," he says and turns back to the Temple, "when not one stone will be left standing on another."

"When is that day?" asks Judas. "Is it a sign of the End?"

But Jesus shakes his head. "It's only the beginning," he says. "Like the leaves of the fig tree before summer comes."

*

There will be wars and rumors of wars, says Jesus. Men who speak in the name of prophets and messiahs will leave the land bathed at least three times in blood.

The apostles' minds reel.

People will starve and plagues will rage and houses will collapse as if under the force of earthquakes, says Jesus. Brothers will hand over their brothers to be killed and

children will turn on their own parents. People will forget the meaning of love.

The apostles' hearts sink.

When fights break out over idolatry, get out! says Jesus.

When the armies come up against Jerusalem, get out at once! he says.

If you see fighters from your housetop, don't go into to the house to put your affairs in order. If you're in a field when the news of war comes, don't go back home to fetch a coat. Just run, immediately, to the safe place over the Jordan.

Pray that your daughters aren't pregnant or breastfeeding then, says Jesus. Pray you don't have to flee in the winter.

Pray that God will make it go quickly so the whole earth isn't eaten up.

When will this happen? says Thomas. How do we know when it's begun?

Only my Father knows, says Jesus. But once it starts it will happen again and again and again. Until the moon is a burned-out candle, and the stars fall one by one.

But don't let it shake you. Go to the farthest ends of the earth and finish the work you've been given.

That's when I'll come again, says Jesus. In a cloud by day and with fire at night.

That's when I'll come.

The apostles' heads spin. They go back to the village and don't say much for the rest of the night.

*

But in Jerusalem, the high priest and his sages talk late into the night, extending their discussion of final holiday preparations to consider the Temple disturbance—and to weigh their options for handling the man responsible for it.

"Who is he?" says one of the sages.

"Trouble," says the high priest.

"For the merchants, certainly, but maybe not for us," says another sage. "Let's talk to him and see what he wants before we act."

"Talk to him?" says the first sage. "And then sit here and deliberate while he starts a riot right at the time when our city is host to guests from every corner of the earth? We should tell the guards at the Temple to arrest him tomorrow if he comes back."

"If you want to see a riot, go ahead and arrest him," says the second sage. "I promise to say the mourning prayers with your widow if his crowd of supporters forcefully objects."

The first sage glares at his colleague, but the high priest raises a hand for calm. "There are more than enough widows in Israel already," he says. "And there's no glory in reckless acts. Either we find a way to disgrace him in the eyes of the crowd, or we find reliable charges and arrest him quietly in the night. Try to find out who he is and what these people expect from him. Listen for him to speak recklessly, or else force him to speak too cautiously for a crowd's taste. Then we can stop him—"

"If he needs to be stopped," says the second sage.

The high priest sighs. "We need to be prepared," he says, "to keep the peace here."

*

Jesus rises early in the morning and climbs up on the young donkey. He asks James to walk by his left side and John by his right, and heads toward the Temple as he promised. And though James hasn't forgotten he's supposed to be humble as a little child, he can't help but feel a little proud and more than a little vindicated that he and his brother are on Jesus' right and left sides on such an important occasion, while the other apostles walk behind.

But James's feeling of pride suffers when Jesus asks him and John to wait at the gate with the donkey until he returns. James had imagined he'd follow his Master into the house of worship, not end up stuck outside with some borrowed, braying beast.

Though Jesus and his apostles have arrived at the Temple quite early, many are already waiting for him there: Simon's friends hoist their palm branches in their air in greeting; the pilgrims from Galilee and men from Jericho cheer; big groups of Jerusalem natives and visitors from overseas point excitedly and whisper; his mother and Mary from Magdala smile at him from across the sea of faces.

Several fully-armed Roman soldiers supplement the Temple guards today. Sullen merchants and money-changers conduct their transactions quietly; new cages of birds have been brought in, and are being sold at standard off-season prices.

A servant of one of the sages walks up to Thomas. "Which one of you is Jesus?" he asks.

"Why do you want to know?" Thomas says.

The servant's eyes shine. "Because there aren't many teachers in these days who really honor God more than men," he says.

Thomas is impressed and takes the man to Jesus.

"Master," says the sage's servant quietly, though still just loudly enough for the people nearby to hear, "what does the law really say: is it right to pay taxes to Caesar?"

But Jesus answers loudly enough for almost everyone to hear. "This man has a good question," he says as he turns to face the crowd. "He wants to know if a holy person can pay Caesar taxes in good conscience. Does anyone have a Roman coin?"

A man in line at the table of a money-changer produces one, and Jesus examines it.

"I grew up in a village where we didn't see coins like this much," Jesus says. He waves the scholar's servant over. "Can you tell me whose face that is?"

"It's a graven image of Caesar," says the man.

"That settles it, then," says Jesus, and Simon sees his friends lean forward in anticipation. But their excitement gives way to disappointment when Jesus speaks again: "If it's Caesar's," says Jesus, "you'd better give it back to Caesar."

Simon watches several palm branches drop.

"If it's Caesar's, it doesn't belong here," says Jesus, and

then, more loudly and clearly: "Give what's Caesar's back to Caesar, and give everything else to God!"

Mary from Magdala is the first to burst into joyful laughter, and a hundred or so Jews from the north, south, and abroad quickly join in. The palm branches go up again and Simon's friends cheer. Jesus hands back the coin and walks with his mother into the easternmost of the inner courts before the foreign soldiers can decide how they feel about what just happened.

*

The twenty-three jurists who sit in the lower court chamber near the treasury can tell by the rising rain-like pitter-patter of coins on the depositories that a large group of people has just arrived in the adjacent court. Two of them excuse themselves: they have special instructions from the high priest to meet someone.

Several men in the crowd fit the rough description they've been given of the one who disrupted the outer court yesterday, so the jurists simply listen to the man everyone else is listening to. They find a place close enough to hear him answer questions and listen to him talk about resurrection in his cumbersome rural Galilean accent. The combination of his folksy dialect and folktale doctrine is almost too much for them to keep straight faces about: they're a little surprised the high priest was worried about such a simple, backward preacher.

"This shouldn't be difficult," says one jurist to the other, and they walk up to Jesus.

"Master," says the first, trying to make the word go out of his mouth smoothly, without any trace of sarcasm, "forgive us for interrupting, but we happened to hear something about the dead coming back to life."

"Surely you've read the scriptures," says the second, "and you know the law: if a married man dies without children, his brother, as the *goel*, marries the widow and makes descendants to preserve the dead brother's name."

But the preacher from Galilee just looks at them and doesn't say a thing.

"Once there were seven brothers," says the first jurist, "and the first took a wife, but died on their wedding night."

"So the second brother married her, but he too died on their wedding night," says the second jurist, "as did the third."

"A more superstitious man might have begun to suspect the interference of some demon," says the first jurist, "and a lesser man might have declined to play the *goel's* part and marry her, but the last four brothers each kept the law —"

"And each," says the second jurist, "died on the wedding night, leaving the woman herself childless until the day she also died."

"Tell us this:" says the first jurist, "if there really is a resurrection — which Moses simply forgot to write about — who will she belong to there? Each of the seven took her as his own."

The jurists smile at the strength of their argument, but the Galilean looks at them with apparent contempt.

"How can you understand the scriptures if you don't know the power of God?" says Jesus. "Moses gave that law for earth: there's a greater law in heaven. You should know at least this: before anyone rises from the dead, the laws of the *goel* will be fulfilled."

All the humor disappears from the jurists' faces. "Come with us," they say, and they lead him up the steps and through the gate into the court of Israel.

*

The two sages who advise the high priest are waiting there, looking out over the court of priests to check the preparations around the altar.

"This is the man who made such a disturbance yesterday in the Temple," says the first jurist.

"And we just heard him disparage the law," the second jurist says.

The first sage turns to Jesus. "Who do you think you are?" he says, "Who gave you the authority to do all this?"

"Answer one question for me," says Jesus, "and I'll answer that question for you."

A large group of strong men begins to file into the shallow court behind Jesus. They watch the first sage until he grows nervous his wife may become a widow if he doesn't choose his words carefully.

"Ask your question," the first sage says.

"Was John's baptism from heaven, or men?" says Jesus.

The first sage sees the trap now: if he says "heaven," Jesus will make him look like a hypocrite for not going out

to the desert. If he says "men," in the presence of so many witnesses, he'll offend anyone who counted John as a prophet.

"I can't tell you," the first sage says.

Jesus nods. "I understand: I can't tell you about my authority either."

"Would you mind answering a different question for me?" asks the second sage.

Jesus looks at him carefully, then shrugs.

"Of all the commandments that have been written," says the second sage, "which comes first?"

Jesus smiles. *"Hear, O Israel! The Lord our God is one!"* he says, "And so you should love Him with an undivided heart, with your whole soul and mind and strength."

But before the second sage can congratulate him on his answer, Jesus goes on, "The second commandment is almost the same: *love your neighbor as yourself.* And there are no commandments more important than these."

The second sage looks over the great altar in the court of priests ahead. "Well spoken, Master," he says. "There is only One, and there is *none other than Him*: to love Him with our whole hearts, with understanding minds and all the strength of our souls, and to love our neighbors as ourselves, is worth far more than all these burnt offerings and sacrifices."

"You're not far from the kingdom of God," Jesus says.

The second sage looks closely at Jesus and speaks softly: "Is that why you're here, then? To bring God's kingdom back into the hands of a son of David?"

Jesus is staring out past the altar toward the entrance of the Temple's holy place. "Why do they say the Messiah is David's son?" asks Jesus. "David himself, filled with the spirit, said: *the Lord told my lord: sit on my right hand, until I make your enemies your footstool.* It would be enough for David's son to bring back his father's kingdom. But what is David's lord supposed to do?"

"I don't understand," says the second sage, but Jesus doesn't seem to hear him. Jesus' eyes are fixed intently on the Temple proper, and though of course it's impossible, the second sage will later swear that he saw in those eyes a reflection of the Temple's eternal flame.

*

The sages don't question Jesus further or issue any penalties for the disturbance on the previous day. When Jesus turns away and asks if he's free to go, they say yes, and he leaves the men's court and goes down the fifteen steps to where Mary from Magdala is waiting with his mother. But before they can ask what happened, Jesus points to something happening on the treasury side of the court: wealthy visitors from far corners of the Empire throw impressive sums of money into the depositories, showing their loyalty to the sacred house and city they've wandered far from. Beside them, a widow throws in two thin bronze coins.

"Did you see that?" says Jesus. "Maybe the others gave the most, but she held back the least."

His mother nods. "That must have been her whole

income. She gave everything she had."

"Then so will I," says Jesus. "For the widows' sake."

And he walks out of the Temple.

Don't regret our breath's use as air, our blood's as oil —
some lamps at last are burning in the night.
                                    -Faiz

Mary from Magdala goes to the market with all the savings she has. For years, she's managed money carefully, feeling that some day she would need it—she never would have imagined, though, she'd be spending her savings like this.

Mary gasps sharply when she hears the price of the myrrh, bites her lip at the expense of exotic cinnamon, tries not to think about what else she could be buying for the amount she's asked to pay for cassia, and responds with numb resignation to the cost of calamus.

She doesn't have enough left for the olive oil the vendors sell in the market, so she walks up the hill and spends the last of her money buying the oil straight from the press.

She pulls her robe in close over the goods and rushes to the village where Jesus will be receiving his guests tonight. She prays not to be robbed on the way, not to lose this gift that means more than any other in her life.

She's too busy praying to notice that Jesus is resting in a nearby garden.

In the upper city, the high priest is feeling restless. He's been working on the puzzle of Jesus all morning, sending out inquiries and gathering information. In the early afternoon, he summons his best informants and advisors, and by late afternoon, they've all arrived.

The servants seat the high priests' guests along the sides of a large upstairs room. The high priest looks around at those he's had summoned: sages, jurists, servants, witnesses, and a spy. He tries not to think about urgent Passover preparations he's neglecting, so he can focus on the matter at hand. Experience has taught him never to let a routine crisis blind you to an unexpected one.

"What knowledge have we gathered since yesterday?" asks the high priest. "We know the man who created the disturbance in the Temple is named Jesus, that he's from an obscure village in southern Galilee—"

"Nazareth," says a young man with a heavy Galilean accent.

"—yes, Nebayoth," says the high priest. "Apparently, in the northern countryside he's quite well known, and many here have heard of him as well."

A few of the high priest's informants nod in agreement.

"But who does he think he is?" says the high priest, "And should his aspirations give us cause for concern?"

"He seemed to me like an honest and compassionate man," says the second sage.

"I don't trust him," says the first.

The high priest turns to the spy. "What do you think?"

The spy brushes some stray hair back from his face. "I can't answer either of your questions," says the spy. "I can tell you that several leading Zealots are excited to support him, but that's all. I don't know how he feels about them or whether he has any plans, and I don't think they know, either."

"He's both careful and clever," says the first sage's servant. "He knows how to be quiet enough to stay out of trouble but still hint enough to encourage his crowd. If he is planning anything, you can't afford to ignore it."

"I agree," says one of the jurists. "People will lay down their lives for a mystery, and he knows how to speak in secrets. If he tells his people they have to take over the city for his secret to be unveiled, they'll do it. And what comfort is it to us then if it turns out there's nothing behind the veil at all?"

"We don't have evidence that he's planning anything," says the second sage, "and we can't act without witnesses."

The young man with the northern accent, who's a stranger to most of the men in the room, speaks up: "Before he left, he told his followers at home he was touring Galilee for the last time. I heard it from the mouths of men who heard him say it. He must be planning to do something here; I just don't know what."

Everyone sits for a moment in silence.

The high priest clears his throat. "It seems we agree that we should be concerned. Perhaps now it's time to answer

my first question: who does he think he is?"

"I asked him in plain terms," says the first sage, "but he wouldn't tell me."

"He's certainly a rebel," says the sage's servant, "but probably the kind who believes we need to purify ourselves before God will bless a rebellion. That would explain the Temple incident."

"Don't imagine he's a purist or saint: he's a blasphemer," says the young Galilean, "a self-obsessed blasphemer. I myself heard him claim the authority to forgive a man's sins."

"And we can stand as witnesses that he disparaged the law," say the jurists.

The high priest turns to the spy. "Who do the Zealots think he is?" he asks.

The spy shakes his head. "They're hoping, of course, that he's the son of David, but they'll follow anyone who might take up the sword."

"And what do you think?" says the high priest to the second sage.

"I believe he's harmless," the sage says. "But I also think he at least wonders whether he is the anointed one."

"Then we have to remove him," says the high priest.

"I don't think he's the kind of man who takes up arms," says the second sage. "If he decides he is the Messiah, he seems more the kind to pray and wait for God to work a miracle."

"And you'll take the dead of this land on your

conscience if you're wrong?" asks the high priest.

The second sage doesn't answer at first, and speaks carefully when he does: "I don't think he'll act on his own, but if you try to take him by force, the crowd might act for him."

"Then we need to find a way to take him when he's alone," says the high priest. "And we need to have witnesses ready to condemn him to death."

The first sage, the jurists, and the young Galilean nod solemnly.

"To death?" asks the second sage. "Why?"

"Where were you," says the high priest, "when Judah and Zadok's revolt ended? You must remember as well as I do how quickly calm returned after Judah had been executed. People will do anything when they think they've found the Messiah, but it's easy enough to bring them back to their senses, because they all know the promised one doesn't die."

*

Mary shows the apostles the myrrh first. Then the cinnamon.

"What is all this?" asks Judas. "It must be worth at least a hundred silver pieces!"

"There's more," says Mary, and she shows them the cassia and the calamus.

"Where did you get all this?" asks Thomas.

"I bought it," says Mary.

"And why did you spend so much money on spices?"

asks Thomas.

"We could've given it to the poor," Judas says.

Mary takes out the olive oil and Thomas freezes. He finally understands.

"Are you sure this is a good idea?" he asks.

And Mary has never looked quite so beautiful to him as when she says, "It's time. Can't you feel it?" Thomas aches. He wants to believe her, but he has such doubts. *This should be a holy anointing oil to Me through all your generations*, thinks Thomas. *And it must be holy to you: whoever makes any like it, or puts any of it on an unauthorized person, should be cut off from the people.*

"Do you think we should anoint him as a prophet or as a king?" says Matthew.

"Both," James says.

"Who should do the anointing?" asks Peter.

"We'll have to ask Jesus," James says.

They all stare at the ingredients for a moment, motionless. Then Andrew moves carefully and begins to mix, trying to match the ancient proportions on this smaller scale. The smells are strong, almost intoxicating, and for some reason, though nothing could be further from the desert's scents, they fill him with memories of his first Master, John.

John should be here for this, thinks Andrew. It's John the Prophet who should pour the sacred oil on the anointed one.

*

Thomas has arranged for Jesus to stay in the largest

house in Bethany tonight, so that he can receive the guests who are eager to visit him: prominent villagers, old friends of Simon, pilgrims from around Magdala and the north end of the lake, relatives of the martyred John. But Jesus went out with only Philip and Nathanael in the afternoon, and the three of them are still gone when everyone else arrives.

The Galilean pilgrims chat contentedly in the center of the courtyard with the locals; Simon's friends sit patiently around the edges, talking more quietly with each other and with Andrew, Judas, and Simon. They all fall quiet with respect when John the Prophet's mother arrives until Jesus' mother greets her so warmly it seems as if they'd known each other for years. The two matriarchs wander off to talk in a more private place inside and leave Peter to greet members of John's father's family.

It starts to get dark. Matthew and Thomas light lamps to illuminate the courtyard, but many of the villagers start to worry they won't have enough oil in their own lamps to make it home if they wait until the dead of night. A few at a time, they begin to excuse themselves. Many of the pilgrims didn't bring much oil, either, and follow their hosts back to their lodgings for the night.

It gets darker. Almost all of John's relatives go, leaving well-wishes for the most famous of the men their kinsman baptized. There's a slight delay as they try to persuade John's mother to go with them, but she insists she'll be all right spending the night.

It's almost midnight when Jesus arrives with the last

two apostles, but Andrew is happy to see that he looks well-rested and more relaxed than he has for quite some time. Jesus greets his remaining visitors while Mary goes into the house to tell Jesus' mother her son is back. The women come out into the courtyard just as one of Simon's friends produces a sword.

He steps forward and kneels down in front of Jesus. "Master," he says, "we've heard you're filled with power like the prophets of old, and we present you this gift in memory of the sword of Samuel." He lays the sword on the ground, hilt toward Jesus.

Another of Simon's friends rises, produces a sword, and kneels in front of Jesus. "My lord," he says, "we welcome you back to the kings' city, and we present you this gift in memory of the sword of your ancestor, David." And he lays the sword on the ground, hilt toward Jesus.

Another of Simon's friends rises and speaks from the scriptures: "*See my servant, who I uphold; my chosen one, who delights my soul!*" he says, "*I have put my spirit on him: he'll bring judgment to the foreign nations.*"

All of Simon's friends rise. The one who has just spoken kneels before Jesus. "We've brought you these two swords in acknowledgment of your authority and power. We also offer our own swords and lives to your service—"

"Two swords is enough," Jesus says.

The man's mouth stays half-open, as if his uncompleted offer were trapped there. Should he push the rest of the words forward, or swallow back the words he said?

Jesus stands up, and offers him a hand. The man bites his lip and then rises. He stands dazed for a moment, and then wishes Jesus a polite good night. Jesus wishes him a safe trip home and asks if he and his men will have enough light.

The apostles and the stunned men mumble goodbyes to each other and exchange awkward embraces. Andrew stays in the courtyard, but Simon and Judas accompany the men out and into the street.

Though he'd like to wait for the two of them to get back, Andrew decides to speak before he loses courage: "We made some oil for you, some very expensive oil. Was that right of us or wrong?"

*

"Why did he reject us?" hisses one of the men at Simon once they're all outside the house. "We would've died for him!"

"I don't know," says Simon, "but he knows what he's doing."

"Does he?" says the man. "What sort of commander shows more concern for your lamps than your swords?"

"You saw him in the Temple," says Simon. "You know he's filled with the power of God."

"The Romans aren't defenseless Temple merchants," Simon's old friend says. "I can't believe we wasted our days and our hope with him."

"What did you expect?" says Simon. "Another sweet-tongued highway robber like Barabbas?"

Simon's old friend spits. "At least Barabbas fought," he

says.

Simon wants to push him, then, wants to shake away all his condescension and pride. But he clenches his fists instead. And he watches old friends walk past him into the night.

But the last man in line lingers. "You're sure you want to stay with him, Simon?" he asks. "It's not too late: you could come with us."

"I'll never leave him," says Simon. "Never."

The man brushes some stray hair back from his face. "Good for you," he says. "But I should warn you: the high priest and his friends are looking for a way to take your Master quietly and kill him."

*

"It's all right," says Jesus in the courtyard. "Don't worry: you've done a good thing."

The apostles exhale in relief and Mary from Magdala goes to get the sacred oil.

"There's one more thing," Andrew says while she's gone. "Since John is dead, we're not sure who should anoint you."

Mary comes back into courtyard, holding the most important gift she's ever given carefully in her hands.

"I want Mary to," says Jesus. "I want her to anoint me this time and the next."

Mary stares, uncomprehending. The apostles begin to protest, but Jesus shakes his head.

"She should anoint my head for the work I have to do,"

he says, "because she's the one who will come to anoint my body when that work has been done."

"Which work?" asks James.

"You'll understand," says Jesus, "soon enough."

Mary starts shaking as she walks toward Jesus. This is an honor for a prophet. Not for a woman.

She's about to begin when she remembers to wait for Simon and Judas.

They come back in. Judas sees her with the vessel of oil held up above Jesus' head. "What are you doing?" he says.

"He told me to," says Mary, and for reasons she doesn't understand, she starts crying as she pours the oil down on Jesus.

*

When the vessel is empty, Jesus turns to Simon.

"Your friends have lost interest in me?" he says.

"Yes," says Simon, "they have."

Jesus looks around at the twelve. "Do any of you want to leave me, too?"

"No!" says Peter. Where else would they go?

"Maybe we should all leave here together, though," says Simon.

"Why is that?" Jesus asks.

"Because I just heard the high priest wants to have you killed," says Simon.

"I'll die when it's the will of God," says Jesus. "Don't worry about what the high priest has planned."

In spite of himself, Nathanael yawns.

Jesus smiles. "It's late," he says, "and it's been a very long day. Go to sleep now, get some rest."

And except for Judas, soon they all do.

*

Judas sits out in the courtyard while the others sleep inside.

Judas wants to pray, but he can't focus.

Judas tries to pray the same thing he's prayed thousands of times: "When is the End going to come? Master of the Universe, when is it going to come?" But when he starts to say the words, there's none of the warmth or excitement he used to feel in response.

Why did Jesus let a woman anoint him? It can't be valid: is he trying to avoid being the anointed one?

Why did Jesus talk on the mountain yesterday like the End wasn't going to come yet, wasn't going to come at all for a long, long time?

Judas's head spins until he has to use both hands to hold it in place, to hold the ache back.

The jar his sister was carrying is broken. Her eyes are blank, and the neck of her tunic is torn.

When is it going to end? thinks Judas.

His sister walks slowly, her shoulders turned in slightly as if she'd like to fold in her arms and draw in her chest.

"When is it going to end?" says Judas.

Judas wants to scream, but the air is trapped in his chest. He should go out with his knife right now and find the one who did this. The one who made him feel this way.

"When is it going to end?" says Judas, "When is this world going to end?"

The angel is sitting across from him.

"You know it's him," the angel says.

Judas nods.

"So why do you keep asking if it's time?" says the angel.

"I need to know," Judas says.

"Not even I know," says the angel. "No one knows but God."

"Who do think I've been praying to?" asks Judas, and the angel is gone.

"Master of the Universe," says Judas, but there's nothing. It's so hard to focus.

He clenches his teeth. He drives his fingernails into his palms hard enough to hurt.

"Master of the Universe," asks Judas, "when is it going to come?"

But God's silence is an echo of his sister's. God's silence is his sister's until Judas's heart suffocates in the thickness of it.

Enough, thinks Judas. And he gives up on prayer.

If God is planning to wait, thinks Judas, then I'll have to force him.

If Jesus wants to go away, Judas will force him to call down a legion of angels first, will force darkness and light into the violence of their final collision.

Judas will force into motion the chain of events that will break this fallen world open, and then what will God do,

what will God have to finally do?

*

Judas walks without lamplight into Jerusalem and through the streets he hates, the broad, greed-lined streets of the upper city. He walks past villa after villa until he comes to the high priest's door.

He knocks, and no one answers.

He knocks more loudly, and the servants tell him to go away and go to sleep.

He knocks until his knuckles bleed and the servants threaten to beat him if he doesn't leave. But the high priest is awake by the time they open the door and drag Judas in, so Judas explains why he's come before anyone has the chance to break his ribs.

The high priest sends his servants back to bed and has a talk with Judas.

Judas walks away in peace a short time later. He walks away in the dead of that night, the moon shining like steel in his hands off thirty pieces of silver.

*

James and John wake in the grey light of the early morning to the sound of several crisp knocks accompanied by their mother's voice. Of course, they think. Every year she's up before the sun to get ready for the first night of Passover.

They pull on their robes against the chill and quietly welcome her into the house. After fussing over them a bit, she asks, "Do you know if he's celebrating here? He's been

252

so busy, I haven't wanted to bother him, but the festival starts tonight and we need to know the plan."

James and John don't know the answers, so they help their mother fix breakfast for everyone while she worries. Will Jesus be celebrating just with his apostles and his mother, or will he have many guests? Does he have other relatives who have come to the city this year?

The owners of the house are surprised to find breakfast ready so early, and the servants are delighted. Mary from Magdala and Jesus' mother help serve the servants first. The apostles join the remaining servants as soon as space opens up, eating as they listen to Salome talk.

Who will be taking the lamb to the Temple? Do we already have enough wine for four cups per guest? That's a lot of wine, Salome says. We'll have to really hurry to make enough of the "bread made in haste" in time, she tells the younger Mary. And is there a good place, she asks the bemused servants, to grate the bitter herbs without making everyone in the house cry?

Fortunately, Jesus wakes before Salome's temptation to wake him becomes too strong to resist. She holds her tongue and gives him time to eat before she asks for any decisions, keeping herself occupied by prioritizing the questions in her head.

When Jesus sits back and praises her cooking, she feels it's safe to begin.

"Are we celebrating here or somewhere else?" she asks him.

"We'll keep the Passover inside Jerusalem," he says.

Peter laughs. "Master," he says, "there must be hundreds of thousands of pilgrims in the city by now. Where are we going to find a free space so late?"

Peter stops laughing when Jesus calls him and John over and gives them precise but improbable-sounding directions on exactly how to find and secure their room. Andrew and Thomas listen and smile as they see Peter's and John's eyes grow wide.

With the issue of space taken care of, Salome asks about guests. Jesus says just sixteen. Salome moves on to the next questions and Jesus makes assignments. Two people should go to get the wine, she says. Jesus sends Matthew and Simon. Who will take a lamb down to the Temple and bring back the meat? Jesus tells Judas to go when it's time. Has anyone purchased a bitter root? Jesus asks James to get one quickly and bring it back. Is Jesus feeling all right? Yes, says Jesus, I feel fine. I just need a little more rest: it's going to be a long night.

"Are all the preparations in the house going to bother you?" asks Salome.

"Don't worry about me," says Jesus, but everyone can see Salome still does.

"Maybe I'll go back to that garden on the mountainside to rest," Jesus says.

Because of Simon's warning, the seven apostles without immediate chores insist on going with him, two of them armed with last night's swords.

Mary from Magdala prepares the fire to cook the thin cakes as she watches the older women make the dough. She admires Salome's bony hands, the efficiency with which they mix and press together flour and water, the ease with which they form the dough into balls of remarkably consistent size. She sits spellbound by the casual, habitual grace of the older Mary's hands as they flatten the dough into circles to bake.

The young Mary thanks God she gets to be close to these two women. She thanks God for the beauty of their grey hairs, the strength of their skilled arms.

Her own hands are hard at work baking matzah by the time James returns with the horseradish root. The older Mary takes it from him, holds it gently and with great care.

And then, before Salome can offer to help her, she goes off to grate the bitter, pungent root alone.

If anyone sees her, they'll assume it's because of the root she's crying.

*

In the late afternoon, everyone meets in the garden. Simon and Matthew, so often tense around each other, are talking and laughing so freely Andrew wonders if they've tried to lighten their heavy loads by sampling the wine. James and the women arrive next with tall stacks of the thin, crisp Passover bread and a little vessel of strong-smelling grated root. Judas comes haltingly: he's having trouble getting the lamb he bought at the market to follow and tries

to drag it until Jesus walks over and advises him on how to patiently guide sheep.

Peter and John are the last to arrive, still wide-eyed with their wonder at having found a servant struggling with a heavy pitcher of water, just as Jesus predicted, who accepted their help with the load and led them to a nice house in the upper city, just as Jesus predicted, whose wealthy owner offered a large second-story room when they told him their Master needed one, just as Jesus predicted.

No one else is nearly as surprised about all this as Peter and John: after all, it's often easier to accept the miracle you only hear about than the one you actually see. As they walk from the garden through the city, most of the disciples absorb the holiday fervor of the crowds, but Peter and John are too busy asking themselves if they really saw the servant right here, if he really led them down this street and into that courtyard. And when their host greets them, they wonder again: did he somehow know they were coming this morning? Was he warned in a vision or a dream?

*

When Judas comes back from the Temple with the meat, they get started. They bless the first cup of wine, wash their hands, and fall through time.

It's spring. After the barren winter, the earth clothes herself in a tunic of new water and a vibrant green robe. We should be happy: the breeze is like wine, breath itself intoxicating. But something is wrong. The renewal of spring comes, but we're still crying, because we're enslaved.

Jesus and Judas dip their parsley into saltwater at the same time.

We're like the caged bird who is moved by the season to gather straw for a futile nest. *And the children of Israel sighed because of their bondage, and they cried, and their cry came up to God because of their bondage.*

*

Jesus breaks a piece of the Passover bread in two, lifts a half high above his head.

"This is the bread of affliction," he says. "All who are hungry, let them come and eat. All who are in need, let them join in the meal with us."

Then he departs from tradition, breaks the half in pieces. "This is my body," he says. "When you eat, remember me."

*

We are slaves in Egypt. We have been thrown into a pit by our brothers and sold.

We bought the blessings of our father for a bowl of soup and now there's hell to pay. We sold ourselves for love but feel the love won't be complete until we're also free.

We're tired of serving idols on the Euphrates and we want God to show us the way to a free land of our own. We ate some fruit, and it tasted good, and the juice was red like our blood against these thorns.

It's spring, but we're still slaves in Egypt.

We were slaves to the Pharaoh in Egypt, and the Lord took us out of there with a mighty hand.

*

This is how it happened, says Jesus. This is how it happened to our ancestors and us.

There was a cup made from the beginning of the world for the price of evil, and drop by drop it fills up with unspeakable pain.

The performers dance in the royal court while the drummer plays a breathless beat. It's the same beat as the rhythm of whips on slaves' backs in the fields; every time the dancers leap, an old man collapses.

Outside the palace one day, the Pharaoh stretches out his arms to bask under the same sun that bakes the slaves' bricks and bodies. The Pharaoh yawns at the same time a slave woman gives birth to a screaming baby he's already ordered to have killed, like so many others.

The slaves are growing too tired even to give their sons names.

Drop by drop, forgotten blood fills the cup.

The mother raises her baby by posing as his wet nurse. The Pharaoh rules his people by posing as their God.

He commissions his wise men to carve his history into rocks, but he doesn't know the overseers' whips are the strongest styluses, that history is being written in scars.

The baby grows up, and tells history to stop. The baby grows up, and kills one of the writers. It doesn't matter. Another will take his place.

The people of Egypt eat and drink and laugh. It's nice to have such cheap bricks.

The man whose mother posed as his wet nurse goes out

to the desert like John. He's tired of Pharaoh. He wants God.

God finds him. God burns like a fire that's shut up in his bones.

The man goes back to Pharaoh. He tells him about the pain in the bitter cup. He tells him to let the slaves go. But Pharaoh has a hard heart. Why does Pharaoh's heart always have to be so hard?

An evil generation looks for signs, so the man shows signs to Pharaoh. But it isn't enough. Pharaoh believes that forgotten blood can stay forgotten: he doesn't believe in the cup.

Jesus lifts the cup high enough for everyone to see, and with each word he spills one tiny drop: *Blood, frogs, lice,* says Jesus. *Flies, sickness, boils,* he says. *Hail, locusts, darkness.*

Slaying of the firstborn.

"This is my blood," says Jesus, still holding the cup. Ten drops on his plate stand for all the suffering of Egypt, but he looks at the whole cup. How many drops are left there? How many thousands of drops?

"Whenever you drink, remember me," he says.

*

Soon Jerusalem's houses and streets and inns and brothels and stables and slums are filled with the sounds of half a million people singing. We've been freed from bondage in Egypt. We've been led by a prophet to a land full of promise, marked by old promises.

I love the Lord because he heard my voice and my prayers! the people sing. *He lowered his ear to listen, so I'll cry out to him as*

long as I have breath.

The apostles' heads are warm with wine. They pour out into the streets and join in the songs. *I will pay my vows to the Lord now in the presence of all his people,* they sing, *Precious in the sight of the Lord is the death of his saints.*

Jesus is going somewhere now, and the apostles try to follow him. In the press of half a million bodies, no one notices Judas is gone.

*

By the time the singing is over and the pilgrims have gone back inside and fallen asleep, Jesus and eleven of the twelve have made their way across the city and back to the garden on the mountainside. They're happy to be here again: the four cups of wine it takes to celebrate this night have made them so drowsy, and it seems like a nice place to rest.

"This will be a hard night for you," says Jesus, and the apostles try their best to listen. "But when it's over, remember the prophets wrote about it: *smite the shepherd, and the sheep will be scattered.* So don't blame yourselves when you leave me."

"I'll never leave you," says Peter, and he starts to get choked up. "Not even if everyone else does, not even if I'm the only one left with you in the world."

But Jesus shakes his head. "Before the rooster crows in the morning, you'll deny me three times."

"No!" says Peter. "I would die with you, but I won't deny you! I'll never leave you, no matter what you say."

So Jesus doesn't say anything, and eight wine-weary men fall asleep.

"Follow me, then," says Jesus to the last three, and he walks deeper into the garden with Peter, James, and John.

*

When they pass the oil press, Jesus starts to shake.

"Wait here," he says. "Just once, I need to know you're here for me."

The three fishermen don't know what's happening, don't know what to say. But they're determined to wait, watching, until their Master comes again.

A stone's throw away, Jesus falls down on his face.

"Father!" he cries.

Peter, James, and John wait and watch, watch and wait, but wine-warm minds make heavy eyes. The night is cool, and the garden feels safe, and the spring is here whispering of a coming sweet summer and the goodness of life.

Peter finds he can keep his eyes open, or his mind from drifting, but not both.

In the olive press, there's a millstone far larger than any man can lift.

How much more than the olive beneath it does the millstone weigh? How might the great stone's weight feel on the olive's back?

"Father!" cries Jesus. "Father!"

Peter, James, and John dream of an olive press. Or could it be that they're awake?

Gethsemane, they call this place. An oil press. An olive oil press.

Jesus shakes Peter, James, and John awake. "Couldn't you wait an hour with me?" he asks.

"We're waiting," they say. "We're awake now, and we're waiting."

Peter, James, and John look out into the heavy darkness of this night.

A stone's throw away, Jesus is flat against the earth again. Fallen before his Father's face.

"Don't make me finish," he begs. "If there's any other way, don't make finish this. But help me finish if this is the only way!"

Peter, James, and John dream of an unbearable weight. In their dream, an angel has to come to protect them from it. To keep it from crushing them.

Jesus wakes them again. He doesn't ask anything, but they still don't know what to say.

Jesus staggers, stumbles, falls one last time. "Father," he says.

Then the weight comes again, all of it, until blood seeps out of every pore like great drops of oil.

Peter, James, and John are deep in a dreamless sleep.

I am like a candle that has gone out on the grave of a poor man.
-Ghalib

Torches shine like scars on the dark, smooth face of this spring night when the clanking of steel against a rock startles eight of the apostles awake. A group of armed men—the high priest's Temple guards and a few Roman soldiers—pass close by, muscles tensed in anxious anticipation.

Thomas and Andrew reach for the swords, only to remember giving them to Peter and James before they fell asleep, though now they can't see Peter and James anywhere. Nathanael starts to ask what's going on, but Simon covers his mouth tightly and pulls him further away from the search party's torchlight.

"We need to get Jesus away from here," Simon whispers.

"Where did he go?" Matthew whispers back.

The eight look as far as they can without moving and don't see any sign of their Master at all. The men with the torches slow down and start fanning out.

"What do we do now?" whispers Philip.

"If they get any closer, we run," Simon whispers back.

The torches get closer. Eight apostles rush to escape.

Peter shakes James and John when he hears men running. Torchlight is scattered across the garden now. Something is wrong. Jesus is slumped down against the trunk of a nearby olive tree. As soon as they see him, the three apostles hurry over to his side, but John trips over a root on the way and falls hard.

Several men shout in the distance about the noise and the torches start moving in Jesus' direction.

"Let's go!" says Peter, but Jesus doesn't even try to stand up. John pulls himself up as the lights start closing in. As the men come closer first their weapons, then their faces become visible.

A torch shines clearly on Jesus, Peter, and James.

The man holding the torch is Judas.

Judas hands his torch to one of the high priest's servants and walks toward the tree. Then he kneels down next to Jesus. "Master," he says, and he kisses him.

Jesus stares as Judas rises, and his voice sounds more tired than Peter can remember. "Did you have to do it with a kiss?" Jesus says.

*

After that, everything happens so quickly it's difficult later to recall. Two of the high priest's servants come, grab Jesus roughly by the arms, and drag him up. James draws his sword and warns them to stop, but they don't. He brings the sword down on one of them with a rough hacking motion. The sword misses the servant's head, but takes off a

chunk of his ear. The servant screams, and men from all over the garden come running. James curses his clumsy fisherman's arms and raises the sword to strike again.

"Put that away!" says Jesus. "Whoever lives by the sword will die by it." Then he places his hand on the side of the servant's head and the bleeding stops.

The servant touches his ear and stares at Jesus. Two of the Temple guards take Jesus' hands and tie them behind his back. James slips back into the shadows and hides.

"I came back to the Temple when you asked me to," says Jesus. "You could have taken me then."

The guards start to drag Jesus forward, and a soldier joins them.

"Have we found any of his fighters yet?" the soldier asks.

"I don't need fighters," Jesus says wearily. The guards laugh: if anyone could use some fighters, it's this prisoner. They're about to tell him so, but he speaks again first. "Don't you know I could call down twelve legions of angels now if I needed them?" Jesus says, looking up into the hollow darkness of the night sky.

And for a moment the guards don't dare turn around, don't dare look up—their prisoner's eyes seem so calm and certain, they're afraid of what they'll see if they do.

A Roman soldier stares at them and at this strange Jew, then shakes his head. He calls in the men who are still searching the garden, and the whole party heads back toward Jerusalem.

In the dark space between two trees, James shudders as he watches their torches grow distant and cold. He doesn't know what to do — or what he's done.

*

Peter follows from a distance, knowing but only half-caring that he might also be caught and arrested. He doesn't want to lose sight of Jesus.

Jesus looks defeated. Though he's walked through the night many times before, he can't seem to keep pace now with the guards beside him. They drag him and push him: Peter hasn't seen them beat or cut Jesus yet, but there are already bloodstains all over Jesus' clothes.

The guards pass by the fortress and head into the upper city. They walk down streets where Peter helped a stranger carry water and pass the house whose owner saved a room for his master, the house where Jesus' mother and the other Mary are asleep. Peter wonders if he should stop and wake them, if he should warn them the world seems to be falling out from under his feet, that everything feels wrong. But he doesn't want to lose sight of Jesus, so he passes the house and follows the guards and soldiers a few more blocks until they walk into the courtyard of the villa that belongs to the high priest.

Peter stands on the street a few houses down. His legs feel empty and his throat is drier than the crisp Passover bread. But he pulls his shawl up around his face, walks into the courtyard, and hopes everyone will assume he's another of the high priest's servants.

*

It's the middle of the night, but the witnesses have already been gathered. A man from Jericho testifies that a hundred or more fighters from his city followed Jesus to Jerusalem and that when the beggars called Jesus the Son of David, Jesus blessed them for it. He says he heard Jesus saying something about secrets on the road up from Jericho and suspects he was making plans for a revolt.

The high priest seems convinced by this evidence, but the attending jurists disqualify the testimony on the grounds that too much of it is indirect, or else relies on unsubstantiated assumptions.

Peter recognizes the next speaker and pulls back further into a shadow. This witness is from Galilee. He used to follow Jesus. He testifies about having heard with his own ears how Jesus offered a man forgiveness of sins, and relates having sat outside a tax collector's home where Jesus was staying one evening while several prostitutes went in. Peter knows he has to hide, but he wants to shout. Any other night he'd be willing to go to prison for the truth, but tonight he knows he can only help Jesus by staying free.

The jurists disqualify the second accusation after learning the man couldn't see into the house to know with certainty what happened there, and the first accusation when they learn that although many have heard from different sources of Jesus' claim to forgive sins, no second direct witness is present to substantiate the claim as required.

Next, the jurists themselves testify they heard Jesus speak against the law in the Temple. But though both are sure this event took place, each of them remembers Jesus' words slightly differently, so they inform the high priest that their testimonies, also, should be considered invalid.

The high priest begins to grow frustrated. "Tell us yourself," he says to Jesus, "did you bring men with you to Jerusalem for a revolt? Do you claim the power to forgive any sins they commit in the process?"

The jurists start to explain that under the most expert interpretations of Jewish law, a confession is not admissible as evidence, but the high priest isn't interested. "Can you explain away the things they're saying? Don't you want to defend yourself?"

But Jesus doesn't say anything. Even if he wanted to defend himself, thinks Peter, he looks too exhausted to speak.

"Who are you?" asks the high priest. "Are you a fraud or a prophet? Are you a lawbreaker or a saint?"

But Jesus doesn't even meet the high priest's gaze.

"Are you the promised one?" the high priest asks.

Jesus looks up, then, and answers—not in everyday Aramaic, but in sacred Hebrew. "Ehyeh," he says, which can mean either "I will be" or "I am."

"Ehyeh asher ehyeh," says Jesus. *I will be whatever I want to be* or *I am who I am.*

Peter hangs his head, but he can still hear the high priest rip his own robe as a sign of shame. It's all over now, thinks

Peter. All over.

"You all heard exactly what words he said," says the high priest. "We're all direct witnesses now of his blasphemy."

The jurists nod solemnly. There's no need to disqualify this evidence.

*

Some of the guards spit in Jesus' face. Others hit him.

When Peter looks away, a young servant meets his eyes. She looks at him closely. "Weren't you with him in the street yesterday?" she says. "Are you one of his disciples?"

Peter wants to get out of this place. He wants to get out, and go tell the others what happened, so he can't afford to be caught.

"I don't know what you're talking about," Peter says.

Across the courtyard, the guards are blindfolding Jesus. They take turns hitting him and shouting "prophesy who did it!" as they laugh. While the young woman watches, Peter slips away to the porch.

He hasn't been there long when he hears another woman whispering: "Isn't he one of them? I'd swear I saw him in the Temple," she says to the servants near her.

"One of who?" says Peter loudly. If he leaves while they still suspect him, they'll tell someone he's running off.

The woman blushes. "I was just saying you look like someone I saw in the Temple a few days ago," she says.

"I haven't even been to the Temple this week," says Peter, and then realizes how odd that must sound at

Passover. "It's just always so crowded this month," he adds.

"Are you from here, then?" says one of the women.

Peter hesitates. Will they believe him if he lies?

"You must be one of them," she says, "I can tell by your accent."

"So everyone with a Galilean mother is a criminal?" says Peter. "I don't know him!" he says, and he swears for emphasis, hoping that will end the conversation.

On the far end of the courtyard, the guards take the blindfold off Jesus. Jesus looks out onto the porch, right at Peter.

A rooster crows.

Peter runs out into the street, and he doesn't stop crying until he gets back to the house with the upper room where the women are sleeping.

*

Morning comes to Jerusalem: the sun's first rays waking the dormant vibrancy of the Temple's white and gold, the dewdrops savoring the twinkling moments in the light before they dwindle and disappear, the birds' songs replacing memory's echo of the Passover psalms.

Morning comes to Jerusalem, but for the scattered apostles, it's as frightening as the previous night.

Simon and Matthew make their way toward Bethany in the darkness and hide on the hillside above the village, waiting for the others. When the light comes, they notice Philip and Thomas are hiding nearby, but wait to make sure they're not being watched before they call to them.

271

Andrew, Nathanael, the big Judas and the little James hide outside the gates of Jerusalem, waiting for pilgrims to enter the city so they can slip into the crowd to look for their Master.

James and John head to Bethphage, where the men from Jericho are staying. They know fifty men don't mean anything against the powers of the city, but they need to feel like they're doing something to rescue their Master, so God can make up for the rest.

In the house in the upper city, Peter tells the women what happened. Salome tears her robe in shame and anger when she hears how the guards abused God's chosen one; Mary from Magdala studies Peter's face as she struggles to accept the impossible words coming from his mouth; Jesus' mother gathers her things and asks where her son might be now.

And outside the sheep gate of the Temple Judas sits, alone: looking tranquilly over at the Roman fortress where Jesus is being kept, waiting for the legions of angels to come.

*

The governor has a problem. Sometimes he feels he's had nothing but problems since he was sent here to the rough edge of the Empire, this edge that always seems on the verge of tearing itself apart. It's a terrible place to have to rule: the Samaritans in the province hate the Jews, and the Jews are prone to riot over any under-punished Samaritan provocation.

And Jerusalem is a disaster. The lower city people hate

the upper city people just like anywhere else, but here they think they hate the Romans instead. The upper city people are terrified of the impoverished lower city people—but instead of finding comfort in the Empire's might, their fear keeps them focused on the order of their old priestly traditions. And because of their shared, strange religion, both kinds of people would rather die than accept something as simple as army banners with standard insignia being brought inside the city walls.

The governor's hope has been to make it through this day without trouble. He's having several petty criminals crucified, but he also has to execute a man who started a short-lived revolt. For that execution, he has the support of the upper city people, but he's been nervous about the lower city people, who take every common robber for a hero sent from their god. So he's been patient. He's waited for a holiday, when attention is focused elsewhere and when an influx of wealthy overseas Jews could add stability.

But the high priest has complicated the governor's day. He's brought in a popular preacher the upper city people also want executed. And when the governor said: I'm busy today, the high priest said: this man is telling people he's the king of the Jews.

The governor wants to be very clear on this recurring point. His firm position is this: Jerusalem is no longer a city for kings. Judea has a governor, and that's all it needs. There's no such thing anymore as a king of all the Jews.

But he hadn't planned on making that point today. And

he doubts he can quietly crucify two popular figures, each with his own supporters and sympathizers, in the same afternoon.

The governor walks out to his balcony, yawns and stretches under the warmth of the morning sun. It's going to be a long day.

*

"Wait here," says Jesus' mother to Peter. "Unless you don't think you can trust the owner of this house—we can help you get out of Jerusalem to find a safe place to hide."

Peter remembers his first meeting with the rich man, how it seemed as if he'd been waiting for word of a visiting teacher, saving the room for the Master that would come. "I trust Joseph completely," says Peter. "But where are you going and why should I wait?"

"I want to be close to my son," says Mary. "But you said they recognized you last night, so it's not safe for you to come with us."

"You were there in the Temple with him, too," says Peter. "Are you sure it's safe for you to go?"

"Don't worry," says Mary, and gives Peter a strange half-smile. "We're women: no one pays attention to us."

*

James and John keep interrupting each other as they tell the story to the men from Jericho.

"Do you know who took him?" the men ask.

James nods. "It was mostly Temple guards," he says, "but there were some Roman soldiers with them."

One of John's old disciples sighs. "Temple guards would be good news," he says. "The religious courts here aren't allowed to kill anyone." He tugs at his beard. "If the Roman soldiers take precedence, though, your Master is in serious danger. This governor isn't ashamed to kill decent men by the dozens."

"What do you think we should do?" asks James.

"I say go straight to the fortress," says the man. "And if Jesus is there, we petition the governor to pardon him."

"Will he listen to us?" asks John

"He's listened to a peaceful protest before," says the man. "Though he did threaten us all with death first. But if he didn't kill us then, he probably won't now."

The other men nod their assent, but the man asks John and James each one more question before they go.

"You're certain they didn't get a good look at you?" he asks John.

"It was late, and I'd fallen, so my face was covered in dirt," John says.

"Then come with us," says the man, "you may be useful." He turns to James next: "You said you tried to cut off someone's ear?" he says.

"I was trying to split open his head," James says. "Cutting his ear was an accident."

"Stay here and don't let anyone see you," the man says.

*

Once they're inside the city, Andrew sends the big Judas and the little James back to the house in the upper city to

make sure the women are safe. Then Andrew and Nathanael start their search for Jesus.

They start by asking people if they've heard anything about a teacher from Galilee who was taken prisoner in the night. They're surprised at how many people immediately ask if they mean Jesus. No one knows what happened to him, but many seem to care deeply: Andrew and Nathanael don't get any news, but find themselves sharing what little they know again and again, until their own accounts start circulating back to them as rumors. Soon everyone they talk to says Jesus was taken prisoner in a garden outside the city. Each has a different way of explaining what happened in the night, but none of the stories tell where Jesus is now.

*

"Do you think your old friends would fight for him now if we asked them?" Matthew says to Simon.

"No," says Simon. "But if the high priest has him killed secretly and thrown in a ravine, they may know where we can recover the body. And if he is still alive, there's a good chance one of them will know where he is."

"He's still alive," says Thomas. "He has to be. Didn't he tell us himself not be afraid of the high priest?"

"Yes, but if Simon's friends are likely to know something, we should go to them," says Matthew.

Simon hesitates. "On the last trip south," he says, "before I knew you as well…"

Matthew nods.

"What happened?" asks Philip.

"I told them about the work Matthew used to do," says Simon.

"I'll stay here and make arrangements for us to get somewhere safe if you can find a way to come back with him," says Matthew. "You three go."

"He never sent us anywhere alone," says Simon. "Thomas should go with you: he knows how to find a safe place. It will be enough if Philip comes with me."

"We'll find a place," says Thomas. "And when you find Jesus, be careful who you trust. Whoever told the high priest's men about the garden probably told them about the house in Bethany, so we wait for each other at the hiding place near the crossroads."

*

The high priest's men tell the governor about Jesus' crimes. He has blasphemed, he's slandered their law, he's claimed divine powers, he's led the faithful astray. Clearly, they're jealous of him. These religious Jews are always jealous of each other's influence: it's like an endless fight between harried priests and sages for control of the whole worthless, downtrodden pack. Following the politics between the various sects and personalities is as exhausting as it is tedious — the last governor tried and rotated through five high priests in ten years. This governor has no desire to create the same instability as his predecessor and does his best to remain aloof from such conflicts. He suspects it will be best to leave this prisoner in the high priest's hands.

"When he says he's king of the Jews, does he mean it as a

political claim — or a religious one?" the governor asks.

"He's told tax collectors to leave their work and follow him," says the high priest.

"Flog him," the governor says to his soldiers.

*

The women are gone well before the big Judas and the little James find the right house in the upper city again. But the owner of the house wants to know what's happening.

They decide to tell him everything. He gets very quiet as he listens.

"I'm an influential man," he says after thinking for a moment. "Do you think there's anything I can do?"

"Do you know the high priest?" asks the little James.

"There were soldiers there, so he might also be with the governor," says the big Judas.

"I've talked with both of them before," says the owner, and he sighs. "Wait upstairs with Peter for now," he tells them. "Tell the servants I said to feed you well if I'm not back by tonight."

*

"The high priest didn't hesitate to give him to the Romans," says one of Simon's old friends before Simon can even greet him. "Now can you see why it's so important to fight?"

"Is he all right?" asks Simon.

"The high priest doesn't need to hand men over unless he's looking for a death sentence," says Simon's old friend. "But as far as I've heard, the governor's only had him

whipped so far. Our man could hear the screams from outside the fort, so your Master must still have been alive."

Philip feels sick. He has to lean against the wall to keep his balance.

"Can you help us?" asks Simon.

"Do you regret how he treated us the other night?" says his old friend.

Simon clenches his jaw so hard his teeth hurt. "I'm sorry I came to you today," he says, and he walks away, back toward the fortress, even after his old friend shouts after him to forget about helping Jesus and watch out for himself instead.

*

John and the men from Jericho gather outside the fortress.

"Are you ready to die for your Master?" one of them asks John.

"Yes," John says.

"Are you afraid of death?" asks another.

"No," says John. "I just don't want to leave him again."

"Good," says the first. "The governor's power comes from our fear. So if his soldiers draw their weapons and we face them calmly, he'll hesitate. Because he can feel he has no power over us."

*

On his way up from the lower city, one of Simon's old friends sees Andrew. "Your Master is being held in the fortress at the north end of the Temple," he says. "Come

with me. I'll get you two weapons you can hide under your clothes, and I'll take you there."

*

The governor sees Jesus' back first, glances at the deep stripes of cuts shaped like letters from an old Persian inscription as he passes. He turns around to face his new prisoner and motions to a soldier to lift Jesus' bent head.

"Are you the King of the Jews?" the governor asks, speaking slowly and clearly in his best Aramaic. As he waits for an answer, he watches closely for signs of character, for anything that might indicate how much of a threat this man is.

He doesn't see any fire in Jesus' eyes, only resignation. He barely notices when Jesus speaks.

"You said it," Jesus says, and the soldier lets go of his chin.

The governor looks at the prisoner's bowed head and the bits of dried blood scattered over the front of his body. "I don't see anything wrong with this man," he says to the high priest.

*

John and the men from Jericho pray to God for protection before they start to sing from a psalm:

God won't sustain a throne of injustice – but they make persecution the law!

They gather against the souls of the righteous, and condemn innocent blood.

They sing those two lines again and again until others fill

280

the square and join them. They keep singing when soldiers come out of the fortress and line themselves up along its walls in formation, and they keep singing when the soldiers draw their swords.

*

When he hears the noise in the courtyard, the governor remembers how much he hates Jewish songs. Songs that praise their god and deny all others, that forecast blessings for the Jewish faithful and curses for the rest of the world. Songs that promise divine deliverance or else glorify martyrdom.

The governor is tempted to have his soldiers charge the crowd before it grows any more, but since there could easily be wealthy citizens of other provinces in the square this time of year, he lets the song go on.

Then the governor gets an idea. He steps out onto the balcony, and motions to the crowd for quiet.

"I want to wish you well on your holiday," he says. "And to commemorate it, I'm going to start a new tradition." He waits a moment while confused whispers pass through the crowd, then goes on. "Every year at this feast-time, I'm going to offer a gift to you people. I know that some of you are upset that Barabbas will be executed today," he says, and watches the square closely. A few people seem surprised, but not many. He's fairly sure no one knew he'd planned on having Barabbas killed today, so he assumes the quiet means most of the people here don't care. "Others are upset about a new prisoner named Jesus, who says he's your king." He

watches the square closely again. More people seem to react to this one—good.

"I've decided to let one of them go," says the governor. He waits for a cheer, but it doesn't come. Maybe he needs to give the announcement some time to sink in. "Tell everyone in the city about the choice of pardon," he says. "I'll come back in an hour and ask who you want."

The governor walks back into the fortress and lets out a great sigh. It's too late to execute anyone quietly, but now he'll be able to execute one of his controversial prisoners with full public support. He'd prefer to be done with the robber from the desert. But if he can't have that, there will be some comfort in seeing the hope-crazy Jews choose to execute a would-be Jewish king.

Maybe he'll be able to salvage this day after all.

*

The crowd in the square starts to break up as soon as the governor steps back inside. Simon's old friends run to spread word to all their kinsmen and supporters about the coming choice. The men from Jericho tear their robes in mourning at the prospect of having to play a part in condemning a man to death, but hold their ground toward the front of the crowd, so the governor will be able to hear them well when they call out for Jesus.

The Galilean pilgrims in the square have heard of Jesus, but want to know who Barabbas is. Most of the Jerusalem natives know about Barabbas, but many have to ask about Jesus. Few of the pilgrims from abroad have a clear idea

who either person is and try to find out enough to know who to call for.

As they move through the square, Andrew and Nathanael find Simon and Philip, then are found by John, the two mothers, and Mary from Magdala.

"What do we do now?" asks the young Mary.

"We stay here so the governor can hear us well from the fortress," says Nathanael.

"We should talk to people in the crowd. They need to know why to ask the governor to let Jesus go," says Andrew.

"I'm a fast runner," says Simon. "I can probably reach Bethany and return with a group of the villagers and our people from Galilee. That will be worth more than trying to persuade people we don't know in such a short time."

"I'll go with you," says Philip. "I may fall behind on the run, but I can help spread the word once we're there."

"Go quickly," says John. "Andrew and Nathanael can talk with the men in the crowd; Mary and my mother can talk with the women." He looks at Jesus' mother. "I'll stay here with you," he says. "We don't want you to get lost in the crowd. You should be the first to greet him when he's freed."

*

Simon and Philip aren't even out of the city when old friends of Simon grab them.

"Where are you going?" one asks.

"That's not your concern," says Simon.

"Our concern is to make sure it's Barabbas who gets

released today," another says, and Simon feels something blunt hit him on the back of the head. He stumbles forward and is shoved to the ground. Someone kicks him in the ribs, a stick slams down on his back, and someone else kicks him in the face so hard he loses consciousness.

*

Peter can't have been waiting in the upper room of Joseph's house for more than a few hours, but he still feels trapped and anxious by the time Joseph returns and comes up the stairs, dressed in his finest robes.

"Did you see the high priest?" Peter asks.

"No," says Joseph. "His servants received me graciously, but he'd already gone to the governor."

Peter doesn't know what to say. He feels weighed down by his worries, as if his soul is made of stone.

Joseph is looking at him intently. "Your Master," he says. "Is his heart as honest as his face?"

Peter meets the merchant's gaze. "No one is purer," he says.

"There's very little purity in our governor's heart," says Joseph. "So I'm hoping he'll let your Master go if I offer him a bribe. My servants are gathering the gold I have here to begin with, but we can promise more if he demands it."

"Thank you," says Peter. "We are in your debt."

"There's no need for thanks," says Joseph. "And no debt to be paid. I've traded enough to know what's worth any price."

"Peace be on you and your household," Peter says.

"For that blessing," says Joseph. "I owe you thanks." He smiles at Peter and he goes back down the stairs. It's not long before Peter can hear him and his servants leave the house.

That's when the weight of Peter's anxiety returns.

"We should go," Peter says to the other two apostles. "There must be something we can do to help him."

"It won't help anything if you get caught," the big Judas says. "Though it might make things worse."

"Tell me what I can do then," says Peter. "Tell me anything."

"Try to get some sleep," says the little James.

*

The governor comes out onto the balcony at the end of the hour. The square must be twice as full as before.

"Who do you want me to pardon?" he asks.

"Jesus!" shouts half the crowd.

"Barabbas!" shouts the other half.

"Who?" says the governor.

"Jesus!" yells half the crowd.

"Barabbas!" screams the other half.

The two factions start to push and shove each other. The governor starts to worry his plan to avoid a riot might end up causing one.

"Since you can't decide, we'll cast lots," he says. "Unless you'd prefer I crucify both?"

The people in the square stop pushing and fall silent.

"Very well," says the governor. "One of them will be

spared." He motions to a servant, who brings him a vessel of water. "You are my witnesses that we left it to the gods to decide their fate. My hands are clean of the crimes of these men and of the verdicts that fall on them."

As the governor washes his hands, his soldiers drag the two prisoners out in front of the fortress. Their hands are tied behind their backs. So that everyone can tell which prisoner is Jesus and which is Barabbas, the soldiers have given Jesus a crown of thorns.

The high priest comes out next with two small stones: one smooth and the other rough. A line of condemned criminals follows to serve as witnesses of what the lots decide.

The soldiers move Jesus to the right and Barabbas to the left.

The high priest throws down the tiny stones.

One of the condemned men takes a close look at them.

"The rough stone fell to the right," he calls out. "The king of the Jews will be crucified."

The soldiers cut Barabbas loose, and push him forward into the crowd. Simon's old friends and their people cheer. The high priest's supporters nod in grim satisfaction.

Jesus' mother clings tightly to John's arm.

*

Though Jesus seems barely able to carry his own weight, the soldiers put the beam of the cross on his back. He cries out in pain when the heavy wood falls across his fresh wounds, but he manages to stagger forward, half-dragging

the cross beam behind him, through the narrow streets of the north end of Jerusalem.

Some soldiers are standing guard at the city's north gate. They seem to be searching the crowd for something: they keep stopping men, questioning them, then turning back some and searching others—the ones with northern accents.

Andrew grabs Nathanael and pulls him down between two fish stands in the marketplace near the gate. "They must be looking for us," he whispers. Then he gets a still tighter feeling in his chest: "And we're carrying weapons."

They don't want to leave Jesus. But they'd rather leave now on their own than be caught on the way out of the city and have Jesus see them get arrested.

The guards are so busy with the men, though, they hardly look at the women. They pay so little attention to them that they don't seem to notice an older woman is leaning for support on the arm of a young Galilean man.

*

When Jesus collapses and can't seem to lift the beam of the cross again, the soldiers make a bystander carry it. He's a merchant, one of the Jews who's been successful enough abroad to make the journey to Jerusalem each year for Passover.

He will never forget this day. He will tell his sons about it and they will never be able to forget the story either.

*

John and the women don't dare come too close to the hill where the soldiers finally lay down the cross. It's an ugly,

lonely, barren hill: short, half-dead grasses cling stubbornly to a thin layer of dried-out dirt over a skeletal outcropping of rock.

They nail his hands and feet to the wood. Neither Mary can stand to watch, but they won't leave him.

The soldiers set up crosses all over the hill. So many men suffer on so many crosses.

Jesus cries out again in pain.

My God, my God, why have You forsaken me? Why are You so far from helping me, and from the words of my roaring?

The sky begins to darken. A cold wind blows and the older Mary tenses, then weeps. Her son is dying: why is she worrying about the cold on his bare skin?

Oh my God, I cry in the day time, but You don't hear me. I cry through the night and never fall silent.

The soldiers are talking and laughing. How can they ignore all the agony around them?

But You are holy, and Yours are the praises of all Israel.

Our fathers trusted You: they trusted, and you delivered them.

One of the high priest's jurists is arguing with a soldier about the sign above Jesus' cross. "Why did you write 'King of the Jews'?" he says.

But surely I am a worm and no man: reproached by men, and despised by the people. Whoever sees me laughs in scorn; they throw open their mouths, they shake their heads and say: "He trusted the Lord to deliver him! If the Lord loves him, why doesn't He deliver him?"

One of the high priest's servants lifts up a cup of wine. "Almighty king!" he shouts. "If you're thirsty, come down from the cross and take a drink of this."

Mary holds on to John's arm as tightly as she can. Someone told her once a sword would pierce her heart, and she can feel it there now, running straight though her chest.

But You're the one who took me out of the womb: You made me hope when I was on my mother's breasts. I was cast on You from the womb: You're my God since before I left my mother's belly.

They lift the wine cup up to him on a stick, but he won't take any.

Be close to me! because trouble is near, and there's no one to help. Bulls have surrounded me, the strong bulls of Bashan. They gape at me with wide mouths, like ravening, roaring lions.

He's been up there for hours.

I am poured out like water. All my bones are stretched thin.

My heart is like wax that has melted down into my bowels.

It gets darker and darker, though it's the middle of the day.

I can count all my bones: they look and stare up at me.

My heart is like wax that has melted down.

The soldiers get bored and gamble for his clothes.
My heart is like wax that has melted.

After six hours on the cross, Jesus cries out:
"My God, my God, why have You forsaken me?"
Everyone stares. It's the first time Jesus has spoken.

"He's calling for Elijah!" says Judas, and he pushes his way past the high priest's servants to fill a sponge with vinegar. He puts it on a long reed and gives Jesus a drink. One of the high priest's men tries to pull him away, but Judas elbows him hard in the ribs. "Leave me alone!" he shouts. "Elijah is coming for him!"

But Elijah doesn't come. Jesus cries out again, loudly.
And he dies.

*

Judas looks up at him.
Judas needs to scream, but the scream won't come out.

Book Four:
Sinai

"The law of the Lord is perfect,
converting the soul."

1.

Andrew and Nathanael hear from the men in the fish market, who heard it from a passing soldier.

James hears from John when he gets back in the late afternoon.

Simon and Philip hear from a passerby shortly after they wake up, panicked, in a filthy alley. Matthew and Thomas hear from them an hour later.

Peter, the big Judas, and the little James hear it from a servant who Joseph the rich man sends.

Their minds go blank. Their hearts break.

They feel weak, when they hear it, and sick to the bottom of their souls.

*

It is spring.

But the whole world feels dead.

It is spring.

But there is nothing to hope for anymore. Ever.

In what strange way has this spring come?

*

The men from Jericho can't bear to stay in the city for the rest of the holiday. It's a festival of freedom, but they're too close here to the crosses on the hill to feel free at all. They

buy some flatbread from the villagers and hurry home.

James's mother leans on him and Jesus' mother leans on John. Mary from Magdala suggests they walk to Bethany to see if any of the others are there.

Matthew and Thomas meet them on the road into the village and show them a place between two trees where Simon and Philip are hiding. Simon's face is badly bruised.

"What do we do now?" asks Matthew.

"We're ready to take you back home if that's best," says Thomas to the women.

As the older Mary imagines the road north, she's filled with an echo of the long-ago dread of realizing, on the way home from the festival, that her son was missing. And she wants to look for him again now, to spend three days searching every corner of the city, though she knows she won't find him this time.

"We can't leave yet," she says. "We have to go back to Jerusalem."

*

Andrew and Nathanael don't know where to go. They waited all day in the market because they could never make it safely out through the gate toward Jesus but were never willing to give up and walk away.

But now that Jesus is dead, there's no real reason to go through the gate.

Which also means the soldiers aren't questioning anybody.

"Where are you going?" asks Nathanael.

"To see him," says Andrew.

Nathanael shudders. "Why?"

"I'll meet you back at the house in the upper city," Andrew says, and as Nathanael watches Andrew walks straight past the soldiers and out the fish gate.

*

Joseph the rich man has spent most of the day waiting to see the governor. But when the governor has time to receive him, it's only because what Joseph wanted to stop has already been done.

"With your permission, I'd like to take Jesus' body and bury it according to our customs," says Joseph.

The governor looks up from his meal. "The king? Is he already dead?"

A captain nods.

"I knew he was harmless," says the governor to the captain. "Didn't even last ten hours."

The captain stiffens and bites his tongue.

"The body is yours," says the governor to Joseph. "Just take it down from the cross."

*

Andrew sees Jesus' body from a distance.

It still doesn't help him believe this could have happened.

Not far from the cross, another body is spread out on the ground, face down and lying almost absolutely still.

"Judas?" says Andrew.

But Judas doesn't turn or answer. Andrew kneels down

beside him, looks him over for signs of wounds—but his only injuries are scraped knuckles.

"Why didn't they come?" says Judas. "It's all my fault."

"Don't talk like that," says Andrew. "We did what we could, there just wasn't time enough."

"You don't understand," says Judas.

"It's going to be all right," says Andrew. "Somehow it will be all right."

"No," says Judas.

"Let's go back to the house," says Andrew.

"You still don't understand," says Judas, "I killed him!"

Andrew takes Judas firmly by both arms. "You didn't kill anyone," he says. "The Romans did this and none of us knew how to stop them."

But Judas pulls away. "You don't understand," he says, and then he turns and runs before Andrew can stop him.

*

Joseph goes home to get a white linen cloth to wrap the body in. He checks to see if the three apostles waiting there are all right and finds ten of the apostles and three women in the upper room.

He tells them he has permission to take the body and that he has a garden outside the city walls with a newly-cut tomb. He says it will be better, in case anyone is watching, if none of the men come with him, but he invites the women.

Salome stays with her sons, but the Marys go.

Andrew is still at the cross when they get there, but no one seems to be watching anymore. He helps Joseph take the

body down. The women wrap it, and then Joseph and Andrew carry it to the tomb.

It's good Andrew is there to help, because the stone at the tomb's entrance is too heavy for Joseph alone to roll aside.

*

Judas doesn't know where to go. He thinks about going to the neighborhood where he grew up, but he's not sure he could bear to be there now. He thinks about going back to face Peter, James, and John, but he doesn't think they'd stone him like he deserves. He thinks about going to the high priest's house, throwing the money in his face, shouting every curse he knows—as if it were the high priest's fault and not his own. As if curses mattered in a world to which the Day of Judgment will no longer come.

He decides to go to the fig tree on the mountainside where Jesus wept.

All the leaves are brown and the branches are brittle. Even the roots have dried up.

*

Joseph, Andrew, and the women make it home just before sunset ushers in the Sabbath.

Everyone says the prayers together, and though they're still devastated, an unmistakable part of the peace of the Sabbath settles over the house.

The Sabbath must be one of the greatest gifts God ever gave to mankind, because not even a tragedy as great as this can take it away.

2.

Late that night, after everyone else is lost in bone-tired sleep, Andrew and Peter talk like they used to, like two young brothers worried about their friends. They talk about Mary, and about Simon's wounds, and about how grateful they are to have Joseph's hospitality and help. Then they fall quiet for a moment.

"I'm worried about Judas," says Andrew, "I wish he were here with us."

Peter doesn't answer.

"I saw him, for a moment, in the afternoon," Andrew says, and he fidgets with the knots on his sleeve. "I think he blames himself for what happened."

Peter bites his tongue. He already hates Judas for betraying Jesus, but now he also hates him for how the truth will hurt his brother. His caring, trusting brother.

"Where do you think he might have gone?" asks Andrew. "How can we find him?"

"Andrew," says Peter, but he can't fit any words out of his mouth. The shapes they take in his mind are too awkward and ugly for his tongue to carry.

Andrew waits in silence. That's the worst part. The way

Andrew is always so willing to patiently wait for him to speak.

"It *is* his fault," says Peter. "He's the one who led them to Jesus."

Andrew doesn't say anything for a long time. Peter feels like there's a fish hook caught in his side and the silence is pulling on it, but he doesn't know how to beg Andrew to say something. Anything.

"Are you sure it was him?" says Andrew at last.

"He was carrying one of the torches," says Peter. "He walked right up to us and pointed out Jesus. That's how they knew who to arrest."

"Why would he do that?" asks Andrew.

"Why do most traitors turn on their friends?" says Peter. "Maybe they paid him well; maybe he carried a silent grudge."

"He feels terrible now," says Andrew.

"Good!" says Peter. "I hope he feels terrible the rest of his life. Maybe someday someone will turn him in, and he can find out how it feels to be nailed to a cross."

"Don't say that," says Andrew.

"He deserves it," says Peter.

"Don't say that," says Andrew. "I'm worried about him. We should find him."

"Jesus is dead because of him!" says Peter. "Can't you understand that?"

"He's my friend!" says Andrew, and he starts to cry.

"He betrayed you," says Peter. "He betrayed all of us."

But Andrew doesn't stop weeping. And so Peter cries with him. He cries for his dead Master, for his dying hopes, for the crushing loneliness of this giant, violent city. But most of all he cries because the pleading tone of Andrew's voice sounded so much for a moment like Jesus last night in the garden.

*

While the Jews of the city are observing their Sabbath, the governor gambles with an old friend who's come to visit. As he rolls the carved bone dice, the governor explains how he convinced half the city to support the execution of a man who claimed to be the heir to the old Jewish kings.

The governor's friend laughs when he hears about the crown of thorns. "Probably the only crown he ever wore," he says—and then he stops laughing, because the dice come up against him.

"Shall we play again?" asks the governor.

"I think I've suffered enough," says his friend.

"Just once more!" says the governor. "You know the whole city's shut down on their seventh day: what else can we do?"

The governor's friend hesitates. It's true that Jerusalem is cheerless today—but that doesn't give him more money to lose. "Why don't you take me to see the king?" he says. "I'd enjoy that."

"You've come too late, my friend," says the governor. "He's already dead and buried. For a king, there wasn't

much fighting spirit in him: he only lasted a few hours. We could visit the tomb, if you like. The man who took the body is quite wealthy, so it should be impressive."

A soldier who's been watching their game speaks up: "I saw where they took him. It is beautiful—a new place in a garden with a freshly carved cave. I think it was meant to be the merchant's own when he died."

The governor's friend raises an eyebrow.

"Should we go?" says the governor.

"Aren't you worried about this?" asks his friend.

"About the tomb?" says the governor. "Why should I be?"

"Does this man you crucified have a son?" says the friend.

"I have no idea," the governor says.

"You should find out," says the friend. "If a man claims descent from their legendary line of kings and is executed, his son is heir to both the kings and a martyr. And since the merchant gave this would-be king a nice tomb, where people can come to offer the wine and gifts for the dead every year—soon you may have big crowds and that grave will be a dangerous shrine."

"Jews don't give anything to their dead after the burial," says the governor. "Except for their one god, they're strict atheists."

"Then maybe they'll pray to their god in the grave or they'll weep at the grave's entrance," says the friend. "Every nation does something. And suppose one day his son—or,

301

who knows, maybe a younger brother? — comes and makes a fiery speech from the tomb. You might have a serious problem."

The governor takes a slow drink of wine and rubs his temples against an oncoming headache. "I hate this place," he says. "We should have left these fanatics to the Persians."

"Do you want my advice?" asks his friend. "Just seal up the tomb now so no one can go in to offer sacrifices and put a guard there a few weeks to keep people away from the entrance. Then they'll forget it. The easiest time to stop a shrine is before it develops."

The governor leans forward, then rises and walks to a window that looks out over the hills to the north.

"Maybe it doesn't matter," his friend says, absently toying with the dice, "but in your position, I wouldn't gamble on it."

*

In the last hours of the Sabbath, Mary from Magdala thinks about her life. About how she stayed at home after all her sisters had married and moved on. About how lonely she felt when her parents died. About all the struggles with both mind and body she had before Jesus came and — with one touch of his hand — drove them out. About how much it meant to her when he said she had great faith.

She thinks about the time she spent following him. About all the people she's told of his work and all the people she's come to love like sisters and brothers. Is that life over now? She can't imagine how it could go on with Jesus dead,

302

but she also can't imagine going on without it. She can't imagine her life without the faith that's made her feel whole.

She thinks about her savings, all gone now, so there's nothing to start a new life with.

But she doesn't regret how she spent it.

"I want Mary to," he said, "I want her to anoint me this time and the next."

And all at once, Mary knows what to hold onto in all her confusion. For tonight at least, her life still has a clear purpose. Jesus wanted her to help anoint his body for its burial.

*

The three women go out after sunset with their own lamps, carrying burial spices and oil Joseph has sent. They sing softly as they go, as they walk out of the gate and see the hill with rocks shaped like a skull:

The Lord is my light and my salvation: who should I fear?
The Lord is the strength of my life: why should I be afraid?

I can do this, Jesus' mother thinks. Women have always done this. I buried my husband and I can bury my son.

I need to do this, thinks the other Mary. If my whole life has only been to serve on this evening, I'll be able to tell God it was enough.

Salome jumps back when her light shines on a figure outside the grave. Two soldiers are waiting there.

"What are you doing here?" says Salome sharply.

Her tone catches the soldiers off guard, and they're not quite sure how to respond. "We're supposed to be here,"

one of them says. "We have orders from the governor."

"Do your orders say to stand in the way of a dead man's mother?" Salome asks, and she gestures at Mary. "She'd like to finish the preparations for her son's body."

The soldiers hesitate. "We can't," says one. "Our orders are to keep people away."

"We're very sorry," says the other.

Salome looks at them. "You seem like kind men," she says. "I know you have your orders, but couldn't you just let his mother in? The rest of us can wait outside if you'd like."

One soldier bites his cheek; the other shifts his weight from one foot to the other.

"We're extremely sorry," the first soldier says, "but they already called in someone to seal the stone. So we really can't let anyone in, no matter how much we might want to."

"We're not even supposed to let anyone linger in the area," says the other. "But if she needs a moment," he adds quickly, "we won't get in the way."

The older Mary takes the other two women's arms and walks right up to the entrance stone. It's sealed all around. They should be able to find a time in the next day or two when the guards are asleep or willing to be bribed, but it will be hard to break in quietly.

Mary closes her eyes for a moment and hopes she looks lost in more typical motherly thoughts.

She nods at the guards. She hopes she appears at once grave and grateful as she walks away.

"Thank you," Salome says to the guards. "I hope we see

each other again someday."

*

Joseph the rich man listens carefully to the women's questions. People don't usually ask a man of his dignity how to break into something, or how much to offer Jerusalem's Roman soldiers for a bribe—which is a terrible shame, because his years of experience on these subjects, from his childhood in Arimathea up through the time when he first established himself here in the city, really should not be wasted. He gives them detailed advice on which tools they'll need to break into the tomb, on how to use a cloth to dampen the sound, on how to walk the fine line between being gouged on a bribe and offending a soldier by showing insufficient respect. He gives them advice on how early to leave the house if they want to start their work when it's light enough to see what they're doing without lamps but still dark enough to keep them from being seen from a distance.

"How do you know all this?" asks Thomas, who's a little skeptical about the whole plan, but Joseph the rich man just smiles. He wonders out loud if the three women, working together, will be able to push the heavy stone aside once they've cut it loose, but they insist they'll manage and that it will be safer to commit a crime if they don't bring any men with them.

Joseph sighs and then settles into helping Mary from Magdala practice some of his techniques with a chisel while Mary and Salome get some rest.

305

She stays up half the night working, Joseph serving as her mentor and a succession of apostles as chaperones, until she feels the plan has been successfully transferred from her mind's memory into her hands'. She's nervous, of course, but she tries not to think too much about that. She's tempted to wait, to plan another day and train another night, but with a dead body to attend to, she doesn't have much time. She has a purpose in life, and if she's going to fulfill it, she has to try now.

The women get up in the last watch of the night to reach the tomb by early morning. Their bodies are exhausted from days of stress and pain but their minds are bright, because their minds are on fire with a love that will burn for the rest of their lives.

*

It's still dim as they approach the garden, so they can't see at first where the soldiers are.

They get closer. The soldiers aren't there.

They move toward the tomb. The entrance stone isn't there either.

They get worried. What's happened? Has someone stolen the body from the grave? Are soldiers hoping the apostles will come: are they lying in wait to arrest them?

Jesus' mother walks into the chamber anyway, the other two close beside her.

*

The body is gone, the linen burial cloth folded neatly where it once lay.

A shining being with eyes bright as lightning and a cloak spun of purified light stands on the cave's right side.

Mary from Nazareth gasps. The angel's face is just like her dead husband's.

"Don't be afraid," the angel says in a voice that feels smooth against their souls. "You won't find him here. He's risen!"

The angel smiles like Joseph used to, and though he doesn't touch her Mary feels lost in his arms. Then he walks out of the chamber and leaps up onto the top of the great stone.

"Tell his friends first," he says. "Then tell everyone!"

Then he leaps again, straight up, higher than any human being could go. The sun starts to break over the hills in the east, and he's gone.

*

The women stare at that first sliver of the rising sun.

Sometimes, it's hardest to believe the miracle you see with your own eyes.

"Should we go back to the house?" asks Salome.

"Yes," says the older Mary.

Mary from Magdala can barely stand, barely see well enough to put one foot in front of the other after the brightness of the angel's light. "I'll wait here," she says. "I should stay and watch so I can warn you before the men get here if any trouble comes."

Salome and Jesus' mother nod and hurry back toward the upper city.

Mary from Magdala falls to her knees, onto the soft, dew-damp soil.

*

"I don't mean any disrespect," says Thomas, "but are sure that's what you saw? Not a trick of the early morning light?"

"Have you ever seen an angel?" asks Mary.

"No," says Thomas.

"Obviously," says Salome.

Thomas sighs. "I know we all would give anything to see him again. But there are some things no sacrifice can buy."

"What if it wasn't our sacrifice?" says John.

*

There's a distinct element of danger. There's a strong possibility the whole thing is a complicated trick, that the high priest or governor didn't think one crucifixion was enough and is looking for more.

There's also a strong chance of further heartbreak. If you abandon your rituals of mourning for impossible hope after impossible hope, how will the mourning come to an end?

But Peter, Andrew, James, and John don't have the patience to listen to reasonable arguments from the others, and they go running to see the empty grave right away.

*

"He was here," says Mary from Magdala when the four men arrive at the tomb. "I saw him. He talked to me."

In court, a woman's witness isn't valid. But the four men who ran believe.

Peter, James, and John run back to the house to tell the others, but Andrew lets himself fall behind. They can bring the good news to the faithful: Andrew wants to find Judas.

When Judas hears Jesus is risen from the dead, he won't be able to shut out hope any longer. And though he'll still carry the guilt of all he's done, the news may give him the courage to come back and be forgiven.

Then they'll work together and they'll pray together until Andrew and Judas stand side by side on the day when their risen Master lifts the veil which conceals the full beauty of the kingdom of God.

Andrew doesn't know where to look, but he needs to find Judas. He needs to tell Judas. He passes the fortress and the Temple and searches through alley after alley. But he finds nothing. So he walks straight to the street where the high priest lives and knocks on the bloody door.

*

A servant answers: it's still Passover, she says. Doesn't he know the high priest is far too busy to talk with every poor pilgrim in town?

"I'm not here for the high priest," says Andrew. "I'm looking for my friend."

"Who?" asks the servant, and Andrew tells her what Judas looks like and when he might have come.

"We haven't seen him," she says. And she closes the door.

But Andrew doesn't know where else to go. So he

knocks again.

The door opens. "Why did you come here?" the servant asks. "Aren't you afraid of what could happen to you?"

"No," Andrew says.

Another servant comes to the doorway. "He was here," the second servant says, and the first servant glares at him. "Are you looking for the money?"

"What money?" Andrew asks.

"You don't know?" says the servant. "Then if you promise not to come back and not to mention any money to our Master or anyone else, I'll tell you where your friend went."

"I promise," says Andrew. "But what makes you so certain my friend won't speak with your Master about it again?"

The servant takes a long look at Andrew. "You didn't hear the way your friend talked," he says. "Or see the look in his eyes."

"Besides," says the other, "We saw him headed for the potters' field."

*

Andrew runs so fast he's afraid the blood will burst out of his veins. He runs so fast he feels he might drown in the exertion.

But he's too late.

Judas's body is hanging from a tree.

Andrew screams out his anger: "Why?" he shouts, "I wanted to help you. Why didn't you come to me?"

Andrew cuts the body down and cries over it. "I was your friend, Judas," he says. "I'm your friend." And he sobs until his throat aches and his mind feels numb.

Then he wraps the body in his coat, digs a grave with his hands through the clay-thick dirt, and says the prayers for the dead.

"Why couldn't he wait just a little longer?" he asks God. "Why couldn't he wait for me?"

*

As soon as Andrew steps back into the house, he can hear the others singing upstairs:

I'll declare your name to my brothers; I'll praise you before a great assembly.

If you love the Lord, praise Him! All you sons of Jacob, honor Him!

Let reverence for Him fill the whole house of Israel —

because He hasn't forgotten or forsaken the suffering one,

He hasn't hidden his face: when the sufferer cried out, He heard.

Only Thomas sits silent, still in mourning, here in the lower level. When Andrew joins in the song, Thomas stands up and leaves:

My praise for You joins the praise of the congregation,

among those who honor him I will fulfill all my vows.

The meek will eat and be satisfied; whoever looks for the Lord will praise him.

Andrew thinks about going after Thomas, but he needs to sing more first. He needs the strength he feels in this

chorus, so he walks up the stairs:

All the ends of the earth will turn and remember the Lord,

people from every nation will come and worship before Him:

Because the kingdom is the Lord's, and He will govern among
all the nations.

Andrew looks around the room at the faces of his brothers and sisters. And he runs his fingers over the knots he tied on the fringes of his shirt.

Our children will serve Him,

We'll tell all His stories to the coming generations:

they will come. And they'll talk of his righteousness to a people
yet to be born: they'll tell them what he has done.

Book Five:
Devarim (Words)

"But Mary kept all these things,
and pondered them in her heart."

1.

Mary's hair is white and thinning by the time the foreign doctor comes to visit; her joints are sore and stiff. He speaks halting Aramaic with a heavy accent; she wishes she'd been educated, so she could talk to him in his native Greek tongue.

People have been talking about her son for decades, but no one has asked her so many questions before, or listened so carefully to her answers. He has some trouble understanding the rural accent she's never lost, so she has to repeat some things several times before he seems able to follow. He says—if she understands him correctly—that he wants to know exactly what happened. He says he's heard more than one version of every story and he wants to get it right. So she tries to tell him everything, but it takes so long, and there's so much to talk about, she soon settles for smiling widely and nodding as soon as he seems to understand the heart of what she's said.

After he's gone through all the common stories and sayings, he asks her about when Jesus was born. No man has asked her about that before. Some men, back in the village, used to look away from her because of whispers they'd

heard about it, but no one ever asked.

So she tells him. About the angel, and the prophetess. About how she almost fell off the donkey when the tightening pains became hard and rapid. She laughs as she remembers trying to tell Joseph to let her get down and have the baby on the side of the street, and explains how frustrating it was that whenever she'd get his attention, the pain would have grown too strong for her to talk.

He asks about Jesus' childhood, but she quickly gives up trying to explain all the places they lived and why they went there. She tries to express instead what a perfect child he was, how infuriating that perfection could sometimes be, and how sometimes, even as a child, he'd say strange things that would sink straight down to the deepest part of her heart, where she'd keep them. Though it wasn't until later, years later, after everything had happened, that she finally understood what he'd meant.

She falls quiet.

"Do you miss him?" asks Luke.

She smiles. "No," she says. "He's not gone."

*

They keep telling the story: from land to land, language to language, generation to generation. The stories change as they travel: people remember the Passover matzah as loaves of their own leavened bread, Mary's son's spring birth gets moved to winter. But the heart stays strong even in such mistakes: it's the darkest time of year when the people of the north celebrate the coming of the Light.

The stories don't mind shifting a little to fill the shapes of their listeners' deepest needs.

And I believe they're all true. Because I've walked into the water, seen John's shape carved across its surface. And that shape is a knife that still opens hearts, so that by the time you reach the water, you're aching to give up all the wrongs you've ever done.

And you tell Jesus: "I can't go on this way."

And he says: "You don't have to."

And you say: "But how?"

And he shows you how to take the stories in your hand, and tear the pride of this world apart.

သာ

သာ

Acknowledgments

Of all those who contributed to this book, special thanks go to:

Bishop Shawn Lucas, who gave me the assignment that started it all.

Abhijat Joshi, who introduced me to Faiz and the ghazal tradition, opening a door on the poetic world of my grandfather's youth.

Orson Scott Card, whose Literary Boot Camp gave me the insights I needed to make my revisions work.

Respondents to drafts: Merrijane Rice, Charles Swift, Janci Olds, Eric James Stone, Lee Ann Setzer, Cavan Helps, Alex Haig, Heidi Summers, Darci Rhoades, Tessa Hauglid, Lesley Hart Gunn, Erin Jackson, Carol Bradley, Ryan Alleman, Cort Kirksey, Marie Mauduit, Vilo Pratt Gill, Vilo Westwood, Heather Westwood, Kira Goldberg, Kayela Seegmiller.

My parents & grandparents, for long-term intellectual support.

My children, for their patience when I was lost in my work.

And most of all, Nicole Wilkes Goldberg, my wife and relentless, formidable editor.

About the Author

James Goldberg has long been interested in how old religious stories can help narrate and give meaning to 21st century experience. His play *Prodigal Son*, which won the 2009 AML Drama Award, dealt with the strain a son's religious conversion places on his relationship with his loving, atheist father. His micro-fiction cycle "Sojourners," nominated for a Pushcart Prize, fused stories of contemporary immigrants with structural allusions to the Jewish liturgical calendar. Goldberg has also presented and published scholarly work on socio-religious themes, ranging from the egalitarian power of religious food traditions to the influence of audience illiteracy on the aesthetics of the world's scriptures.

The Five Books of Jesus is his first novel.